FEB 23

Lola
AT
LAST

Lola AT LAST

Also by JC Peterson
Being Mary Bennet

Lola
AT
LAST

JC PETERSON

HARPER TEEN
An Imprint of HarperCollinsPublishers

To Jackie; I like you so much better than Jill

Lola AT LAST

ONE

IT IS A TRUTH UNIVERSALLY acknowledged that boys make for the best mistakes.

Speaking of. I clink glasses with the boy across from me and tip the shot back, my gaze tipping with it. From his white teeth, up to the white mast of the boat, up to the twinkling white stars pricking the midnight sky.

Someone jostles my shoulder, and the boat sways under the soles of my platform sandals. My attention tilts back down to find Jasmine has pushed the boy aside, Meg in tow. Meg Grant and Jasmine LeGrange are two of my oldest friends. I mean, currently they sort of hate me, but . . . semantics.

"Lola!" Meg says, all toothy smile and loose limbs, probably thanks to the vodka bottle hanging from one pale hand. I came late and alone, and she definitely did neither of those things. Meg squeals at someone behind me and hauls my twin sister in for a hug that makes Kat grimace. Or maybe that's because she was caught trying to sneak by me with four beers for her new friends. Meg, though, grins and tilts her cheek against my twin's long golden hair. "You both made it!"

The cheap bourbon shot is still clawing down my throat, and I have to cough to clear it out. "Of course I made it," I say with a practiced shrug. "It's not a party without Lola Barnes."

Everyone knows that. Or they did. Kat snorts and squeezes the bottle necks in her grip, but that's easy enough to ignore. Or actually . . . I snatch three of them and press the cold-slicked bottles toward Meg and Jasmine. Maybe they all just need a reminder of how much fun I am.

"Hey, Crenshaw Day!" I shout, howling over the noise. "We're gonna be seniors!"

All around me, my Crenshaw classmates cheer. The feel of their eyes on me seeps into my skin and warms me up better than any cheap liquor. I spear Jasmine with a look.

"See, Jas? Like I said. Not a party without me."

Jasmine blinks slowly but doesn't respond. Point for Lola.

Because that's what every decade-long friendship runs on, right? Points and grudges. Whatever. Worming my way back in with Meg and Jasmine means being popular again. Because, honestly, I'm too fabulous to be unpopular.

Meg clinks the neck of her bottle against mine. "You always

make it fun," she says, and my heart swells. She's the only one who even takes a swig of the beer I generously procured, but maybe this is it, the night my friends are finally going to forgive me! We'll go back to how it always was! Me and Jasmine shopping while Meg and Kat rate the boys walking by. The four of us—

"Just, like, don't sink Daddy's yacht, okay, sweetie?" Jasmine's words are honeyed and hard as rocks.

My heart crashes, and my hope sours. Next to Meg, Kat picks at the peeling label of her untouched beer and is distracted by the crowd. So it's still like that. "Best friends" who refuse to forgive me and a twin sister who's moved on. I hone that soured hope into something sharp and snag Jasmine with a look.

"It's super cute you'd call this a yacht, Jas," I say, smile serrated like a knife.

It is, at best, an aspirational dinghy.

"That's why Daddy sold it for a bigger one." She waits a beat, inspects the nail polish of one spray-tanned hand, and slides her gaze to Kat. "And Kat, maybe go check on your friends. They're really bringing down the whole vibe." She loops her arm through Meg's, trills "Costume change!" and drags her off.

We used to plan every outfit together, but now I'm only wearing these slouchy jeans and cropped sweater and have no idea what she has planned next. I swallow against the ache in my throat and refuse to remember the time in eighth grade when we convinced our whole group to wear evening gowns to school.

We were all sent home early; it was fantastic. I have to clear my throat again, even though the bourbon's long gone, but when I turn to Kat, trying to force out something sarcastic about ridiculous costume changes, she's gone.

Great. Really great. I spot her long blond waves disappearing through the crowd. My own hair, chopped above my shoulders and lavender this week, sticks on my lip gloss. I flick the strands away and stomp after Kat, only to spot her sliding onto a white leather couch near the prow with her shiny new friends. Who are all total nerds, by the way. The party teems around them, but they look like they're discussing Kafka over black coffee. They don't have their extra credit summer work out, but I bet it's in the car.

Kat glances up from the conversation, spots me hovering, and freezes. Like she's been caught. Or maybe like she doesn't want to be found. Too bad, sis, I found you in the womb. I sidestep the "CLOSED (FOR TWINS)" sign and plop onto the couch next to Joon Park. Everyone stops talking, record-scratch style.

Across from me, Ezra Reuben lifts his hand in a sort of half wave, then clearly thinks better of it and tugs at the collar of his short-sleeved floral button-down. His cheeks blaze and he drops his chin, and I feel, for the barest of seconds, like I get it. That sense of not knowing how to connect. But I swipe that feeling aside because I'm on a mission to regain my spot in the Crenshaw hierarchy, not plumb the depths of my psyche.

Joon sort of gets a pass because he's the best player on the soccer team and is from London, so he insists on calling it football in this gorgeous accent that's all soft at the edges. But he's also captain of the debate team and wears a tie to school every day. Wash Carson is his boyfriend, an über-smart geek who transferred sophomore year after he transitioned and the people at his Texas high school became real dicks about the bathroom he was using. And Ezra, well, he once did a science project on the mystery of male nipples and then got called Ezra Booben for nearly two years.

Kat shoves the toe of her sneaker against my shin. "What are you doing?"

"Like, generally? Or . . . ?"

Kat's been all about her new friends for months now, but I've never been invited to join. I mean, not that I want to. But it'd be nice to be asked. Kat rolls her eyes and sits back with a huff. She's got the better pout by miles. She's all curves and big eyes. Everything about me is sharper, including my tongue.

"You guys quizzing each other on the periodic table?"

Kat scowls.

Ezra hooks his elbow behind the couch, stretching the shirt across his chest and shoulders, and actually meets my eye. Okay, he's pulling off the Hawaiian print better than expected, but also, I'm halfway to drunk so maybe don't trust me. "We're talking about Tahoe."

"Who's a ho?" Wash says, cracking up at his own joke. These are the people Kat has chosen over me? People who make puns?

I consider heaving myself overboard.

Joon pulls Wash's hand into his lap and threads their fingers together, knitting Wash's darker skin with his lighter tone. "My darling boy," he says sweetly, which I'm pretty sure is British for *do be quiet.*

Across the deck, Jasmine and Meg have reappeared from belowdecks in matching terry-cloth rompers and roller skates. People are cheering for them, and it's like spiders crawling down my skin.

"Have you been to Lake Tahoe?" Ezra asks.

The last time I spoke to Ezra was during the month I suffered through honors genetics freshman year, when he couldn't even look at me without his face glowing with embarrassment, which made being lab partners pretty difficult. He accidentally smeared disgusting FlyNap on my science notebook and it smelled like a drugged fruit fly for the rest of the semester (which was in life sciences with Meg and Jasmine, by the way).

This is going about as well as that.

"There's a rad section of the PCT over that way," Ezra continues.

"Never been," I say, not really listening. Jasmine just twirled. She looks ridiculous. Why didn't Meg tell me to bring my skates? We bought matching iridescent ones last year.

"Yes, you have," Kat says, interrupting my thoughts. "Three years ago with Grammy."

"Oh, right. Sure."

Skating on a deck would be pretty rad, honestly. They're posing for photos now, and my legs twitch.

Wash starts again. "I read this article—"

I surge to my feet, the need to move, to join the crowd, like sparklers at the ends of my nerves. "Gotta go. Just heard my name."

"No, you didn't," Kat says, one eyebrow arched.

"I definitely did."

Kat rolls her eyes. "Whatever. Go chase after them, I guess. Like it's gonna work."

The sting of her words blooms across my cheeks. I spin away from them and stomp back into the tangle of bodies at the center of the deck. Back where I truly belong. The only person to acknowledge me is some rando who backs up into me and spills beer down my front.

It used to be that *I* was at the center, not Meg or Jasmine. It used to be that Kat was right at my side, flirting outrageously with boys and giggling at all my jokes.

But then last year happened. And that leaves me . . .

Well, right now that leaves me pissed and not wanting to think about it.

Instead of thinking, I choose something much better. I stride through the crowd and stop directly in front of the mast, the thick white pole bolted to the deck and studded with metal rings and dangling rope. Let's see Meg and Jasmine try this with those ridiculous skates on.

"Bet none of you can do this," I challenge everyone within shouting distance.

I kick my shoes off and reach up. A wet breeze off the Pacific licks my exposed stomach, but the mast is even colder. Yet the metal rings are sturdy—I push one foot upward, and another. Then I'm stuck, clinging to the pole with my chin wrenched upward along its tapering length. Behind me, someone snickers. Mom and I once took a sunset cruise off the coast of St. Lucia, and a lumbering man from New Jersey was able to climb to the top and hang out there pretending to be Jack Sparrow for a full half hour before the sailors coaxed him down. If he could do it, I sure as shit can.

My knees clench, and I muscle my way up, like I'm shimmying up a tree trunk. Until the people around me forget the low-rent disco that can't hold their attention like I can. I'm above their heads now, the wind off the ocean tugging at my pastel hair and pricking goose bumps from my skin. The world around me is dark with night, but a floodlight perched at the top of the mast bathes me in a yellow glow. I'm *literally* in the spotlight, right where I belong.

I can feel the way they're watching me in my bones. In the pit of my stomach. It fills me with this insatiable craving for *more*. Below, a couple of boys cheer, and I throw them a smile. Screw Kat and her new personality that leaves no room for me. Screw Jasmine and Meg and their roller skating. This party would be so lame without me. They'd have nothing to talk about, nothing to remember. I look out past the low hump of the cabin, past the stubby end of the boat roped to the marina slip, past the bigger, better boats next to it.

Until I see him. Loping up the dock and sucking all the air from my lungs. Douche, ahoy.

TWO

YOU KNOW HOW I SAID boys make for the best mistakes? Well, here comes one of my biggest.

Tully.

Shit. Tully.

He shoots his arms overhead and hops onto the deck of the boat, and I can feel the mast jerk between my legs.

"What's up, losers! I'm back!"

Every face that had been turned to me whips to him.

Tully: The reason sloppy photos of me making out with someone else's boyfriend live on in an awful corner of the internet. The reason Meg and Jasmine iced me out and Kat found new friends. The reason my parents shipped me off to France to "get some space" from my mistakes.

Embarrassment and shame and a whole lot of anger whips into a storm in my gut, lightning forking down my nerves. I've worked so damn hard since I schlepped home from France to make them all forget. To stop being the *label* and just start being Lola again. And now it'll all come crashing down thanks to freaking Tully showing back up?

The last time I was face-to-face with Tolbert Grimes Harrison III almost exactly one year ago, I threw a lasagna in his face and was suspended for a week. He graduated, I failed at remaking myself in France, and I came home to clean up the mess we made. What the hell is he doing on Jasmine's dinghy?

All the drive that pushed me to climb up the mast and over my classmates' heads drains to my toes, until I'm a just a girl clinging to a metal pole, not entirely sure how to get down. But it's not like anyone is watching anymore to see me struggle.

Or make that almost no one. I shimmy and fumble my way back down the mast and plop the last couple of feet onto my butt, only to see Jasmine staring down at me. She scrunches her face in concern.

"Ooh, Lo. Are you okay that Tully's joined us?" She's still on her skates, so I have to crane my neck to look up at her.

She grabs hold of a railing and offers her hand, and I let her haul me to my feet. "Why the eff is he here?" I ask, straightening.

Jasmine shrugs, and her bright brown eyes find mine. "He got back in town a few weeks ago. Didn't you see that on Insta?" She lets the question hang in the night air, and I fidget. "Oh shit.

I forgot. Didn't he block you after the whole . . ." She shuffles back and forth on her skates and waves her hand through the air, mimicking . . . what? A cheating scandal, an anonymous take-down account called "Lola Barnes Is a THOT," a lasagna to the face?

"Anyway," she continues. "I guess he spent the last year hopping around his parents' houses. You know, total PJ lifestyle or whatever. Ugh, the dream."

PJ. Private jet. The words drill through my thick skull and ooze into my brain. The mistakes Tully and I made were done together, but while I got labeled a slut and a whore, he was . . . on vacation? I grab Jasmine's arm, nails sharp against her skin. "Wait. Are you serious? He never got in trouble for what went down between us?"

Jasmine grimaces. "Hon, it's not like you got in trouble. You were at a freaking boarding school in France. I know I wouldn't have left early if I had that chance."

I throw back my shoulders and jut my chin. "Yeah, well . . ." Well what? Jasmine and I built our friendship on bickering— first over American Girl dolls, then sparkly eye shadow, then guys—but I can't find the line anymore. The tether between us is frayed beyond recognition. Her lips quirk upward into a triumphant smirk, and I wonder, if I rolled her over the side of the boat, how long would it take to find her?

Jasmine skates off before I can continue scheming. And, okay, obviously I'm not that obtuse. I know anyone should be thrilled to spend a year in France. But, the thing is, most people picture Paris, or, like, the Riviera. I was in a tiny village in Normandy with more sheep than people and two hours by train to Paris. It was an all-girls school where everyone in attendance had summered together since infancy and had names like Turmeric Tarringall-Buttocks-McFafferton. My family has a lot of money, but they're California rich, not "my name is in some big book of landed gentry" rich.

And right now, I blame Tully for *Every. Second. Of it.* You know what? I'll just ignore him. I'll look at him like Mom looked at that poor valet who accidentally brought around a Honda Civic at the club one time.

But before I can so much as give him my most basic sneer, Kat is at my side. Her fingers wrap tight around my wrist. "Let's go. Wash can drive us home. Don't move, I'll be right back and we'll leave. I mean it, Lo."

But I can't do that. I can already feel people watching me, waiting to see how I'll react to Tully. They probably have their phones already in video mode to capture us making out slash murdering each other. No, to leave now would look like I was running. And ew. I don't run.

Across the deck, Tully's being greeted like a damn prodigal. People surround him, howling with laughter while he pretends to throw Meg over the side even though she's slapping at his arm. A shiver works its way down my spine, but I grind my molars together to hide it.

Then his eyes find mine, and a smile unfurls across his face. I'm rooted to the spot. Dammit. I should have been the one to make the first move. Establish dominance, you know? Like a lion.

Tully sets Meg down and walks away from her, and my heart jumps the tiniest bit. Which is, like, super annoying.

Tully, with his carefully windswept sandy hair and wide shoulders. Tully, who laughs harder the wilder I get. Or he did. He did when I kissed him that first time even though he was dating Crenshaw's most popular senior, who happened to be a friend. I don't even know why I did it. Maybe because it made Tully laugh. Maybe because it made me feel invincible.

Everything from last year is all too hard to think about. So I don't. Think, I mean. It's one of my better qualities, if I'm being honest. Along with flawless makeup and the ability to cry on demand.

"Hey, Lola," Tully says, drawling and lazy. Behind him, Meg and Jasmine—who have now managed to change out of the roller-skating getup and into coordinated sundresses—scurry closer. My heart twists. I should have them, and Kat, on my side, not be facing Tully alone like this.

"Don't you have any college friends?" My lip curls. "I won't be caught dead at a high school party next year."

Tully's laugh thins, and his hazel eyes search the crowd. Ha! Point to Lola.

"Had to come make sure you guys know how to party without me. Has your sister finally stopped being so clingy? It'd be so much easier to get in your pants now."

"Oh my god, Tully," I shoot back. "I don't want you anywhere near my pants."

Tully shrugs, and it's so nonchalant, so empty of emotion, that I want to scream.

I can sense my twin shoving her way closer before I see her, but she stops dead a foot away from where Tully and I square off. "It's time to go, Lola."

Yet my attention doesn't leave Tully. If I back down now, he wins. And okay, don't ask me what he wins, because I can't quite say. But I do know that if I turn away, I look like the loser.

"Nah," I say to Kat, my focus on Tully. "Things are finally getting interesting. Go home without me. Sorry."

Kat's voice issues sharp and clear. "Lola Barnes, you are many things. But sorry isn't one of them."

Tully slings an arm over my shoulders as Kat stalks away. "That's my girl."

I duck out from under him. "I'm not your girl."

Behind me, someone whispers loudly, "No, you're the side piece."

Tully swings his attention between me and the crowd that's formed to watch this little reunion, and his mouth drops open. "Oh shit, man! Is this about last year? I'd totally forgotten all that."

I need another drink. Hell, I need an entire keg to deal with Tully's sudden reappearance. So new plan. Don't just ignore Tully. Get so drunk I can't even see him. I'm full of good ideas tonight. I walk away from him, stalk down the stairs into the cabin, and am already fishing through a jar of maraschino cherries before I realize Meg followed me. Her orange blossom perfume is the same one her mom always douses herself in after tennis at the club.

"So, um," Meg begins. She sways a tiny bit on her bare feet and says in a rush, "Tully and I—"

I arch one eyebrow and pluck another cherry, sucking it into my mouth, waiting for her to finish. She's always hated awkward silences.

"So," she starts again. "Tully and I are sort of hanging out."

"He just got home," I counter.

Meg rolls her lips together and plays with the edge of a paper napkin stacked on the bar table. "Yeah, but, um . . . you know how we went to Mammoth over New Year's? We stayed with his family. And, um . . . other stuff."

Right. Because Tully's been living like nothing went wrong last year. Because he's a guy and gets applauded for the same things that apparently get me ostracized. Sweet.

The cherry pops between my canines and squirts a satisfying bright red across the strap of Meg's dress. She hisses through her teeth, but at that second Tully hulks down into the cabin, his ego taking up as much space as his body.

"Is there about to be a girl fight over me?" He shoves his hands overhead, punching the curved, low ceiling. "Yeah, girl fight!" He bellows it, and above us on the deck, feet shuffle closer.

I purse my lips and reach across Tully for a beer, then look him up and down. "Don't flatter yourself." I loop my arm through Meg's and drag her forward a few steps before she gives up and climbs the stairs with me.

"You really don't mind?" she asks.

Faces turn our way back up on the deck, and I throw my mouth open in a loud laugh that draws in even more. I deposit Meg onto one of the banquette seats bolted to the deck and perch at the back of it, twisting to look down at her. "Oh, god, Meg, not even a little bit! Tully is . . ."

Well, he's reappeared, for one thing, his mouth hanging open as his attention jostles between us. "Tully is all yours."

A smile curls across his lips and he drops onto the banquette, knees spread wide. He slings an arm around Meg and slides his other palm along my leg. "I just unblocked you on Insta. Can we be friends again?"

I cross one leg over the other, out of reach of his hand. "Not likely."

His shoulders bunch in a laugh. "Ouch."

"So why are you back?" I ask.

Tully drags his arm from behind Meg and rubs a hand against his chin. "My dad's being a hard-ass about college and shit."

"As in, making you go?"

Meg steps in. "He's going to UCLA in the fall."

Tully shrugs. "I guess. School sucks."

Meg looks like my sister Marnie when someone disparages books. Honestly, Meg can do way better than Tully. If she didn't low-key hate me now, I'd tell her that. Instead, I decide to walk away from all this crap. I've made my point. Now no one will think Tully got the best of me again.

I make to stand, but an elbow jabs me from behind. My arms flail, grasping air, and I topple directly into Tully, my butt landing neatly between his thighs and my beer sloshing into Meg's lap.

"Shit, I'm sorry, Meg!" I squeak, and I actually mean it.

But her mouth is tight, and she won't look at me. She jolts out of the banquette, swiping at her dress and pushing her way through the crowd.

Tully jolts too. He dumps me onto the deck and jogs after Meg, calling for her.

And everyone—*everyone*—sees.

Heat starts deep in my chest and flames higher up my neck, into my cheeks. It burns up my nerves, until I'm raw and restless. I need to do something that'll make them forget what they saw. Because of Tully. Again. I shove to my feet, still searching for a way out of this, but it's not like there are a ton of places to hide on a damn boat.

I pound down the steps into the cabin, frantic for a distraction. My vision is edged in black and my heartbeat whooshes in my ears. What if they feel sorry for me? The thought of their pity makes me shiver with disgust. It's even worse than being ignored. My chest is tight and my throat stings with a scream that wants to unleash. I wrench open the narrow door to the bathroom and shove out the white girl who was reapplying lipstick.

The white porcelain sink is cool, and I curve down and press my forehead to the lip, but red draws my eye. Shoved into the corner beneath the pedestal is a plastic emergency kit, the word *FLARE* written in giant letters on the outside. I mean, I have always had flair. I squat down, rip open the kit, and grab the red flare gun. It sits heavy against my palm, the long, wide barrel tipping down and the trigger teasing my pointer finger.

The scream pressing against my chest thins to laughter. It's all for fun, right? This party was boring anyway, might as well kick it up a notch. Make it memorable, you know? Trust. Jasmine will definitely thank me.

I trot up the stairs and wave the flare around like a stubby baton. "Hey, wanna see some fireworks?"

Across the decking, Jasmine holds up her hands. "Put the flare down, Lola."

Tully, though, pushes to the front of the crowd and pumps his arms. "Dude, do it!"

My eyes are on Jasmine. "What—you afraid?"

"Of you shooting that thing in my face on accident? Uh, yeah." She's smiling, but her eyebrows are drawn together. She strides closer and I waggle the flare gun at the end of my loose wrist.

I tip my head back and laugh, spinning around in a circle, the flare pointed straight out in front of me like the weirdest game of pin the tail on the donkey ever. People spread out in a circle around me, some of them cheering. See? I'm not Tully's tragic leftovers. I'm fun. I'm a goddamned supernova when I want to be.

My fingertips fizz, and I feel light as air. Kat accused me of not really being sorry. And you know what, I'm plenty sorry about a bunch of shit. But not this.

Out of nowhere, Jasmine grabs my arm, wrenching my hand to try and get the flare, and my fizzy fingers slap against the notch of the trigger. There's a dull *thwump* and a kick and time slows down.

The flare streaks through a gap in the crowd and disappears down the stairs to the cabin. And if my stomach wasn't twisted up so tight in horror, I'd be pretty damn proud of my aim. There's a phosphorescent bang and an explosion of red sparks that ricochet up the stairs and spiral everywhere. Everyone dives out of the way as sparks streak black along the decking, tear through the canvas sheeting, and burn holes, ironically, in the banquette seating where Tully shoved me so gracelessly aside.

I drop the red plastic canister with a clatter and my hands fly to my mouth. That wasn't supposed to happen. People are scattering everywhere, screaming. The boat tilts back and forth under their feet, then dips precariously to one side. Shit. Shit.

But suddenly Tully's at my side, and he's practically cackling with glee. "God, I've missed you, Lola!"

He grabs my hand, and we jump straight into the moon-limned water.

THREE

"CONFIRMING, SIR. IT WAS THE yacht at slip twenty-seven—"

"It's really more of a dinghy."

The Santa Cruz Yacht Club security guard glares at me and turns his back to continue speaking into the phone. "Correct, Mr. LeGrange. The yacht—"

"At best, it's a speedboat."

Next to me, Meg rams her shoulder against mine. "Shut up, Lola. My god."

Fine. I wrap the disgusting, scratchy blanket tighter around my soaked body and kick my bare heels against the curb. Behind me, yellow lights from the guard's car flash off the boats still floating in the marina. I mean, the *Smooth Sailin'* is still "technically" afloat. It's just sort of . . . listing heavily to one side and slightly smoldering.

I'm not sure how much time has passed since Tully practically shoved me into the water. He's lucky I wasn't attacked by a shark. He's gone awfully quiet, hunkered down next to me on the concrete curb. The rest of the partiers have scattered— some as sopping wet as me, but no one else besides Tully and Meg has been detained by a security guard with entirely too much mustache and too little chin. Jasmine was certainly quick to point me out as the culprit, even though (let's be honest) everyone will be talking about her party now and that's only thanks to me.

The security guard is back, and he's scowling so hard into the phone his bushy blond mustache flutters. "I hadn't received notice of that, sir. And your daughter had the gate key. Before the boat caught on fire, everything was—"

There's a bunch of muffled shouting, and the guard's pasty white face goes alarmingly red. He looks like he's two seconds from shoving me back in the water. Perhaps if he'd done his job better, we wouldn't be in this mess.

"I, uh, let her leave the premises."

More shouting. I press my lips together, which are probably blue from the oncoming hypothermia. At last I'll die happy knowing Jasmine isn't going to shuttle all the blame onto me so easily. I'll put it on my gravestone: "Dearly Departed, but Not as Dead as Jasmine."

"Should I call the new own— Right, of course— Yes, I'll—" He stops short, grimacing and growling and generally huffing angrily while dialing a new number. I can hear the press of many voices over the line before it goes quiet and someone speaks. The guard repeats the whole mess over again, how a bunch of students from Crenshaw Day School in San Jose snuck onto the boat—yes, the boat this mysterious new man apparently bought, like, yesterday. I mean, terrible timing, dude.

"Their names?" the guard says. "Er, I'm not sure. Want me to— Right, of course, sir, I'll ask." The guard puts a hand over the bottom of the phone and fluffs his mustache in Meg's direction. "Uh, you. What's your name?"

"You don't need her name," I say, tilting my dripping head toward Meg. "I don't even know why you grabbed her." I let my teeth chatter, then add, like an innocent little lamb, "And why would you need my name?"

Tully grumbles and Meg groans. "I just want to go home."

There's a prick of fear at the back of my neck. I've been kind of numb from the cold, but the prick is quickly turning into a jab. Out in the marina proper, a floodlight illuminates a trail of smoke rising from the canvas sheeting. You'd think they'd make that less flammable. But really, the boat is still, you know, floating.

"Hey, did you hear me?" the guard shouts. "What's your name?"

My name? It's stuck in my throat. It's a big lump of regret with a sprinkling of anger that—once again—I got myself into an absurd mess.

"Her name's Lola Barnes," Tully grunts out. Which, thanks for that, Tully. My hero.

The security guard repeats my name, and the line goes suspiciously silent. He uses the intervening quiet to glare and adjusts his overstuffed utility belt. Really, how many walkie-talkies does one man need? He jumps to as the new boat owner speaks again, and the guard's little eyes volley between me and the boat as he listens.

"Uh-huh. Of course, sir. They won't move an inch, sir." He hangs up and turns on us.

"Was that your mom?" I ask.

He splutters. "You know it wasn't Mother."

"I need to use the bathroom." And by bathroom, I mean I need to call a car. Thank god for that waterproof upgrade, right? Dad finally caved after the second time I tried to use my phone in the pool. How was I supposed to know my oldest sister's triplets would jump in?

"You're not moving, young lady."

"What about me?" Tully asks. "I didn't do anything."

On my other side, Meg's chin jerks Tully's way. I'm pretty sure Tully would have shoved a baby out of the way to get onto a *Titanic* lifeboat.

The guard bristles and checks his phone. "You and the other one"—he jabs a finger toward Meg—"were at an unsanctioned party on private property. This is the Santa Cruz Yacht Club, not some public marina."

Well, la-di-da for you, sir.

The seconds tick by, marked only by the steady drip-drip-drip of my hair onto the gross blanket around my shoulders. It's quiet enough to hear the gentle slap of water against the other boats. It's also quiet enough to hear my own thoughts, which is not at all welcome.

Look, if there's anything I believe in life, it's that looking back is for losers. But sitting here, once again in trouble, with Tully beside me, I can't help but try to untangle how I got here. Tully and I started out as friends. I guess that's where it all begins. When Meg, Jasmine, Kat, and I started freshman year at Crenshaw, we were folded into the popular crowd of sophomores and juniors. Because, duh, we were hot and rad. But then the sparking sort of back-and-forth between Tully and me slid from friendship into flirting. I don't honestly remember when it happened, but suddenly every time we were around each other, the air was tense. And dammit, it was exciting. Which, ugh. Then near the end of my sophomore year, I decided his girlfriend was in the way, that they were going to break up anyway when they both graduated, so why not.

Why not? Because it kicked off a bunch of shit that has ruined my life. Because of my, as Mom dramatically calls it, "affair" with Tully, I went from popular to punching bag overnight. And I'm getting pretty damn sick of everyone refusing to move on.

My fingers clench the blanket to my chest, my serpent ring glinting dully at me. It winds around my ring finger, two tiny raw emeralds for eyes and minuscule etched scales along its body. I found it in a vintage market in Rouen, and it's the one good memory I have of my months in exile. I rub my pinkie against the smooth gold, shifting the ring back and forth, back and forth.

"So," I say, eyes still on the remains of the *Smooth Sailin'*. "When are you moving to LA, Tully?"

He shrugs again and grunts. "My parents finally let me take over the pool house at the back of the property. I've got a sweet setup. You should see it."

Meg sucks in a breath.

"I mean—" Tully stumbles into an excuse. "With everyone else. Like, you, Meg, obviously, and, uh, others. I messaged some of the guys from soccer now that everyone's on summer break."

Tully was a soccer star in high school and played with Joon. I used to catch nearly all his games. Regret swells behind my ribs, remembering how it was before I decided to make Tully mine—piling into a car with friends to cheer the guys on, staying up late with fast food and movie marathons, the gorgeous chaos of a half-dozen girls getting ready in a single bathroom for a night out.

But it's not like I can change any of that, and introspection sucks, so I'm almost glad when the guard's phone rings again. He answers faster than Mom judges *The Bachelor* contestants. He listens for a second to whatever is being said, then turns and stomps over to me. This can't be good. Foreboding crawls up my throat to roost.

"It's for you." He pushes the cell phone into my hands and

continues to glare. I blink away the shock, clear my throat, and lift the phone to my ear.

"H-Hello?"

"Hello, Lola," says an all-too-familiar voice.

Well, shit.

"Will."

My brother-in-law sighs, and I picture him as one tight line, his mouth, his shoulders, his asinine morals. He's so uptight I don't know how he can walk.

There's a long, pained silence. How the hell is he even on the phone right now? Does he have a bat signal for whenever I'm in trouble? My fingers ache where they clamp the scratchy blanket shut around my shoulders, and they wrench even tighter when Will says, "You sank my damn boat, Lola."

Oh.

Oh.

Well, how the hell was I supposed to know Will bought a boat? And yeah, I do now recall my older sister Lindy saying something about how she and Will were thinking of buying a sailboat and cruising around for the summer since she stepped back from her documentaries to heal after her accident, but I mean. What are the odds it was *this* boat? I mean, okay, I guess Will and Jasmine's dad work together. But other than that. Will interrupts my thoughts.

"Honestly, you're lucky it doesn't still belong to LeGrange. He's very litigious."

God, does Will expect me to thank him? What an ass. My voice goes acid bright. "Oh my goddddd, Will! What would I do without you! I am so glad you married Lindy and completely fu—"

"I could have you arrested."

My lungs shrivel up to walnuts.

"It's not even that damaged, Will. Just, like, lightly scorched."

"It was vandalism and willful destruction of property. Also, cops could tack on B&E since Jasmine definitely didn't have permission to host a party on, let me reiterate, *my boat*."

"She thought the sale wasn't done," I shoot back. "It's not my problem Jasmine's dad doesn't have open communication with his daughter."

Will's voice dips dangerously. "Lola."

"Fine. What's my punishment, since you seem to love that, you perv." I haven't forgotten it was his idea to send me to France last year after everything that happened with Tully.

"I am seriously two seconds from hanging up and calling the cops, Lola. I flew to Hawaii this morning for this tech conference and I'm wiped and have been schmoozing for hours and now suddenly I'm getting a call about you burning down my boat. But . . . but I have a proposition for you."

"Oh, goody. A proposition," I deadpan. He's probably going to make me alphabetize his record collection.

"I'm sure you remember my sister, Georgia. I'm on the board of her nonprofit."

My breathing shallows. Where is this going? This is the South

Bay; you can't toss an organic pine nut without hitting five people who serve on nonprofit boards to "diversify their optics."
I can feel Tully, Meg, and the security guard all watching me
closely. I should have chucked the phone in the water. I could
have claimed it was a bad connection when Will shows up at
my house jet-lagged and totally pissed. But it's pretty obvious by
now that I'm not very smart.

Oh god, he's still talking.

"So here's my proposition. I will not file charges . . . if you
complete a summer-long program with Georgia's nonprofit,
Hike Like a Girl."

"What like a girl?" Surely I heard him wrong. The
hypothermia—thanks, Tully—is affecting my hearing. Kite Like
a Girl? Sure. I'll even Fight Like a Girl. Hell, sign me up for Bike
Like a Girl. I still have that vintage Peugeot cruiser I begged Dad
for the summer after freshman year when I decided I was going
to bike everywhere and buy local flowers from the market and
store them in a cute basket. I did use it as a prop for some rad
Insta posts, I guess.

But hike? As in, with bears and shit? No, thank you.

"Hike Like a Girl," Will repeats, like I have ever, in my entire
life, shown an interest in nature. God, this is worse than France.
At least there I could wear good shoes.

So I do the only reasonable thing. "Whatever," I say to Will,
then hang up on him.

FOUR

THE SUNLIGHT STREAMING THROUGH MY bedroom window is being a real asshole. It's a cheese grater against my sandy eyes. But that wasn't what woke me up.

My bedroom door bangs against the wall. "Lola," Kat barks again.

Ah, there it is. I grumble and dig for my phone hiding somewhere in the tangle of blankets. I pull it up to one cracked eye and groan.

"It's not even one p.m., Kat. Totally unacceptable."

I flop over onto my side to glare fully at my sister, but she's determined. She barges into my bedroom and plants her bare feet wide, her arms crossed.

"Unacceptable? You're seriously trying to lecture me after what happened last night?"

My sister avoids confrontation like an Olympic sport, so I kind of have to give it to her for pressing on. The last time she actually yelled at me was two days after I got home from France and tried to throw myself a welcome home party. Attendance was sparse and she was pissy the whole night.

Kat sets her jaw and glares back. When it's pretty obvious I'm not going to respond because, seriously, I haven't even had any caffeine yet, she squeezes her eyes shut and bursts out with, "You tried to burn down Jasmine's yacht!"

One corner of my mouth scrunches. "I wasn't *trying* to do anything. And also, it wasn't Jasmine's boat, turns out?"

Kat's jaw drops. "Well, then, whose was it?"

I scrub at the tip of my nose and say to the wall over her shoulder, "Lindy and Will's?" She chokes on shock—like, actually starts choking—so I scramble to say, "Okay, but, I mean, it was barely a sailboat."

"Are you serious?" Kat rubs her temples. "You tried to burn down Lindy and Will's new boat?"

I kick my covers off and squint toward my window. Who the hell forgot to pull my shades yesterday? It's absolutely blinding in here. "Again, I didn't go there with, like, an arson plan. And if you think about it, I was doing them a favor. Now they can probably get insurance money or whatever and buy a better boat."

"Oh my god, so not the point," Kat says.

"Well, it should be."

"Stop trying to change the subject."

One of the worst things about being a twin is that they know all your tricks.

Kat jabs a finger at me so hard it makes her fluffy blond bun shiver. "You should have left with us. Instead you let Tully turn you brainless. Again."

"So sorry I didn't want to go play Trivial Pursuit with your new friends."

She throws up her hands. "We got Korean barbecue!"

My stomach growls so loud Kat smirks, but she grinds it down into a frown. "I hate how you act when you're trying to get their attention." She waves her hand toward my invisible audience . . . *them*. "You're not popular anymore. Get over it."

"I'm not popular *at the moment*. And I don't know why you don't care anymore." I'm not whining. I'm not. It's totally a coincidence that my voice goes all shrill.

She stills, her mouth forming an O to blow out a slow breath. Kat got super into yoga and intentional breathing (whatever that is) while I was stuck in France. Sorry, I mean she got super into yoga, intentional breathing, and *forgetting she had a twin* while I was stuck in France.

"I don't care because I remember what they all did to you," she says, voice measured. "And I remember how much it hurt you."

Scratch that. The worst thing about being a twin is that they know all your secrets. You're like all soft underbelly and they hold a fluffy warm blanket in one hand and a knife in the other.

The only question is which one they'll use on you. Apparently Kat brought the knife with her today.

Does she really think I don't remember? Of course I effing remember. I remember the photos, the way they zoomed in on my open mouth, on Tully's hands gripping at my thighs under the frayed hem of my shorts. I remember the comments, especially from the people who I'd thought were my friends but all sided so damn fast with his ex. I remember Mom weeping about having a "fallen daughter" like it was freaking 1813 and Will quietly offering his contacts to get me into the school that would solve everything. The problem is, everyone else remembers too. And I don't want that—*that*—to be all I ever am.

And now Tully's back, and I oh so predictably slid into my old patterns. The push and pull. The race for attention. I feel like sometimes I can't see anything past what's right there, the immediate, and when I wake up with the consequences I'm so full of regret my bones groan with the weight of it.

"What I care about is *you*," Kat says. "You'd be so much happier if you just moved on."

Debatable. But also . . . "Wow, is the sainthood in the mail? You *do care* about your effing twin, despite how terrible I am? Please clap, everyone."

Kat rolls her eyes. "You know what I mean. You've never even asked me what *my* life was like when you were gone."

I glare at her and say in a voice meant to rot teeth, "Hey, Kat. Tell me about *your* last year. Did *you* have to eat snails and smelly cheese every night for dinner?"

My sister screeches in frustration and throws her hands in the air. "I don't want to tell you now!"

My laugh is mean. "Of course you don't. Gotta save it all for your new friends."

What the hell happened to us that Wash and Joon—that *Ezra*—know my sister more than me?

"Just leave, okay?"

"Wait, Lo—"

"Holy shit," I spit. "Just go."

I hate myself the second it's out of my mouth. And I hate it even more when Kat ducks her chin and slips away. I flop back to my pillow. On the wall by the door, a giant corkboard is pinned with dozens of old photos of me, Kat, our friends. There's no photos of me alone, because I never was. And now . . .

Why is it so wrong that I want things to be like they were before? I liked being popular and having lots of friends. I liked spending more time with Kat than apart, sharing our life and our secrets with that weird twin shorthand. Everything was so much *easier.*

An ache blooms behind my eyes, so I squeeze them tight until it passes. I tug my comforter back up over my head, but sleep has decided to become a coy witch. Typical. I pull my phone up to my nose and scroll through Instagram and freeze when Tully's latest post comes up. I'd totally forgotten he'd unblocked me.

I hesitate for only a nanosecond before selecting his handle.

Come on. Of course I'm going to cyberstalk him. A year of—as Jasmine called it—living that PJ life scrolls past me. Skiing in Mammoth. Surfing in Baja. A rooftop in LA and a garden party in the Hamptons. So far as I can tell, none of his last year included a drafty castle with Stone Age plumbing and a dirt lane—dirt!—to reach the nearest coffee shop.

And then the unthinkable happens. My finger slips and I accidentally like a post from nine months ago. I shriek, wrench back my covers, and chuck my phone across the room. It hits the pile of clothes dumped on my Eames chair and vibrates.

Shit. Shitty shit shit. My heart crawls up into my throat like a frightened chipmunk and starts clawing at the inside, trying to get out. My legs get twisted up trying to get out of bed and I crash to the floor. I haul myself toward my phone and the new message laughing at me.

As in, literally. Tully has texted back *Ahahahahaha*.

Followed by a half-dozen eggplant emojis because it's Tully.

I roll over onto my back and pray for a quick death. But instead, all I get is this tomb of a room pressing in around me. Four bright white walls except for the Technicolor pink-and-green palm tree wallpaper behind my headboard. An orange-neon sign above my bed that scrawls the word *dreams*, except it turns out falling asleep awash in the hazy orange glow and buzz of neon is nearly impossible, so I have to unplug my dreams every night. I've had enough English teachers to know they'd say something about metaphors, but it's summer break so

I'm not about to analyze it.

The house goes silent around me. Not even the vibrating announcement of more eggplant emojis. Silence makes me twitchy. I stretch out and reach for the TV remote half-hidden under my bed, but the first thing to pop up is a Netflix show with a dozen unwatched episodes I've been saving to watch with Kat. They've been waiting for months, and the snide little "continue watching?" is a reminder of how fractured our lives have become. Instead, I command the smart speakers in my room to play a new album and try to let the music drown out my thoughts.

But it's all still there. Stubborn memories.

The thump of my butt hitting the deck when Tully dumped me off his lap in front of everyone . . .

The sizzle of the flare shooting away from my hands, red and angry and promising destruction . . .

The wild light in Tully's eyes when he grabbed my hand and yanked me into the ocean . . .

I press the heels of my hands against my eyes, hard enough to force pops of white in the blackness. If I could snap my fingers and make the "affair" with Tully disappear, I would. But the only way I can comprehend to make things better is to convince my old friends and my sister that I'm worth forgiving. Yet every time I feel like I'm getting close, I screw it up again.

Beyond my bedroom, the doorbell rings. There's a beat of silence, then the unmistakable sound of my older sister Lindy bellowing my name.

FIVE

"LOLA! GET OUT HERE!"

Naturally, I turn the music up. So loud I can't even hear Lindy knocking on my door and shouting my name.

See? Everything's fine. I didn't accidentally burn down the strange impulse purchase of two people who are still trying to get over loss by definitely dying at sea. Really, I probably saved their lives. Or at least saved them the embarrassment of breaking news about the indie documentary darling and tech scion being rescued at sea. Yet Lindy, who we've established is entirely ungrateful, pounds on the door again. Are she and Kat in this together?

Up goes the volume. The song is synth-heavy pop with a female vocalist and sort of reminds me of the single time I went out with the girls from Ecole d'Excellence, which I'm pretty sure is French for Lame-Ass Boarding School. We went into Rouen to a club and I very thoughtfully found a group of guys to buy us all drinks, but when I went to find the girls, they'd left. Without me. And that's how I made three sworn enemies from the British aristocracy.

They can join the club with Lindy, who at this second slams my door open. I feel the stomp of her feet through the floorboards, the not-so-gentle kick of her toes against my hip. The music abruptly stops and I'm left with the auditory aftereffects pulsing in my ears.

I squint up at my older sister, whose square jaw is practically quivering she's scowling so hard.

"Are you going to tell me it's time to face the music? Because I swear to god, I am not here for your puns today. I nearly died last night."

That scares a rush of harsh laughter out of her throat and she holds out a hand. When I don't take it, she squats down, forcibly grabs my arm, and yanks me up to stand. I help by letting my muscles liquefy. "I've brought you a medal of bravery," she says, grunting to keep me upright. "It's out in the living room, why don't you come see?"

Lindy walks me out to the great room like a golden retriever about to get bopped on the nose for piddling on the slippers again. At the dining room table, my parents and Will are seated and holding their metaphorical rolled-up newspapers.

"Where's Kat?" Lindy asks, peering around. "I assume she

was your partner in crime last night."

I bark a laugh and slump into a chair next to Mom. "So you're still on this bullshit?" I say, glaring at Will. His eyes are bloodshot and his face is drawn. That's his own fault for riding his high horse all the way across the ocean last night.

"Language, Lola," Dad says.

Mom pats my hand. "Lola, darling, did you really try to burn down Lindy and Will's new yacht? That hardly seems like you."

I love you, Mom. But it totally seems like me.

"Mom, come on," Lindy says from across the table. She flaps a hand at me for emphasis, like I'm over here holding a match to a model of the *Smooth Sailin'*.

"Julia," Dad says to Mom, "I drove down earlier to take a look at the damage myself."

"Okay, but that doesn't mean Lola did all of it." Mom turns to me, her eyebrows high. "Was there an emergency? Did someone make you shoot off that flare, darling?"

It's only now that Kat joins our little party by shouting from down the hall, "No one made her do anything."

Et tu, Kat-e?

Will turns to me, all brooding, stormy eyes and wild dark hair and severe mouth. I have no idea what Lindy sees in him. "Lindy and I really don't want to press charges or sue for damages. You're family, and that doesn't make us feel right."

"But," Lindy adds, leaning onto her elbows. Apparently shanking family does feel right to her. "That doesn't mean there are no consequences, Lola. You're lucky we happened to have already signed the paperwork so you have a chance to redeem yourself here instead of being handed over to the police."

Mom gasps.

"Tell me about this program you mentioned, Will," Dad says, ignoring the way Mom is now massaging her heart. "You said your sister founded it?"

"Hike Like a Girl was launched two years ago to teach young women self-reliance, confidence, and cooperation. It's also a feeder program for tech, helping to recruit more women to the industry." Will sounds like he's reading from an exceptionally dull website bio. Oh god, there he goes again. "Over the course of the summer, the small group—capped at five participants"— he pauses, glancing at me—"well, six this summer. Anyway, the *six* participants will build their hiking endurance and learn backpacking skills, all culminating in a fifty-mile, weeklong backpacking trip on a section of the Pacific Crest Trail."

Whoa, whoa, whoa. How many miles?

"Fifty miles!" Mom blinks at that number. "All this talk of hiking alone in the woods. It makes me nervous."

"Me too, Mom," I whine, letting my lip quiver for emphasis. "I'm scared what'll happen to me."

Lindy rolls her eyes so hard I'm surprised her chair doesn't tip over backward. "Come on, Mom, she's not going to be alone. Georgia lived out of her van for six months hiking and climbing routes around the West, and she's hiked this entire trail before.

And Lola," she says, turning her piercing gaze my way. God, she and Will are made for each other. How revolting. "Don't act like this isn't entirely your fault. Take some responsibility for once."

Pressure builds in my chest, tightens around my lungs like a vise. I'm trapped. There's no escape, no way out of this mess. My face feels hot, and I struggle to draw in a breath. My only option is to go nuclear. I mean, obviously I'd prefer not to, but they've forced me into it. I clutch Mom's hand and whisper to her, "It's like they're not even listening to our concerns."

"And when does this start?" Dad plays his part by ignoring us and addressing Will.

"In two days," Will answers.

My fingers go tight around Mom's hand.

"Two days!" Mom's voice is as clenched as my hand. She shakes her head in disbelief, stares around the table looking for sympathy. "This isn't . . . I can't believe . . . Tom, look at her!" Mom waves a hand at me and appeals to Dad. "She can't *camp*!"

Okay, maybe give me some credit. Camping can't be that hard, right? When we all stayed in that casita on the Riviera Maya a couple of years ago, I slept in a hammock next to our private plunge pool one night. That's basically the same thing.

Mom pushes back out of her chair and stands. "It can't have been that bad, surely! It's just a boat!"

Her voice climbs higher and higher, right on cue. A classic Mom Freakout is my only way out of this. But more than that, it works a change in me, like a pressure valve in my chest releasing all my fear and anger and incredulity that one dumb mistake could turn into basically a summer prison sentence. No, you know what? Mom's right! I can't camp! I mean, look at me. My hair is lavender. The term "sports bra" offends me.

"This is outrageous!" Mom presses a hand to her chest again, and it makes my own heart jump.

I surge out of my seat and face my traitorous family. Tears spring to my eyes, and I let them fall freely. God, I am so good at this.

Lindy and Will are competing to see whose mouth can pinch the hardest, and Dad is massaging the bridge of his nose.

"Do you want her to get eaten by a bear, Tom? Have you not considered what that would do to me if my youngest child is consumed by an animal?"

"Julia," Dad says, deploying his most soothing voice, but, like, read the room, Dad. Julia Barnes is beyond soothing. "No one is being eaten by a bear."

"Out there?" Mom shrieks. "Anything could happen. How can you stand by and say you don't care if your daughter is eaten by a bear!"

"Julia. Lola—" Will attempts.

I ignore him. Obviously. "You know where I don't have to worry about bears? At home."

Dad tilts his chin. "Actually, the threat here is mountain lions, because they come after dogs."

"Oh my god, Tom!" Mom sobs and sits down heavily, her

hands fluttering near her chest.

Lindy straight-up lays her forehead on the table and Will has both hands up, pleading for reason.

"There are murderers out there!" Mom bursts out, since no one seems to care about the bears. God, I'd be a prize for a serial killer. "And . . . and snakes! And cliffs!"

"Mom, calm down," Lindy pleads, her voice muffled against the table. "Please."

"Oh, don't you dare tell me to calm down. I am concerned for my child." Mom grabs me about the shoulders and holds me close because she actually loves me, unlike all these people who wouldn't care if I got swept off a waterfall out in the wilderness. Also, she's kind of choking me, but in a loving sort of way. "Don't any of you care about her? Don't you care about how I'll worry with her gone?"

Will holds up a palm. "The overnights are only after proper—"

Mom barrels on. "None of you have even thought how this will affect me!"

"I have, Mom," I say, snuggling into her shoulder to get a bit of clearance for my airway and looking out the corner of my eye in triumph at Lindy.

Mom coos into my hair. "You're the only one, darling."

"Will you both stop," Lindy snaps. "This is ridiculous."

I wheel away from Mom and glare. "Since you all want me to go away so much, I'll just go live in the woods right now.

Will that make you happy?"

My chin juts, and I stomp past Dad and out through the sliding glass doors behind him. I stomp all the way to the grove of trees at the corner of the yard, where a rickety ladder leads up to the old tree house Dad built for me, Kat, and Marnie. I'll probably get impaled by a broken rung, but I haul myself up the ladder and into my new home. It's a dusty mess up here, the walls lopsided and the wind chimes we hung from the overhead branches creaking like the opening bars of a horror movie. I collapse back against the rough trunk that runs up through the center of the tree house and splay my feet out.

All the fight leaks out of me. But I'm left with a hefty helping of petulance. I can't believe I'll have to live here now out of spite and I didn't think to grab a blanket or some snacks. My stomach grumbles, reminding me all I've got in there is old beer. If they actually do go through with making me do Hike Like a Girl, this will be my life now. I'll probably have to subsist on beans . . . or learn to hunt rabbits. This is all so unfair!

I thump my bare heels against the probably rotten floorboards and hiss as pain ricochets up my ankles. But the boards knock back. Great. I'm being haunted now.

But it's not a ghost who sticks her head up into the tree house. It's Kat.

Kat clambers up into the tree house and stands over me, arms crossed.

I pull my legs in, making room for her.

"Is this your plan? Hide in the tree house?"

I answer her with a shrug and pick at a clump of bark that's hanging from the tree. "I'm not hiding. I live here now."

The bark pulls away, and I try to press it back into the trunk, but it just crumbles into my lap.

Kat's nostrils flare dramatically. "They're trying to help!" She pinches the bridge of her nose, looking alarmingly like Dad for a second, and when she speaks again, it is forcefully measured. "People could have died, Lola. You realize that, right? You're better than this."

But am I? Because it's now twice in the space of a year that I've made a big enough mistake that my family has had to convene a war council to figure out what to do with me. The thought that I'm not capable of any better . . . that this is me. It's sour at the back of my throat. Heavy in my stomach.

I crane my neck to look up at my twin. Open my mouth to admit the unthinkable—that she was right about last night. I really should have gone home. But there's another knock on the floorboards, and I crunch my jaw back together and swallow down anything resembling remorse.

"Lola?" Lindy calls.

"Occupied!" I shout down at her.

Kat peers down the opening before kneeling in front of me. "You have to do this."

But all I see is our knees pressed together. We used to sit like this with thread pinned to our pants, braiding friendship bracelets for each other.

She leans forward and grabs my hands. "Seriously, Lo. You don't have a choice."

"It's bullshit."

"No, it's not. It's the price you pay for making mistakes. Actions have consequences."

My eyes flick toward the ladder. "I don't like these consequences."

"Yeah, well, I don't like some of your actions. No, be quiet." She squeezes my fingers fiercely when I open my mouth to argue. "Sometimes it's like you want people to think the worst of you so . . . what? So they'll never expect anything? It sucks because I know how much you could accomplish."

"Okay, but hiking?"

"Lo, come on," Lindy's voice calls, thin with exasperation. "Can you please come down?"

Eyes locked on me, Kat calls out, "Just a sec, Lindy, she's coming."

"No, I'm not," I counter, shouting toward Lindy. "This is my new home. I'm accepting no visitors at this time."

"Yes, you freaking are going down there." Kat's tone is low and urgent, and my will to cohabitate with squirrels starts to ebb. "I'm serious, Lo. You can sit up here and feel sorry for yourself and repeat the same mistakes over and over, or you can actually take charge and do something to make things better."

"Are you coming down or what?" Lindy calls from below.

Kat's right in front of me, her fingers tight around mine, but I miss her so much it's like an ache that's gnawing inside my gut. We used to get in trouble together. For the silliest shit. Like the time we reordered and taped up all Marnie's books so they spelled out swear words. But for the past year, ever since I got caught with Tully, I've made these mistakes on my own. There's been no one to run away with, giggling and tripping over each other. No one to stand next to as one of our sisters or a teacher or our dad lectures us. And now she's sitting across from me telling me to own up to my mistakes, to do better.

"I'm gonna have to do this hiking shit, aren't I?"

Kat nods. "Yeah, you are."

I let her haul me to my feet to go face Lindy. I wonder if she'll stand by my side when Lindy lays into me. But when we get down the ladder, she drops my hand and walks away.

SIX

AFTER MUCH THOUGHT AND CONSIDERATION, I go with the gold lamé high-tops. I might be forced to go hiking, but I still have some dignity.

According to the horrifically cheery welcome email from Georgia Drake—I'm immediately suspicious of anyone who is this excited about forests—Hike Like a Girl meets at a picnic spot west of San Jose. I've been told to look for the orange VW bus, which, no, thank you. A surfer once tried to hit on me at Half Moon Bay, and I was nearly tempted until I saw him walk back to a gross camper and realized he was living in it. Like, where do you go to the bathroom, sir?

So when I pull up to Georgia's orange VW bus and see her handing out T-shirts from the side of it? I mean, all signs point to yuck. There are five girls hovering around her, sort of introducing themselves and tugging the branded tees over tank tops. No one else is wearing gold lamé high-tops or a floral romper and wide-brimmed black felt hat. I can confidently say I'm going to hate this.

"Lola!" Georgia jumps out of the open sliding door of her bus-slash-home and strides over to me. She walks like her brother and has the same peachy-pale skin. Strike one against Georgia. I met her at Lindy and Will's wedding, obviously, but she pulls me into the type of hug you reserve for old friends. Her shock of wavy brown hair gets all up in my face and a few strands of it stick to my lip gloss when she pulls away.

She drags me over to the group. "Everyone, this is the last member of our crew, Lola."

I rub Georgia's hair germs off my mouth and say, ". . . Hey." The five girls just smile and wave even though I'm giving them every clue that I'm here under duress. It's still and quiet under the blue-green shadows of the eucalyptus trees, and it makes me want to crawl out of my skin. Everyone is staring. Is this over yet?

"We've all already introduced ourselves," says a white girl wearing hideous brown hiking boots. She's got the sort of posture that reminds me of the overachievers at Crenshaw. Like, the clipboard isn't there, but it's there. "I thought it was just the five of us, but we must have been super tight with the application rankings, I guess. Let's all go around again and—"

"Hold on, Beth," Georgia says, jumping back out of her orange bus with a wadded-up T-shirt in her hands. "We'll do proper intros in a sec."

Ha! Guess you're not the boss around here, Beth. I immediately decide to launch a personal vendetta against Beth. My heart warms the tiniest bit for Georgia, but then she attempts to toss me the T-shirt and it freezes right back over.

I watch the tee bump my elbow and fall to the ground. "Gotta be a bit quicker on your feet around here!" She eyes my shoes. "What size do you wear?"

"Uh, eight?"

"Same size as me! Want to borrow a more appropriate shoe?"

I look down at her "appropriate" footwear and cringe. "I'm good."

She blinks at me and barrels on. "Okay, then. That's your Hike Like a Girl tee, Lola, and I've got a bunch of other goodies we'll use out on the trail."

"These are voluntary, right?" I grab the tee and hold it out for inspection. It's the color of a mandatory PE uniform and emblazoned with an orange VW bus with the mountains behind, the name in a circle around the illustration with a pair of hiking boots hanging off the bottom of the G.

Georgia ignores me and claps her hands twice to get our attention. Strike two.

"Okay, girls! Welcome to a life-changing summer!"

A shiver works its way around the group, but I stop that shit dead.

"No matter if you're here because you're working toward a tech career or if you love nature like me—"

"Or," I interrupt, "because of some light arson."

The Chinese American girl next to me scoots away. Georgia laughs nervously.

"The point is," she says, trying to regain control of the conversation, "no matter what brought you here, out on the trail, we're all the same and we're all in this together. So! First!" She holds up a finger and jogs around to the back of her bus and returns with an armful of . . . sticks? Is this the part where we pick one name and club them to death? I vote Beth!

Georgia moves around the circle handing them out, choosing each stick according to the girl's height so they come up to our ribs. Mine looks like a low-rent wizard's staff, all gnarled and knotted, but the wood is pale and feels almost glossy under my fingertips. I mean, still totally ugly. Obviously.

"These are your hiking sticks, and they'll not only be a lot of use on the trail, but they'll also measure your progress. When I climbed Mount Fuji"—she pauses and the other girls ooh and aah appropriately—"you used a walking stick that you stamped with the elevation and station you'd passed. It's a really special way to remind yourself that you are making progress, even when it doesn't feel like it, and to remember the challenge."

At this, Georgia holds up the last walking stick that's still in her hands and shows off the elaborate symbols inked onto the stick. Show-off.

"So for each milestone we achieve over the next six weeks,

you'll earn a different colored leather thong to tie around the handle of your own walking stick." Georgia holds up her fist, where dyed leather thongs hang like a My Little Pony horse tail. "Be creative with it! I've had some girls add beads or wrap the grip in interesting patterns. You'll earn these for our first hike, first five-miler, first overnight, first fire, first full pack, first night on the trail."

My goal, obviously, is to not earn any of these. Though the faded pink one is kind of pretty. Wonder what it's for? Hopefully for quitting once Will has forgotten this ridiculous punishment.

"This is so amazing, Georgia," Beth enthuses. "I'll treasure mine forever."

I am going to murder Beth at the first opportunity.

Across the circle, the girl next to Beth—the one with light amber skin and a curly topknot—gives Beth a sidelong glance. Ooh! She can be my accomplice!

"Okay!" Georgia claps again. "If I could get a couple volunteers to help me haul some gear"—five hands rise in an obvious scrum to be teacher's pet—"let's go find a shady picnic table and get started! Then we'll get out there for our first hike!"

The gear in question includes a bunch of nylon bags full of mysterious shit, a metal contraption with legs, some sort of pump, and a little shovel with a stubby handle. I bring up the rear, helpfully toting my T-shirt (still not on) and a bunch of disdain. The last person to wear my high-tops must have walked through bacon grease, because I'm skittering over the gravel trail like they're Baby's First Stilettos.

Finally, down in a dusty gully next to a river, we make it to the picnic table, which is legit disgusting. My palm gets dirty wiping off the slats before I sit down. Thank god I didn't bring my Celine bag, opting instead for a low-key Madewell mini-backpack. Speaking of, I shove the T-shirt deep into the bottom of the bag and hope to never see it again. The girl next to me—not Beth, praise, but a South Asian girl—is wearing a purple backpack with some sort of hose sticking out of the top. She sticks the rubber hose in her mouth and drinks. What in the hell am I doing here?

We're seated three to a side, with a lineup of bullshit between us and Georgia standing at the head of the table. She claps her hands again.

"So, before we get into what all this is for," she begins, waving at the gear like she's about to unveil birthday prezzies, "let's get to know each other. I'd love to hear where you go to school and the number one thing you hope to gain from our summer together."

The girl next to me with the backpack slash drinking fountain goes first. "I'm Priya. I go to Albion Prep and study chemistry, and I guess I'd like to gain resiliency." She turns to me expectantly, and I almost feel bad for letting her down so fast. She's got an open smile, but it drops when I say, "Pass."

Georgia cocks her chin in my direction, but recovers quickly. "We'll come back to you, Lola. Tavi, how about you go next."

On my other side, Tavi is ready to go with "leadership skills." She pushes long twists over her shoulder and explains that she's a sprinter at St. Pius but wants to pivot to coaching after focusing on marketing and communications in college, Stanford hopefully, but Loyola is her backup school. I don't even know what I want to eat for dinner tonight.

When Beth opens her mouth to start talking loudly and confidently about . . . wanting to gain confidence, I pull out my phone, scrolling through social media under the table.

Georgia clears her throat. "No one needs a phone out," she says, looking at me but not saying my name. "Give your respect to your crew." My lips compress to a thin line as I drop my phone into my bag, where it lands with a dull plop.

"Beth, go on."

Beth does go on. And on. Next to me, Tavi inspects her nails. Priya's going to have to find a bathroom soon with how much water she's sucking down. Finally, after approximately forty-five years, Beth finishes her speech and somehow stops herself from standing and taking a bow. Next to her, the girl who scooted away from me after I brought up arson says her name is Mei and that she wants to build strength. Despite her anti-arson bias, I like her already because she didn't accompany that with a two-thousand-word personal essay. Corinne, the girl with the topknot dyed a deep auburn with dark roots, runs a finger along a knot in the wood and says connection with family and meeting new people. God, I'd be embarrassed for such a confession if she wasn't also wearing the hell out of perfect winged eyeliner.

And that just leaves me. Everyone stares, expectantly at first and then with increasing unease. I'm never at a loss for words, but suddenly my mouth has gone bone dry.

"Lola?" Georgia prods.

"TBD," I finally say. Georgia raises her eyebrows. I shrug and tack on, "I mean, I'm not sure what I'll gain yet. But . . . but I'm open to the possibilities."

I am definitely not open to possibilities, but it's enough to get Georgia off my back. She claps again and directs us all to check out her lineup of weird stuff. "Okay! Who can name any of these things!"

"Is the shovel for digging our own graves when we realize we're stuck in the woods with no signal?"

Across from me, Corinne goes *heh* and I'm not sure if it's a laugh or disapproval, but, I mean, who cares.

Georgia smiles, but it's strained. Give me five minutes alone with her and I'll have her in tears. "Okay, so this is a shovel, like Lola pointed out, but hopefully we won't be using it to dig any graves. Everyone signed their waiver, right? Ha!"

The other girls laugh obediently. Chumps.

"I usually ease into this discussion, but since Lola brought it up, let's get into it. This trowel is used for digging a grave . . . for your poop." She grins and shoots finger guns. God, being a goober must run in the Drake family. "That's right, let's talk pooping in the woods."

"I won't be doing that," I say quickly, clearing up any misinformation that may be floating around.

"Come on, we're all going to do it. Now, who's heard of 'pack it in, pack it out'? When we're out on the trail, we've got to get used to doing our business in nature. And a really important aspect of that is not leaving behind any garbage. So you use your trowel, do your business, cover up any solid waste, and make sure to pack out your used wipes or toilet paper."

Pack out . . . as in . . . my eyes fixate on the trowel as the meaning sinks in. This isn't what I expected. This isn't a bit of a walk and camping for the 'gram with some artfully arranged boho blankets and a s'mores kit. The realization makes my skin go cold. You know what? The only thing I'm about to pack out is myself. Like, right now. Nope. Sorry. Strike three goes to bringing my own dirty toilet paper home with me like literally the shittiest souvenir ever.

I clap my hands—Georgia should love that. "And I'm out. Sorry, I can't do this." I shimmy a leg past Priya and climb away from the picnic table. I can barely spot the parking lot through the trees and gross underbrush, but I speed-walk back toward my sweet, sweet escape.

I'm nearly back to my car when a voice calls out.

"Hey!" Without breaking stride, I hold up a hand in a good-bye and grab my door handle, but the voice calls out again. "Hey, hold on!"

I turn reluctantly to see Corinne. The only reason—the *only* reason—I give her a second is because I respect her eyeliner game.

She jogs to a stop in front of me and huffs out a laugh, holding out my forgotten hiking stick. "Hey," she says again. "You forgot this. And it's not that bad."

"Shitting in the woods? Yeah, I'm going to say it is that bad."

"No, I mean, the whole program. I can tell you're, like, not on board, but I did a ton of research into this program, and Georgia's legit."

She looks like she's about to keep going, so I hold up a palm. "No, dude. No. Don't give me your hiking cult sell. I don't want to buy any of your illegal kombucha."

Corinne gapes at me, so I jump in my car and toss the hiking stick at the passenger seat. Before she can react, I push my oversized, mirrored sunglasses onto my face and leave her standing alone in a parking lot.

SEVEN

I HAVE NO IDEA WHERE I am.

I mean, that's pretty normal. Google Maps never gives me good directions. Like, turn now, Google? Right now? Into this river?

As long as I'm not stuck with a bunch of weirdos who chose to spend summer surrounded by rocks. And it's not like I can go home yet, where everyone will ask me a bunch of prying questions.

But also, I legit am lost. I dive across two lanes of traffic to the soundtrack of blaring horns and bail on the expressway. I veer into the first gas station on my right, get all turned around, exit the wrong direction, and get stuck on a side street of bungalows before being spit out onto a random wide road that looks like every other road around here. Wait, not some random wide road. That's the turn to the valet parking in front of the Prada entrance at Valley Fair—Mom's favorite mall entrance.

It's so old-school, but I unironically love the mall. I am my mother's daughter, after all. Maybe shopping would relieve this awful pressure at the back of my ribs. A smoothie and a quick jaunt through the makeup counters at Nordstrom to see if the elusive C.Rahmani+Co Blond lip palette is back in stock. Great plan, Lola.

But the car continues straight; oddly I am choosing to drive away from Valley Fair. Which makes no damn sense. Except . . . except the thought of being alone at the mall makes me shiver. What if someone I knew saw me? God, I might as well be my sister Marnie, who once declared she had no need for friends because she had books, except even she now has a boyfriend and a rad best friend and I'm . . . I'm driving away.

Until the road dead ends at some sort of complex smashed between the snarl of Caltrain tracks and the green ribbon of the river park. There's a building that looks like a mountain of over-sized shipping containers stacked one on top of the other, the containers sticking out like spokes and one big wall of windows in the center reflecting the sunlight. Out front, there are a bunch of dirt mounds and weed clumps where people are mountain biking for some reason, and a giant bronzed statue of a bear on its hind legs where a family is posing for selfies. I have no idea why. Maybe they're into weeds and shipping containers.

I throw the car into reverse, but someone honks, and I realize there's a line of cars behind me, waiting to turn into a narrow parking lot. I guess I live here now. One last parking spot down at the end opens up, and I swing the car in and shut off the engine. It's only now that I see a huge metal sign drilled into the side of the ground-floor shipping container.

BASECAMP, it declares, and underneath that promises *Adventure*—gross—*Gear*—but why?—*Education*—no, thank you, this is summer—and *Caffeine*—okay, I can work with that.

Between the family posing with the bear statue and the white guys in bandannas giving each other high fives as they wait their turn on the mountain bikes, it's all so . . . wholesome. Probably none of these people lit a boat on fire within the last week.

Indecision pins me to my seat. I tug out my phone, ignore the missed messages in my Barnes Sisters group chat, and open Instagram. The first thing that pops up—because of course—is a photo of Jasmine, Meg, and Tully at his pool. They would never expect me to use a poop shovel.

Before I can think too hard about it, I DM Tully. We've only talked once since the Boat Incident, when I told him about HLAG. **Wut r u doin? Bailed on stupid hiking.**

He responds almost right away. **Hell yeah! Knew you wouldn't last.**

Knew. You. Wouldn't. Last.

Right. I get out of my car and head inside.

Okay, focus. Caffeine. The sign promised caffeine. I can figure out my next move after some coffee. The heavy glass door opens into a dimly lit hallway flanked by stylized trees, a variety of outdoorsy crap hanging from the limbs. There are even nature sounds piped in, like I'm walking into Backwoods Disney. The hallway opens up into a central atrium, and at the far end I spot people scrambling over a fake rock wall studded with colorful handholds and jangling ropes. I mean, ew. Why would someone climb a wall when the stairs are right there?

"Welcome in!" a guy wearing a name tag says, jumping out from behind a display of flashlights that hang off some sort of stretchy band. "How can I help you discover adventure?" He's wearing cargo shorts. I have made a huge mistake.

"No, thank you," I say to him, walking away. The only thing I want to discover is a nap. But also . . . wow, it is so freaking obvious I am not meant to be here. How could I ever have thought I could do this? Mom and Tully were right.

But my feet drag me farther into the store, past nylon jackets, over a fake river, and onto a fake island surrounded by fake trees. There's a campsite in the center, with a neon-green hammock, navy-blue camp chairs, and a squat burnt-orange tent fluffy with black sleeping bags. There is absolutely no cohesion to the color story they're trying to tell. I swing the hammock with a slap and crawl into the tent and sit. At least that's real.

I pull out my phone for a bit of doomscrolling and regret it immediately. The ignored texts from the Barnes Sisters group chat blink at me. There's twelve years separating us, from my oldest sister, Joss, down to me and Kat as the youngest, and a lot of the time I feel that separation, not any connection, especially since my oldest sisters are both married and my middle sister, Marnie, is about to move away for college. But the group chat puts us all on even footing. Or it did, until I read the following.

Joss: How'd it go, Lola? I read all about Georgia's program and it sounds lovely!

Lindy: Heh

Marnie: I tremble to think what those poor women are in for.

Kat: I tremble to think what nature is in for.

Marnie: Can you imagine Lola facing a bear?

Joss: 😊 😊 😊 The bear wouldn't stand a chance.

Lindy: Taking bets. How long will Lola last before storming off into the woods?

My fingers fly over the keypad. **U all suck. I could be dead at the bottom of a cliff and ur making fun of me.**

Lindy: Oh god, she's haunting us!

Marnie: Lola, I love you, and there is no way you last more than five minutes in the wilderness.

I grit my teeth and mouth the words as I type: **Well, I don't love u and u wouldn't last 5 minutes w/o ur nose in a dumb book.**

Marnie: Hmm? Sorry, I was distracted by my hot boyfriend currently making out with me.

I audibly gasp.

Kat: Gasp!

Lindy: Damn! Get it, Mar!

I hate u all. I'm doing an amazing job n they've already voted me head girl. I hit send and slam my phone down onto my knee.

Dammit. Dammit! My shoulders sag, and I hunch forward. The air mattress underneath me is slowly losing air, and my high-tops, though freaking rad as hell, are turning into a real trench foot situation.

There's this horse that lives on the farm next door to Joss and her wife, Edie. They call it the Pouty Pony, with its long, sad face and blond forelock always covering one eye. Right now, I feel like even that horse would take one look at me and tell me to buck up. I paw at the ground in discomfort and tug one of the sleeping bags over my lap.

I'm so lost in thought—not recommended—that I don't even notice an employee squat down in front of the tent. "Um, miss?" She's a perky brunette with two tight French braids, her green tee says "BASECAMP" and her name tag says "Sheena— Assistant Manager." "Can I help you?"

"Neigh."

Sheena's smile falters. "Okay, well, I'd be stoked to help you discover adventure. We've got some great sleeping bags rated to negative thirty on sale right now." Pause, pause. "Okay, well, if you're sure."

I blow a big raspberry breath out of my lungs, and Sheena hoofs it. Ugh times a million.

I'm doing a super great job feeling sorry for myself when someone else squats in front of the tent. He's got the same forest-green T-shirt and name tag, but when I look up into his face, I blink in confusion.

Ezra Reuben sighs, crawls into the tent, and sits down next to me.

EIGHT

EZRA CROSSES HIS LONG LEGS under him and leans his elbows onto his knees. The light through the orange nylon bronzes his unruly light brown hair and deepens the tone of his skin, already tan with summer. I swear to god, if he asks how he can help me discover adventure—

"So my shift manager said there was a girl in here neighing at people."

I should have known Sheena was a narc.

"You neigh at *one* person . . ."

A corner of his mouth lifts a fraction, then falls. "Are you okay?"

Ezra's question takes me by surprise. I pick at the sleeping bag draped over my lap and say, "You heard about the boat?"

I assume he left with my sister, but Crenshaw Day is a small school. Even nerds like him eventually hear all the gossip.

Ezra presses his lips together. "Yeah, I heard about the boat."

"Okay, but it wasn't, like, on purpose. And I probably wouldn't have even set off the flare if Jasmine hadn't tried to grab it out of my hand and—"

"Lola," Ezra cuts in. He tilts his chin and widens his eyes behind his glasses. "Why are you sitting inside a tent in an adventure store in San Jose?"

"Oh. Right. That." I sigh and twist my serpent ring around my finger. "My parents are making me do this summer hiking program to, you know, make up for the whole boat thing. And I guess it just feels like it's setting me up for failure. Again. I mean—" I peek up at Ezra, but he doesn't say anything. This close, I can pick out a constellation of light freckles across his cheeks that I've never noticed before. I shouldn't be saying all this to him, but he crawled in here and sat down next to me, so I guess this is a therapy tent now. "I mean, it's just— Not even my mom thinks I'll be able to do it. And that sucks, you know? But she's probably right! I should go tell them that it's too hard and I can't do it. But also, I don't want to quit and confirm everything they already think about me."

Wow. Okay, so that was a lot. I roll my lips together and stare down at my lap. After a minute, Ezra's voice fills the tent. It strikes me that it's deeper than it was when we were lab partners freshman year. Less reedy and more confident.

"Do *you* think you can do it?"

No one's asked me that. Um, well . . . "Honestly? Probably not."

Ezra shrugs. "Why not?"

I wave a general hand over myself. "Have we met?"

"We have." He clears his throat, then says, "Can you promise to not make it weird if I tell you something?"

Curiosity makes my pulse jump. "This is the sharing tent, go right ahead."

A smile drifts across his mouth. "You probably don't remember, but freshman year, when we were in honors genetics. People used to call me . . . a name."

"Ezra Boo—" He cringes, so I pull it back. "Right, I remember."

"Yeah, it sucked. But the first time someone called me that in class, you stood up and told him that it was dumb and to never say it again. Just like that. I know we haven't, um . . . been around each other in a long time, but yeah . . . You used to not give a shit what anyone thought." Ezra pauses, his face turned down toward his lap. He fists his hand, and I watch a cord of muscle tighten in his forearm.

Until this second, I'd forgotten about standing up like that in class. And it didn't make people suddenly stop teasing him. He was still Ezra Booben, still the skinny nerd with the glasses and backpack weighed down with homework every Friday when the rest of us were making plans. But also . . . he's right. When did

I become someone who cared so much what others thought of me? The realization makes me shift with discomfort.

"I'm definitely gonna be weird about this," I say, more to move on from these uncomfortable thoughts than anything.

Ezra groans. "I knew I—"

"Hey, no. I'm joking. Thanks for telling me that."

He looks up at me with clear gray eyes, and my heart skips a beat. "You're welcome. Just . . . You're capable of way more than you think, okay?"

Something in his words takes that tiny little seedling that wanted to prove everyone wrong and gives it room to grow. Everyone thinks I'll fail. But not Ezra.

Dammit. I'll do this. And I'll become the best effing hiker or camper or whatever Hike Like a Girl requires. And I'll do it purely out of spite. The way all good decisions are made.

Across from me, Ezra glances at his watch, a sensible thing with a faded green band and utilitarian face. I eye him. With his clearly-well-used hiking boots and slim, well-worn pants and all around Boy Scout looks.

"So anyway," he says kind of awkwardly. He pushes his wire-frame glasses back up his nose. "My break just started, and—"

Instead of letting him finish, I crawl out of the tent. Ezra scrambles out after me, but peers past me to the big climbing wall.

"Like I said. It's my break, and there's this route that's been destroying me, so. Um." He nods at the wall—again, there are stairs *right there*—and slides his hands into the pockets of his dark pants and rocks onto his heels. Neither of us move.

"What do I need?" I blurt it out and scrunch up my nose. "You're obviously the expert here, and if I'm going to do this hiking thing, I'll probably need, like, gear and shit. So . . . what do I need?"

Ezra looks from me to the wall, then back again. His lips press together, digging dimples into the creases on either side of his mouth, before he sighs and says, "Come on, follow me."

He grabs a canvas shopping basket and leads me back around to the nylon jackets. We pile in a black water-resistant shell, wool socks, a black ball cap with a mountain patch on the front, and a metal water bottle when I flat-out refuse something called a CamelBak. (Though the mystery of Priya's backpack drinking fountain is solved.) We've woven in and out of four of the "containers" spoking off the main atrium, and as we're walking toward the shoes, he pauses to throw in a few more essentials from the gear section: flashlight, the headlamps I noticed earlier (note: I will choose death before I wear a headlamp), first aid kit, waterproof matches, and a pocketknife.

At one point, he tells me to hold on a sec and jogs over to an older couple poking at a row of bright yellow kayaks balancing on their points. I nudge the overflowing shopping basket at my feet and watch the way Ezra's hands move when he talks to the other customers. They smile up at him like he's the mayor of Basecamp, and, I mean, he does kind of fit the role perfectly. He looks like he pees pine scent.

Ezra glances back at me, holds up one finger to make sure

I'll wait. He grins, and my god it's so adorable in that moment that my cheeks prickle with heat. Obviously I've gone too long without a proper boyfriend if a guy who owns a Hawaiian shirt is making me blush.

"Sorry," he says, jogging back over. "I was helping them earlier with the kayaks, so I wanted to see if they'd made a decision." He smiles again, and my stomach flips. I follow him like a puppy up a set of stairs and into the shoe section.

"Okay, so I think this should be the last big thing you need for hiking," he says, signaling for one of the employees—oh god, it's Sheena—to come help. She measures my feet and heads off, and Ezra grins, the dimples reappearing. Which is, like, so annoying. No one should be allowed to have gorgeous hair and a pretty mouth and dimples.

I heft the canvas shopping basket off the ground, and *oof.* "You've definitely earned a new Boy Scout badge for this."

Ezra laughs. "Oh, I earned my community service badge years ago."

"Wait, are you really still in Boy Scouts?"

Red creeps up his neck, but he clears his throat and shrugs. I watch the way his Adam's apple bobs when he swallows. "Um, it's Eagle Scouts now. Over spring break we did fifty miles of the CDT."

I assume CDT is a drug.

"Continental Divide Trail," he amends. "It's actually really rad."

"Oh, Ezra," I say, giving him the same gentle smile I give Joss and Edie's triplets when they're super proud of their block towers. "No one would ever accuse you of being rad."

That pulls a deep laugh from him. "True."

"Okay, so giant, enormous, unreasonable hikes. What else are you doing this summer?"

He peers around right as Sheena rejoins us with her own block tower, this one of shoeboxes. "Um, this."

"Well, we've already established that I'm, like, on my way to becoming an ultra-athlete, so I'll probably be back. But, like. Um . . ."

Oh my god, what am I doing? Are these . . . nerves? No way. It's probably that it's been a while since people have wanted to actually talk to me, and man, realizing that is not great for the ol' self-confidence.

Sheena clears her throat in a highly irritating way. Like, a perky throat clearing. "Hey, Ezra. Unless my watch is wrong, your break ended five minutes ago."

"Oh, he's helping me," I cut in. I mean, duh. Read the room, Sheena. Then leave it.

She smiles brightly and I imagine kicking her. "Well, now I'm here to help you! Let's take a look at these awesome shoes I've pulled for you!"

Ezra shrugs and backs up a step. My heart tugs suddenly, and I'm aware that I really don't want this conversation to be over. "Sorry about the rock wall," I say. I honestly didn't realize he'd spent his whole break with me.

He waves me off. "I'm there practically every day. I can skip once." He's still backing up, eyes on me.

"Okay," Sheena says, sliding in between us and blocking his face from mine. "Thanks for helping out this customer, but I can take it from here." Her smile seems like a challenge, and I decide to be the customer she has nightmares about until the day she dies.

Ezra leans around Sheena and flashes me a quick smile, adding, "Backpack! You'll need a backpack. Later, Lola."

He turns and hustles down the industrial iron steps, and I'm left with Sheena. Who is, we've established, the worst.

She bounces on the balls of her feet and claps. I should introduce her to Georgia. "I think you're going to love some of these shoes!"

Doubtful. All of them are objectively hideous, but after twenty minutes of complaining and indecisiveness that wipes the smile from Sheena's face—victory!—I end up with a pair of light brown boots that hit just above my ankle and have bright red laces. They were, I hope she's noticed, the very first pair I tried on. Finally, I lug all my purchases over to the backpacks and stare. I never knew there were so many backpack options.

From where I'm at, I can peer into one of the shipping containers where rows and rows of those sleeping bags Sheena was trying to shill hang. Ezra's got another couple rapt and nodding at him, their hands rubbing sleeping bags. It's . . . weird seeing him like this. Confident, I guess? Freshman year, he was shy and gawky. Sophomore year I was preoccupied with Tully. And junior year I was either in a different country or busy trying to reclaim my spot in the Crenshaw hierarchy (a work in progress). But in the nearly three years since I've interacted with Ezra . . . I shake my head and focus on the backpacks in front of me.

I grab a mini Fjallraven Kanken in a washed-out red and a multicolored, retro-style hip pack that I've actually seen on some of my favorite Insta influencers.

After paying for my piles of stuff and tossing it all on the back seat of my car, I perform a pretty graceful twelve-point turn and drive back up the road and screech to a stop at an intersection. On the dash, Google Maps tells me to turn right. Right leads home. Left leads back to Georgia and Hike Like a Girl.

Snippets of some random poem we read in school float up in my subconscious. Two roads diverged in a wood or whatever. A car behind me honks, which I'm pretty sure didn't happen in the poem.

Right or left? Comfort and giving up, or risk and possible reward?

I glance at the hiking stick lying against the passenger seat, flick on my blinker, and turn left.

NINE

GEORGIA AND CORINNE ARE PACKING up the orange VW bus when I come careening into the lot and park sideways next to them. They both pause and stare as I casually amble over, trying my hardest to look like I was out on a coffee run and didn't go streaking off into the night.

"Hey."

Georgia takes her time stowing the last of the gear in cubbies built into the back of the van. It's actually kind of neat, now that I look closer. There's a compact kitchen setup, with a cooktop, sink, and mini-fridge fitting into a sleek blond wood design, and everything looks tidy and kind of . . . cool. God, no one tell Will Drake I find anything about his little sister cool.

Except, well, changed into tough black boots and dark jeans, she's even making the ugly Hike Like a Girl T-shirt seem like a whole "look." With her thick, wavy hair tumbling down and her dark sunglasses, I'm struck that she's the sort of person I'd try to emulate if I wasn't committed to loathing her.

"So, I'm still suspicious that this is all a front and I'm going to wake up in six months wearing caftans and eating dandelions for every meal, but . . . I'm in."

Georgia pushes her sunglasses into her hair and stares at me with such obvious contempt that I nearly run away shrieking. That is such a Will look I want to die. Earlier, she was buoyant and radiating smiles. Now all she radiates is cold disdain. Corinne tugs at one of the springy curls tumbling over the knot of her yellow headband and stares back and forth between us.

I try for a laugh, but it turns to dust in my throat. God, did she and Will go to How to Stare in a Quietly Menacing Way school? I wither under her glare and pick up a vintage saucepot tucked away in the kitchen cabinet. It's painted around the outside with lemons and is kind of obscenely adorable.

"Don't touch that," Georgia says evenly.

My eyebrows crawl high, but I replace the Queen's Cooking Pot. I rock onto the outside edges of my high-tops and stare at a poop shovel secured in a cubby like it's high art.

"Okay, but I'm serious," I finally say, unable to stand the awful silence any longer.

She stares before saying, "About . . . ?"

Seriously? I think I made it very clear, but Georgia quirks one eyebrow and waits. "I mean, about giving Hike Like a Girl a try. It's, like, good for my character."

Supposedly.

Georgia takes her time locking things into place, and I'm half tempted to explain to her that she wouldn't have to worry about her cutlery sliding away if her home didn't have wheels, but I keep my mouth shut. She swings down the back gate of the bus and leans against it, arms crossed. She is an awful, awful person and I wish I could intimidate people half as well as she can.

"How can I prove it to you that I'm serious? Like . . . is there a craft project I should do?"

Georgia sort of snorts. "This isn't Brownies, Lola."

Okay, okay. I roll my lips together, thinking. A terrible pastime, I know.

"I mean, I could hike. Like, do a hike on my own before the next meeting? Would . . . would that work?"

Georgia takes a long time considering my proposal. "You missed the first hike today, so didn't earn your milestone." She gestures at Corinne's hiking stick, which I just now notice leaning casually against the wheel well of the bus, being a total asshole with its pale pink leather thong wrapped around the top.

White-hot jealousy flares in my heart, but I shrug and say with perfect boredom, "Okay?"

Georgia blinks slowly, holds up a finger. "At least two miles. I'll want to see it logged on a tracker app. And I mean outdoors and not on pavement, Lola."

Ugh. Georgia, you are the worst.

"Duh, what else could you mean?"

One side of Georgia's mouth pinches. She climbs into the driver's seat and cranks down the window.

"Oh, and if you bail on this one more time, you're unwelcome in the group and I'll be in touch with Will about the next steps."

Next steps, as in an orange jumpsuit. A police record. Shit.

She smiles in the same way a crocodile cries—predatory and only to terrorize. "And Lola? Next time, wear your T-shirt."

God, can this day get any worse?

Oh, wait. It can. Because when Georgia's bus lumbers away and I let my shoulders finally droop, Corinne comes to stand next to me.

"I promise you, I'd never eat a dandelion." She grins, but I'm pretty sure she'd eat a whole field of dandelions if it meant impressing Georgia. "I'm happy to share some of my favorite easy hikes in the area, if you'd like. I once dragged an ex-girlfriend on a trail that was too hard, and I'm not saying it's why she broke up with me, but . . ."

Corinne is nice, and I can't deny that I'm seriously a bit envious of this winged eyeliner she's perfected. But also, she smiles in this open way that is so eager it makes me take a step back. What are you peddling, lady, because I am not interested.

"Nah," I say. "I'm good. I mean, how hard could it be?"

It turns out, really freaking hard.

Because the next Hike Like a Girl meeting is tomorrow and

the only place I've hiked is: 1) from my bed to the backyard pool; 2) from the parking lot to my stylist for a color refresh (we went for a rooted ombré that fades from ash blond to cotton-candy pink); 3) from the car to the patio café of the club. Which is where we're currently sitting, because Mom was all "Oh, I just want to swing in to say hello to Susanna, she's just had her nose done, you know," and "Look, girls, my favorite table is free and Paolo is working."

So I'm perched on the edge of the wicker patio chair surrounded by ladies in twinsets while I'm wearing brown hiking boots and a sports bra, which smashes my boobs to my chest, dropping them in the rank of my most enviable possessions. Guess I'll have to cultivate a sparkling personality to make up for it?

Paolo arrives with a white wine spritzer for Mom and club sodas for me and Kat. Without a word, I trade my lime (Kat likes extra) for her straw (I like the extra fizz from two tiny straws).

"Mrs. Barnes, I swear you look younger every time I see you," Paolo says, lying outrageously through his dazzling white teeth.

"That'd be the Botox," I say sweetly.

Mom glares at me before turning back to Paolo with a blinding smile. They must have the same cosmetic dentist.

As soon as Paolo leaves, I push my drink back. "Mom, we really need to get going. Georgia will murder me if I don't do this hike for HAGs." (I decided sometime in the last six days that Hike Like a Girl has a silent *L*. It's been HAGs ever since, and I am deeply proud of myself for this.)

Mom waves at Susanna a few tables away. "Susanna's new nose is a disaster," she says, smiling at the woman.

"Mom, did you hear me?"

"Shall we order some food?"

So that's a no. Kat pushes her phone toward me. "What about this one?"

She's been avoiding conversation by searching area hiking trails since we got in the car. But, I mean, at least she's here. Ever since she yelled at me the morning after the Boat Incident, things have been eerily calm between us. She didn't even put up a fight when I invited myself to go get coffee with her, Joon, and Wash. Though that calm sometimes feels like "cordial," which should only be a word used to describe the experience of shaking hands with the priest during your twice-yearly attendance at Mass.

I predict some bonding over Mom's inevitable trail freakout. We'll find our way back to each other by sharing exasperated eye rolls. As one does.

Kat curls her fingers around the sleeve of her overlarge sweatshirt and nods at the trail description pulled up on her phone. "It says it's got epic views from the top of the ridge."

I push the phone back. "Sure. It's close?"

"Yeah, and it's marked yellow on the guide, so that means it's less than one thousand feet of elevation, which doesn't seem bad, right?"

Before I can comment that climbing one thousand feet does kind of sound like a lot, Mom says, "What are you girls scheming about?"

Kat hunches down further in her sweatshirt. "We're not scheming, Mom."

Mom waves at someone at another table. "That's what Dad and I always said, the twins and their scheming. You two are always planning something together, so what is it this time?"

I wave at the map open on Kat's phone. "Duh, the hi—"

But Kat says over me, "Oh my god, Mom. It's not like that anymore. We're not little kids."

Like planning something with me would be awful. Like this terrible distance between us is a good thing. My insides hollow out and I shred the cocktail napkin under my club soda.

"Oh, that's right, your little walk," Mom says, apparently not noticing the frost creeping between us. She sighs loudly. "You know I adore Will"—the feeling is in no way mutual—"but this Georgia person is making everything much too difficult. She shouldn't be expecting so much out of you!"

Okay, yeah, I'm not president of Georgia's fan club either, but it continues to smart that my own mother expects so little of me.

Speaking of low expectations, that's the moment Tully rounds the corner from the tennis courts, glowing in his whites and burnished from the sun.

"Tully!" Mom waves him over and shades her eyes to beam up at him. If she remembers he's the reason I was sent to France, she doesn't show it. My cocktail napkin is turning into a snow flurry.

Tully's mom, Janeth, throws an outrageous Patriots & Poseurs Fourth of July bash every year at their mega-mansion, so it appears Mom is already buttering Tully up for an invite. (Each invite is delivered by a man in a powdered wig. Two years ago they set up an aviary full of eagles and were reported to the ASPCA.)

"Talk sense into Lola about this silly hiking thing," she says, pulling her mouth down into a frown and patting the open chair between us. Tully drops into the offered seat and glances at my legs. I tug at the hem of my ratty tie-dyed shorts and scowl at him. If I'd known we were going to be entertaining visitors, I would have worn my formal cotton pajama shorts. "Maybe she'll listen to you better than her own mother."

I glance at Kat to share a bonding eye roll, but she's buried in her phone again. Annoyance zings through me.

Tully holds it together for maybe two seconds before bursting into the sort of loud laugh that draws attention from all the surrounding tables. "Whoa, whoa, you didn't quit that lame hiking thing?" He rounds on me and guffaws.

"See?" Mom crows. "Tully agrees with me."

"Tully doesn't know what he's talking about," Kat snaps, each syllable hard.

Mom flaps a hand. "Oh, like you could hike either, Katherine. I'm looking out for what's best for you two, and you act like I'm a monster!"

They snipe at each other, and Tully takes the opportunity to duck his head close and whisper in my ear. "I'm having a few people over to the pool house tonight. You should come. Do something you're *actually* good at, like wearing a swimsuit and looking pretty."

His words drag me down. But it's when I'm drowning in the muck of Tully's expectations that Ezra's confidence throws me a lifeline. What did he say? That I shouldn't worry about what they thought. That I was *capable*.

"Mom, get the bill. We're going hiking."

Tully snorts. "Sure you are, Lola."

TEN

SURE YOU ARE, LOLA.

Two hours later, I am hiking, and it turns out I regret everything I said about capability.

I made it through Mom ordering food and a second spritzer, but stormed off in a rage—dragging Kat with me—right around the time she asked Paolo if Liz could squeeze her in for a quick manicure. We left her sitting in a massaging chair with Liz starting to trim her toenails and the closest greenery topiaries, which vaguely resembled penises.

And I can't even complain slash bond with Kat because all my lung power is currently devoted to gasping and swearing.

The trail is narrow and rocky, and the Murder Boots strapped to my feet feel like they're lined with razor blades and regret. I bat away an annoying, low-hanging branch and am rewarded with a face full of spiderwebs. Ezra is obviously deeply disturbed if he finds shit like this enjoyable.

My thighs are burning and my heels are burning and everything is burning and, oh god, I'm going to die out here. Behind me, Kat is sort of . . . wheezing.

"There's a sign," Kat pants.

All I manage is a shrug, because every ounce of energy is diverted toward survival and anger right now. Besides, what the hell can the sign say to cheer me up? Taco Bell to the right? This way to learn Georgia Drake's deepest secret and how to use it against her?

"Lola, come on. Stop. I think we have to go that way."

I turn around with the grace of an oil tanker and sort of grunt in Kat's general direction. Sweat drips behind my knee, which is a new and exciting achievement. This is such a great experience! Look at us bonding! Kat's cheeks have turned the corner from red to purple, and mascara streaks under her eyes.

"What?"

She jabs her thumb toward a smaller path nearly swallowed up by ferns. "On the site, it said something about a fork in the trail."

I stare at the narrow trail that definitely leads to a serial killer's lair. "That's not a fork. That's certain death."

Kat rolls her eyes, but weirdly it doesn't make me feel closer to her. "Don't be dramatic."

"It's the only way I know."

Kat blows out a big breath and drops her half-empty water bottle. She tugs her sweatshirt over her head with jerky, irritated motions. Telltale signs Kat is pissed. My stomach drops.

"Sorry," I blurt as she yanks the sweatshirt sleeves around her waist and knots them with a severity I imagine she'd like to use on my neck right about now. "Hey, you're probably right. Let's take that trail. Looks great. All those ferns! No idea where it goes around that corner. Can't wait."

She glares at me, but scoops her water bottle back up and starts down the trail.

The trail that is definitely not the right way. Which becomes pretty obvious when it stops being a trail. There's a clearing off to the right, and what looks like a circle of stones that I'm guessing is where they do the human sacrifices, but nothing in the way of a trail.

In front of me, Kat screeches and whips around. Her olive-green sports bra is ringed with sweat. Though I shouldn't comment. It feels like there's a lazy river between my boobs right now.

"Soooooo, the other way?" I try to smile at her, like *Hey! We're in this together!* Didn't Georgia say something like that? But Georgia doesn't know what she's talking about, because Kat shouts "Shut up!" and stomps past me.

Cool. Great. This is so much fun.

I jog to catch up and walk next to her once we rejoin the

actual trail. "Hey, it's a dumb hike. That hiking website you found sucks. It said the views would fulfill my soul which is, like, ew. Don't be gross."

We're still marching forward as I talk, Kat's strides stretching out, almost like she's trying to get away from me. Up ahead, the trees seem to be thinning, and sunlight makes a patchwork of the dull, brown dirt. I match Kat's strides, hopping a bit to try to keep up. "Hey, I—"

Kat grinds to a stop. "Oh my god, shut up. Shut. Up. All you do is complain and I am so damn sick of it. I'm sorry I picked a hike that you hate, but you weren't doing anything to choose one."

"I was just trying to make a joke."

I was trying to make her laugh like she used to. Like she never does anymore. Not around me, at least. I reach out toward her, but she steps back, away from me.

"Well, it's not a joke. Stop being so effing selfish and whiny and think about how you make *others* feel for once. If this is really how you're going to act around those girls and effing ruin their summer, then quit, okay? You'd be doing everyone a favor."

She shoves past me and takes off down the trail and all I can see is her running away from me again. Leaving me behind.

"Hey, Kat! Wait!" I jog after her, but she keeps walking like Mom trying to be first in line at the club's Saint Patrick's Day open bar. Shit. What do I do? "Please! Come on! You're not going to just hike off into the wilderness! We need to stick together."

She disappears around a corner, and fear spikes in my gut.

"Kat!"

For the second I can't see her, the forest grows teeth. It growls and snaps and looms over me with intent. My fingertips buzz with adrenaline, and suddenly the pain in my feet, the ache in my muscles, is gone. Vanished. Like my sister who has definitely left me to perish in the woods. A big, rolling sob catches at my chest, and I break into a run. A real run. I swear to god, if I die running I will haunt Kat forever.

My feet pound down the path, skirt the roots, and there—finally—I spot her.

She's paused, peering over her shoulder toward me. Like she wants to make sure I'm still following behind the tantrum-in-progress. The fear hardens to seething anger. I'm the whiny, selfish one? She's the one who acted like the biggest insult possible was Mom saying we were planning something together.

"Fine!" I shout at her as she starts speed-walking again. "You can get eaten by a bear and I won't come to your funeral!"

"I wouldn't want you there!" she shouts back over her shoulder.

"I'll tell Mom you hate her new nose!"

She answers that one with a stiff middle finger raised above her head.

I follow her another, I'm going to say, five hundred miles give or take, until the trail twists away out of the trees and opens to a steep hillside. Kat stops dead, and I do too. Ahead of us, the trail zigzags up the side of a meadow to a windy ridge, and I don't know if it's the blistering sun or the way the trail doubles back on itself as it climbs or the fact that I'm seriously considering sistercide, but I'm done. Just absolutely done.

Go to the woods they said.

The trees are so peaceful they said.

Nature can go fuck itself.

I stop at the edge of shade and collapse down to the dirt, my back to a tree. Sharp, stabbing pain has been dogging every step, but now that I've stopped, I realize the throbbing in my feet feels hot and wet. I'll never be able to wear sandals again, probably. A doctor will have to chop my feet off, most likely. Thanks, HAGs.

"I'm done," I announce to the trees.

The trees shake their leaves in triumph.

Kat mops sweat from her face and chews on her lip for a second before lifting a foot and nudging my knee. "Don't tell Mom I hate her new nose, okay?"

"Only if you'll let me give the eulogy at your bear-mauling funeral."

She chews her lip again. "Sorry I called you whiny. I think . . . I think you need to work on being tenacious."

"Tenacious sounds like something you need a prescription cream to clear up."

That makes her giggle, and I feel so absurdly proud that I'm honestly ashamed of myself.

"Check the tracker app Georgia made you download. I bet we're done."

I dig through the little zippered pouch slung around my hips and unearth my phone. Surely it'll say somewhere between eight and ten miles. At least. The screen lights up and the number 1.87 flashes at me. Okay, so not as far as I thought, but still! Nearly two miles! That's all Georgia wanted, and I've done it! I've struggled up nearly two miles of this godforsaken mountain, past annoying waterfalls and meadows of bullshit wildflowers and all these awful trees, but I've done it. And I only threatened my sister once and even made her giggle!

Energy surges through me, and I push to my feet. They scream in protest, but who cares! Maybe I already am tenacious! I can work hard at things! I've hiked two miles and now . . .

And now . . . I need to hike back.

The realization is a free fall off a cliff, a high cliff where you have a good long while to face reality. What, did I expect a moving sidewalk to appear and haul me back to the car like I was headed to baggage claim at SFO? Maybe a Cinnabon would pop up and a duty-free next to it? I blame it all on the trees. And also Cinnabon for not considering "middle of the woods" as a franchise location.

We hike back to the car in defeated silence.

All I know is, hard work sucks. I mean, it's right there in the name: work. It's not like anyone calls it hard vacationing or hard lounging. It's work, and it's not for me. Tully and Mom are right about me. I don't know why I expected Ezra, some guy I barely know, to understand anything about me. I'm not capable. I never have been.

The car finally appears out of the trees like a mirage. I'm dirty, sweaty, tired, and I've nearly finished mentally penning a manifesto against nature, sunlight, and air. We don't say a word on the drive back, but I've made up my mind.

I might have to complete Georgia's awful, unfair punishment this summer, but I refuse to like it.

You know what I will like? Tully's pool party.

My swimsuit cannot get wet.

I know, I know, but it looks really good on me. And as nature demonstrated earlier, I need to stick with the things I'm *actually* good at: wearing a swimsuit and looking pretty.

I twist side to side in front of my full-length mirror to inspect my look. The suit is pale pink, like the newly dyed ends of my hair, and has a plunging halter neck and cutouts at my waist. And it's leather. Not, like, Medieval Times leather, but sleek and modern. And thus not suitable for actual swimming.

But after what I've been through today, I don't give a shit about things like "practicality" or "making basic sense."

There's a quiet knock on my door, so I yank my black batik-printed cover-up over the suit. Kat sticks her head around the door, her shower-wet hair curling down to her elbows. A frown burrows between her eyes.

"Are you . . . going out?"

I shake out my freshly washed hair and look at her from the mirror. "Nothing major. Tully's having a chill thing at his house."

Kat balks. "You're kidding me."

"Today sucked, okay? I want to hang out with some friends."

Kat's laugh is just this side of mean. "So why are you going there? Plus, don't you have Hike Like a Girl in the morning?"

I roll my eyes and turn back to the mirror to apply a rose-colored lip stain. "Those HAGs won't go anywhere without me, don't worry." I blow myself a kiss in the mirror. There, perfect. Now I simply have to ditch my sister so she'll stop judging me.

"Okay, but"—oh god, there she goes again—"didn't Georgia say she'd turn you over to Will if you bailed again? There's no way you're going to pop in to say hi to Tully and be home to actually get some sleep before Hike Like a Girl tomorrow morning."

I'm throwing keys, lip gloss, and my wallet into a straw tote, but pause. "Thanks for the reminder, Mom." I straighten and grab a pair of gold studs from the little porcelain dish on my bedside table and stick them in my ears. "Actually, Mom would tell me to go. I had a hard day and want to do something for myself."

Kat snorts. "Yeah, because you *never* do anything for yourself. God, stop being so melodramatic and selfish."

I should have absorbed her in the womb.

"Drop the concerned sister act," I snap. "Why don't you go back to being fun for once instead of a total bore. I liked silly, boy-crazy Kat a hell of a lot better than this sanctimonious shit."

Kat jerks away like I slapped her, and an apology gathers at the back of my throat, but she spins away from me and rushes out of my room. I shouldn't have snapped. But also, she shouldn't stick her nose in where it's not welcome. I shove down the desire to go knock on her door and instead gather up my bag and stride down the hall toward the front door.

It's quiet in the rest of the house. Mom's at a charity auction, and Marnie's in the city with her boyfriend. I'm halfway to the door before I notice Dad, curved over a book in his favorite armchair by the fireplace.

"Oh, uh, hey, Dad! I'm not going to be late."

Dad doesn't look up from his book but kind of hums his agreement.

My hand's on the door when Dad finally speaks up. "How's it going with Hike Like a Girl?"

My shoulders droop, but I tug them back high. "Oh, great!" My voice is so bright I'm probably giving Dad a sunburn. "Yeah, it's, like, super life changing! Georgia's a real peach!"

Dad sets his book down and rubs a large hand against his jawline. He's tall and broad-shouldered, but prematurely stooped from forever being bent over books or computers. I mean, he's a total nerd, obviously. You have to be to single-handedly build a tech empire by the time you're thirty-five and retire by fifty. He's always around, puttering in his shed out back—that's where Mom stashed all his old equipment when she had the house remodeled a few years ago—or volunteering for a million things. So, yeah, always around but always sort of preoccupied. At least where it comes to me and Kat.

"You know," he begins. I hold my straw bag in front of myself, hoping he doesn't notice I'm not actually wearing what would traditionally be called "clothing." "I hope you appreciate the gravity of the situation here. You really could have hurt people on that boat, and Will and Lindy are fully within their rights to press charges. They didn't need to give you a chance to redeem yourself."

They didn't need to, true. But where else would Will find his finely honed sense of moral superiority?

"Something to think about as you make your choices, Lola," Dad says, and turns back to his book.

This is where I'm supposed to change plans. Go back to my room and put on sweats and get a solid eight hours of sleep.

Like that's going to happen.

ELEVEN

FLOODLIGHTS BATHE THE HEDGEROWS AND eucalyptus trees outside Tully's mansion, throwing shadows against the nouveau-French turrets studding each corner. My BMW inches up the long driveway till I reach the end of the line of cars. Tully's beloved chrome Audi R8 isn't in the lineup. He used to leave it outside, but ever since a certain revenge incident a year ago that I can't go into for legal reasons, I have to assume it's in the six-car garage on the other side of the house. Tully loves that ridiculous car more than his Gammy Harrison, the woman who bought it for him when he turned sixteen.

I park only partly in a hedgerow, straighten my gauzy black cover-up, and try not to wince when the strap of my sandals rubs against one of my lovely new blisters. Since I saw him last,

Tully has apparently abandoned the family mega-mansion in favor of the pool house, a two-story, modern loft with a party shower and a pool table in the living room. But as I skirt the Harrison estate, I can still picture the interior, remembering the parties that were thrown there: giant-sized cream furniture, drapes and tassels everywhere, and the family portrait hanging over the marble fireplace that Janeth commissioned to mirror Louis XVI–style opulence. Mom is obviously insanely jealous, but I've always preferred our house to his.

A paved walkway snakes through the formal garden and past a grove of trees before depositing me at the edge of shadows, the pool house glowing eerie blue before me. There's a handful of Crenshaw Day alumni who graduated with Tully, but I'm surprised to recognize most people as current Crenshaw students. They lounge around the squiggly edges of the outdoor portion of the pool, and I can see a dozen more through the panes of the angular glass house encasing the indoor pool.

And no one—no one—is wearing a swimsuit. What the hell kind of pool party is attended fully clothed?

I'm hit, suddenly, with the same overwhelming sensation as earlier, the sense of not belonging. I definitely didn't belong in the woods (because I don't have a thing for storing nuts or living in hollow stumps), but this doesn't feel quite right either. I tug the tassels of my cover-up, pulling it closer against my skin and shivering in the breeze. In the weak light, the green stone eyes of my snake ring wink up at me. I rub at them, searching for calm or defiance or . . . something.

But the only thing I get is the sound of people coming up the path behind me. I let go of the tassels, ignore the scrape of sandals on raw skin, and march into the light of the party.

A few girls from Tully's class stand in a clutch by a potted palmetto, sporting red Solo cups and sneers. They all left super nice comments on Lola Barnes Is a THOT last year. Love seeing them again! I walk past, limping as little as possible and ignoring the overheard sound of my name.

Through the glass, Meg and Jasmine lounge on a chaise, scrolling through their phones, and my stomach drops with relief at the sight of friends. But then it twists right back up again. They might not have left comments, but they weren't exactly throwing We Support Lola parties.

Meg nudges Jasmine when I step through the glass doors, one side of her mouth moving. Their eyes dart to me, then Jasmine huffs and lets Meg haul her to her feet. We meet halfway with all the warmth of Antarctica.

"Tully mentioned you might stop by," Jasmine says, glancing behind me. "Yay."

I tug at the tassels of my cover-up. "He said it was a pool party."

Meg swipes her hand through the air. "He should have clarified. We decided, I don't know, it'd be more chill without swimming?"

Jasmine rolls her eyes at Meg. "But quite a bit less like a pool party."

I smile at Meg. "No, it's a good idea. Chill is, um, good. Did you secure all the emergency flares?"

My joke fizzles out like a defective flare gun. What the hell is wrong with me? This is Meg, the girl I helped buy tampons for the first time. I stood outside her bathroom reading the instructions through the door. This is Jasmine, with whom I created elaborate secret handshakes in fifth grade. Why am I trying so hard?

"Anyway," Jasmine says, "we promised Tulls we'd help him host, so we better make the rounds. There're drinks on the pool table. Thanks for coming, Lola."

Jasmine hooks her arm through Meg's and leads her away, the two of them hissing with whispers the whole way. And I'm . . . I'm . . . oh god, I've been given the brush-off. By the two girls who are supposed to be my oldest friends. They don't just sorta hate me in that friend way where you know the reconciliation is inevitable. They . . . they've really moved on. Humiliation sears the backs of my eyes, prickles in my throat. I'm standing here at the entrance to the swim-less pool party looking ridiculous in a pink leather swimsuit and people are glancing at me and not in a good way and dammit why did I come?

I twist in a circle, trying to go for a whole *I'm definitely not freaking out that no one wants to talk to me* insouciance. I mean, come on. I didn't *only* hang out with Meg and Jasmine. There was a whole group of us, and yeah, some of them graduated with Tully and most everyone else sided with his ex. At least one of them was responsible for the chili dumped on my head during the cafeteria blowup. But there's got to be . . . someone.

There. Standing in the corner with another soccer friend, Joon catches my eye and nods. Relief is like a warm shower cascading down my skin. I grin and wander over in a totally cool and nonchalant way. Sure, Lola, sure.

"I'm gonna need you to take off your clothes," I say instead of hello, dropping my bag on an empty chair behind me.

Joon chokes on a laugh. "Pardon?"

I ignore his soccer friend when they clap a hand on Joon's shoulder and walk away. I wave a hand at his T-shirt plus cardigan combination. He's got clothes to spare and I'm . . . I pick at my cover-up. "I can't be the only one in a swimsuit here." Then I shake out my cotton-candy hair and laugh with a look over my shoulder at the two rising junior girls who're watching me. "I mean, look at me. I don't want to make everyone jealous." My eyes find Joon's. "Please?"

Joon smiles kindly, and I want to shrivel up and die at the pity in his face. But also, I'm very excited to put this cardigan on. He shucks it and is about to hand it over when his attention snaps to something behind me and—

"Lola!" Tully shouts, and suddenly arms are hauling me off the ground in a bear hug. "Now the real party can start! Bring any more fireworks?"

He drops me roughly back to the ground and my feet hit concrete with a gentle pop of blisters. I tug my cover-up down my legs. All around us, people are watching. Their attention knits confidence into my bones—I can change the narrative here, give them something fun to talk about. I simply have to take charge. I turn back to Tully and poke him in the arm—it looks playful, but I don't hold back with the jab. "I left them all on Jasmine's little boat," I say with a laugh. Someone snickers, and I pull my shoulders back. "You still have that dartboard? I bet I can beat anyone here." I look around as I say it, a challenge.

Tully snorts. "Last time we played darts, you speared my finger on accident."

I tilt my chin at him. "How sweet of you, thinking it was an accident." I let the words hang there and twist away to go find someone better to talk to. I won't let Tully be the one to leave this time.

But he grabs me around my waist and swings me up into his arms before I can make it even a step away. "Nah, dude. I don't want to play darts." He lumbers over to edge of the pool, holding me out over the water. "How about swimming. Since you came dressed for it."

"Tully!" It comes out like a shriek, which makes him roar with laughter and jolt his arms like he's going to let me drop.

But I'm not laughing. I'm suddenly pissed, and I'm absolutely certain coming here was a mistake. I've got to drag my ass to HAGs tomorrow at the absurd hour of eight in the morning, my arms are covered in scratches, and my feet look like they've gone through a meat grinder. Exhaustion sits like an overstuffed Neiman's bag on my gut.

"Tully, come on. Put me down."

I glare up at him, and he sighs, his face going soft. He takes a step away from the edge, but a voice cuts the humid air behind us.

"Didn't you hear her," it says. "Put her down, you jackass."

Tully turns toward the voice, his arms still clamped under my back and butt.

Everyone in the pool house is staring.

Staring at us and . . . Ezra?

Ezra. Here. At Tully's party. His feet are planted wide and there's murder in his face.

"Oh shit, it's Ezra Booben!" Surprise and laughter mingle in Tully's voice, and I can feel the shake of it in his stomach where he clamps me close to his body.

Ezra's mouth is a slit, his eyes hard. "Don't be a dick, Tully. She asked you to put her down."

I blink at Ezra and try to telegraph intent. Tully is a bear, a big, dumb bear. You don't poke a bear; you make it complacent with honey. And also, what the hell, Ezra! I don't need some dude I've barely talked to trying to play Prince Charming.

Tully takes a big step back to the water's edge and laughs, his voice loud and fast.

I make myself squeal playfully and grab hold of his neck, grinning up at him. "If I'm going down, you're coming with me."

"Oh, you're going down? Let me grab my phone."

Shock sucks the air out of me. There weren't pictures of any-thing like that, but the memories of what *was* on the site . . .

"Come on, Tully. You're all big talk, but we both know you suck at the follow-through."

Tully grimaces, but his arms soften and my nerves with it. He won't actually . . . and that's the moment Ezra snaps again. "I swear, if you drop—"

And Tully lets go.

Time slows down enough for me to feel flames of anger lick through me before my back smacks the water and I plunge into the pool. Bubbles froth around me. Above, there's a muffled shout and two more bodies slam into the water. I surge upward with a couple of strong kicks and break the surface to see Ezra and Tully spluttering for air. People edge the pool, silent and staring.

I give myself a second to gather my voice and force a laugh. "Get in, you jerks! The water's great!"

Bless them, a couple of the dumber ones jump in fully clothed, and the commotion gives me a chance to slice through the water and haul myself up a ladder at the pool's far end. It's warm and humid, but my skin still stings with cold. Joon is there, and he hands over his cardigan without a word.

Gratefully, I grab it and swap it out for my sopping-wet cover-up. I'm going to have to cut this swimsuit off my body at some point.

Joon leans close. "Are you okay?"

"I'm fine," I grind out. Except I've got to track down Ezra or Tully—whoever I spot first—and murder them. I spin away . . . and smack straight into Ezra's soaking-wet shoulder. Anger is a fire in my belly.

"Lola," Ezra says, reaching out to touch my elbow. I snatch my arm away from him and glare.

"What the hell, man!"

Ezra's gray eyes go big and he takes a step back, but, like, there's nowhere to hide now. It's your own watery grave.

"You barely know me. And yet you decided you knew what was best for me? I can make my own damn mistakes, dude."

Ezra shakes his head in disbelief and looks to Joon, who demonstrates how smart he really is by keeping quiet. Ezra's voice is clipped and low when he snaps back, "I wasn't trying to decide what was best for you. I didn't care who the hell Tully was tormenting. I saw a bully bullying. The end. I don't give a shit that it was you he was holding over the water."

The force of his anger nearly makes me take a step back, but I square my shoulders. "Well, screw you."

"God, this was such a mistake to come. Sorry, Joon, man. I'm leaving." Ezra breathes hard and rakes a hand through his hair. And I hate that I notice it—like, really hate it—but the way his chest expands with each breath, the way his soaking, dark T-shirt clings to his lean frame. A trickle of water slides down the front of his throat.

"Yeah," I force out, reeling myself in. Come on, Lola. Now is not the time for lustful thoughts. I'm supposed to be alive with righteous fury. I face Ezra dead on and stare at him. "Yeah, it was a mistake."

Ezra spins on his heel and strides away, and Joon whistles. "Damn. Right, Lola, I know this probably isn't the time, but you didn't see the way Ez tackled him into the pool. It was . . . I mean, if I didn't have a brilliant boyfriend right now . . ."

I swipe a hand through the air, trying to erase the image of Ezra tackling Tully, of the way he looked all wet from the pool. Normally, I'd say two guys fighting over me was, like, best case scenario. But it all felt gross and wrong and like I was a prize to capture.

And what a prize I am. Encased in a leather sarcophagus, hair dripping wet, eyeliner probably smudged to hell. I push through the crowd and finally locate the drinks Jasmine promised. I grab a bottle of tequila, my purse, and lock myself into the second-floor bedroom to get to know Mr. Cuervo on intimate terms.

TWELVE

BEEP BEEP BEEP.

Kat's alarm won't shut up.

Beep beep—

"Shut up," I bellow.

Beep.

Well, now it's just being rude. I feel around for my other pillow to jam over my ears and my fingers run through some sort of . . . fringe? What the hell? Did Mom buy new pillows? My bed doesn't . . .

I bolt upright, and the room sways around me. Heavy celery-green curtains. A cherrywood four-poster bed. A room, but certainly not mine.

I'm in the guest room. Of Tully's pool house. My head pounds in time to my incessant alarm, and it takes too long for the meaning to chip its way through the hardened tequila encasing my brain, but realization eventually trickles through me.

I've got HAGs today. And I'm hungover and wearing a "UCLA Class of '92" tee I dug out of a drawer sometime last night along with enormous navy sweatpants and an extreme lack of underwear. Lying over the threshold of the en suite bathroom is my ruined leather swimsuit. My sandals are MIA.

And I am so, so screwed.

I stumble out of bed, paw at my phone until the alarm finally goes silent, and lurch to the bathroom to puke. I almost make it to the toilet. Sorry not sorry, Tully.

My forehead slumps against the cool porcelain and I roll it back and forth. Okay, think, Lola. Think. It's—I check my phone—quarter to eight, which means I have fifteen minutes to get home, change, and drive fifteen minutes south. This is fine! Everything's fine! I'll be a few minutes late, which I'm sure Georgia will understand. Unless she's at all related to Will Drake.

And there's that little matter of promising to turn me over to Will if I bail again. A sticky groan rolls up my throat and I consider splashing my face with toilet water.

I tilt to my left and flop my hand around until I turn on the shower, puke one more time, and sort of roll my way under the blast of hot water. I fail to remove my clothes, so, still sitting, I yank everything off and toss them with a wet plop out of the shower. I don't get around to using soap or shampoo, but the needling water helps slough off the hangover. Sort of.

After toweling off, I dig up another tee ("Señor Frog's Cabo '93!") and some black athletic shorts that hang below my knees. I grab my phone and purse and tiptoe barefoot through the quiet pool house toward freedom and/or the executioner. My phone declares it's now quarter after eight. It'd probably be a good idea to text Georgia that I'm running late, but it'd be an even better idea if I had her phone number. There is no world in which I'll be contacting Will about this latest screw-up. I mean, eight a.m. on a Saturday? He and Lindy are probably on, like, hour two of a bracing seaside walk. I picture them both wearing binoculars around their necks and sparring about the merits of James Joyce. It's their form of foreplay and it's revolting.

It's ten minutes to home, and I sneak in through the garage, grab a semblance of clean clothes out of the laundry room—Kat's maroon yoga pants, a pair of period underwear, my new black sports bra, and the damn Hike Like a Girl tee—and rummage through the mudroom bathroom for bandages and use a whole box on my chewed-up feet. With only a moderate amount of swearing, I put my hiking boots on and lace them up.

I'm almost back to the garage when I hear a door open somewhere in the house.

"Lola? Is that you?" Mom's sleep-rough voice filters down the hall.

"No!" I call, then trot back to the car.

It's pushing nine—nearly an hour late—by the time I come

screaming into the picnic area and gracefully jump a curb tearing across the lot. But Georgia's orange VW is nowhere to be found.

Crap. Crap crap crap.

My heart is beating a staccato against my ribs and my fingers tingle where they've gripped the steering wheel. I yank out my phone and check my email for any clue to where they've gone, but nothing. Instagram—nothing. There's only one option to track them down, and the thought of it makes me long for the run-of-the-mill tequila pukes I had earlier. My fingers are fat sausages as I scroll through my contacts and press call.

He answers on the third ring. "Hello?" Will's voice is gravelly. Was he . . . sleeping in? What a slacker!

"So, listen. I need Georgia's number. Or, um, if you know where she was planning to go with HAG— I mean, Hike Like a Girl this morning, that'd be great."

". . . What?"

"Oh my god, dude. Where is Georgia?"

Over the phone, I hear rustling and my sister groaning about something, and the visual of them lying in bed . . . or, oh god, *cuddling* makes me want to die. There's a grunt and a creak of feet on wood floors before Will finally speaks.

"They're at Sanborn Park, site twelve."

"Site?"

"Campsite. Lola, why aren't you there?"

"Okay, thanks, Will, byeeee!" I hang up as he's still talking, wrench my car into reverse, and take off.

Sanborn County Park burrows into the forested hills south of me. It's a horror show of redwoods and rivers, and I'm having major flashbacks to yesterday's hike. The campsites—which, ew—are spread out under the shade, and I crawl down the road searching for number twelve. And there it is, the hideous orange bus glaring at me as I park next to it.

My fellow HAGs are gathered in a circle down a treacherous slope littered with pine needles, but Georgia is nowhere to be seen.

"I'm here!" I wave my hands and skid down the slope toward them. "I'm here!" Faces turn my way, and I realize they're all standing around a campfire.

I wedge my way in between Priya and Beth to join the circle. "Did anyone bring s'mores?"

I'm greeted by silence.

Mei tugs at her dark bangs and says, "We're learning to build fires."

"Mei means we already learned, because we weren't late," Beth adds.

"Okay, well, I can learn now." I reach for the box of matches Beth is holding, but she jerks her hand away.

"What are you even doing here," she challenges.

I wave at the fire. "I'm learning to build fires and camp and shit, like you."

I try to catch anyone's eye in the circle, but no one will look at me. Not even Corinne. Tavi lifts her chin at me. "You're being disruptive to the group."

"I'm not even doing anything!"

Next to me, Beth snorts. "Yeah, exactly. How did you even get into Hike Like a Girl? Not to be shitty"—oh, she absolutely means to be shitty—"but this is a really exclusive program and you . . . don't seem the type."

I splutter and throw my hands up, the picture of offense. How dare Beth—who is currently wearing a backpack with some sort of seat belt system and two severe braids—decide what sort of "type" I am.

And also, I mean . . . they're not wrong. I don't belong here for about a thousand reasons. I didn't apply or get references or write an essay about how great trees are or whatever. All I had to do was burn down my brother-in-law's boat. But they don't need to know that. I open my mouth to argue, but Georgia chooses that moment to come stumping out of the woods with an armful of sticks. She stops dead and stares at me.

"Lola, you need to leave."

"But I just got here!"

She makes a big show of putting the sticks down and checking her watch, like, okay, Miss Punctual San Jose, I get it. "Exactly."

An excuse flops around on my tongue. "I— I—"

"I don't have time for this," Georgia says, leading me away from the group and back toward my car.

"No, but I do! I promise!" I'm begging. Totally not a good look.

But the specter of Will and Lindy actually pressing charges . . . of proving everyone right *once again* . . . A shiver rolls down my spine. I mean, I broke down and called Will! I had to stand here and listen to Beth yell at me! It can't have all been for nothing!

"Wait, look." Words and emotions collide and I'm not sure whether I'm going to cry (probable) or scream (definite). I fumble with my phone and shove it toward Georgia.

"I hiked yesterday." Georgia glances at my phone. "No, really, look. I tracked it and everything and it sort of destroyed me, like, I can barely walk, but I did it and then I slept through my alarm, but I wasn't trying to bail on you or anything and I . . . I mean . . ." The words have flopped out of me and landed with a wet splat on the ground. Moved: Georgia is not. I swallow hard and say, quieter now, "I'll do better next time."

I about sixty percent mean it.

Georgia holds out her hand. "Let me see that." She inspects my hike, and I watch her jaw work back and forth. Without a word, she hands back my phone, pulls out her own, and sends a text that hopefully says something like, *JK! Lola is here and an absolute credit to her name. I love her like a daughter.*

"Okay, you did the hike. But you were late today, and I am not in a forgiving mood. So, I'm sorry, you are not welcome to join us today, but I look forward to you being on time when we meet again on Wednesday."

"But, I— You can't—"

Georgia shakes her hair out behind her shoulders—damn her and her great hair—and looks at me through half-lidded eyes. "I can, and I will. You're cutting into everyone else's time with this tantrum, so I need you to leave. And before you come back, I expect a real apology for wasting our time."

Behind me, five pairs of eyes are wide and staring. They definitely heard all of that. Beth's shoulders are squared as she stares down her nose at me, and Tavi and Priya share a look. No! We're supposed to share exasperated looks about Beth! Not me! Mei is chewing on her bottom lip, and only Corinne has the decency to try for a weak smile. I can feel them watching me all the way to my car and as I turn it on, back up, lightly run into a stump, and drive away.

Cold shame prickles up my neck and pools in my eyes. I flick away a tear and grip the steering wheel. God, how embarrassing. The way they all looked at me. The way they're probably all talking about me. The trees close in on either side of the car and the road curves, empty and quiet. I veer off into a tiny dirt lot and shut off the engine.

The air outside my car smells like dirt. Like the time Joss dragged me to a greenhouse to pick new plants for her garden and I ended up lost in a bunch of ferns.

There's no plausible explanation for why I reach into the back seat, grab my new backpack still stuffed with gear Ezra helped me pick out at Basecamp, and start walking. There's a little wooden sign at the end of the lot that says "Backcountry Sites" and a dirt trail that disappears into the deep forest. Because I apparently want to be miserable, I follow it.

The ground is weirdly soft under my feet, like it's springing back with every step. On either side, freakishly large trees have rendered me tiny and insignificant, which is a real dick move on their part. It's horribly still and quiet, and it's one hundred percent everyone else's fault that I'm out here all alone. If Kat hadn't goaded me into going to Tully's in the first place, I would have slept in my own bed. If Ezra hadn't shown up last night and made Tully drop me, I wouldn't have gotten drunk and slept through my alarm. If Georgia wasn't such a hard-ass whose only love in life was punishing me, I would have been bonding with the other girls. (Okay, okay, that one isn't true.)

And if I'd made different choices basically every step of the way for the last seventeen years, I wouldn't be alone in the woods with no clue what I wanted to do next.

The realization hits me with the force of a mountain lion. I spin around to make sure a real mountain lion isn't stalking me, then continue down the path. I have no one to blame for this but myself. You know what? That really, really sucks. This would all be so much easier if I could convince myself I'm totally innocent. Ugh. I should probably actually apologize to Kat and Ezra and Georgia and, I don't know, give a blanket apology to everyone who had to escape a burning boat.

I'm so lost in thought that I don't even notice the trail splitting ahead until I nearly run into the marker. Randomly, I choose the right fork and head toward backcountry sites four through seven. Going to be honest here, I don't entirely know what a backcountry site is, but I'm really hoping it involves some sort of indoor plumbing and maybe a juice bar.

Spoiler alert: it involves none of those things. Site four is nothing but a cleared patch of ground and a stone circle with some charred wood piled in the middle. Mei's admission earlier today comes back to me. They were working on building fires before I came screeching up. Maybe that could be a way to show Georgia I'm not a total loser. I can learn how to build a fire. I mean, I nearly burned down an entire boat, so a tiny little camp-fire should be a breeze.

I kneel on the soft ground and disgorge my bag to find the box of matches. The sticks in the firepit are already kind of flaky and whitish black, so that probably means they'll burn easier. I strike a match and hold it against the log until flames lick my fingers, but nothing happens. I drop the match with a hiss, and it snuffs out immediately. My next step is to gather a few sticks and other material. There are ferns ringing the cleared area, so I bend off a few of the green fronds and throw them under the fresh sticks. Let's try this again.

But it's another failure.

And another. And another. Soon the pile of spent matches is nearly as tall as my pile of sticks, and I've got nothing to show for it except singed fingertips and a thin curl of gray smoke. If this is camping, I want nothing to do with it. This is shit. I'm shit. Everything is shit.

Okay, so I can't build a fire. Maybe I'll be better at . . . the other stuff. Like building tents or fending off bears. Surely I'll be good at *something*. I stand and douse the fire ring with water in case there are any surviving embers—I mean, I may be the Bay Area's biggest dum-dum, but I did grow up in California, so I know not to start a forest fire.

Back in the car, it doesn't matter how fast I drive or how high I crank the music, I can't smother my thoughts. That I suck. That I'm not wanted. That I need to apologize for it all. That's the scariest one of all—agreeing with Georgia and recognizing that I really do need to apologize. Apologies mean admitting guilt, and the only way this whole Lola Thing works is if I never admit guilt, never stop moving forward. But now that the realization has invaded my brain, I can't escape it. I owe some apologies.

I'll start with Kat. She's my sister; it's not like she can ignore my apology.

Yet the house is still when I push through the front door, even though it's barely noon. And when I knock on Kat's bedroom door, she doesn't answer. I wander through the house looking for anyone to talk to, anyone to distract me, but it's empty and silent. Finally, I curl up on my bed and fall asleep, all alone.

THIRTEEN

MY BEDROOM IS SOFT WITH dusk and thick with silence when I rouse sometime later. I strain to listen, but the whole house seems entirely too quiet. Georgia's insistence that I apologize sits heavy on my chest. The truth is, I don't know how. Not how to do it and mean it, anyway, without this awful, prickly sensation that apologizing for my actions means apologizing for who I am. That it means who I am is *wrong*.

Instead, I roll onto my side and palm my phone, idly scrolling through social media. I'm not above admitting that I start following Hike Like a Girl, hoping for some brownie points. My feed is mostly highly curated images of influencers and beautiful people, but the next photo makes me sit up tall and blink fast. Joon posted fifteen minutes ago; it's a shot of him, Wash,

Kat, and some rando from debate posing with putters in front of a mini-golf windmill. And behind them, trying to line up a shot, is Ezra. Okay, so I stand by what I said last night—I *don't* need anyone fighting my battles for me—but I probably could have been a bit nicer as I explained that. Maybe I can apologize to him and Kat at the same time! A two-for-one apology!

My fingers fly over my keypad with a text to Kat, kicking off my covers as I go. **Where r u? Can I come too? Is Ezra still there?**

I vault out of bed, peel off my clothes, and barrel into my walk-in closet. I've just tugged on a pair of washed-out cutoffs and selected a slouchy, cream-colored sweater when my phone buzzes. I jump over a pile of shoes and grab my phone off the dresser.

Please don't do this to him is Kat's response. What, apologize? God, way to stand in the way of my emotional progress. I poke gold hoops through my ears and text her back.

Wut apologize?

Kat's response comes fast: **He's a good person, Lola.**

He's a good person. I worry my serpent ring around my finger. My sister doesn't want me around Ezra Reuben, Good Person. Cool. Great.

Won't get my bad person vibes on him, promise. Where r u?

She doesn't respond.

Stop being annoying tell me where u r.

I finish getting dressed and check my phone again, but still nothing.

R u into him or something? WHERE ARE YOU?

I'm halfway through swiping on some C.Rahmani+Co boy-friend brow and some mascara when my phone finally dings again. But it's Joon sharing their mini-golf location, not Kat. Whatever. I'll deal with that betrayal later.

All I know is, it feels great to have momentum. A reason not to be alone in this giant, empty house. They're at a mini-golf place in Mountain View I only vaguely remember from a birthday party in, like, third grade. It's properly dark by the time I park, select a golf club and ball, and track the group down at hole eleven. Kat, I notice, is gone. She must have begged a ride from the debate club girl. I raise my hand in a wave and head straight for Ezra. Eyes on the prize and all that. But Joon intercepts me.

"Hiya, have you talked to Kat about anything?"

Down at the other end of the green, Ezra takes a step toward me, then away, before turning and scrubbing his hands through his hair. Way to ruin my entrance, Joon. What was he going on about? Oh, right. Kat.

"The only thing I've talked to Kat about is all the shit she wants me to change. Did she seriously run away? And she thinks I'm the one who needs to grow up?"

Wash straightens the cuffs of his olive-green bomber jacket and doesn't quite meet my eyes as he says, "She said she was late to something."

– 117 –

"*Mm-hmm*, yeah," I say, not buying it. "The stab your sister in the back convention."

Joon shares a look with his boyfriend.

"What do you know that I don't?" I demand. You know, other than *anything about her life since I came home from France.* My chest is tightening, my skin hot. I can feel my particular brand of snappish, cutting anger bubbling up in me.

But that's not why I'm here. I squeeze my golf ball so hard one knuckle pops. "I'll talk to Kat later, okay?"

Joon and Wash share another look. The ball is basically a diamond at this point, I'm squeezing it so hard.

Yet the sight of Ezra at the other end of the green makes me take a steadying breath. Since I've walked up, he's putted three times and missed three times, and red is rising up his neck. It's so dorky and also somehow cute? Okay, focus. I came here because I latched on to the idea of apologizing for personal growth—and as "ideas Lola latches on to" goes, it's not terrible. I mean, better than the time in fifth grade I decided to become known as the Mermaid Girl and started drawing glitter gills on the sides of my neck. It totally became a mini-trend at Crenshaw Day's lower school, by the way.

Joon and Wash are still staring. Ezra is pointedly not. I blow air out of my nose and smile. "Hey, but I'm here now, and I bet you don't know this about me, but I'm super good at mini-golf. Junior mini-golf champion for three years in a row."

Wash snorts. "You are?"

I break and laugh. "No!"

The boys relax, the night air between us settling. Almost like they were on edge around me. Like I'm not a good person.

Kat's last text is a poltergeist in my ear. *He's a good person.*

Well, maybe I can be too.

"First person to get a hole in one buys ice cream?" I propose. See? I'm offering ice cream! Would a bad person offer ice cream?

I gently hip check Joon out of the way, line up my shot, and send the ball curving down the green. It bumps against the cup and rolls to a stop a few inches away. Oh my god! Maybe I am a junior mini-golf champ and didn't even know it!

Behind me, Wash goes *huh* with surprise, but I ignore him and stride down the green toward my real target.

Ezra's standing along the brick outline of the hole, knocking the metal head of his golf club against his toe and acting like he's super interested in whatever is happening in the non-Lola part of the putt-putt course. Nerd.

"I'm sorry," I say without a hello, standing in front of him on the short turf. "About last night. You had no way to know Tully would react like that."

Okay, phew. I did it. And you know what? I said sorry and literally zero apocalypse horses showed up. Maybe that's what I'm good at? I can be the official apologizer.

Ezra bites down on a smile. "Yeah, I'm sorry too. I didn't mean to come off like an ass."

Wash's highlighter-yellow golf ball bounces off the side of

my canvas sneaker, and he whines in the background, but I'm focused on Ezra. He rolls his lips together, and instead of looking at me, he steps off the brick and tries to hit his tangerine-orange ball into the hole right next to me. It misses by a mile.

"You make me nervous," he says, his eyes flicking up to mine.

"I'm not that scary, Ezra."

He sinks the ball and leans at the waist to pick it up. I definitely don't take a peek at his butt except that I definitely do. Because I'm a human with eyes. He stands, a small frown tugging his brows together, and his voice dips low when he says, "I didn't say I was afraid of you."

And holy wow, there's something in his tone, in the firm line of his jaw when he looks at me, that makes my skin go tingly. I shake it off and follow him toward the next hole. Okay, so Ezra Reuben has gotten cute.

Hot, a voice in my head says. *Ezra Reuben has gotten hot.*

Cute. Hot. Whatever. It's not like I'm into him. That would be absurd. He's way too smart for me. I prefer boys I can easily manage.

The path to the next hole curves around a waxy green bush heavy with pink flowers that smell like syrup. I peek over at Ezra as we walk, at the way his neck bends as he watches his step and the mix of sharp and soft in his profile—sweeping curls, strong nose, curving mouth, solid chin. We stop outside the light illuminating the next hole, and he turns to me, the glow framing his unruly hair.

"So did you—" he starts, at the same time I say, "I meant to tell you—"

"Sorry, go—"

"No, you . . ."

Ezra's cheeks stain pink and he pushes his round glasses back up on his nose. A flustered sort of sigh pushes past his lips and he scratches at his hair behind his ear.

"Well, that was awkward," I say, a grin working its way across my lips.

That pulls a laugh from him. "Ah, my specialty."

"You shouldn't feel awkward around me."

Ezra rolls his golf club between his palms. "Sure, but you're you and I'm—"

He clears his throat and is back to not quite looking at me. And what is he? Because, okay, we all know he had a bad nickname and spent most of freshman and sophomore years being shoved into lockers. But he also smiles like he means it and gives good pep talks, and in his slim, dark shorts I've noticed there's a V of muscle above his knee that is doing things to me. Like, am I a leg girl now?

But also, I can't be a leg girl or any sort of girl who's into guys like Ezra because my number one goal since I got home from France was to reclaim my place in the social hierarchy of Crenshaw Day and that's basically impossible if I start hanging out with Kat's new nerd friends. Ugh, why is this so hard! Why does my stomach shimmy all over the place when I look at Ezra?

I take a big step back, away from Ezra and his good legs and cute smile. As Wash and Joon round the corner toward us, I line up my putt, take a swing, and sink a hole in one.

The ice cream stand boasts the name Kiwi Kones scrawled in hot-pink neon, and it promises us something called New Zealand ice cream. I order four Kiwi specialties (mixed berry dusted in crushed honeycomb) and find the guys sitting on low wicker chairs in front of a wall of fake green moss studded with brightly colored wooden sugar cones. Wash and Joon are . . . rapping back and forth to each other about a hippo? I nearly rescind their offer of free ice cream.

But then Joon falls back laughing and grins up at me when I hold out his cone. "Thanks, love."

Ugh, a British accent ruins any chance at staying annoyed. I sink into the last open chair next to Ezra and take my first lick of ice cream. At which point I decide I'd die for crushed honeycomb.

"Holy shit," Ezra says around a mouthful of ice cream. "This is so good." He closes his eyes as he takes another lick and sort of moans. It is, frankly, obscene. My skin heats up from the inside out, and my lightly boiling brain is the only excuse for what I say next.

"Will you take me hiking?"

Ezra chokes. "What?"

"Forget it. I was talking to the honeycomb."

I watch his jaw working back and forth, a teaspoon of worry in the pit of my stomach. I know he heard me, but if he pretends he didn't . . .

Look, I've never struggled with any of this. Fitting in, making friends, any of it. But the last year has felt like I'm knocking on doors, and I can hear people inside, but no one ever lets me in. It's weird and discombobulating and makes me feel all spiky with worry and uncertainty. But if I stop knocking, then what? The thought of being forever outside makes my blood go cold.

"Anyway, the honeycomb said no," I say, prompting him. "So I'll settle for you."

"You really want me to take you hiking?" His voice has gone rough at the edges, and next to us, Wash and Joon scurry away with an excuse about more ice cream. He leans forward and looks at me, gray eyes soft and hopeful. "Seriously, Lola. You're not screwing with me?"

My heart jolts, and I realize I want this boy to take me hiking so much it's a little bit scary. I knocked. He answered. But if I go through this door, will everything else be shut in my face for good?

"It's part of this Adopt a Nerd program I'm starting," I say, trying to joke. Trying to relieve this awful soup of emotions sloshing inside me. But the second it's past my lips, I regret it. Ezra's face shutters. His mouth goes hard.

"I don't need *adopting*. Jesus, Lola."

Shit. *Shit*. He was being sincere and kind and I bailed at

the crucial moment. He stands and strides over to a compost bin to toss the last few bites of cone. When he comes back, his hands are shoved into his pockets, and his arms are taut. "I don't care what any of them think of me. I don't want them to like me."

Them.

"You mean me," I say, keeping my voice even. Because you know what, it was just a bad joke. And he's turned it into something more.

A defeated laugh tightens his shoulders. "I mean *them*, but if you still care about being one of them, then yeah, I mean you too."

I stand up and face him, my nerves lighting up with anger at him, at me, at this awful position I'm in. "That's kind of really fucking unfair. They were my friends for *years*. What do you expect me to do? Just walk away from all that?"

Ezra shakes his head. "I don't expect you to do anything, Lola. All I know is that it's bullshit. It's chasing after a reaction to remind yourself that for that tiny bit of time you were still in favor. It's all just so . . . *disingenuous*."

I blink at him. "Sure, dude. Because this whole thing"—I wave a hand toward him, with his curated *I don't care about popularity* look—"is *totally* authentic. You might be cute, but your little lecture was super condescending. We're all just trying to figure our shit out and hope that people like us."

Ezra scrubs a hand down his face. "You're right." And for a

second, the buzz of anger in my chest fades, but then he looks at me and says, "But a lot of us can do that without stepping on everyone else."

And I'm out. I walk past him and throw over my shoulder, "Yeah, well. Apparently not me."

FOURTEEN

EZRA'S WORDS CHASE ME ALL night.

Which is incredibly annoying because I'm super pissed at how last night went down. I apologized! I bought everyone ice cream! And then I didn't even get to finish my cone because Ezra effing Reuben decided to lecture me about the problems of popularity.

I roll over in bed and massage my temples. Look. I can't help it if I'm universally beloved and popular. Or used to be. Or am but with the little hiccup that no one knows anymore. *Ugh.*

Somewhere down the hall, a door slams. I lie flat and stare up at my ceiling and feel *very* aggrieved. Except.

Except I can't get one thing out of my head. I stand by my statement that we're all just trying to figure our shit out. And maybe I'm doing that while also being (formerly) invited to parties, and maybe Ezra's doing that while going to Boy Scout camp, but it's the same thing. Right? Except the way he said some of us figure it out without stepping on others . . . well, it's all I can think about.

Which really sucks when I'm determined to feel self-righteous.

Being alone with my thoughts is *the worst*. I roll out of bed and pad down to Kat's cracked door. Okay, so I screwed up with Ezra. But maybe I can fix things with Kat. Joon and Wash implied I didn't know what was going on with her, so might as well pry.

Except her bed is made and she's gone.

Gone all day, in fact. It's not until Marnie comes sneaking in at damn near ten o'clock that I learn Kat has gone for an impromptu visit to Joss and Edie's home near Sonoma. Which makes zero sense because their next door neighbor—they of the Pouty Pony fame—is a purveyor of artisanal goat milk products, and Kat is terrified of goats. It's a whole thing.

The next day, the late June weather melts in the middle, and I meld with the couch during a marathon session of watching the sort of television that makes me feel better about myself. By the time evening rolls around, I'm so bored I let Marnie read a passage from *Anne of the Island* to me, yet when I predictably collapse to the ground and feign death, she starts going on about someone named Lydia Bennet, to which I say *Who?* and she screeches *ExCUSE me?* and I'm left with no choice but to clean my room, which someone has let get appallingly messy.

Once that's finished, there's nothing left to do but lie on my freshly vacuumed bedroom rug and text Meg.

Wut r u doin?

The bubbles of death blink at me for an eternity before she responds. **Don't be mad.**

Well, too late for that, darling.

A new text pops up. **We're on Jasmine's new yacht. Her dad said you weren't allowed.**

My hand flops to the ground and I groan. This sucks. Everything sucks. I have HAGs in two days and exactly zero yachts on which to lounge. Or friends to lounge with. I flip onto my stomach and swipe to Insta. A photo of Meg, Jasmine, Tully, and a few others posing on a yacht pops up in my feed. The comments are all some variation of *OMG so jelly!*

So I type, **Looks like you're ready to go Moby Dick around at sea.**

Look, it makes me giggle and it makes me feel a bit better about myself. A little thrill zings down my skin at the thought of Jasmine seeing the comment and pouting. Of others seeing the comment and laughing.

But no one does.

No. One. Does.

New comments pour in, burying my joke, which doesn't garner a single like. The zing turns zappy. It's a jellyfish sting that makes me squirm with discomfort.

I just did the *exact damn thing* Ezra accused the popular crowd of doing. Of stepping on everyone else to feel like you still belong for one tiny second. I went for the reaction because it felt good in the moment. But it didn't last, and I'm right back where I started. Lying on my floor in the dark feeling shitty.

I eventually just fall asleep there and wake up sometime later to crawl into bed.

It's not until the next morning that I realize I missed a series of texts. They're not from a number I recognize, but I frown and open it anyway.

Two days in a row being a total dick. I'm really sorry.

Maybe you do scare me.

If the honeycomb still says no, I'd like to go hiking with you.

It's Ezra, by the way.

Afternoon sun glints off Basecamp's metal exterior.

The excuse I'm using for being here is that I want to buy apology gifts for the HAGs. That's what I told Wash and Joon when I picked them up, two of the only people who will apparently answer my texts these days. (When I asked Marnie to come, she mentioned a bookstore, so I disinvited her.)

"I think this will be the perfect apology," I say to them, pulling into a parking spot. It's definitely not because I'm still trying to figure out how to respond to Ezra and am hoping for an "accidental" run-in.

"Uh-huh," says Joon.

"I'm serious," I say, voice ratcheted high. "If I can't win these HAGs over with my charming personality, I'll buy their love."

"Here's a thought," says Wash from the back seat. "You could stop calling them HAGs."

"The *L* is silent!"

"The *L* is most certainly not silent," Joon counters. "You're being obstreperous."

I set my jaw and refuse to acknowledge his ten-dollar word.

"Maybe try just talking to them?" Wash offers.

"And what, have to learn about their lives? No, thank you." Wash sits back in a huff, so I meet his gaze in the rearview mirror. "Do you want to wait in the car? I can crack a window."

"Hush," Joon says, already getting out. "We're coming."

The hallway of trees and nature noises isn't as annoying this time, and I even make it halfway into the atrium before I crane my neck for any sign of Ezra.

Joon one million percent notices. "Ha!" he crows. "You fancy him."

"I'm intrigued by him." My heart thumps . . . with intrigue.

Wash pushes past Joon to lay a hand on my arm. "Don't listen to Joon. I heard how Ezra tackled Tully into the pool last week."

My cheeks heat at the memory of it.

"And then she yelled at him for it," Joon reminds us.

Okay, thank you, Joon. Yes, yes, I'm a monster. I shouldn't

have yelled at the first person to ever stand up for me like that. But also . . . I don't know. Ezra standing up to Tully for me was admittedly hot. But I can also defend myself. I've never had any issue voicing my opinions, concerns, and general comments, and maybe I'm afraid that someone else standing up for me implies I should be quiet.

Also, it's not like he's a meek little lamb. I square my shoulders and glare at Joon. "Yeah, and then he yelled at me for being popular."

Joon scrunches his nose. "Are we still calling you popular?"

His words wriggle into the cracks in my mask, but I slap on some stage makeup and say, "More popular than your British ass."

And I am, right? As long as I stay the course and prove to everyone I'm worth it, they'll accept me again. The loneliness will go away. Right?

Joon shrugs, but his smile is soft when he glances at Wash. "But I'm happy, and I think that's better."

That word—*happy*—sticks at the back of my throat.

I . . . I'm not . . . A ripple of pain starts at the back of my neck, but Wash interrupts my thoughts, thank god.

"He's not working today," he says, face tilted toward his phone.

I'm not disappointed. *I'm not.* This is for the best, really. Because now I can focus on getting back on Jasmine's and Meg's good sides, where I belong. Ezra was a distraction. Just like Hike

Like a Girl is a distraction. But since I can't get away from the HAGs (not yet, at least), I'll get rid of Ezra. Great plan.

"Like I said," I say, shrugging, "I'm only here to get gifts for the HAGs."

I totally believe myself. And if all my energy dribbles out onto the floor, that's only because I need some coffee.

"What are we buying?" Wash asks.

Shrug.

"What do your HAGs like?"

Shrug.

"Do you want to hear all the dirt on the girl Ezra took to winter formal last year?"

Now we're talking. Fifteen minutes later, and with exciting insider info about a girl on the swim team named Jessica who was discovered with a notebook full of sketches of Ezra, my mood is markedly improved. Apparently one of the sketches portrayed him as a centaur. I died.

I mean, only because it's a good story. Not because I'm, like, invested in Ezra or anything.

To prove it, I finally text him back once I'm home.

Hey, I'm probably a no on hiking. Thanks though.

FIFTEEN

I'M EARLY. TEN MINUTES EARLY.

"I'm early," I helpfully point out to Georgia. The tip of my walking stick *tap-tap-tap*s on the ground for attention. "And I came prepared with an apology for everyone. Just like you said."

She pauses, mid-hair-braiding, and arches one eyebrow. The morning sun is streaming through the trees at this small roadside park north of the Los Altos Hills. It dapples Georgia's VW bus in golden light that almost makes it look rad. Almost.

"I'm just, like, really committed," I add when she still doesn't say anything about my achievement in time management. I'm wearing my hiking boots and sensible ball cap and have thoughtfully packed my mini-backpack with water and the apology gifts for the girls.

A long, slow breath filters out of Georgia's nose and she continues to ignore me. Someone needs to work on their leadership skills.

"So, I just thought you'd notice my commitment."

She turns away and braces her palms on both sides of the open bus door.

"I mean—"

"Stop."

My mouth snaps closed.

"You showed up on time and without complaint once, Lola. Right now, that's an aberration, not a pattern."

I hook my thumbs through the thin straps of my backpack and stare. I don't know why Georgia has such an attitude this morning, but it hardly makes me want to recommend her program. I open my mouth to say as much, but Beth and Priya's arrival interrupts. Ugh, why is Beth so early? Kiss-up.

Georgia steps close to me, and her eyes are hard when she says, "You are here as a favor. You didn't apply or pay like the rest of these girls, and I refuse to let you hijack my program or destroy their summer. Is that understood?"

I— What I mean is—

Well, shit. I don't have anything to say to that. I give Georgia a small nod and stand there blinking at the ground as she strides away from me. Embarrassment rustles over my skin, prickles behind my eyes. She doesn't want me here. Just like everybody else. Yet I have to stay, knowing she thinks I'm a bother, an aberration.

The humiliation burrows into my bones and hardens, turns angry. She knows I'm stuck doing this, so why provoke me? As leaders go, that's a fairly shitty move.

She wants me to not be a problem. Cool. I'll do more than that. I'll make them all like me, just to prove her wrong. And I've got the start hiding in my backpack. Determination becomes a steel rod jammed up my spine. Will would be so proud.

As the rest of the girls arrive, I act as the welcoming committee, waving and smiling and saying hi. Most of them look at me like I've got a whole farm of broccoli stuck in my teeth, but Corinne answers my high five. Georgia calls us over and demonstrates some bullshit about setting up a tent and how to work a camp stove and wilderness survival blah blah blah to get us ready for the first overnight in a couple of weeks, and I smile and nod along while fantasizing about making her cry in front of those she most respects.

"Okay!" Georgia claps her hands, and I clap too. She glares at me, so I give her a smile so sweet it'd make honeycomb jealous.

"Hold on, Georgia. Can I interrupt really quick?" I don't wait for her to respond, but stand and unzip my backpack.

"Actually—"

"So, crew. I just wanted to say I really appreciate you all so much. I know I've got a lot to learn, but I'm excited to do it alongside all of you. I hope you'll accept these little tokens as an apology for arriving late last week." All the girls are holding their walking sticks. Every one of them has earned their pale pink first hike thong but me. No matter. I pull out my ticket to acceptance: lipsticks for all of them I bought after we left Base-camp. It's, like, a really good gift. I chose each one specifically to match individual skin tones and the colors they wore at our (short-lived for me) first two meet-ups.

I turn to Georgia and, because I am at heart a petty asshole, make a show of looking in my backpack. "Oh, gosh, Georgia, I must have forgotten you."

Georgia stands and swipes dirt off the butt of her leggings. "If you're done." She eyes me for a second before turning a winning smile toward the others. "We have a fantastic hike lined up today that includes a big surprise. So, let's get in the bus and head out, crew!"

I give her a little salute and she looks like she wants to slap me, which fills me with triumph. We pile into her bus, three to a side on Creamsicle-orange upholstered benches. There's an oval fold-down table between us, and curtains printed with lemons against each long window. A soft floral rug is laid over the composite wood flooring and cream pillows embroidered with orange-and-yellow birds at our backs. Ugh, no one tell Georgia this, but it all kind of works. Like, in a vintage cool way. I expected it to smell like Great-Grandma Barnes's house: old perfume and wine coolers. Instead, it's an orange grove. Annoying.

"So what does everyone think the big surprise is? Group therapy, maybe?"

Beth sighs very loudly and crosses her arms over her chest.

"We worked hard to get here, Lola. Hard enough that Georgia chose six of us instead of five. Why is this such a joke to you?"

I press a hand to my heart. "I would never joke about hiking."

I would absolutely joke about hiking.

"I love the opportunity to pretend modern plumbing doesn't exist."

It's at this point I remember my vow to trick everyone into liking me so Georgia and my family all realize how much they've underestimated me, so I probably shouldn't make fun of these HAGs's, like, passion or whatever. I make a show of zipping my lips.

Beth rolls her eyes. But next to me, Corinne smiles, and Mei leans around her to tap my knee with her tube of lipstick. "I really like this, Lola."

"Oh, good! You wore that pretty floral scrunchie the other day, so I thought a nice rose color would be great for you."

I give the other girls plenty of expectant silence to also thank me for the gifts, but no one utters a word.

Priya swallows a gulp of water from her ever-present Camel-Bak and leans closer over the table. But I'm on the end of the bench seating, so I sort of have to shove in to hear her. She doesn't look at me but to the others as she whispers, "Can I be honest? I'm not really into hiking."

What the what now?

"I'm here because of Georgia's connections, and I know Beth is too."

Beth looks at the other girls aghast, but her resolve to lie obviously crumbles. "Ugh, Priya, why'd you have to tell on me. Yeah, I'm here for her brother."

I blink at that. Does Georgia have another brother I'm not aware of? "I'm sorry. What?"

No one acknowledges me, but Tavi shares a look with the others. "Okay, so I'm actually here because I do understand the benefits of getting outside and it'll make me more well-rounded for my future business. But, also . . ." She makes big eyes toward the front of the bus, where Georgia is humming along to some indie rock band probably singing about granola.

"What is happening." Do these people, like, *like* the Drake family?

Mei finally throws me a bone. "Don't you know who she is?"

Beth sneers. "Yeah, did you not do *any* research when you applied?"

Okay, calm down, Beth. Around the table, five pairs of eyes bore into me. Right. Because they all think I applied to become a HAG.

I sit back and fold my arms across my chest. "Georgia? Yeah, I'm familiar."

Georgia. Species: *Drakien dumbassien*; habitat: the woods; diet: my last damned nerve.

Beth sighs loudly. For the first time, I notice her tee says "Swift Student Challenge 2021." I've never heard of it, but I assume it's for self-serious assholes who dream of one day writing "polymath" in their Twitter bio. "Are you seriously saying you don't know her brother funds one of the foremost feeder programs for women in the tech industry?"

Mei bites back a grin. "And he's cute."

"Gah! He's, like, a hundred and five." I swallow this morning's brekkie back down.

Tavi tilts her chin. "Have you ever seen Will Drake?"

"What are you girls talking about back there?" Georgia eyes us from the rearview mirror.

Six girls hiss in unison. "Nothing!" Beth shouts.

Corinne crosses her arms. "I'm only here for the hiking."

"Hey," I say, holding up my hands. "I can promise you that I'm *definitely* not here for some surly nerd who probably eats Grape-Nuts for breakfast."

I realize that I could score some points by telling them exactly how I know Will. But that'd probably come with the admission that I'm only here as a favor to make up for my own epic screw-ups. Something that I don't think will go down too well with the Overachievers (Un)Anonymous in the bus. But also, how do you casually drop in that the guy they're all gushing over is actually your annoying brother-in-law.

So I don't say anything. Besides, it's not like there's any way they'd find out. And who cares if they do. I only have to tolerate these hippies for a summer, then it's so long.

The VW bus lurches its way up the twisty roads of Mount Tam north of the Marin Headlands. I've never been, because I have so many better things to do, but Lindy's always going on about it.

Joss sort of generally lives up this way too, and I crane my neck to peer out the window, like I might see my wayward twin walking along the narrow road. Obviously, I am losing my mind.

Finally, the bus trundles into a parking lot, and we pass a giant cross section of a tree that says Muir Woods National Monument. I'm the last out of the bus, and as I'm hopping down, a shiny silver tube left on the bench seat catches my eye.

A wisp of sadness curls in my chest. It's the lipstick I got for Beth.

I clear my throat and leave the lipstick behind. Whatever.

When I'm out of the van, I take a look around. We've parked in a small lot, surrounded on all sides by thick forest. The grove is shadowy, and if I were the sort who cared for this kind of thing, I'd notice that the air is threaded with the scent of rich earth. But I don't care, so I don't notice. Not at all.

What I do notice is how the sunlight slanting through the trees turns the air sparkling gold because it's most likely full of pollen. I lift my nose and look up, waiting for the inevitable sneeze, but it never comes. Instead, I follow Georgia and the others deeper into the redwood grove and closer to a big sign with a map of the area.

"Okay, crew!" Georgia claps, and we gather round. Her backpack has a seat belt around her waist like Beth's, which is deeply dumb. "Everyone remember what I said last time about reading the map at the trailhead?"

Um, no. And follow-up question: What is a trailhead?

The other girls take turns snapping photos of the map, so I do too. For, like, the memories?

Georgia keeps going. "Great! So a photo is the basic way to remember a trail, but it's definitely not a good option all the time. Once we work up to longer hikes, we'll start using legit topo maps. But this works for today. Let's talk about today's trail. This is our five-miler, so you'll be earning your next milestone."

I slide my palm up my hiking pole, hiding its nakedness. Georgia's gaze flicks from my hand up to my face, so I give her my sweetest "Lola will kill you later" smile.

"Round trip, we've got a little more than five miles with about four hundred feet of gain and"—Georgia pauses, grins at us—"I've got quite the surprise lined up for us at the halfway point."

She's talked up this surprise so much over the last couple hours, I'm going to be severely disappointed with anything less than a pop-up spa.

But right now, I'm mostly surprised Georgia would pick something so . . . nice. As we start walking, I realize this isn't some dirt track in the middle of nowhere but a wide, flat board-walk teeming with people. And is that . . . a gift shop? I breathe easier knowing I'm within shopping distance of a souvenir tee and a magnet with my name on it.

The boardwalk gently curves around enormous redwoods, ferns dripping with morning dew and moss clinging to fallen logs. There's even a fawn nestled in among the ferns, which immediately makes me suspicious. Like this hike is trying to lure me in. I'm onto you, clearly fake fawn and—oh god!—it yawns and I swear I see hearts. I shake my head. Nope. Not gonna work.

Right on cue, Beth shrieks and jumps back from something, then tries to cover her freakout with a cough. I peer around her shoulder to see a disgusting banana slug sliming up the place in the dirt right next to the trail. See? Nature is an abomination.

But so is Beth, so I take the opportunity to blow gently on the back of her neck and grin when she jumps out of her skin and slaps her neck. She whips around to me.

"It was just a spider," I lie. "But I got it. It had a red hourglass on its butt? Not sure what species that is."

Beth's eyes go big and she sort of sobs and laughs at the same time, and if I'd known hiking would be this much fun I wouldn't have bailed that first day.

Corinne pokes my arm. "There was no spider, Beth. Lola was kidding."

Beth stumbles away to walk next to Georgia, and I glare at Corinne. To think, I'd thought she could be an accomplice. And her eyeliner game is so strong!

Corinne watches Beth scurry away and slides a look my way. Her bouncy curls are swept back by a knotted headband today, and her flawless eyeliner is eggplant purple. "Beth isn't made of the same stuff we are. Go easy on her."

"I'm made of shopping and pool lounging, so I doubt we're the same."

Corinne shrugs. "Me too, plus makeup tutorials and hiking."

Huh. I'm about to ask about her favorite tutorials, but she skips ahead to ask Priya about the giant camera she's pulled out of her backpack.

The trail forks, and we leave the boardwalk and the comforting familiarity of the gift shop area for a packed dirt path that slowly crawls up the slope of a ridge. Before long, I'm alone at the back. Ahead of me, the other girls huff and talk, snippets of conversation—of the getting-to-know-yous—filtering back toward me. The soles of my feet itch to close the distance and hear more, but that's probably the developing athlete's foot.

My legs already ache, and I can feel one of the dozen Band-Aids still plastering my feet dislodging. We stop for water at a bend in the trail, and I can see it zigzagging up a steep hill in front of us. It's like that awful field I faced with Kat. I am *so glad* I got rid of Ezra and that ridiculous idea to go hiking with him. I think I've proven I am absolutely not a hiker.

"What the eff am I looking at," I pant between gulps of water, flapping a hand at the trail.

Corinne, who hasn't even broken a sweat, has the audacity to laugh. "They're called switchbacks," she says. "To make the incline more manageable."

"Cool. Can we *switch back* to something easier?"

She glances at me and frowns. ". . . No?"

From her perch on a rock, Priya looks up at us and shrugs. She's still got that hose in drinking distance from her mouth. "Think of it this way," she says. "What goes up must come down. The elevation will eventually even out because we have to make it back to the van."

"Yeah," I counter, "but it can still suck on the way up."

Georgia cuts in. "Let's have a positive attitude, girls."

"I enjoy the challenge," Beth adds, with a pursed, pleased smile. "It's called the growth mindset."

Georgia blinks slowly and rises from her own super comfy Tempur-Pedic rock. "Okay!" she says, clapping. "Let's keep going. Only a little farther to the surprise."

I swear to god, the only thing that keeps me going is the hurt on Beth's face that Georgia ignored her.

Yet, the thing is, it doesn't *entirely* suck. I mean, let's not jump to any conclusions here. I would so much rather lounge in AC with a smoothie. But beyond the switchbacks—on which, for the record, I persevered harder than anyone else in human history—the forest is shaded and cool. The light is moody and golden, making it feel a bit like I'm walking through a dream. I wonder if Ezra's ever hiked this trail?

This trail . . . that comes with giant-ass birds! I shriek and jump back (and don't miss the way Beth snickers) as an enormous bird alights from a tree not five feet from where I'm standing and soars down an open ridge. It's terrifying and kind of wildly cool at the same time.

"A golden eagle," Georgia says, her voice awed. "Aren't they magnificent?"

And, well, now that it's not trying to peck at my eyeballs, I do kind of marvel at it. I don't think I've ever seen one before. What the hell else is hiding out here?

Another mile down the trail, we find out. And it's not at all what I expected.

It's a chalet.

In the middle of the woods.

And I can smell the grilling meat from here. My mouth waters and I have to blink to make sure I'm not hallucinating.

"Surprise!" Georgia is obviously so proud of herself, and I want to roll my eyes at her, but also if this surprise is truly a bratwurst with mustard, I will propose marriage on the spot. To be clear, I mean to the bratwurst.

It's still a ways off, separated from us by a shallow valley alive with wildflowers, but I find that just seeing the chalet motivates me, helps me push past the tired muscles and aching feet. It's at least two stories, from what I can see. There's a flag snapping in the breeze from the ridgeline of the roof, and the chatter of people talking and tools hammering is odd to hear in the middle of the forest.

We reach a gate, painted a faded sea blue, and Georgia turns to face us. "So! Welcome to the Tourist Club of San Francisco! Our little woodland lodge is private, so please respect the space.

I'm here to volunteer for a workday as one of the members, but I invite you to grab some food and drinks and enjoy yourself in the meadow. We'll head back in an hour."

I am . . . well, I'm speechless. I don't know what I expected, but it wasn't this. And she keeps the surprises coming. Georgia hands out our next milestone, a leather thong dyed pale green. As is tradition, I'm the last through the gate, and Georgia glances over her shoulder to make sure the others have moved on before she speaks.

"I was about to send you back alone for a while there."

"That hardly seems safe," I reply. I'm on the threshold of the property, but Georgia guards the gap of the little blue gate and won't step aside.

"Your attitude affects everyone around you, okay? Don't make this all about you."

I open my mouth to argue—why isn't she pulling Beth aside to tell her to stop lecturing everyone to death?—but she holds out the pale green leather thong *and* the pink one I missed.

"You earned these. Be proud of them."

I'm obviously very unproud. But the leather is soft and warm, and the two colors side by side wrapped around the top of my stick looks kind of great. All the other girls and Georgia have cleared out by the time I finish wrapping my stick, and I take a second to myself to feel the smoothness of the wrap under my palm before remembering I don't care.

A shaded, narrow walkway leads between the steep hillside

and the alpine lodge, perched above the forested hills and val-leys of Muir Woods. I can just spot the back of Georgia's dark, messy braid up ahead, so I follow her around the front of the chalet, past intricate paintings along the chalet's lintels, doors, and eaves. Inside, the other girls are already gathered around a big bar, listening to an elderly man dressed in Von Trapp cosplay list items off a menu.

Some of the members are serving food, but most of them are a flurry of movement—brushing on fresh coats of paint to railings or repairing wooden tables, and there's even one group trimming bushes outside.

"Welcome!" The man behind the smooth oak bar has a face like a walnut, but his voice is deep and loud. For the first time I wonder how they all got here—did they hike here like us? "We've got brats, German potato salad, cucumber salad, a few more schnitzels, and latkes. And beer! But not for you!" He laughs at his joke and starts taking orders.

A few minutes later, I take my plate outside, only to find the rest of the girls have formed a tight little circle in the meadow. There's no spot for me, and I don't care. I *so* don't care. But from here, I can hear the trip and tumble of their conversations and see flashes of smiles. My first instinct is to tell them to shove over and just start talking, because if I launch the conversation, I'll be guaranteed a place in it. But my first instincts, I'm slowly realizing, are mostly shit. Would I be making it all about me, like Georgia just said? Or would I be stepping on others in my effort to get attention, like Ezra said?

Beth looks up and notices me hovering there, notices me waiting for my place among them, but she goes back to her food and chatting. My insides wither.

Fine. Maybe this is the reminder I need that these HAGs aren't for me. My focus is on—

"Hey, Lola," Corinne calls. My chin snaps up, and I see her instructing the others to budge up. She pats the grass next to her, and my chest fills with gratitude.

I fold myself into the spot. "I was going to FaceTime my friends," I lie, "but I guess I can eat with you all."

We eat in silence for a few minutes, then I say, "Did you like the lipsticks?"

I didn't know fishing was part of today's adventure!

Mei's already got hers on, and Corinne smiles wide. "It was really nice!"

She takes hers out and slicks it on; Priya does too.

Across from me, Tavi kicks out her long legs and leans back on her hands. "I'm usually not into white girls trying to buy makeup for me, but you did pretty good."

Beth, I notice, has gone silent and surly. It warms the cockles of my cold, dead heart.

"If you could be anywhere in the world right now, where would it be?" I ask. It takes some effort, but I don't answer my own question first. I slowly eat every last speck of my brat and latkes and listen to the girls. Like, actually listen. It's hard! Even when Corinne says "New York" and I've got this amazing story about getting mistaken for—

No, you know what? I'm just going to listen. At the end, Corinne asks my favorite spot, and the feeling of be asked, of being listened to . . . it's kind of great. There's this sense that I'm part of a conversation, not bulldozing my way through it.

I say Saint-Tropez, but, well, I don't know if there were drugs in the brats or if the hiking has scrambled my brain, but I kind of want to say right here in this meadow. There's this peaceful sense of . . . happiness swirling within me. Kind of like how it felt shopping with Wash and Joon the other day. Like I have nothing to prove.

Around me, poppies flutter in the sunshine, a blanket of creamy orange, and deeper in the shade of the surrounding trees I spot spikes of lavender and light blue. It's all so freaking bucolic I might be sick. I set my empty plate aside and stretch out on my stomach, long grass tickling my ears and the sun beaming warm and golden on my head. It almost reminds me of this pretty field I could see outside my dorm window in France. It was bursting with late-season wildflowers, and one time I spotted ponies running through the meadow. I had this vision of wandering the meadow picking wildflowers for my windowsill, but instead I stepped in horse shit in my brand-new Bensimons.

I wonder, if I'd gotten past the shit, could I have found something like this?

SIXTEEN

"LOLA, DARLING, ARE YOU EVEN listening?"

I wasn't. Mom huffs at me and shoves another handful of spinach into the juicer. My phone dings with a text from Corinne about tomorrow's Fourth of July pool party, an impromptu idea I had on the drive back from the Muir Woods hike a few days ago. I even invited Beth, and if that isn't a sign I'm becoming a better person, I don't know what is. I go to answer Corinne, but Mom stares at me until I put my phone down.

"Anyway," she continues, assured of my attention. "Susanna went to the retreat with Janeth and they're raving about it! I'll have to ask them about it tomorrow. Are you still hosting those girls from Georgia's little hiking group? Dad and I expected you to quit by now, which obviously I'd understand."

It's entirely too early for Mom to be speaking so loud. And it makes me squirm on my chair that she so obviously doesn't think I'm cut out for hiking and camping. My phone dings again, and I peek at it to see another text from Corinne. Three days ago, Corinne implied that I was made of the right stuff to handle all Georgia's outdoor exploits. At the time, I scoffed. But now . . . remembering the hike I conquered and the weird pride I felt at the end, I kind of . . . don't want to quit. Even if Mom expects it.

I wish I could tell Kat about it, but she's been gone for five whole days. Has she just, like, moved in with Joss and Edie? Let me tell you, having only Mom, Dad, and Marnie for company is not recommended. Marnie woke me up this morning and asked if I wanted to go to the library. At nine in the morning. In the summer. I pray for a quick death.

"Apparently it's all holistic and spiritually cleansing," Mom continues, even though I've only grunted in reply. "You take this jade egg, and you insert it into your—"

Behind Mom, the front door opens and I nearly vault over the island to escape what she was miming. But then I realize it's Joss and Lindy coming through the door, and I pull up short, stuck between a rock and a traumatized jade egg.

"I've got a cat delivery," Joss announces, smiling at her own joke. Dork.

But she opens the door wider, and Kat shuffles into the house, hauling her giant leather tote.

My heart bursts and my legs pinwheel. I bowl my twin over so hard her tote goes flying, spilling clothes and treats from Edie's bakery.

"Kat!" I screech at the same moment we hit the back of the couch opposite the entryway and go flipping over it onto the cushions in a tangle of limbs and hair. "Kat, never leave me ever again!"

Okay, so I was going to play it cool. And I am definitely still aggrieved she basically said I was a bad person, then ran away from mini-golf. But it's Kat! Kat! She's the best! We can figure out the hard stuff later.

I disentangle myself and bounce up and down on the couch. Kat's smile is tight, but I'm not about to let a little thing like apathy stop me. "What do you want to do? Want to hang out? Mom's going on about a vagina egg and she made smoothies and I can share with you, what do you think?"

Joss's tinkling laugh fills the entryway. "Mom's got what sort of egg?"

I can see Kat biting the insides of her cheeks to hold back her grin. She's always been crap at grudges.

"Oh, be quiet, girls," Mom grumbles. "I'm looking after my own health like you all should. Now, who wants a smoothie?"

Lindy glances at us and produces a brown paper sack. "Or we could destroy these breakfast burritos we picked up from Moe's."

Screw my twin. I clamber back over the couch and grab the

bag from Lindy. Scents and steam waft up from the bag when I open it, and soon we're unwrapping foil and plating four burritos with avocado salsa. Mom announces she'll only have a tiny bite, then eats three-quarters of Joss's burrito.

I wiggle in my seat with excitement to have Kat home and peek at her as she takes a sip of the green smoothie between bites of burrito. Joon telling me to talk to Kat pops up in my mind, but I push it to the side. I will talk to her, but I also want to bask in her presence and apologize to her about the things I said before Tully's party and tell her about the mysterious German beer garden we discovered with Hike Like a Girl and finally act very gracious when she apologizes for implying I'm a bad influence on Ezra, even though we're not even friends so it shouldn't even matter. Basically, everything is better, and nothing will ever suck again now that Kat's home.

Lindy swoops in to disprove me right away. Because of course. "I take it you found Georgia the other week? Why were you late?"

My eyes careen over to Kat, who definitely doesn't yet know about the fallout from Tully's party.

"It was a bit of miscommunication."

Lindy's stare is what you would call hard.

"I hiked all the way to this alpine lodge!"

Joss nibbles at the remains of her burrito. "Oh, that's wonderful, Lola! You should be proud of yourself!"

"Did you really? Honestly?" Lindy points her fork at me, and it takes every ounce of control not to swat it out of her hands.

"Yes, Lindy. Honestly. Maybe have your husband go ask Georgia if you don't believe me. Or, I know!" I snap, giving in to Peak Pissy Energy. "You could install a tracking device in my butt!"

Lindy glares, so I glare back, until Mom plucks the last bite of burrito off Joss's plate and declares that our sniping gives her a headache. Lindy breaks first and rolls her eyes, and the tension between us dissipates.

An hour later, Mom has left for a charity luncheon—it's either pro-bat or anti-bat, Mom didn't seem very clear about it—and Marnie has returned home with an armful of library books but has been convinced to bring them out to the back deck. We lie on the tiered patio, stretched out on loungers in the shade or on towels next to the pool. I feel like a cat, warm and lazy, one paw drifting idly in the water. The summer sun is wonderfully hot on my shoulders, and the spicy scent of California sagebrush mixes with the sweet pink primroses starting to bloom.

"It's too hot," Lindy groans, throwing her forearm over her eyes. From her perch under a big umbrella and an enormous sun hat, Joss hums a response. I roll over onto my stomach and reach to poke Lindy's foot.

"You and Will are very strange, do you know that? Who doesn't love the sun?" Lindy and Will live in an enormous weathered beach house north of San Francisco that clings to the ocean cliffs and is always depressingly gloomy. No, thank you.

Give me a bluebird sky any day.

"Me," Marnie says from behind her book.

Kat splashes her foot through the pool and scrunches her nose. "I think I agree with Lindy and Marnie."

"No, you don't. We're twins, we have to agree on everything."

Kat frowns, so I shove up and scoot toward her, letting my feet dangle in the water like hers. The pool water is cool against my toes and glints sunlight up into my face.

"Okay," I say, nudging her with my shoulder and speaking quietly. "Not everything. But I think we can agree that I was a complete asshole to you before I went to Tully's, right?"

Kat peeks at me, her mouth pinched. I can't see her eyes behind her dark sunglasses, but I can imagine them narrowed.

"Just please don't go live with Joss and Edie," I continue. "I couldn't stand it if you left me behind."

Again, if you left me *again*.

"I don't think you even understand how much it hurt, what you said," she says to the pool.

"So tell me."

"But would you even listen? You only ever want to talk about *you*."

Her words sting, and I bite back the instinct to reply with something that'll sting her just as bad. "I'm listening now," I say gently. "I'm trying."

She keeps her eyes on the pool and her lips tight. Joon pushed me to talk to her, and here I am trying, so why won't she respond?

There's this deep restlessness in the very bottom of my stomach that she won't tell me what's going on. It almost feels like . . .

"Did something bad happen? While I was gone?"

Kat jerks. "What? No. It's not . . ."

"Then—"

"Ugh, it's too hot," she cuts in, speaking loudly. "Lindy's right." She pulls her cover-up over her head and slips into the water. I try very hard not to let disappointment creep in, but it's unbearably hot against the back of my neck.

"Yeah, totally," I say, and jump into the water after her. I float on my back, concentrating on the way the cool water laps at my warm skin, at the way I swallow back the fear that something irrevocable has changed between us.

She swims past me and jackknifes under the water, her butt in the air and legs glued together like when we were younger and spent hours pretending we were mermaids. I dive down too, twisting in the water and watching my pink hair cloud in front of my face. But when I surface, Kat's already climbed out of the pool and taken a seat in the shade with Joss, Lindy, and Marnie.

"Want to learn how to set shit on fire with me?"

The sun is setting, and us Barnes sisters have moved from lounging on the back deck to lounging in the living room watching the sort of TV that Mom says rots our brains. (Not like the Mensa-quality murder shows she never misses.)

Lindy pushes up to her elbows from her spot on the couch

and frowns at me. "Um, haven't you done enough of that?"

"Yeah, yeah." I hold up my phone, where I've got a bunch of fire-building videos queued up. "It's for Hike Like a Girl."

"The lesson you missed the day you were late?"

I cut her with my eyes. "Yes, Lindy, what I missed on the day I was late." I stand up and act like I'm going to huff out. "Never mind. I'm just over here bettering myself on summer break and, like, exercising my brain or whatever!"

"Okay, okay!" Lindy says, palms up.

Joss unfolds her legs from some sort of pretzel-y yoga pose and stands up. "I know where Dad keeps the wood for the brick pizza oven."

Twenty minutes later, I've learned exactly two things: log cabin beats lean-to, according to a bearded gentleman named Kodiak on YouTube; and Lindy is utter shit at building fires. I know, sisterly affection, etc. etc., but it makes me absolutely cackle with delight to see Lindy struggle to light a match without yelping and throwing it in the firepit.

But it turns out Kodiak—despite the fashion choice of "floppy camo hat"—is actually decent at teaching. Before long, I've successfully arranged, lit, and managed a campfire. Pride flickers in my chest. Never tell Georgia.

It's fully dark by the time Joss and Lindy leave, and Marnie wanders back inside mumbling something about books. It's the first moment I've been alone with Kat since we fought last week. I toe at the grass and peek at her, suddenly . . . shy? It's this strange hesitation that rustles along my nerves. And it's something I'm definitely not used to feeling around anyone, especially my twin.

"So," I say, like a girl in a movie with first-date jitters.

Kat looks up from her phone. It bathes her face in blue light from below, kind of giving this totally normal interaction a sense of foreboding. Which is ridiculous. "Hey, good job with the fire," she says, a note of distraction to her tone. Her eyes go back to her phone. "Sorry," she says, "Wash is coming to pick me up and—"

"Are you into Ezra?" I don't know why I ask. But I also don't know why she wanted me to stay away from him, so maybe it's that? "I mean, you usually won't shut up about whatever new guy you're into, but you haven't dated anyone since I've been home, so . . ."

Her eyes are hooded. "I'm not into Ezra."

"You're sure?"

"I'm sure."

I shouldn't pick at this wound. And yet here I am. "But, I mean, why didn't you want me around him?"

Her phone buzzes. "Listen, I gotta go."

"What?"

She pushes back the sliding glass doors, and I'm a stray puppy following her inside. I watch her dump her phone into her bag and slide her bare feet into a pair of leather sandals. "Joon got tickets for this late-night showing of some old campy horror film, so . . ." She strides out the front door, but I follow, still feeling a bit hazy.

Wash's black Land Rover is idling in the circle drive, him and Joon in the front seats and two others in the back. Kat glances over her shoulder and frowns at me. "What are you—"

Ezra jumps out of the back, and my heart jumps with him. *Dammit.* He made it plain what he thinks about popularity. And I made it plain that's my only goal. And it was . . . it *is* . . . but then why are my muscles and bones working against me right now and trying to drag me closer to this boy?

He stands there. Stares at me. I said no to him. I finished whatever was happening between us. Regret groans through me, but I refuse to give in.

Except then he roughs a hand through his hair and walks closer, and I'm a goner.

"Are you coming?" Hope floods the corners of his voice.

"There's not room," Kat says. Agitation ripples off her like waves from an old radio tower. Frankly, it all makes me pretty annoyed. Like she *wants* me to stay the selfish mess of a girl I've always been because it makes cutting me out easier. But there's something changing in me, and I'm only just now realizing that might be a good thing, whether or not Kat will acknowledge it.

Ezra tilts his chin at her. "We could drive separate."

Kat splutters in frustration. "I don't care," she says shortly. She walks away, waving dismissively at us, and climbs into the back seat next to Joon's debate club friend who facilitated Kat's mini-golf escape.

Ezra steps closer to me. The porch light glows over his face and shoulder, but the rest of him is soft in the darkness. My agitation settles, even as other parts of me are getting all out of sorts.

"Sorry I missed you at Basecamp," he says, voice low. "Let me know when you're going back and I'll meet you there."

"I won't be going back," I manage.

"But if you did . . ."

"If I did?"

"Lola—" My name melts on his tongue, and I melt with it. Whatever's happening, I want this. I want to feel like this.

I want to be happy. And I realize very, very suddenly, that I've been looking in the wrong places for my happiness.

"I lied," I say suddenly.

His breath catches.

"I do want to go hiking with you, if you're still offering."

Light falls over the column of his throat, the bob of his Adam's apple when he swallows. "You have no idea how much I'm still offering."

Shadows move, and the very tips of his fingers brush across my arm. My skin ignites, so suddenly, so powerfully that I don't know whether I want to jump him or run away.

"Come with us tonight," he says. He hooks my pinkie for one lingering moment, then lets go. "Please?"

But before I can answer, Wash lays on the horn and Joon hangs out the window. "Get your arse in the car, Ezra."

In the back seat, Kat stares straight ahead, like if she concentrates hard enough, I'll vanish. I blink away the hurt and step back. He might want me there tonight, but the most important person in my life doesn't. "Next time."

And I actually mean it.

SEVENTEEN

I'M ANXIOUS. ARE THESE ENOUGH flamingos? Is there such a thing?

And also, when can I see Ezra again?

And also *also*, why didn't Kat want me to hang out with her last night?

No. Flamingos. Concentrate on the flamingos.

My HLAG (turns out, the *L* probably isn't silent) crew is coming over in an hour, and I only have three flamingos and two pink-frosted sprinkle doughnuts blown up and floating in the pool. I raided Mom's party closet and ran to Target this morning for novelty sunglasses, Popsicles, and a bocce ball set even though I don't technically know how to play. In years past, Kat and I would cohost a pool party for the Fourth while all the parents were at Tully's. Last year, I was in exile in Arizona with Grammy while Will helped Mom and Dad negotiate my move to France. I'm definitely not thinking of that now and wondering what Meg, Jasmine, Tully, and the others are doing. Or what Kat did last night that had to be sister-free.

"One more flamingo," I announce.

From underneath the deck umbrella, Kat *mm-hmm*s vaguely and continues painting her toenails. Not positive, but I believe the shade is called Color Me Indifferent, and isn't she just?

I grab a flamingo and start blowing. Don't think about Kat. Don't think about the fact that she ran off instead of having a conversation with me last night. Stay busy. Get this flamingo looking perfect, and definitely don't think about it.

The flamingo inflates with the speed of a French rail employee, and my vision is going black at the edges by the time the floppy neck finds the will to stand up straight.

"Thanks for your help," I gasp at Kat.

She *mm-hmm*s again. My blood starts simmering gently. I ignore it and set out the coconut cups and leis on the long patio table, then fill the cooler with Popsicles and bubbly waters. My sister focuses on her nails, and at this point it's on purpose, right? Nobody concentrates that hard on nail polish.

No matter! Look at this cute setup! There is no way the girls won't have fun and fully accept me as one of their own! Which I definitely don't care about except that I definitely do! I check Insta, but no one from school has posted any pics yet. They're probably all bored without me throwing the usual party. Sure, Lola.

The doorbell rings, and I hop through the sliding glass doors, thrown all the way open so the entire back wall of the house leads onto the patio. I smooth my pink-and-orange pool cover-up and paste on a smile. Being surrounded by others will be exactly the thing to get over this weirdness with Kat.

But when I pull open the door, I feel Kat sidle up next to me.

"Hi!" she says, suddenly locating her voice.

Priya and Beth look between us. "Oh, that's right. You're twins," Priya says. She's in a lavender terry-cloth romper with a floral beach towel sticking out of her big tote.

"Must be fraternal. You really don't look alike to me," Beth adds. Her towel is brown, and that in no way surprises me.

"Come on in!" Kat beams. She introduces herself and leads Beth and Priya through the house.

What the hell? Is she . . . hijacking my party? Is this payback for trying to go with her last night?

I'm still standing at the door, gaping, when the next car pulls through the circular drive. Tavi and Mei get out, and Corinne is not far behind.

"Sweet house," Tavi says, tugging off her sunglasses as she walks inside. "I dated a guy who lived over this way, but turns out he was an entitled ass."

That pulls a laugh out of me. "Yeah, that tracks. It was probably my ex."

We walk through to the deck, and Kat is there handing out

leis like she's the damn host. It bugs me way more than it prob-ably should. Those are my leis. (That I found in Mom's party closet. Semantics.) I worked hard on this and it's like Kat has suddenly turned on her human host protocols and is acting like this was a joint effort when she's made it pretty damn clear she is no longer interested in joint anything with me.

"This is going to be so fun!" I say way too loudly, try-ing to snatch the attention away from Kat. She keeps chatting with Corinne, and jealousy flares in my chest. These are my maybe-friends. Not hers. She can have Beth.

I grab Corinne's wrist and very subtly drag her over to the cooler. "You want a Popsicle? Or a bubbly water?"

Corinne frowns. "I'm fine."

"Okay! Well, whatever you need! So excited you're here!"

My nerves snap and sizzle, my muscles twitch, wanting to move, to act. So I rip my cover-up over my head, scream "Cannonball!" and jump into the pool. When I surface, Tavi is diving into the deep end, and Beth is trying to climb onto a flamingo without actually getting any part of her body wet. Mei—love her forever—giggles and pushes Beth in. Never, in the history of H_2O, has anyone entered the water with less grace. Only Corinne is still chatting with Kat, but I'll get to her later.

Except after I show off my perfect shallow-end handstand, I come up to see Priya is chatting with Kat now too. And Kat's laughing and talking with her hands and generally acting exactly like she used to. Except she's ignoring me.

It all feels so . . . weird. This sense of being slightly off, like I'm a puzzle piece that doesn't fit with everyone else around me. And no amount of slightly-too-loud joking or cannonballs or trying to force mocktails in half-coconut shells on the girls is sanding down my edges to make me fit.

I drift to the corner, back into the shadow of the house, and ache with loneliness. I thought . . . ugh. I swipe under my eyes. How absolutely pathetic, what I thought these girls could become. The ache builds, and I sit down heavily on a lounger. I miss Meg and Jasmine. I know I shouldn't, but I do. I miss what we were. I miss the history and the bickering and the way we were a *unit*.

I wrap myself up in a towel and watch my pool party go on without me. Mei and Priya are playing cards. Beth's pulled out a book. How would Meg and Jasmine fit in here if I blended my former friends with these girls? I chew on my lip, heart sinking. Jasmine would be her particular brand of shitty, putting people down with a smile and a twist of the knife. And Meg would let her. And me? Would I stand up for them like I did for Ezra freshman year? It's blazing hot, but a shiver ghosts down my spine. I know the answer, and I hate it.

A shadow falls over me, and I squint up at Corinne. She's got a gauzy tie-dyed caftan on over her black swimsuit and a totally naked face save for the most epic bright pink lipstick. She pokes at my towel. "You okay?"

"Just having a bit of an existential crisis."

"Love those!" She sits down on the lounger next to me. "Wanna talk about it?"

I shrug in my towel, but then say, "I think I'm a mean girl."

Corinne barks with laughter. "Um, you're just now figuring that out?"

My face scrunches up. "I don't want to be, but I'm afraid it's my default setting."

"Nah, I don't think so. Your default setting is to want to be at the center of it all, but that doesn't make you a mean girl unless you let it."

It all sounds alarmingly like what Ezra said a couple of weeks ago, that we might all be figuring our shit out, but some people can do that without hurting others. My stomach twists. I *don't* want to hurt others. I just want them to like me.

I stare past Corinne toward the girls. Tavi and Beth are now wearing novelty sunnies and posing for Priya and her fancy camera. Mei and Kat are in the pool spinning their frosted-doughnut floaties. "I've been shitty to everyone. Do they hate me? I'd hate me."

Corinne stands and holds out her hand. The sun is sinking toward the horizon, and it makes her curls glow golden like a halo. "So change their minds."

Right. So that's kind of a yes to the whole hating thing. And also, Corinne's advice sounds *hard*. Maybe too hard. Isn't there, like, an easier way? But if I was able to convince Crenshaw's board of directors that the dress code was sexist (with some *very* glittery poster boards and a dramatic reenactment), then maybe I can convince five girls to be my new friends. I take hold of Corinne's palm and let her haul me to my feet.

It's only later, when the house is quiet, that this giant hill to climb feels insurmountable. I'd kill for some switchbacks (or an elevator). Kat's digging for food in the fridge, while I'm slouched at the kitchen island, eating sour gummy worms and scrolling Insta. I pause on a photo of Meg and Jasmine in matching American flag bikinis under shortalls, smiling, cute. It all looks so easy. The sour gummies are a lump in my stomach.

I tell myself they took five hundred shots before Jasmine let Meg post it. Then I cast my memories back, digging for the last truly good one with them, but I'm coming up short. We made it all look easy, we did. But that doesn't mean it was *good*. Because, now that I think about it, it hadn't been *them* who made me happy in a long time, but what they represented. Which sucks to realize about two of the people you once counted as best friends.

"What's your favorite memory with Meg and Jas?" I ask Kat idly, holding up my phone to show her the Insta post.

"Seriously?" Kat shakes her head and walks past me.

"Yeah. Like, we *did* have fun together, right?" I click on Meg's handle and start scrolling through her feed. The pictures all look the same.

Kat's voice is hard-bitten when she says, "I can't believe you're still obsessed with them."

"No, I didn't mean—"

"You know why I don't like being around you anymore? Because of *that*," she snaps, glaring at my phone, still lit up with Meg's post. She stalks closer, and I can see splotches of red crawling up her neck. "The second Jasmine decides you're back in, you'll drop everyone else and run back to her. You're using the others."

Well, this took a turn. And by turn, I mean Kat's being a real asshole and twisting my words. I sit up straight and glare at her.

"Watch out," I spit at her. "You're acting *melodramatic*. Thought you were better than that now."

Kat rolls hers eyes and turns away with a muttered *whatever*, but I jump off the stool.

"No," I say, grabbing her wrist. "What the hell did I do to make you treat me like this?" She tugs at me, but I refuse to let go. "You've freaking abandoned me when I really could use you."

Kat yanks away from me and squares her shoulders. "Yeah, you could have *used* me. That's exactly it. You never once asked about *me* while you were gone. It was only ever about you. *Oh, France is awful! I live in a castle and get to travel around Europe! Boo-fucking-hoo for me!*"

Okay, her perception of what I was doing in Europe is wildly off, but we'll get into that later.

"So I'm asking now!" I press her. "Tell me anything. I *want* to know!"

Kat sneers. "It's too late for that."

"No, it's not. You've, like, decided you're done with me even though I'm trying my hardest. And that's really shitty."

Kat pokes her finger out at me, her face rigid. "Or maybe it's shitty that you hijack everything. I want something just for me, okay?"

That makes me laugh in her face. "You mean you and your new friends."

"Yeah," she shoots back. "That is what I mean. They're not *your* friends."

Her words are frost on my heart. "You know what? You keep going on about Jas and Meg hurting me, but *you're* the one who's made sure I feel unwanted."

Kat laughs, harsh and shrill. "You're so effing delusional."

And what she says next makes me shatter.

"Jasmine started the account."

That can't be right. *It can't be.* We made friendship bracelets and daisy crowns. We told each other secrets and comforted each other's tears. A great, rolling sob is a tide in my throat. Choking and salty.

"You're lying."

She has to be. Jasmine wouldn't go that far. She may be low-key evil, but we were always *us. Us.* And now I'm . . . Loneliness is a winter wind in my chest. But before I can set my storm loose, the truth hiding in Kat's words freeze me.

"You knew and didn't tell me."

Because worse than Jasmine's betrayal is the one standing in front of me. It disassembles everything I thought about myself, my friends, my sister. But I knit myself back together with rage.

"You fucking knew."

Kat sucks in a breath. "I didn't want—"

"Jasmine was my friend, but you're supposed to be something more. A *sister* wouldn't keep that from me." I lift my chin and spear her with a glare. Beth was right—there's no resemblance. I don't recognize any bit of me in my twin.

"Lola," Kat tries, reaching for my arm. Yeah, too late, *sis*.

I shove past her. My bedroom door slams behind me, and every ounce of anger that'd kept me upright leaks away. I crawl into bed and yank the covers up. I want to wallow, to feel pathetic. But something deeper groans through me. I'm in *mourning*. I've wasted a year—a whole damn year—convinced that there was some magic combination that would make everything go back to "normal." Because it was easy and safe and all I'd come to know. But it was never going to happen. Jasmine and Meg made that decision a year ago, and Kat knew. They stood by and watched me suffer and grasp. They *enjoyed* it. Because it's just like Ezra said—making others suffer is a perverse little reminder that it's not *them* on the outside. I swipe at my eyes, embarrassed, angry. But more than that, more than anything, I'm hollow with loss. I wish I could burn up everything other than my anger, but I can't. I can't rid myself so easily of missing what we were.

It's a very long time before I'm finally able to chase down sleep. It comes long after I've shut off my dreams.

EIGHTEEN

TRADITIONALLY, PEOPLE SHOW THEY'RE IN mourning by wearing black.

My mourning is taking a slightly different form—that of sabotage. I'm pissed at Jasmine, but Kat . . . I expected better from her. So since she did me dirty, I'll return the favor. I think some dead guy said something about not going quietly into the night, and I'm pretty sure he meant that in the context of getting retribution against a terrible sibling.

In four days of sabotaging Kat's life, I've racked up some impressive stats: three (3) favorite protein bars eaten by me; five (5) Hulu shows I've turned on just so she'll lose her place; one (1) hideous throwback photo I've posted that I know she hates.

Who's not missing her twin? THIS GIRL.

Kat has responded with chilly formality, but I heard her swear in front of the cupboard yesterday when only the flaxseed protein bar was left. Today, though, she gets a break—unless she discovers that I'm wearing her favorite leggings and cropped tee—because I'm off on a new assignment with HLAG.

I've almost forgotten the deep sisterly betrayal when Georgia pulls the VW bus up to a tall building splashed with a crazy colorful mural of a dude rock climbing. Which is not what I expected when I woke up this morning. Georgia twists around in her seat and grins at us.

"Rock climbing!"

A vision of Ezra flashes in my mind. Guess I'm about to see what's so great about "ladders but make it worse." He'd probably love it here. And then I think, *So would Kat.* She's never had a fear of heights, and when we went zip-lining in Antigua once, she was the first to volunteer for the Tarzan swing.

But movement next to me pushes the sister who I definitely wasn't thinking about out of my mind. Corinne sits back hard, even as the others are leaning forward.

"I went rappelling in Costa Rica with my dads last year," Mei says in a rush, her eyes bright.

"And I watched that doc about the guy who climbed El Capitan without ropes and it was . . . whoa," Tavi adds. "I definitely thought he was going to get smashed on the rocks."

Corinne sort of groans.

"Hey, guys, maybe none of that," I say, slicing my eyes toward Corinne.

Georgia is twisted in her seat, giving us the rundown on this rock climbing gym, and hasn't noticed that Corinne is currently doing some sort of breathing exercise.

"This is how I got my start climbing, at gyms like this. Rock climbing takes trust, not only in yourself, but in your gear and your crew. So let's head in and learn more about what it takes to get to the top, then we'll pair up and get climbing!"

Around us, the girls start moving, but Corinne has turned to stone. I pause for a second before nudging her shoulder. "Will you be my partner?"

Her eyes take a second to focus, but she presses her lips together and nods. It gets her moving too, and soon we're out of the bus and into a little room for a safety briefing. A white guy with dreads teaches us how to secure our harnesses, the how-tos of belaying, plus a series of commands. For Corinne's sake, I make sure to actually listen.

Inside the climbing silo, it's bright and chilly, and the air smells weirdly dusty. And it's tall. The wall Georgia leads us to looks to be about the same height as the one at Basecamp, but they get way higher from there, so tall it kind of makes my mind swim to tip my neck and squint for the top. There are people up there, scaling the heights and scrambling for holds.

A curious feeling thrums through me, watching them. My blood sings with it. My stomach flips. I want to get up there. I want to see what the world looks like from the top. Huh. The surge of emotion and energy surprises me, and when I turn to Corinne, I'm practically bouncing on the spongy floor mats.

I tug at the harness giving me a spectacular camel toe and grin at her. "I'll go first, okay? You can see what it's like before you try."

Corinne flicks her eyes up the wall and squeaks in reply.

Even this shorter section of wall looks a hell of a lot taller from close up, and I crane my neck to peer up at the top. An instructor hooks my harness to the top rope and stands close by to make sure Corinne isn't going to pass out and let me plummet to the ground. On either side, Tavi and Beth are also facing the wall, and I nod at both of them.

"Race you to the top?"

"We've never done this before, don't be ridiculous," Beth snaps.

Tavi glances at me. "Slow and steady. It's not a race. There's this great TED Talk about—"

"It's definitely a race," I interrupt, because I'm really trying here and nothing will make me roll my eyes harder than a secondhand account of a TED Talk.

"It's not a race," she says harder.

Pssh. "Three, two, one, go!"

I grab a handhold and heave myself up. Then up again, and again. Hey, this is easy! On my other side, Tavi's scaling the wall slower than me, scanning all the various handholds like it's a math problem. Beth has already jumped back to the mat and is stomping like a little Beth Baby.

I scramble upward until I'm well above her head. My arms quiver from hauling myself up, and my fingers already ache.

And . . . I'm stuck. I sort of crabbed sideways, and the next handhold is three feet to my left and above my head. My feet are reversed, so my legs are nearly crossed at the knee, and there's a jut of false rocky wall bumping my hip out. I glance down at Corinne to see her watching me, her hands ready on the belay line. I take a breath, clench my stomach, and surge up for the handhold.

I miss by a mile and my heart jumps as my body slips off the wall. There's a swoop and a lurch and I'm suddenly sitting in my harness, floating above the ground. I let out a whoop and land gracelessly on my butt when I hit the padded floor. But the smile on my face feels so wide my cheeks hurt.

"That was amazing!" I grin up at Corinne and accept her hand when she offers to pull me to my feet.

"Whatever you say," she says, voice tight.

I'm already eyeing the wall. "I'm serious, it's so cool up there, and there's this crazy second when you start falling that makes you feel like . . . like a bird or something! It's so fun!"

Though maybe not as fun for Beth. From above our heads, she shouts and swears loudly and Priya lowers her back to the ground.

Corinne watches her and says, "I'm good right here."

On my other side, Tavi sets her hand on one of the holds and nods at me. "Slow and steady sucks," she says with a sly smile, the callout clear.

"You're on."

We fall several more times, but every time I make it a little higher, find my footing a little more surely. Priya switches in for Beth, Mei for Tavi, but Corinne begs off taking a turn.

It's my fifth time attempting the climb when I pause a few feet off the ground. I've noticed it feels a lot better when I use my legs for leverage instead of trying to muscle up the wall with my arms. I stare at the wall and the handholds above me, and chalk my hands for better grip. Instead of blindly scrambling, I take my time, choose each handhold precisely with a thought for what lies ahead. Little by little, the floor falls away. Until I'm higher than any of the other girls. The air is cool and the top of the wall inches closer and closer. Until I have only a couple of handholds left. I carefully place my foot sideways, splayed out like a ballet dancer, and push off, reaching for the last hold. There. Right . . . there.

Triumph ripples through my muscles and I lift my free hand to slap the top of the wall. Chalk dust puffs up from under my palm. Far below me, I think I actually hear Tavi and Priya cheer. I give myself a second to revel in this feeling of accomplishment before I sit back against my harness and rappel down the wall.

Georgia's there, and when she gives me a high five, I don't

even care how dorky we look. I unhook the lead and hold it out toward Corinne.

"You've got to try it. And I'll be right here to catch you."

Corinne chews on her lip. "I can't." She's shifting back and forth on her feet, and her skin looks practically green when she glances up at the wall. "I just can't."

Georgia peers at Corinne. "There's a bouldering room down that hall," she says, pointing across the gym. "It's as hard as rock climbing, but without the height."

I have no idea what bouldering is, but I nod at her and grab Corinne's elbow. I peek into the other rooms down the hall—one has angled ceilings so the climbers are practically on their backs, and another has these, like, upright treadmills with handholds that rotate as you climb. Past locker rooms and a utilitarian cafeteria is one more area tucked away into the far corner of the building.

It's like walking into a cave. The lights glow golden and the air is warmer than in the main gym. The squishy mats sink under my feet, but that's the only thing that looks man-made. The walls are covered in realistic boulders that curve and pile and twist to form shelves and recesses. But none of it is more than maybe six feet high. I turn to Corinne, and a wide smile lights up her face.

"Oh, this is perfect!"

She's crap at first, but so am I. Without the bright handholds, it's a lot of feeling and guesswork to figure out where I can get a good grip and where I can't. We try and fall, try and fall. But there's a lot of cheering and even some laughing too. Within minutes, I'm sweaty and breathing hard, but I don't want to give up. That feeling of triumph when I reached the top of the wall out in the main gym, there's nothing like it.

But it's a different sort of triumph in the bouldering room. There's no point where I can tap the top of the wall and declare that I've won. It feels like I'm pushing to outdo *myself*, not the wall or the other girls. And, shit, I kind of like it.

Corinne flops back onto the mat and starfishes her limbs, breathing hard. I jump down from a ledge and sit next to her, tired and sore, but weirdly happy at the same time. It's strange and new.

Corinne tugs at the end of her curls, fluffing them up, and grins up at the ceiling. Even after all this climbing, her mascara remains perfect.

"Okay, I can't hold it in any longer," I say. "Your makeup game is flawless."

Corinne purses her lips. She's got a fat line of olive-green eyeliner on her top lid today, paired with full, curved nut-brown brows and mascara that won't quit. "Oh, thanks." She pushes up to sit cross-legged opposite me and adds, "My mom is a makeup artist. Colette Rahmani?"

I gasp so loud I swear chalk dust lodges permanently in my lungs. "No way. The lip kits she did last year were, like, the best. I'm on a waitlist for the new one. And those tutorial videos on eyebrows? Life changing." I tilt my face back and forth, show-ing off my C.Rahmani+Co boyfriend brows. Colette Rahmani is a French expat who started selling her makeup commer-cially after clients begged. Like Fenty, she became known for her inclusive range of tones that came from her own need to mix makeup growing up since French beauty counters catered to white women.

Corinne's cheeks are pink, and she looks somewhere between embarrassed and pleased. "Her new lip kits are rad. We've got a bunch all over the house she's been mixing and matching to prep for launch in a couple months."

"I'm not going to lie, I'm totally starstruck right now."

Colette Rahmani is exactly the sort of person I thought I'd become in France—elegant, witty, and insouciant—and though she's lived in the States for like twenty years, she's always so impeccably French.

"It's kind of weird," Corinne says. "I mean, she's just my mom, you know? After my parents divorced, she moved us out here and started selling the makeup all her clients loved and everything really took off a couple years ago. It's . . . an adjust-ment." She tilts her chin to the side, regards me. "Can I ask you something? What you said about arson . . ."

A *heh* chuffs out of me. "Yeah, not a lie. I, um, accidentally burned down my sister and brother-in-law's boat. I mean, not on purpose, but, um. It was definitely my fault." I pause, scrutiniz-ing Corinne—my secret sits on my tongue, but I need to know first: "And you're really not here because you hope Georgia will put in a good word for you with Will Drake?"

Corinne shakes her head. "My dad is really into hiking, so I thought it'd be something we could do together. I don't see him as much anymore, and . . . I don't know. I want us to have something in common other than just him being my dad."

"Okay, so I'm going to tell you something, but I don't want the others to find out." I take a breath. "I never applied to this program. I didn't even know it existed until two days before it started. But, um, well. Will Drake is actually my brother-in-law. I'm only here because it was his boat I burned down."

Corinne's mouth drops open for a second before she snaps it shut. "Holy shit."

"It's weird, hearing the other girls freaking out about someone I've known since I was twelve." I shudder, and Corinne laughs. "And, like, Beth has made it clear that it was really hard to get in and, um. I just . . . don't want everyone to know I didn't earn my spot. Especially now."

I pick at the seam of my leggings. Maybe it's what I learned about Jasmine and Kat, or maybe it was something growing before that, but being around these girls makes me feel not so lonely. They make me feel part of something bigger.

Corinne nudges my shoulder. "I promise to never say out loud that Will's hot."

She laughs when I roll my eyes, but she says, quieter, "I won't tell anyone."

I can't quite say why, but I believe her.

NINETEEN

I'VE GOT CHALK DUST EMBEDDED under my nails, but I've also got a need for tacos in my heart. And to prove to Corinne that I really am a changed HLAG, I ask the rest of the girls to join me.

So it's a real kick in the vagina that only Priya agrees, which means Beth is coming too since they drove together. Okay, so not my first choice, but maybe we'll get to know each other better and discover we all . . . Right, I'll figure out what we have in common after I eat my weight in Jorge's street tacos. I pile the girls into my car, and we set off for the taco stand near my house.

First thing we don't have in common: they both go to Albion Prep in Mountain View, which is one of those schools where a panel of experts has to decide you're a genius to enter its halls.

I was never in danger of attending. Apparently, they applied to HLAG with another classmate, Carissa. Except Carissa didn't get in, so I'm left with a lovely gnawing sense of guilt that I somehow stole Carissa's spot even though I know I'm the tacked-on person this year.

Second thing we don't have in common: Beth has declared repeatedly that she doesn't drive because of its impact on the environment, but she sure as shit isn't having any qualms about trying to drive from the back seat. Every two seconds Beth says helpful things like "Stop sign, Lola" or "There's a pedestrian right there, Lola." She's about to become a pedestrian herself if she doesn't pipe down.

I grip the steering wheel and bare my teeth in a smile. "Thanks for the reminder, Beth," I manage, glancing at her in the rearview mirror.

"Brakes, Lola!" She flaps a hand at me. "Brakes!"

I look forward and slam on my brakes before the car in front stops me instead. I don't swear at Beth. At least, not out loud. Please, perceive me.

Outside Jorge's, the line to order is twenty deep and the main street is packed with cars, so I have to park around the corner. But the taco proximity makes my stomach groan with the promise of al pastor and carnitas with an ice-cold strawberry Jarritos to wash it all down, so I can't complain too much about the parking.

But then my stomach groans again, this time with utter dread because I've spied Tully's unmistakable, chromed-out Audi R8 only a few spots away. And as we round the corner, I spot him at a prime table, Meg and Jasmine sitting at his side. My skin goes cold.

"What's wrong?" Beth demands when I freeze in the middle of the sidewalk. "Are you carsick from your bad driving, because I am."

I don't acknowledge her or her critique of my driving.

"Beth," Priya hisses. "Be nice."

"Maybe she doesn't know she's a bad driver. I'm helping her improve," Beth hisses back.

A thin laugh crackles across my tongue. I'm afraid of how they'll treat me, and afraid of how I'll react. I could turn around right now and play this off. It's not like there aren't a thousand other taco places in the South Bay, and most don't come with betrayal.

"Lola?" Priya asks softly.

No. You know what? I'm *more* afraid of what it means if I can't face them without breaking. I shake my former friends out of my thoughts. "Come on, let's get in line."

Tully proceeds to belch loudly and tip back onto the legs of his chair so the people in line have to curve out of his way. If he notices, he doesn't react.

He, Meg, and Jasmine haven't noticed us yet either, but the inevitability of it prickles at my neck. The place where I kept Meg and Jasmine in my heart still feels so raw, and there's this horrible confusion of wanting to not give a shit about them, but absolutely still caring what they think, despite everything.

The line inches forward, and I squeeze my eyes shut tight and blow out a long breath.

Knowing what I know about them now, it means I'll truly never be popular again. And I think . . . I think I'm okay with that? Or will be? But also. I kind of wish I were facing them with someone *other* than Beth and Priya beside me. Which, I know, means I still suck. I'm a work in progress, okay?

Priya's wearing a baggy black T-shirt like the free ones Dad brings home from tech shows. This one says in big white letters "Don't Be Na Cl Y." Next to her, Beth's hair is scraped back into two tight French braids that are only missing gingham bows and a cow to milk.

Then it happens: Tully spots me. Embarrassment lances down my spine. But I push my shoulders back.

"Lola!" Tully shouts down the line at us. I lift my chin at him. I wonder if he knows it was Jasmine behind the account, or if he is even aware of its existence. Honestly, I wouldn't be surprised either way. "You puked all over my bathroom floor and left your swimsuit under the bed. The maid was pissed."

My mouth turns to dust under the sudden attention of fifteen people in line who are definitely picturing me nude and covered in vomit.

"And what the fuck was Booben doing there?" Tully bellows. Meg whispers something sharp at him, but he waves her off.

The line shifts forward, until they're only a table away. Jasmine's smile curls. "Tulls, don't make fun of Ezra," she says, full of fake concern. Her eyes slide to mine. "Josie W. saw you on a cute little ice cream date with him. I mean, one of his friends is an amateur magician, but whatever makes you happy."

"Who's Ezra?" Beth asks.

Old habits blah blah blah, because I smirk at Jasmine and say, "Someone I could make super popular if I wanted."

"Wow, illuminating," Beth grumbles.

"Who's the amateur magician?" Priya asks. "Is he in the league?"

I sort of hiss at Priya to be quiet, but that makes Jasmine smile wider. Discomfort curls through my stomach, embarrassment tangling with guilt. Why should I care what Jasmine thinks? Except I do. It's so super annoying, but I do.

"Sweet shirt," Jasmine says to Priya, trying a new tactic.

Priya frowns down at her tee, but you know what? Under the nerdy AF clothes and alarming revelation about magic, Priya takes the most gorgeous photos. And Beth . . . okay, Beth is still Beth. *But she's crew* is what whispers through my brain.

"Jas, sweetie," I say, matching her sickly sweet tone. "Maybe it's time to stop obsessing about who I hang out with. It's getting weird."

She blanches, but schools her expression fast. But not quickly enough for Meg to look between us, frowning. She blinks up at me and starts picking at her nails—an old nervous tic. "I . . . ,"

Meg says, half standing. "I think I've gotta go."

But Jasmine grabs her wrist and tugs her back down to sit. "What are you talking about? You can't go to Big Sur without me and Tulls."

Tully watches all this dully, his little eyes still returning to me. "We're taking the PJ to Big Sur. You should come, Lo. Come fuck shit up with me."

No mention of our history, of what happened last time we fucked with some shit. It's in the past, and Tully's not the sort to ever look behind. That's the thing with him—he can be such a good time when he wants. But it never ebbs, never changes.

"I'm good, Tulls. Thanks for the invite, though." And I mean it. Taking his plane anywhere with him on board sounds awful.

"We wouldn't have room for you anyway," Jasmine adds.

Tully shrugs. "You could have stayed here, Jas."

Her face drains of color, and not gonna lie, it feels good. Look, I'm trying to become a *better* person, not *the best* person.

Mercifully, the line continues, and when I glance back a minute later, they're already gone.

It's a door slamming. Nearly twelve years of friendship, and it really is over. The truth is sour in my stomach, but it doesn't take me down. It doesn't break me. And maybe . . . maybe something new, something better, is standing right next to me. (I mean, aside from Beth.)

Priya watches Tully's Audi speed past. "So that was weird," she says. "Are those . . . your friends?"

I roll my lips together. The easy thing to do here is lie. But it doesn't feel fair.

"They used to be. Not anymore."

Beth is still for a moment before saying, "Do you want to talk about it?"

Grateful. That's what I feel. A wash of gratefulness that flushes out all the embarrassment and guilt. We step forward in line, and the guy behind the counter awaits our order.

"You know what, maybe later." And I mean it. "Right now, I want every taco available."

Beth nods, a nerd on a mission. She literally orders one of every taco on the menu.

A few minutes later, my fingertips slipping along the condensation on the glass neck of my strawberry Jarritos, my mind whirs between a couple of new things. One: I survived my first encounter as an Officially Not Popular person. And two: I'm going to make this hike with Ezra happen.

TWENTY

HEY. ABOUT THAT HIKE . . .

I text Ezra as soon as I get home (after placing gummy worms in the toes of all Kat's shoes). My phone buzzes almost immediately, which should turn me off this new flirtation with Ezra, but it's just so wholesome that I can't help but be flattered. Actually acting like you like the person you like! Who knew!

Sorry. At work. Hold on a sex.

Sec!

I meant sec.

I'm not saying I'm cackling, but . . . The typing bubble pops up and Ezra's back. I imagine him: crawling into that tent, hunched over his phone, hiding from Sheena. Are his cheeks pink from the (Freudian?) slip? It makes me grin to think so.

I make a split second decision and FaceTime him. He answers and immediately drops the phone.

"Sorry," he says, fumbling for the phone and lifting it up so I can see him. His face is sort of obscured between black sheeting. "I'm hiding from Sheena in the sleeping bag display."

"Ol' Sheena's a real dick."

Ezra chokes on a laugh.

"So I've been thinking about this hike," I say.

His mouth pinches just the tiniest bit. "Yeah?"

"Yeah. So. Today?"

"I thought—" There's a muffled noise in the background, and his eyes dart to something I can't see. "Shit, I just got paged. I'm working the rest of today. Tomorrow?"

Tomorrow. It's weird how much I'd hoped for today, but I say, "Sounds great."

His eyes dart again. "Great. Sounds good. I'll—" I can hear someone calling his name. He leans closer to the phone, so close his face blurs and all I can see is the movement of his lips. "I'll text you," he whispers. "Bye, Lo."

Never has a person anticipated a hike so much. I say that with confidence and a total lack of information on the national popularity of hiking. I'm so enthusiastic, I don't even go through with my newest petty idea to annoy Kat (changing all the car radio presets to smooth jazz).

The next day, I'm only five minutes late to the trailhead. I pull in beside Ezra, who's leaning against the passenger-side door of an enormous old Volvo station wagon. My stomach jolts at the sight, the casual way he's got one brown boot hooked over the other, the nonchalant rise of his hand in hello when he spots me. I grab my backpack and sling it over my shoulders as I walk closer.

The navy of his pullover tips his gray eyes toward blue, and his hair is still wet from showering. He smiles, dimples creasing the edges of his mouth, and my heart goes jackrabbiting out of here. I breathe long and steady out of my nose and attempt for bravado to paper over the fact that I'm basically losing my mind over him. Look, I'm as surprised as anyone that it's taken this turn.

"Wow me with nature," I say instead of hello. I peer around the, frankly, very nondescript trailhead and squint up at the noon sun. A wooden railing delineates the dirt parking lot from the dirt trail, and the air is warm and dusty. Gray boulders pile on the ground beyond the fence with no thought for symmetry or layout. "So far, I'm unimpressed."

Ezra laughs and holds up his hands, palms out. "Give it time. I promise, this hike is killer."

My mouth shuffles over to one side. Doubtful. And I'm also so damn drawn to Ezra. It's a weird mix, is what I'm saying.

He grabs his backpack from the back seat of his Volvo and slides it on. It's also of the seat belt variety like Georgia's, but he doesn't buckle in for safety. That's got to be a demerit.

"It's a little over seven miles round trip, but not too much gain except for one big hill. Ready?"

My nose scrunches, and I say, "Yes?"

We head out, the trail a thin ribbon of pale dirt. It skirts the edge of a sunbaked meadow before burrowing into a wall of pines. It's cooler under the dappled shade, and quieter. I crane my neck, peering up toward the swaying tops of the giant pines. Greens and browns bleed together, and the wind unites it all, turning the forest to music if I tune my ears the right way.

Yet right now, I'm tuned to Ezra. To the quiet, steady huff of his breath and the way he watches the trail, deliberate in every step.

"Why is this your favorite hike?"

Ezra smiles in a way that turns my heart to mush. It's something intimate to be invited into the thing a person is passionate about. But I wonder—right now, if Ezra asked me to show him my favorite place or thing, what would it be? Sometimes I feel like my opinions have bent toward what others find worthy without asking myself if I agree. That extends to how I think of myself too, which isn't a very comfortable thought.

"I want to keep it a surprise," he says with a grin.

"You should meet Georgia Drake. I think you two would get along." When he cocks his chin, I explain who she is.

"Is that going any better?"

I shrug and chew on my thoughts for a moment. "I am still very unsure about the actual hiking, but I kind of really like the girls I've met."

Ezra is nodding. "It was the same with me at first. My parents put me in Scouts because I was super shy and not exactly athletic. I probably never would have stuck with it, but I made really good friends. The love of hiking and camping and all that . . . It came later."

"So you're saying there's hope."

"There's always hope, Lola."

He says it lightly, but the words sink into my heart. I twist my serpent ring around my finger, feeling the warmth of the metal against my skin for a comforting moment.

"We're doing our first overnight soon, which is giving me stress dreams," I admit. "It's actually at some old Scout camp out by Henry Cowell State Park."

Ezra cuts a glance my way. "Shaw Camp? I'm going to be out there next weekend with some friends to do a gear shakedown."

"Ooh, maybe if we're there at the same time we can . . ." All my thoughts straight-up flee my brain at the look Ezra gives me, at the way his chest suddenly rises with quick breath and the warmth pooling in his eyes. "Never mind," I chicken out. "You'd probably be busy anyway."

"If you were there, I'd make time for you," he says, his voice soft and rich like the ground under our feet.

"Yeah?" I somehow manage even though my lungs have lost all oxygen.

"Absolutely."

Is it hot in these woods? No? Just me? After a moment of silence, in which I'm definitely not thinking of backing him up against a tree and devouring him, Ezra clears his throat and nods at something down the trail.

He slows, his fingers reaching for my arm. They wrap around the soft skin inside my elbow, ignite my blood from the inside. I blink at his fingers—four soft points of contact that I swear I can feel pulsing all the way down to my toes—up to his warm, open face. His lips twitch in a quick smile. "Come here, I want to show you something."

And I'm not saying that in this moment I'd follow him anywhere, but I don't hesitate even a second before letting him lead the way off the main trail to a narrow path cutting into the trees. The grasses are tall, and these giant, puffy flowers—like dandelions on steroids—sway in the breeze. I pluck one and carry it with me, toward Ezra and the growing sound of . . . something. A deep, resonating rush.

The trees fall away, and we stop short at the edge of a cliff, a wild river cutting through the rock below us. The water is a living thing, tumbling over itself in the rush downstream, and the air rising from the water snaps with a misty cold.

It's all so pretty—pretty in a way I've never considered the outdoors—that it almost aches. A playful wind tugs at the fluffy flower still in my hand, so I lift it to my face and blow. The tiny seeds are sent into the air, dancing at the end of their downy parachutes. They catch the golden light, whirl in the wind . . . and blow straight back into my face.

Just a big middle finger from nature. I splutter on a mouthful of seeds and pick them away from my lip gloss. Next to me, Ezra lets out a giant laugh, and I turn to him, pouting.

His laugh softens to a smile, and he reaches out, runs the pad of his finger along my cheek. It's nearly impossible not to lean into it, lean into him. He lifts another puff from my cheek and grins.

"That was spectacular," he says.

"This is what I get for trying to be, like, one with nature."

Yet if Ezra stays close like this, heat radiating off his skin so different from the bright, cold air, I'm about to become one with nature in a whole new way, if you follow me. My fingers ache to grab him, reach out toward him, and the tiny hairs on my arm stand with the anticipation of it.

But he takes a step back and nods toward the trail. "Come on, let's keep going."

We lapse into silence, but it settles like a soft blanket around me. Usually, silence makes me jumpy, but there's so much to concentrate on out here—watching my steps for roots, following Ezra's hand as he points out birds, running my fingers across all the different textures of bark, fern, rocks, leaves. For all the silence, I feel like every other sense is working overtime.

My lungs, too, are working as hard as my legs. We turn a tight corner, and looking ahead, I notice a slow, straight climb across the face of the hill, followed by another sharp turn. My breath hitches, and I pause for a drink of water. It's exactly like the switchbacks that defeated me on that awful hike with Kat.

But, I remember, I conquered them during the five-mile hike with HLAG.

Sweat beads my hairline, so I scoop it up into a messy ponytail and nearly sigh with the relief of a bit of breeze against my skin.

Ezra has peeled off his pullover and shoved it in his pack, and his gray T-shirt sticks to his stomach. He yanks up the hem and wipes his forehead, and I nearly pass out. It's totally just all the hiking. Definitely. It's not the sight of his toned stomach and the soft trail of hair leading from his belly button down into the band of his underwear sticking out from the top of his shorts. No, definitely not that. Thank god I'm a sweaty mess so he can't see the way my cheeks are practically pulsing with heat.

He drops his T-shirt and catches me staring. I become very interested in the edge of a leaf and he clears his throat, and I can feel every inch of open air between us. I've been with two guys (and kissed a few more than that) and I know what lust feels like. But this is different. A peculiar mix of lust and like, which I don't quite know how to handle.

"This is the tough bit," Ezra says roughly, breaking through the tension. He clears his throat again and focuses on the trail in front of us.

"Is there an elevator option?"

He laughs at that and glances at me. But a strange thing happens. He lifts his chin and looks at me fully. Almost like he's making himself not look away. "Lola, I don't know many people who just decide to hike seven miles. Half the guys in my old troop would have already been whining so damn much. You're badass."

"Huh." It's not a question, more an acknowledgment. Of something I've never really considered about myself.

"Once we're at the top, we're nearly there. And it's downhill nearly all the way back to the cars."

However, getting *at the top* is easier said than done. My thighs are screaming by the time we crest the ridge, and my heart is thumping with the effort, but I can't seem to corral the grin that's gone galloping all over my face. I look down the face of the hill in triumph.

I did that. *I did that.*

Ezra and I high-five because apparently I live in a movie musical now, and after a water break, it feels good to stretch my legs, lengthen my strides. Honestly, I can't believe how far I've come in a matter of weeks. A month ago, I played the part of Torture Victim #1 on a two-mile hike, but now I'm going to end up doing seven miles round trip and I don't feel defeated. I feel exhilarated. Like I can't wait to see what the next mile brings.

The trail slips and slides down into a ravine, the river shallow and wide as it meanders along the base of a wavering, golden-colored cliff. The trail is narrow here, with the hillside of trees on one side and the river's edge on the other, and sound doubles back and around us as we walk single file. But it's wonderfully cool and wet next to the river, and I'm half tempted to tug off my shoes and wade in.

Ezra stops suddenly and turns to face me. His eyes are bright and his hair is a wild mess of curls gone more than a little untamed.

"Okay, are you ready?" He grins and tips his voice low and dramatic. "Prepared to be amazed."

"God, you're very weird."

That only makes his smile grow brighter, and he does something that sends a shower of sparks across my skin. He reaches out and oh so gently wraps his hand around my wrist. My pulse quickens, and spikes of energy go switchbacking up my arms from the spot he touches me. Hand around my wrist, he pulls me forward, around a bend in the river.

My gasp is so loud it takes me by surprise. I dissolve into laughter, and my hands go to my mouth.

"Oh, Ezra," I breathe.

Because, dammit. I wasn't sufficiently prepared. We're standing at the mouth of a rounded hollow, water tumbling over the edge of a smooth, short cliff and lifting mist into the air, where it splashes into a clear pool. Sunlight catches and casts rainbows in the mist, turning the scene so damned magical that I think I might cry.

"Do you like it?" Ezra asks, his voice hopeful.

I slap his shoulder. "You idiot. This is amazing! This has been basically in my backyard the whole time?"

He laughs and bends to unknot his boots. "No, it was installed last year. Wait till you see the laser light show."

"Oh my god, shut up. Let me revel without your sarcasm for a second."

I revel. Then I kick off my boots, peel off my socks, and wriggle my toes against the edge of the pool. Ugh, this is gorgeous. I'm going to have to talk about this and tell everyone how awesome it is, aren't I?

"Come on, there's something else I want you to see."

He steps into the water, picking his way very carefully. He keeps to the shallow edge, but the rocks are slick, and the going is slow. I feel my way forward, one foot, another. Then—

"Shit!"

My foot slips on the rock, but Ezra's there. He grabs my hand to steady me, and we walk the rest of the way with our palms pressed together. Heat builds deep inside me, and it's hard to find a full breath. Hand in hand, we follow the curve of the cliff as it inches closer and closer to the falls, before noticing what looks like steps worn straight into the rock.

Ezra hauls himself out of the water and up the step to a stone lip, then turns and offers his hand to help me up.

It's a cave. Sort of. Like a giant scooped his hand along the side of the cliff and gouged out a chunk. We follow the shallow opening until we're directly behind the tumble of water. In front of us, the waterfall courses over the side of the cliff, the spray sending droplets into the still air. But back here . . .

My stomach twists and my blood sings. "I've never seen anything like this," I breathe out, completely overcome. "It's—"

Ezra is standing close, to ensure he can hear me over the roar of the waterfall, and when I look back at him, his clear eyes are focused directly on me. "Unforgettable," he says.

The next thing he says tumbles out of him like the waterfall over the edge of the cliff. "I went to Tully's because I wanted to see you. I asked Joon if I could come with him. Because, Lola, I always want to see you. Ever since you were my lab partner. I always want to see you."

My heart cracks against my ribs and my lungs don't seem to be taking on any more air and my skin is alive with every sensation happening around me right now. But it's Ezra's eyes on mine that make everything else disappear. So I do the only sensible thing. I grab hold of his T-shirt and drag his body against mine.

He blinks fast and pauses for one agonizingly long second, before threading his fingers up into my hair and tilting my face up to his. There are droplets of water caught in his eyelashes, beading the ends of his messy hair. His tongue runs along the seam of his lips and I watch it. Want to follow it with my own tongue, to kiss the freckle dotting the edge of his mouth.

And that—that second right there—is when a troop of a dozen effing Scouts rounds the corner and catches us. They're in their matching brown button-downs and sewn-on patches. And they're staring like they walked in on a unicorn humping a dragon. Even over the rush of the waterfall, I swear I can hear their leader clear his throat.

We jump apart, guilt pulling nervous laughter from us. Ezra roughs his hands through his hair in obvious frustration, which is so damned cute I might ignore the impressionable young Scouts and jump him right there.

"I have never been more disappointed in Scouts than right this second," he grinds out, voice ragged.

I tilt my chin and flash him an innocent smile. "Why?" I tease.

He groans, but suddenly balks. "But I didn't expect— What I mean is, I didn't bring you here to . . . Obviously, I wanted to, but I don't want you to think—"

He's pacing, his expression stricken. That's pretty cute too, honestly. "Ezra?"

He stops muttering and faces me. I stretch out my cupped hand under the fall and splash it into his face. He splutters and gets these puppy dog eyes that make it hard not to laugh. The first Scouts are splashing through the water to reach our little not-so-private haven. I poke his shoulder and grin. "There's plenty of opportunity to try again. Maybe next time we can have a flock of nuns swing by."

But his eyebrows draw together, and his eyes drop from mine. And even though I try my hardest not to let it eat away at me, I keep thinking about that look. About how despite what I'm feeling, he clearly doesn't think we have plenty of time.

TWENTY-ONE

THE AIR SMELLS DISGUSTINGLY FRESH.

A deep breath sucks straight to the bottom of my lungs, filling them with pungent pines and rich dirt. It's so gross I take two more deep breaths and wonder if my heart is really in it to continue hating nature. After hiking with Ezra a couple of days ago, it's hard not to appreciate the make-out potential of the woods.

Georgia's got her eyes closed, her face tilted up toward the sunlight streaking through the branches overhead. And, okay, it does feel kind of nice, the way the air is still cool with morning dew while golden sunlight reaches summer-warm fingers through the forest.

Yesterday, Georgia emailed us with a bunch of fire emojis

along with GPS coordinates that Dad helped me decipher. Which is how I've ended up here—at a small parking lot within Portola Redwoods State Park. It sits snug between the mountains west of San Jose and the ocean, and I have to admit that the drive here was spectacular if you're into things like natural beauty.

"You're early again," Georgia says, clipping her backpack's seat belt, which I still don't understand. Is she going to attach side mirrors to her ears next?

My mini-backpack did not come with a nylon belt. I tug at the band of my high-waisted seafoam-green leggings and matching longline sports bra and tighten the knot on my hiking boots. I've stopped needing the Band-Aids, actually, though that hasn't made them any cuter.

Beth—also sporting a backpack with a glorified seat belt—arrives next with Priya, and both girls stop to chat. Priya's got her giant camera out, and Beth absolutely flips a kiss-ass switch when Georgia ambles over. This girl's got a thing for authority figures that is, frankly, not healthy. Suddenly, she's gushing about the trees. She's never seen such beauty! Such raw nature! What a humbling experience it is!

And yeah, she was actually pretty supportive at Jorge's, but here's hoping she humbly falls over the side of a waterfall.

Okay, I shouldn't think that. Here's hoping she humbly falls over the side of a *small* waterfall.

Soon, everyone's arrived. As Corinne joins us, I can't ignore the bubble of happiness in my chest. But then it bursts into a thousand rainbows of pure joy, because she smiles big and pulls out from behind her back . . . a coveted C.Rahmani+Co lip kit.

I shriek so loud birds scatter from the limbs overhead. But they're probably just jealous, because Corinne—bless her—brought me Blond Nudie Picks, one of the limited-edition lip kits that has a six-month waitlist.

"Oh my god." I pet the satiny smooth cover and lift it with the sort of reverence usually reserved for rare jewels. Inside, six shades of matte nudes for cooler skin tones like mine await.

"We had one at home," Corinne says. "And fair warning, shade 006 has been used once."

"This is seriously the best thing I've ever seen in my entire life."

Corinne grins wide. "Rad."

"Girls," Georgia interrupts.

I look up, sort of dazed, surprised to see we're still in the woods.

"If we're done at the makeup counter," Georgia begins.

I scoff. I will never be done at the makeup counter. But I tuck the kit into my car and rejoin the group as Georgia's explaining that today's hike is a six-mile lollipop loop, which, unfortunately, comes with zero candy. Nature should have a better cross-promotional consultant.

But what it does come with is a beauty that honestly takes my breath away. It's all terribly inconvenient when I started the summer vowing to hate everything about nature. How rude of the trees to soar quite so high and the ground to feel so springy underfoot. And how audacious of the cascading waterfall to spritz my face in a cooling mist. Even the wildlife is in on the assault, with a family of deer prancing through a meadow and a woodpecker showing off its bright red head.

Nature's bounty is damned enraging.

"You know," I say to Corinne, who's right behind me on the trail. My muscles ache from the elevation gain and the straps of my tiny backpack are digging mercilessly into my shoulders, but each step forward feels like progress. "That first time I went hiking, I made it less than two miles before I wanted to die."

"My dad once dragged me on this hike that had, I swear to god, a thousand feet of gain over two miles. It was brutal."

The trail widens before us, sunlight dappling the ferns like we're on a damned movie set. God, Nature, we get it. You're embarrassing yourself at this point. Corinne's words trickle through my burgeoning grudge. "Wait," I say, remembering the details of that two-mile hike Kat chose for us, "so a thousand feet really is a lot?"

Corinne nods, walking next to me. "It depends on how it's spread out, but yeah, that's a lot of climbing."

One Katherine Lucille Barnes is going to be hearing from my lawyer.

"So you really, truly do like hiking?"

She nods again. "I grew up hiking and camping with my dad and my aunts and cousins, but he spends a lot of his year on the

East Coast. It's kind of . . ." She frowns and rubs at the end of her nose. "I don't know, ever since I grew boobs and told him I was bi, it's like he doesn't know how to handle me. So I thought this could bring us back together. You know about the family hike, right? He's going to fly out for it."

One: I did not know about the family hike. Lord save us from an episode of *Julia Barnes: Into the Woods*. And two: I have a visceral reaction to Corinne trying so hard to connect with her dad. It's a twist in my gut and an overwhelming sensation of sadness that reminds me very, very much of a certain twin who shall remain nameless.

"I bet he's going to lose his mind seeing how amazing you are at all this," I say, tipping toward her to nudge my shoulder to hers. "Beth is up there going on about how much she loves nature, but I definitely saw her kick a fern out of the way coming back from the toilet at the trailhead."

We fall back into silence, and the soundtrack of birds in the trees overhead soothes its way into my brain. A contented sigh issues from my mouth, and I look around fast to make sure no one heard. I'd lose all my street cred if it came out that I was maybe, sort of, perhaps enjoying myself. Who knew nature could be so amazing? Okay, don't answer that. A quick Google search would be like, *Everyone knew that, Lola. Everyone.*

Behind me, Mei is definitely wearing the lipstick I bought her and chatting with Priya, and behind Georgia at the lead, Beth has dragged Tavi and Corinne into some sort of camp-off.

I kind of wish she didn't feel the need to try so hard, but also can definitely imagine how she'd react if I said anything because I have lived my whole entire life with Marnie as my older sister.

"Did you do THINK?" Beth is asking Tavi and Corinne. "I did that two years in a row. And Interlochen one year because I'm very gifted at clarinet."

Of course she is.

She ticks off three more camps she's attended, demurely skipping her stint at modesty camp. Corinne sort of half-heartedly responds about a Girl Scout camp, and Tavi straight-up ignores her. Beth slices a look over her shoulder and focuses on me.

"What about you, Lola? What camps have you done?"

"Um, none?"

She nearly trips over a tree root in shock. "Wait, you've never done a camp? How did you get your extracurricular references for the Hike Like a Girl application? How do you prepare for the next school year?"

I'm going to go ahead and slide over that first question. Instead, I say, "I usually ignore the next school year until it's time to pick my first-day outfit. Because I'm normal."

Beth shakes her head. "But—"

"Oh, wait. I did do a camp once." I'd honestly forgotten it because my one and only camp experience was short and not what we'd call a success. "My parents spent six weeks in Greece when I was eight, so they shipped us off to spend the summer in Arizona with our grandparents."

Here's what happened. It was a Bible camp of indeterminate origin. Not Catholic, I remember that, because my family is nominally Catholic, and this wasn't. What it was, I suspect, was a convenient way for Grammy and Grampa to get me, Kat, and Marnie out of the house for a few days. Anyway, on the first night we gathered in the gym slash worship hall and I noticed there were bars on the windows. I, trying to impress the older and therefore cooler camp counselor next to me, made a joke about the bars locking any nonbelievers inside. She was . . . not amused and told me God didn't like jokesters. They sent us all home early because—oops!—they forgot about the residency requirement.

Tavi's mouth is hanging open when I finish my story, and Corinne throws her arm around my shoulder. Even Beth kind of clears her throat and changes the subject.

"What? I thought it was funny!"

"That camp counselor sucked," Corinne says. "You know that, right?"

"Yes! I didn't mean . . ." But a frown tugs my eyebrows together, and the buried memory sticks like tar to my thoughts. All my life I've been told to be quiet or stop being silly or dramatic. Because I was the youngest in my family or the classmate with an opinion or the girl trying to make jokes at the wrong time. Like I have audacity for taking up space. Maybe I'm loud and dramatic to prove I can be, to prove that I exist on my own even though sometimes it feels like everyone around me wants something different.

Corinne's arm is still around my shoulder, and her fingers squeeze me. "Hey, I'm serious. No one should tell a little kid they're wrong or not worthy of love just because they're not like everyone else."

I give her a smile and chew on what she said. I was always a different child, at least compared with Marnie, Lindy, and Joss. Maybe I should embrace that a little bit more. I've always been confident—and I love that about myself—so maybe I can be confidently different too.

I swipe sweat from my forehead and keep walking, the steady rhythm of my feet giving me space to think. Before I quite realize it, Georgia has stopped us back near the trailhead. Through a gap in the trees, I can see the glint of my blue BMW.

"You girls have done fantastic today! Really, I'm impressed!"

Her eyes crawl over me as she says it, and pride pings in my heart. Though accompanying the pride is a whole lot of sweat, seriously aching shoulders, and legs that feel like overdone spaghetti noodles. I suck down some water and look at her backpack seat belt with envy. Her straps are padded like clouds and I want to rub my cheek against them.

"So now, it's time to earn our next milestone." She pauses for drama, and dammit, I'm leaning in. "Down to our left, I've reserved three campsites that come with three fire rings." As Georgia speaks, she walks down the line of us and hands over a long lighter. "I want you to pair up and build a fire. The first to complete the challenge will win two one-hundred-dollar gift cards to REI."

"Partner?" I say, eyebrows raised in question at Corinne.

She twists her fingers together. "I kind of sucked at the fire-building clinic Georgia led."

My face breaks into a wide smile. "Well, lucky for you, I've watched like eighteen hours of how-to videos to prepare and have also successfully burned down a boat."

It feels kind of amazing to take charge. I dump the contents of my mini-backpack—one half-empty water bottle, a candy bar, and gum—into Corinne's bag and instruct her to gather pine needles and twigs in my bag. I scan the ground as we walk, building an armful of thicker branches by the time we've reached the fire ring.

Thanks to Kodiak (god, who am I becoming?), I know to lean the longer branches against the fire ring and stomp on them to snap them into more manageable lengths. I get to work building my log cabin, my knees in the dirt and my hands ashy from previous campfires. It's basically like playing with Lincoln Logs with Joss's triplets, except with the rush of destroying my competition at the end. I mean, I honestly like Priya, Tavi, Mei, and even on occasion Beth, but I will rub their faces in my perfect example of a log cabin fire before too long. Soon, I've got a little four-sided structure of larger sticks with a sort of raised floor of smaller sticks balanced in the middle.

"Okay, put a pile of the pine needles on those sticks in the middle," I instruct Corinne.

On either side of us, Mei and Beth are arguing about their shoddy lean-to design, and Priya and Tavi can eff right off with their poorly constructed teepee.

"It's about the airflow," I explain, setting a final layer of small sticks from Corinne's stash across the top of the structure. I carefully fit the lighter down into the pine needles. "With dry wood like this, the log cabin has much better airflow, which means the pine needles will work like embers and the larger stuff will have time to catch."

Corinne stares at me like I've grown a third eye. I grin, light the kindling, and bend close to blow on the adorable little baby fire taking root in the pine needles. I twist my face away from the catching fire to suck in a big breath and dip in close to blow at the base of the flames, the pine needles glowing red.

There's a beautiful crackling noise, and the sticks on top catch.

"Ha!" I jump up and throw my arms above my head. "Done!"

Look who's just won an REI gift card. Seat belt backpack, here I come.

But then I do something that surprises even me. I spend the rest of my time giving pointers to the other girls, and soon we've got three merry fires hissing and popping. Georgia slaps me on the back, and I feel such an absurd rush of triumph when I twist my newest leather thong (dyed red) around my walking stick that I'm damn near ready to buy everyone a round of tacos.

Turns out, nature: maybe the best?

I spin to Corinne as we're finishing up the last quarter mile of the day's hike. "Want to come over tomorrow? We can go use our gift cards and then I can have my dad pull out the portable screen in the backyard to watch movies."

Corinne grins. "Totally."

TWENTY-TWO

THE SKY IS STREAKED PINK by the time Corinne and I leave REI the next day. I'm now the proud new owner of a backpack with a seat belt, and it's joining the growing pile of hiking and camping gear that's stacked in a corner of my room. Three-quarters of the stuff is still in boxes, but I'll have to remedy that at some point before Thursday for our first attempt at IRL camping. Like, in the woods and shit.

The REI trip was kind of the best. Being able to talk and laugh with Corinne while we tried on backpacks felt like this release, like I could breathe all the way to the bottom of my lungs for the first time in months. I confessed my almost-kiss with Ezra and Corinne talked about being an only child. Not in like a *woe is me* way or anything, more like getting to do fun things as her mom's plus-one. But I couldn't help but picture what my life would be like without my sisters. And the fact is, I think it'd suck. All alone with Mom and Dad? Gross.

A dark part of me wonders briefly if that's what Kat wants. The thought hurts in a way that's hard to name. It's something deep and raw. But also . . . too bad for her? I'm not going anywhere. Though maybe it's time to ease up on the sabotage. (Just yesterday, I snipped every single one of her hair ties so they'd break halfway through her day.) I'm still angry—at her, at Jasmine, at Meg—but the truth is, I survived the break with Jas and Meg. It's hard and it sucks, but I'll be okay. But with Kat . . . A shiver ghosts down my arms that I have to shake free.

So when Corinne and I cram through the front door at home, REI bags rustling, I'm on a mission to convince Kat I'd be a super cool addition to her friend group. I'll ask them insightful questions and listen to their answers. I'll give them sincere compliments without expecting any in return. I'll kiss Ezra a ton, which will definitely help group morale.

Absently, I toss my paper bags over the back of the couch, but the bags land with a squeak.

Marnie pops up from the cushions and glares.

"Didn't see you there," I say. Past the glass patio doors, Dad's setting up the projector.

"Never do," Marnie grumbles.

Corinne taps my arm. "Hey, I did AV back at my school in New York. Mind if I go ask your dad what he's using?"

I flap a hand at the big sliding doors. "Have at it." I go to pluck my REI bag off Marnie's lap, but she's already rifling through it. She pulls out the burnt-orange backpack, frowning.

"This is . . . unexpected."

I snatch my new backpack away from her. "You try hiking several miles without proper shoulder support. It's super distracting trying to appreciate a waterfall when your shoulders hurt."

Marnie's eyes go big and she scrambles up to her knees on the couch. "Oh my god," she whispers.

"What?"

"Oh. My. God."

"What!"

She opens her mouth and starts absolutely cackling. "You like something! *Earnestly* like something!" She shrieks, then gasps and points at the big windows to her left. "Look at that bird out the window!"

And, dammit, I look because Marnie never jokes like that, but the little shit was lying! I don't see any birds!

"Gah!" she cries. "You're fantasizing about trees right now, aren't you! I can't believe it!"

Obviously, when someone besmirches my good name like this, I've only got one choice. I vault over the couch, grab a decorative throw pillow, and whack her in the face. She shrieks again.

"You love nature!"

Well, that's it. I'll have to prove I don't love nature by

single-handedly driving a small woodland creature to extinction, except major oil and gas companies already called that one. We're handling this in a totally mature way by smacking each other with pillows when Kat stomps down the hallway and snaps at us.

"What are you two doing?"

I use Marnie's shock to thwack her one more time and pout. "Marnie thinks I have a big boner for flowers."

Kat narrows her eyes and says incredulously, "You?"

All the fight drains out of me. I sit back hard, a giant *huh* clearing the last bit of air from my lungs.

Kat stomps back down the hall, muttering something about trying to nap, and I stare at the bit of space she left behind. Marnie's voice is soft beside me.

"You need to talk to her."

"Tried that," I say, still staring down the hall. "She's not interested."

"Then try again." I twist to look at her sitting next to me, a pillow hugged against her chest. She smiles sadly. "I used to be so jealous that you had each other and didn't seem to need me."

"Of course we need you, Mar," I say. "I think my English teacher would say you're my foil."

"Okay, very uncool." Marnie rolls her eyes, but her smile grows bigger. "But also, nice command of English comprehension and analysis."

"You are, seriously, the worst," I say, grinning.

She wriggles her foot toward me, then shoves me off the couch. "Go! Talk!"

The walk down the hallway toward Kat's room feels about thirteen miles long. I usually don't shy away from confrontation—a bit of a scream and a good cry is healthy for the blood—but *knowingly* heading toward confrontation when you've already been rejected . . . it's not easy.

I carefully turn the knob and speak into the crack of the door. "Kat?"

She grunts.

"Can I come in?"

"I was trying to nap."

I open the door wider and lean against the frame. She's starfished on the bed with her eyes closed, but also she forgot to flip off her phone when she dropped it on the rug so it's still blinking a bright game at me. "I mean, you're not."

"I'm trying to."

Her dresser is against the wall right next to the door, and it's topped with a white porcelain lamp in the shape of a cat that would probably have a really nice weight if I picked it up and chucked it at the wall. Maybe then she'd stop "sleeping" and actually talk to me.

Okay, breathe. Don't smash the lamp.

But maybe smash the lamp?

No, Lola.

I need to show her I'm putting in the effort. But . . .

Fear is a bitter nut in the bottom of my stomach. Hard and knotted and there—always there. She's already told me in anger that she doesn't want me in her life. But if she repeats it now, when she's calm and in charge of all her mental faculties . . .

Perhaps I shouldn't have slightly opened all the caps of her favorite flavor of bubbly water.

I rub at the sparkling green eyes of my serpent ring and remember the way Ezra said there was always hope. But he's an intelligent, hardworking guy whose only strife in life is that he tried to kiss a girl and got caught. His life is nothing *but* hope. What if he's wrong about me?

"Hey, sorry Marnie and I disturbed you. Dad's setting up the projector and Corinne's over. Wanna split some popcorn and watch a dumb action movie?"

I'm such a chicken, I might as well go live in a coop and lay eggs all day.

Yet Kat actually sits up. "This isn't like some ploy to get me out there only to realize you've sabotaged all the butter popcorn and put that gross powdered cheese on it?"

Hope blooms in my chest. I think of Ezra and smile. "One," I say to Kat as she stretches and grabs a sweater to pull over her sports bra, "that cheese is a goddamn delight. And two, I might be ready to end the sabotage."

She follows me down the hallway to where Corinne is chatting with Marnie.

"Kat! Hi!" Corinne smiles wide and holds up a selection of

movies. "You choose. Explosions on a ship. Explosions in space. Or explosions with Brendan Fraser."

"Duh." Kat grabs *The Mummy* from the stack.

Marnie meets my eye and raises her brows in question. I shrug and follow Kat and Corinne out to the back, only catching the end of their conversation. Something about a waterfall and a Scout troop and a kiss cut off before it even started. I jolt and run to join them, but it's too late. It's plain on Kat's face that she knows exactly who Corinne is laughing about.

I make a show of laughing too. *Oh, ha ha ha! I didn't try to make out with one of your precious friends!*

"Didn't I tell you about that, Kat? Yeah, it was wild, but the hike was legit super pretty!" I sling an arm around her neck, but her shoulders tense. She lifts my wrist and removes it. The air between us is sticky with all the things we've stopped telling each other.

On Kat's other side, Corinne's eyes go big. "Oh shit, I assumed—"

"No! Totally fine! I've been busy so I haven't had a chance to say anything yet and . . ." And I have no good way to end that sentence.

"Well," Corinne says, obviously trying to smooth the tension. In front of us, Dad has pulled out the enormous beanbag chairs from the triplets' playroom in the basement and is fiddling with the equipment. She clears her throat. "It sounds like he's really into you, Lola."

Between us, Kat stiffens. She lets loose a laugh that's hard at the edges. "Oh, guys go nuts for Lola. Probably because they don't have to live with her."

She says it with a laugh. But the words are a battering ram straight to my sternum. I feel them reverberate through me when I collapse back into the beanbag chair, when the movie starts, when I get popcorn. Pretty soon, they're all I hear.

TWENTY-THREE

SCHLEP MY TENT BAG OVER to the flat bit of ground between the trees.

Oh, guys go nuts for Lola. Probably because they don't have to live with her.

Toss my mess of a backpack in the dirt—*oh, guys go nuts for Lola*—and scoop my hair off my neck—*probably because they don't have to live with her.*

I'm about to pull a Beth and go kick some ferns. Anything to interrupt my mind repeating Kat's oh so casual takedown of my life, which has dogged my every second in the last three days. I'm totally blaming Georgia and her insistence that we become better people for that, because two months ago, I probably would have thrown a drink in Kat's face and run off with the first available warm body to prove her wrong. I wouldn't still be turning over her words in my head like a stone in my palm, wearing them smooth from constant attention.

And dammit, I like Ezra! Like, really like him! And now every time I think of him and his smile and forearms and the sound of his voice and his laugh and his confidence in me . . . Kat is there like a bad smell. I haven't seen him since our almost-kiss behind the waterfall, and I glance around, wondering if he's here in the woods somewhere. If he's looking around for me too. Or maybe he's already realized what a mistake I am. I can't scrub from my mind that split second of uncertainty that flared in his eyes when I said we had plenty of time. Maybe he already knows we can't last. Maybe Kat was right.

For the millionth time, I try to press down the thoughts and focus on the present. Weird, right? I'm in this clearing in the woods in the middle of an old Scout camp attempting to erect my own tent precisely because I couldn't consider anything beyond the moment I was in when I was on Jasmine's boat all those weeks ago. Now I remove the tags from my minuscule tent and pull everything out of the stuff sack to lay on the ground in front of me like Georgia's taught us, trying to keep my mind in the present, to not focus on all the other thoughts racing around my head.

It's like looking at ancient hieroglyphs. Nothing makes sense. I look from the visual directions to the items in front of me and back again.

"Help?" I shout in Georgia's general direction. She looks up from where she's been talking Beth down off the ledge and trots over.

"What've you got?"

"A mystery," I respond.

Across our clearing, Tavi shouts "Done!" and wiggles in a circle while Corinne groans, one step behind her. Both their small orange tents mock me.

"One step at a time," Georgia says, using the same voice Joss puts on when she's trying to get the triplets to put their poops in the potty. I stick my tongue out at her before mumbling, "Sorry."

"Hey, setting up a tent is something totally new. It's normal to be kind of overwhelmed. But I promise, it gets easier each time you do it. Okay, take a look at your directions. What's your first step?"

I stare at the instruction card and attempt to decipher what appears to be a pictograph of jellyfish washed ashore. "What's a rainfly?"

"That's not the first step, Lola."

Right. Okay. Take a breath. Focus. I read the directions and spread out my rust-orange tent on the ground, orienting it so it matches the illustration. Georgia pats me on the shoulder and wanders back to Beth, who's trying to jam the end of a pole into the dirt.

The poles are easy enough to assemble, but it takes three tries to get them clipped in correctly, and the first time I try to actually yank the tent upright it lists over to one side, and I trip over my backpack and hit the dirt with a grunt. The tent goes *pfff*, and I bite down on a scream.

Focus.

From my spot in the dirt, the little grommets at the corner of the tent wink at me. I forgot to secure the ends of the poles into the grommets. I get up and try again, doing it right this time. Finally, I bend the last pole into place and slip it into the grommet and let go. The tent is up! And it's tiny! My god, I have to sleep in this thing!

But whatever! I did it. I constructed my very own bedroom and—wow—I am, like, very independent and amazing. I peer around in triumph and realize I'm the last person to actually pitch their tent. But they can't start a fire without me, so sit tight, ladies. Plus, I haven't even thought of Kat in the last few minutes. I mean, who? I didn't think that. Moving on.

I finish the last couple of steps (sort of) quickly, staking the tent into the soft earth and tugging the rainfly over the top and clipping it in. I deserve so many s'mores. I dig through my backpack to stage my space: sleeping mat, blow-up pillow, sleeping bag, LED lantern. Then I bring out the real essentials: forest-green pennant banner I found at a local market to string from my tent to the nearest tree; small tasseled Pendleton rug unrolled outside my tent flap to welcome guests; vintage (nonworking) lantern to set next to the rug; and tiny foldable stool topped with a white enamel pitcher with a dried flower bouquet for vibes.

"Are . . . you for real?" Georgia asks, walking up.

"We're camping, Georgia, we're not dead."

"You had all that in your backpack?"

I grin at her with pride. "I just had to take out my rain gear and the first aid kit. Also, I'll need to borrow your pots and pans. And food."

Corinne comes to stand next to me and shakes her head. "Lola, you are—"

"Amazing, I know." I duck into my tent and rustle around in my bag, then reemerge with a blue speckled enamel mug printed with her name and stuffed with a hot cocoa packet and marshmallows shaped like squirrels. "I have one for everyone!" I announce as the rest of the crew gathers round, obviously awed by my styling skills and creative genius. I pluck one last mug and hold it out to Georgia. "Even you."

Georgia's features scrunch together and she hesitates before accepting her mug. "This is really sweet, Lola. But when we're actually on the trail and hauling everything in our packs—"

"I know. I won't be able to bring all this."

"Any of this," she amends.

"Most of this," I counter. "And really, I know. But it's my very first time camping! I don't know, I wanted to make it special."

Around our site, we've circled up seven small teardrop tents with tall pines at our backs and ferns and toadstools enclosing us. The trees turn the air soft blue and cast everything in a dreamy sort of half-light even though it's the afternoon. In the center of our circle, a big ring of stones awaits a campfire with thick bench logs laid out in a hexagon around it.

Mei pokes around my setup. "I wish I had signal!" she squeals, taking photos of the lantern-table-flower arrangement.

"Wait!" I say, remembering the last thing, my black felt hat with the wide brim I wore to the first HLAG meeting. I hang it artfully from the stubby bit of broken branch where I tied the pennant banner.

Soon, everyone is taking turns posing for photos until Georgia sighs very loudly and offers to take a group shot.

"Okay, three, two, one . . ."

And that's when I spot boys in the distance, carrying a canoe. Like, an honest-to-god canoe. Hair wet, shirts off, arms taut where they grip the—need I remind you—canoe. And leading the way is Ezra. Like an em-effing demigod, light burnishing his skin, sparkling off his hair. Holy. Shit.

"Cheese!" the other girls say.

"Fuuuuuck" is what I go with.

It's all very special.

I don't go racing after him, and if you want any sign I'm truly a changed woman, that's it. But I've got a campfire to start and some hungry HLAGs to feed.

If you don't count the time Joss and Edie tried to have us all over for a big bonfire meal and Mom (in charge of bringing the meat but on a health-food kick at the time) supplied us with Belgian endive to roast over the flame, this is my first campfire meal.

Dusk settles like dove feathers over our clearing, and even though Georgia is being very annoying by reminding us over and over that most trail food won't be like this, it's damn near the best meal I've ever tasted. Roasted hot dogs that are charred to perfection, corn that was steamed directly in its husk and is dripping with butter. Grilled pineapple and watermelon cooked on a little grate Georgia props between two stones, and s'mores that ooze. I pop two more marshmallows on the end of a skewer and squat in front of the fire—which I built like a freaking fire goddess, by the way. The tendrils of orange flame curl up into the twilight, embers twirling above our heads. I tilt my chin up and up, watching them cool from orange to yellow to gray.

My face is warm, but a cool breeze is at my back. For one spectacular second, I feel like a cork bobbing in the ocean. Calm and peaceful. Letting myself be a part of my environment without fighting it. I love that I'm sharing this with my crew, and I don't want this to be it. I'd like to do this again with them, again with my family even though they'd complain heartily, again with Ezra and that tiny tent where—oh no!—we'll have to share the narrow sleeping pad.

"Fire, Lola!"

Sigh. How true. My thoughts are aflame with thoughts of me and Ezra in that little—

"Seriously, fire!" Beth's words bring me back, and I snap my chin down toward the flames. My marshmallows are little burning suns. I lift my skewer and blow them off. The outsides are charred, but the insides are perfect as ever, and that's probably a metaphor for something, but I think I'm done with the deep thoughts for the night.

I'm shoving the second marshmallow into my mouth when the log underneath me jolts and Priya scoots in close. She holds out her big camera and shows me a shot pulled up on the screen. It's of me in front of the fire, my face tilted up to the sky and my eyes closed, my mouth soft.

"Isn't it great?" she says.

"Oh man. Can you send that to me? I love it."

I just look so happy. Happy in a way I haven't felt in a very long time.

I also feel . . . very much like I need to pee. But the vault toilet—the forest version of a porta potty—is hidden down a short, shadowy path. It goes without saying, but it's a path full of bears and mountain lions and serial killers with a thing for public urination.

"I need to pee," I announce. And wow, if those are my last words, I'm going to be so disappointed.

"Oh thank god," Mei says in a rush. "Me too."

"I'll go too," Corinne adds.

"Bring your headlamps, girls," Georgia advises. "There's not going to be a light."

So here we've reached a crossroads. Because I swore on my life that I would never use a headlamp, but also, do I really want to die by falling in a porta potty? It's a real lose-lose situation. I settle for a flashlight, because at least I can use it to fend off an attack without resorting to headbutting. Though, true story, the two years my parents had me in soccer as a kid, the only things I excelled at were headbutting other players, then subsequently crying.

We conquer the trail like a trio of totally calm mountain women who know how to wrestle panthers. Jokes! We smash against each other so hard we've basically reverted to a single-cell organism and shriek at every breath of breeze or rustling leaf. In the middle of our amoeba, I swing my—on reflection—tiny as shit pocket flashlight back and forth along the trail. Finally, we reach the vault toilet. It's a little box with a pitched roof and the lovely scent of chemicals wafting off it.

"I'm not going in there alone," Mei whispers.

"I'm sure as shit not staying out here alone," I whisper back.

Why are we whispering? Are stalking bears usually hard of hearing?

"My dad told me once that he sat down on a vault toilet in the dark and something bit him," Corinne adds.

"Why the hell would you tell us that!" I whisper-hiss at her.

I mean, seriously.

"I just meant, like, check the toilet seat before you sit down."

"There is no way I'm sitting down now. This one's definitely going to be a hover," Mei says, jumping back and forth on her feet. "But I really have to go."

"Fine fine fine," I say in a rush. "I'll go in with you, Mei, and keep my flashlight on the seat to scare off any spiders, then you do the same for me. I'll come out and Corinne will get her turn and you'll help her. Deal?"

Truly. Peace in our times and all that.

In what can only be described as a bonding experience, Mei and I do our business. I switch out for Corinne. But that makes it plain that I'm out here all alone. Like a fool. Like a delicious amuse-bouche of a fool.

A twig snaps behind me, and I whip around, swinging my dainty-ass flashlight with it.

And bash Ezra right in the shoulder. He chokes out a string of whispered swear words and rubs at his shoulder, and in my rush to make sure he's not permanently damaged, I manage to sock him in the jaw too. This is going super well.

"What are you doing here?" I hiss.

"I saw you earlier," he hisses back.

We sound like a pair of horny cockroaches.

"So you followed me to the porta potty?"

Ezra groans. "No, I was following this trail to your site. I'm down that way."

I swing my flashlight—Ezra winces when I do—and see that the trail continues on past the vault toilet and into the woods. It's at this point that Mei and Corinne pile out of the toilet and stare, surprised that our single-cell organism has done some evolving.

"Who the eff are you?" Corinne snaps.

I sigh. "This is Ezra."

Her eyes go big.

"Could you give us a second?" She grabs Mei, but I add, "Don't go far. I don't want to walk back alone."

They walk exactly one foot and stop. I turn back to Ezra. "Did you have a plan?"

"It wasn't to be attacked by a flashlight."

In the distance, Georgia calls for us. Was she timing our potty break?

Ezra scrubs a hand down his face and groans again, and I'm suddenly remembering the way he looked tromping through the forest, hoisting that canoe, water dripping from his wet hair and tracking down the lines of his stomach. Okay, okay, I couldn't see that, exactly. But I could imagine it.

"There was something rad I wanted to show you, but I've made such a mess of it. When I talked it out with my friends—"

"You've talked about me with your friends?"

He clears his throat. Behind me, so does Corinne.

"Girls!" Georgia calls again, closer now.

"I'm the tent with the welcome mat and flower arrangement. Come find me later, okay?"

His face breaks into a wide grin. He nods and melts back into the twilight.

TWENTY-FOUR

THE PROBLEM WITH WAITING FOR a cute boy to come sneak over to your tent is that every sound could be him . . . or it could be a mountain lion.

A few minutes ago, Georgia reminded us how to douse the fire and said she was headed to bed. Now only a couple of the girls are still up, sitting around the glowing flames and chatting. I'm lying on my sleeping pad with my tent flap rolled open so I can watch the fire when a sort of scratching tap shakes the nylon behind my head.

I jump a foot and crawl out of the tent to see Ezra waiting just beyond the light of the fire, the reflection shining in his eyes. "You weren't kidding about the flowers."

"I'd never joke about aesthetics."

Across the stone ring, Corinne catches my attention and nods. She agreed to stay up, and I promised her I wouldn't do anything rash. It helps that she admitted Ezra's cute.

I grab my flashlight and turn on the beam as we start down the trail, but Ezra shakes his head. "It's a full moon," he says. "Let your eyes adjust. It's pretty amazing walking through the dark."

"Says the guy."

He tilts his chin at that. "Point taken. Whatever makes you comfortable. I already know you can take down an ox with your flashlight."

"Or, like, a single dude who recently discovered light weights."

A laugh huffs out of him. "That is . . . prescient."

Gonna be honest, I have no idea what that means, but also, I trust Ezra. I turn off my flashlight and freeze as the entire world goes black. His hand finds mine in the darkness and I hold on tight.

"Give it a second," he says, voice low and close to my ear. "I'm right here."

After the longest second in the history of time, forms begin to take shape in the darkness, needles and leaves and trunks limned in silver. He keeps hold of my hand, our palms whispering together as we start walking through the dark forest. With my vision dimmed, I'm acutely aware of everything else. The scent of the pines, almost like the butterscotch cookies Edie makes in the fall. The far-off hoot of an owl. The way Ezra's hand is larger than mine, his movements steady where he threads our fingers together. The feel of him works its way up my arm, through my chest, down to my toes. The nearness of him a whole separate sense that makes my skin tingle.

We walk a short ways, past another campsite burrowed into the trees and another campfire with a couple of guys sitting around it, until we reach a meadow. It's surrounded by hulking, dark trees, but the tall grasses shine silver in the moonlight. In the center, there's a big oak tree, and when the wind picks up, a hollow thrumming weaves through the air.

Closer now, I can see a big swing hanging from one of the lower branches, and the sound—a sort of woody hum—pricks at my ears again.

"Wind chimes," Ezra explains. "One year a camp counselor here really went on a homemade wooden wind chime bender, so we hung some in the tree."

It's a haunting sound, yet also sort of quiet and lovely.

"It's . . . I don't know, I think it's a cool place," he says, his fingers still tight around mine. He looks at me, his face half in shadow, but I can see the hesitancy in the lines of his mouth. "I, uh, have a lot of good memories here, coming for camp and everything."

It's so sweet, I can't stop myself. I tip closer to him and kiss his cheek. "It's great, Ezra. Thanks for showing me."

His voice is rumbly and creaks at the edges when he speaks again. "Yeah, of course."

We're at the rope swing now, and I pull away from him to sit, pushing back and forth on my feet as I move in a slow, idle way.

"I think I get why you like this nature shit," I say, running my palms up and down the rough rope. "Earlier, I had this moment of, like, calm. Everything inside me usually feels so tightly wound. But it was kind of amazing. Everything unspooling so it felt like I was floating."

"Lola, I—" He says my name in a breath, in a rush of feeling that quickens in my chest. He's standing in front of me, his feet wide and the bit of moonlight catching at the way his shoulders are moving up and down with his breaths.

Then he strides across to me, his hands wrapping around mine and his hips between my thighs. The gentle force of it has pushed me back on the swing, so I'm on my toes and leaning into him. He stops a breath away from my mouth, and even in the darkness I can see the question forming on his lips. And, look, I know the right thing to do here is to ask permission and give permission, but also if I don't finally kiss this boy I think I'm going to scream, so it's me who closes that last bit of distance.

His mouth melts against mine, and I swear I can taste mountains and meadows and sunshine and water. His lips part, and his tongue slips along the edge of my mouth, tasting me. I want to taste him too. I suck at his bottom lip and drag my teeth gently against his skin and shiver when he groans against my mouth.

He pulls away, his forehead tilted close to mine and our chests rising and falling together. Without a word, he slides his hands from my fingers, along my skin slowly from my wrists to the insides of my elbows, up and over my shoulders, like he's learning the shape of my body for the first time. There's something so reverent about it, the way he's so clearly taking in this moment between us. His fingers whisper up the side of my neck, soft and featherlight, and yet the sensation carries deep, deep inside me. I suck in a tiny breath, and his voice catches on my name. He wraps his arms around my waist, holding me tight. I tip forward, off the swing, and he sets me on the ground. My knees have been reduced to jelly, my stomach doing somersaults, my heart splitting itself into a million pieces to beat just under my skin, at every juncture of my body.

I snake my hands up to his shoulders to keep myself steady and drag his mouth back down to mine, deepen the kiss we started. Until Ezra gives up every bit of hesitancy in his body and folds me tightly in his arms.

And wow. He's good at this. How did he get so good at this? It's unlike anything I've ever felt. Kissing Ezra makes me feel like all my parts are coming undone and piecing back together in a new way, a way that also finds room for him. With Tully, with the other boys I've kissed, it felt like a dare. All exhilaration and conquest. But Ezra feels equal parts give and take.

We stay wrapped up in each other for a long time, exploring the way our lips and tongues fit together. The way my body fits against his. I've got my hands in his hair and his scent pressed into my skin. And I never, ever want to stop.

When we do finally break apart, Ezra is breathing hard, and I notice how he clears his throat and has to adjust how he's standing as we face each other properly. That makes me feel powerful. But, for the first time ever, I want a boy to recognize how he affects me too. I let him see me catch my breath. Let him feel the heat of my cheek when he brushes the side of my face with his fingers.

"Um," I say, my voice rough. "That's a weird way to end a hike. I would have gotten into hiking long ago if I'd known that's how you do it."

Ezra laughs, and his voice cracks. "Yeah, I don't know why they don't put it on the trail maps. Best spot to make out with the girl you haven't been able to stop thinking about."

His words hum through me. He hasn't stopped thinking about me. And the truth is, I haven't been able to stop thinking about him either. So I tell him that.

Ezra groans and closes the distance between us, his arms threading along my waist to tug me against him. He bends close, his warm breath fluttering against my hair and tickling the curve of my ear. His lips press, the gentlest touch, against my earlobe, before he dips his mouth lower.

I lift my chin, leaning into him. Wanting him.

And then, oh so suddenly, wanting not to be seen anywhere near him.

"Lola?" My name carries through the woods, and we jump a mile apart.

"Shit," I squeak. "Shit!"

Ezra grabs my hand, and we race together back through the forest, in the direction of Georgia's voice. Finally, we skid to a stop close to the vault toilet and Ezra reaches into my back pocket—not now, dude!—but it's only to grab my flashlight and switch it on. He nods at me, thrusting his chin toward the sound of Georgia's voice.

"I'm here, Georgia! I'm so sorry!"

"Where?" she calls.

Ezra's eyes get big.

"I got lost going to the bathroom! Um, emergency! But I'm done now!"

Oh, Jesus. Now he won't be able to stop thinking about me and this toilet.

Ezra bites his knuckles to stop the laughter threatening to overtake us both.

"It was a disaster!" I call out toward Georgia, pressing my face into Ezra's chest to muffle my laugh.

Ezra lifts my chin and tilts his mouth to mine in a fierce, fast kiss. I let my hands roam greedily, trying to feel all of him in the few seconds we have left.

"Well, are you coming?" she calls.

A groan rumbles in Ezra's chest, vibrates under my palm.

"One sec!"

I kiss him back, pull away, then grab his hand and yank him closer again for one more. The beam of Georgia's flashlight bounces through the trees, so I plant one more quick kiss against Ezra's mouth and dash away. I almost run into Georgia around the corner.

She sighs loudly in exasperation and grabs hold of my elbow. Hopefully the flashlight doesn't pick up on my kiss-swollen lips or this toilet story's gonna get weird.

"Do I need to tie a bell around you when we're out on the trail?" Georgia marches me back to our site and Corinne's still at the fire, basically looking like the concerned face emoji.

I roll my eyes Georgia's way and say, "I'll just moo really loudly."

"Oh, great idea. Really sound like a wounded animal. That'll keep the predators away." She claps and says, "Okay, to bed. I'll douse the fire," before practically shoving me toward my tent.

My heart is still hammering while I finagle my way into pajamas—it is seriously tight in here—and wriggle down into my sleeping bag. I imagine Ezra in his own tent, his heart hammering too, his mind back on the way we kissed under that tree. I press fingers to my lips, searching for any trace of him still there.

I wish I could say I fall into a deep sleep, carried away on dreams of kissing Ezra. But it's a long time before I can tune out the sounds of Nature At Night, which is truly next-level terrifying when you're by yourself and encased in what amounts to a bit of plastic wrap rendering you a ready-to-eat sandwich.

When I wake up in the gray morning, I'm relieved to not be the contents of a bear's stomach and even more thrilled at the chance to pick up where Ezra and I left off.

TWENTY-FIVE

BUT IT TURNS OUT IT'S hard to pick up where we left off when Ezra's gone for five days on a backpacking trip before heading to Vancouver to see family, and the day he returns I'm packing to head out on my own camping trip.

Where are you hiking? Ezra types the morning I'm leaving. It's a totally unreasonable hour to be DMing with him, but he's apparently sitting at the Vancouver airport and I'm in my living room facing down an enormous pile of stuff that needs to fit into one (1) internal frame backpack. Georgia wasn't kidding that I'd need to nix the Insta setup when we were actually out on the trail. There's no way I'll be able to fit a fold-up stool and vase in here. I'll be lucky if I can cram in extra underwear.

Ezra's message stares up at me, so I respond quickly. **Alamere Falls in Point Reyes.**

Oh shit. You're going to love it. One of my favorites.

That pulls a smile to my face. **Just once, I want to hear u roast a hike. Can't all be winners.**

Fine, he responds. **Yosemite is just a big rock. Eff off, Yosemite.**

I giggle, and Marnie glances up from her book. She's been curled up like a cat at one end of the couch since I hauled all my gear out here. "What's funny?"

I ignore her and type back to Ezra. **YES. Thank u Ezra u beautiful, positive ray of sunshine. I'm finally corrupting you.**

He responds with a bunch of ellipses, and my cheeks warm. But the alarm starts dinging on my phone, dragging me back to the task at hand. Georgia will be here in an hour to pick me up, and I have packed exactly zero things.

Gotta go, I type back. **Text when I get home.**

Have fun!

And a moment later, **I'll be here awaiting corruption.**

Oh my god, I am going to kiss that boy so freaking hard next time I see him. Reluctantly, I put down my phone and face my backpack. This is what Georgia is calling our shakedown hike. It's our last milestone before the big fifty-miler along a portion of the PCT and will earn us our blue walking stick thong, to join the pink, green, red, and orange that we earned after surviving the first night camping.

Today we're driving to an overnight somewhere closer to the trailhead, and tomorrow we'll be hiking with full packs and doing five miles to our campsite, followed by five miles the next day back to the trailhead. And I have a single hour to pack everything up. Can this backpack truly fit a tent, sleeping bag, inflatable sleeping pad, camp stove, cooking supplies, and water purification pump on top of all my normal hiking gear? No or no?

"What's a WhisperLite?" Marnie peers over the top of her book and points at the camp stove.

"Backpacking stove," I grunt, trying and failing to fit my metal pot into a side pocket. I palm a red-and-gray cylinder plus tube contraption and hold it up. "And this is the water purification pump. It's actually kind of cool. It—"

But Marnie's focus has wandered back to her book. Her long blond hair is secured in a loose braid, and her fingers idly stroke the ends. Oh god, she's probably reading about Gilbert Blythe and fantasizing. I mean, ew.

"Cool," I grouse to my still-empty backpack. "Sorry to bother you with present-day information when obviously you can learn so much more reading a smelly old book about made-up people."

Marnie's eyebrows slash in annoyance. Ha! "Anne is real if I hold her in my heart."

"Oh my god, how is it that you have a boyfriend and I don't?"

My older sister carefully marks her place—with a bookmark, not a dog-ear, because she believes anyone who does *that* is a monster—and sets her book aside on the couch. "Lo, would you like to talk?"

Ugh. Sort of? I'm really proud of how far I've come with Hike

Like a Girl, but no one is acknowledging it. Kat is talking to me like I'm a roommate she found on Craigslist, and Mom asked me the other day why I hadn't quit yet.

I plop down next to Marnie on the couch and toss my stocking feet up onto the glass coffee table. It's covered in art books that no one has ever opened and three vases finger-painted by the triplets.

"You were right when you accused me of liking all this hiking and nature crap. I do like it, and I'm proud of myself," I grumble.

I bet when the triplets finished their big accomplishment (i.e., the vases), Joss and Edie showered them with compliments and probably little gold stars. For my big accomplishment, I'm getting surprised looks and absolutely zero gold stars. And I know it shouldn't matter, but I'm excited to share this amazing new thing I've discovered with friends and family and, like, strangers on the street. I've become all Nature! Who Knew!

Marnie pats my hand. "You should be proud. It sounds like you've really pushed yourself with this program. Sorry I haven't been around a lot this summer. I didn't know it mattered this much to you."

This is where I should snap, *It doesn't matter*. Instead, I slump sideways and grab my sister around the neck for a bit of forced snuggling. She is tepid, at best.

"What's the city got that we don't?" I whine into her hair.

Marnie pets my head. "Do you want the list alphabetized or geographic?"

I yank back and stick my tongue out at her. "Yeah, we both know that list begins and ends with Whit."

"It doesn't! I mean, it is lovely to get a summer simply to hang out with Whit, but we've gone to museums and taken Sir Pat on wonderful walks, and—"

"And probably banged a ton even though you dress like a librarian, and not the fun kind."

Marnie's cheeks go spectacularly pink. And, okay, yeah, I'm trying to be all New Lola or whatever, but getting a rise out of my sister is exactly what I need in this moment. She clears her throat. "Would you like some assistance packing?"

"Yes. God, yes. And I still need to shower and change."

Marnie shoos me off. "Go. I'll handle this."

I pad down the hallway and pause at Kat's door. It's cracked open, and I can hear music playing inside. I knock and push it open. "Hey, I'm going."

She looks up from where she's sitting against her headboard with her phone against her folded-up knees. "Have fun," she says, distracted. But then she pauses, puts her phone down, and actually looks at me. Like, eye contact and everything. "Really, have fun," she says again. "Let's . . . let's hang out or something when you get home."

"Yeah," I say. "I'd like that."

We're saying all the right words, but it feels like we're relaying them through a crack in a wall. And you know what? That sucks. It sucks to feel like this with the most important person in my life. But Georgia will arrive in less than an hour and I have to hope Kat will still be here when I get home.

I'm blow-drying my hair when the doorbell rings and Marnie's voice calls down the hallway. "Georgia's here!"

The front door shuts and Georgia's voice rings out. "Lola, girl! The bus is leaving!"

I tug a hoodie over my longline sports bra and grab my shoes on the way out my door. In the living room, Marnie is standing next to my fully packed backpack, triumph in her face. Ugh, she's a saint. I hope she gets a hundred Gilbert Blythes.

"Hey, you're up!" Georgia's got her thick dark hair piled into a bun on top of her head and is wearing the dorkiest pair of swishy cargo pants I've ever seen. I think they . . . oh god, they do . . . they unzip at the knees. I take back everything good I said about HLAG.

"Didn't get lost on the way to the bathroom again?" she asks, laughing at her cleverness.

"Yeah, yeah. It's too early for jokes, Georgia. Calm down."

"I'm excited! Will and Lindy have a big dinner planned for us tonight. We'll hit the trailhead by their house nice and early."

I'm sorry. What?

"What do you mean, Will and Lindy?"

Georgia laughs and slugs me on the shoulder. "Lola, you need to read your adventure emails closer. They're hosting us tonight at The Shack! Should be fun. They've got plenty of room and the girls will get a chance to talk to Will about his women in tech initiative."

No. No no no. I've been liking HLAG and having fun with my crew. And if they know I'm actually related to Will, everything will fall apart. They'll realize I lied, that I never earned my place with them. That I'm not really one of them after all.

Oh shit. *Shit.* And now I have just a single bus ride to figure out how to nonchalantly drop into the conversation that—whoops!—I actually do know Will Drake and that Beth was totally right about how I didn't earn my spot. It's that or think of a way for Will and Lindy to play along. But they definitely won't because they have, like, standards. Maybe I can knock them on the head with a rock for some convenient amnesia when we get there. Cool. Great plan. What can go wrong?

I heft my bag, take one last look down the hallway toward Kat's open door, and follow Georgia outside. She stows my backpack into a roof box as the side door slides open and Corinne jumps out.

She pauses, glancing at Priya and Beth inside the bus before saying quietly, "So, what's the plan?"

"Plan?"

"Yeah, you said you don't want the girls to know how you're related to Will, but we're driving to his house."

From somewhere underneath my panicking, the realization that Corinne never told my secret emerges. I never could have expected the same from Jasmine or even Meg. I mean, it doesn't actually solve any of my problems, but it's a nice feeling.

She's looking at me expectantly. "How can I help? Maybe you should just tell them now."

"Oh yeah, that. Um." I scrunch up my nose. "I think I'm going with 'pretend it's not happening.'"

Corinne chuffs a laugh. "That's a terrible plan."

I roll my eyes at her. "Get in the bus and play along."

TWENTY-SIX

"DO YOU THINK HE'LL BE there?"

The whisper from Beth to Mei unfortunately carries over the rumble of the VW bus trundling up the desolate, misty freeway toward Bolinas. Okay, think. It won't be that big a deal if they find out I know Will. And really, if you think about it, I barely know him! Like, I have no idea how he prefers his toast in the morning. (Ugh, it's seeded multigrain with a scrape of unsalted butter and a smear of raspberry preserves. I hate myself.)

Priya leans around me, ignoring my agitation. Her T-shirt today says "There's No Place Like 127.0.0.1." I'm not going to even ask.

"Definitely, right?" she says to Beth. She nods toward the front of the bus and adds, "I heard she does a night at their house every year. Can you believe we'll actually be inside Will Drake's house? I've heard it's gorgeous."

Mei giggles. "He's gorgeous."

A groan creaks past my teeth, and Tavi looks at me sharply. "Are you carsick?"

"Something like that."

Corinne presses her knuckles to her mouth and swallows down a giggle. I hope she's enjoying my agony. No one has ever suffered as I have.

Tavi continues. "His wife is crazy talented too."

Oh good. Let's add Lindy to the mix. An ominous burp rumbles up my throat. Priya scoots away from me in a totally obvious way. I shall puke on her first.

"My parents took me to her first doc a few years ago, and it was so beautiful," Tavi says. "I think she shot it somewhere on the coast. Dune Reef? Something like that."

"Duxbury Reef," I say automatically, and immediately regret it.

Lindy's first documentary, *Something or Otter*, was nominated for an Oscar and Mom didn't shut up about it for months.

"What was that, Lola?" Corinne asks innocently.

"Nothing, Corinne," I say back. She shall also be puked upon.

Beth looks between us and rolls her eyes. "I know you two don't care," she says to us, "but I heard that last year, Will put one of the HLAG girls in touch with the innovation team at Invigor, his father-in-law's old company. She's only a freshman in college, but she's interning there now."

Perfect! Now Dad has entered the conversation! I hope these girls are prepared for some projectile vomiting. I slouch in my seat and try to disappear.

Objectively, I know my family is Bay Area famous. When Edie debuted rainbow macarons for Pride last year, people lined up down the block and the photos were all over Insta. Lindy and Will are Silicon Valley plus Indie Hollywood famous, and Dad is "old guard of the tech industry" famous. Mom once famously started a feud with Tiffany & Co. because her diamond-encrusted watch broke when she wore it in the hot tub for a photo shoot for *San Jose Gossip*. Even Marnie—Marnie!—got featured for a fluffy piece in a San Francisco weekly magazine about her program, Bark Books.

And I . . . embarrassed my family with a cheating scandal and burned down a boat. Yeah, when you put it like that, perhaps I want to become known for more than being an epic screw-up. I groan and cradle my head in my hands.

"Lola, what is going on with you this morning?" Priya asks at the same time Georgia calls from the front seat, "We're here!"

That's what's going on with me.

Okay, tell them. Say, *Hey, not sure if I mentioned it, but these weirdos are actually my sister and brother-in-law.* No big deal, right?

Instead, when Beth starts giving us stats about their eco-renovation, I turn in my seat, pretend this is the first time

I've ever seen The Shack, and say, "Ew, I think it's kind of ugly."

Everyone ignores me.

The Shack is a freaking enormous beach house that squats in a field of heather and thistles at the very edge of the ocean. It's moody, and Marnie would call it romantic, but Marnie is one thousand percent wrong. It's gloomy. The wood siding has been artfully weathered by the wind and an architect who called himself a storyteller. The house is on one level, but the ceilings inside rise to soaring rafters that hold minimalist chandeliers. Outside, a circle drive sweeps along a wide, flagstone porch dotted with yellow and white flowers in big pots on either side of a tall front door, painted glossy yellow. They have a door knocker shaped like a bumblebee and a patch of weeds sprouting among a pile of rocks on the side of the house they call a pollinator garden. Everything is terrible.

The girls shuffle and jostle as they clamber out of the VW bus and stand in a line like we're about to be received at Downton Abbey. I jump down from the bus, my boots landing hard on gravel, and issue a long, very aggrieved sigh. I don't know whether to cause a scene so maybe we can get out of this whole thing or curl up into a little ball and make Corinne carry me around like a pet hedgehog in the hopes no one will notice me. I mean, both great options.

But Will and Lindy, damn them, take away both options by tugging the giant front door open and shouting "Welcome!" in sync. They definitely practiced that. The worst. *The worst.*

Beth tramples Priya in her fervor to be first in line to shake Will's hand, then Lindy's, and introduces herself with her full name and where she attends school. Will and Lindy go down the line, greeting everyone, and I stand at the end in full-on panic mode.

Scream!

Run!

Dive into the ocean and pray the mermaids accept me!

Oh shit, Will and Lindy have arrived in front of me.

Will looks like he's going for a hug, so I do some quick thinking and instead yank his arm down and shake his hand. "Pleased to meet you." I duck to tie my shoe to evade Lindy. I can feel her pausing above me, but I watch her shoes—sensible boots that look a lot like mine—shift away from me. When I finally stand, Georgia and her brother are staring at me like I've sprouted a second head, so I ignore them.

Will recovers first with a sardonic quirk of his brow. He turns to the others and graces them with a fleeting and rare Will Smile. Down the line, Beth practically swoons. I'm about to swoon her right off a cliff; that'll probably shift focus nicely.

"Welcome to The Shack, everyone," Will says. He's speaking in a strange, sort of clipped tone in a deeper register than normal, and I realize it's probably his patented Silicon Valley Golden Boy Voice. Gross. "I thought you could get settled— Georgia will show you to your rooms—and we can share a nice meal before your big day tomorrow. I'm interested to hear what you think about the program so far."

Annoyance ripples down my spine. Why are Will and Lindy being so gracious? What sort of hosts asks their guests all these prying questions? Just let us in to rifle through your private belongings like normal people.

Some of us, apparently, can't wait to share.

"It's astonishing how far I've come in so short a time. I'm so astonished by the way I've been able to push myself. The others too," Beth says loudly. "Nature is astonishing."

Last weekend she shrieked when a butterfly landed on her arm.

"It's been very rewarding," Tavi adds.

"And Lola?" Lindy asks, kind of gently.

I shrug. "I would say astonishing, but Beth already used up the day's allotment of that word."

Will's smile vanishes and I feel an absurd sense of accomplishment. Astonishing!

Lindy shakes her head, but she's grinning. She cuffs me on the shoulder and drapes her arm around me before I can sprint away into the fields. "There's the Lo we know and love."

Somewhere in the distance, a record scratches. Confusion turns to accusation on the other girls' faces.

"Wait, what?" Mei says.

"What?" Lindy says brightly. Her smiles fades. "Wait."

"Wait. Just, wait." I hold my hands up to my crew, who are looking at me with big eyes. "I can explain?"

Lindy's arm drops from my shoulder, and I've got to admit, I'm sort of feeling really terrible about it. Will recovers first and turns away from me. "Why don't you all head inside and relax for a bit. There's a nice den with books and a big deck out back that looks out over the ocean. Lola, a word?"

But the girls don't listen to Will.

Mei is staring. "I don't understand."

Corinne squeezes my wrist and whispers, "Lola, come on."

By now, Beth, Tavi, Mei, and Priya have formed a horseshoe around me, staring at me, waiting for me to explain myself. My heartbeat echoes, but it feels like every drop of blood in my body has drained to my feet. My brain sways, I squeeze my eyes shut, and I blurt, "We're related."

Beth's face curdles. "But we said—" Her eyes dart to Will and away, and her cheeks burn. Her eyes turn to murder, and I swear I can see every cell in her body start quivering with rage. "Are you fucking kidding me!"

The force of her anger makes me flinch. Also, whoa with the language, Beth! Next to me, I'm vaguely aware of Will and Lindy mumbling something about giving us a moment before they shuffle back inside. Georgia, damn her, hovers nearby but doesn't step in to defend me. Ugh, she probably thinks I need to, like, stand up and face my own mistakes.

Beth is breathing like an ornery bull about to charge, and I realize I'm wearing red. "Holy shit, Lola. All this time you let us believe you'd earned your spot, but it was all fucking nepotism! I should have known a program this competitive didn't just magically add another spot because it was too hard to choose. Do you know how hard I worked to get here?"

"I know," I say quietly.

"No," Tavi snaps, her words all right angles. "You really don't."

Beth jabs a finger at Corinne, still next to me. "And you knew too!"

Blindly, I scrabble for Corinne's hand. "Don't blame her, I asked her to keep it a secret."

Priya is blinking fast, her eyes wet. "But why keep it a secret?"

"Because I didn't want you to treat me different."

And underneath everything else, I know that's true. Because if they knew I was only here because of Will, they'd figure out the boat incident, and France, and Tully. They'd know I wasn't worth their time.

Beth juts her chin. "So did you apply like the rest of us?"

I rub at the end of my nose.

Beth sneers. "Fucking unbelievable. Have you even thought about the people who actually deserve to be here? All because you're some privileged, selfish—"

"Hey now," Georgia interrupts, but I hold up my hands and talk over her.

"But that doesn't mean I don't want to be here," I say, talking fast and shrill. All that blood that was pooled in my feet is suddenly electrified, spiking through me and making me afraid I'll actually burst. "Please, I promise. I—"

"Be quiet." It's Mei. She hasn't said a word until now, but she glares at me, face tight and mouth hard. "Listen to what we're telling you. We worked our asses off to get into this program and we've given it our all. But not only are you here because it turns out you're related to Georgia, you didn't even try for most of this summer. You've made this worse for all of us. Do better."

My mouth opens and closes, my tongue and teeth and throat useless and empty and completely without excuse for what I've done. Mei's words—*do better*—pound behind my eyes.

The girls (*my crew*, my brain whispers) leave me behind, standing alone in the driveway. Corinne is the last to go, and she looks from the back of Tavi stalking through the front door to me.

"Give me a minute, okay?"

She nods and slips through the front door just as Lindy comes back out. My older sister stops in front of me, and I brace for impact. But she just says "Oh, Lola" like my name is another word for disappointment and nods for me to follow her along a narrow path around the side of the house.

The air is heavy with brine and the clouds hunker low above us, but I peer down the little path worn into the stubby grasses and find my feet itching to move. To do something to get my mind off what happened.

The path skirts the headlands, the cliffs to our right a tumble of rivulets and pale gold stone all the way to the surf. The plants are the hearty, stout sort that can survive the constant, buffeting wind, and I feel like an intruder on the land. I pull up the hood of my sensible rain jacket and tuck my chin.

The trail slopes gradually to a point where the cliff dips toward the water, and Lindy starts descending a set of metal stairs bolted to the rock face in a way that can only be described as "foolhardy." This thing looks one stiff breeze away from crumbling.

We still haven't said a word to each other, but the quiet has given this awful, jumpy energy in my bones a chance to calm. I've always given Lindy and Will shit for making their home in such a gray place, but there's a windswept, lonely beauty to it. Down on the rocky beach, the gray sky is reflected in the tide pools, and the bleached driftwood twists into natural art.

It sort of reminds me of this farm we went to in Normandy with my cohort. They produced sheep's milk cheese on rolling, wild land at the edge of the ocean and it was said you could taste the sea salt from the grasses the sheep ate. But I refused to try any because of the smell in the barn.

Lindy crouches at the edge of a tide pool and peeks into it. "You see that purple sea urchin?"

I squat next to her and crane my neck to see where she's pointing. The sea urchin is stuck to the side of the rock, a lavender shock of spines. I haven't poked around a tide pool since I was small, and the sense of discovery is kind of thrilling. A small crab scuttles past the urchin and disappears under a ledge. Ezra would love it here.

"I once spent an afternoon watching this family of sea otters go bananas on a crop of sea urchins," Lindy says, eyes still on the tide pool. "They'd snap off all the spines, chomp the thing open, and slurp out the insides." She smiles at the disgusting memory and stares off into the ocean, her eyes bright. "That was such a great filming day."

Since her accident last winter, she hasn't talked as much about her documentaries, and it fills me with warmth to see that light in her eyes again. She may drive me insane, but we're still family. Despite what Kat thinks, I swear I'm not really a monster. And if I say it enough, it'll be true, right?

"Why didn't you tell those girls the truth?"

Well, this conversation took a hard left. I want to be prickly as that sea urchin. But that'd probably make Lindy the otter in this analogy, snapping off my spines and slurping out my insides.

"Because I'm a messy bitch who lives for drama?"

Lindy blows out a big breath. "Come on."

I make myself look at my sister. We're about as opposite as two sisters can get, her dark-haired and witty and Dad's obvious favorite. Me blond and prone to outbursts and Mom's partner in histrionics. But both of us have sharp chins and sharper eyes, and right now when I stare at her, I can't help but see those similarities.

I pick up a piece of driftwood and weigh it in my palm. It's surprisingly light, and the swirls of weathered wood are etched with strange, curving designs.

"I didn't want them to look at me different."

Lindy nods. "Because of who we are."

"No, I mean, sort of. But . . . they all assumed I'd applied and everything, that I was supposed to be in the program. They didn't know about how I got in, which meant they didn't know about the boat, or France, or Tully. I don't know, it was nice to not feel like the screw-up. Not to be looked at like I was this . . . inevitable disaster."

Lindy nods again, but it seems like she actually gets it. "You were getting a fresh start with them."

"Yeah, and at first I definitely didn't appreciate it. I mean, that's what France was supposed to be, but I screwed that up. Because I'm a mean, bitter screw-up." I tap the driftwood against the still surface of the tide pool, and tiny fish scatter.

"You're not any of those things, Lola."

I swipe my hand through the air. "No, I am. But . . . but I don't want to be. And those girls, even Georgia . . . they're helping me realize that. I want to do things that mean something. I want friendships that aren't a fucking nightmare of backstabbing and pettiness."

It all rushes through me, like the tide surging. But what's left behind feels scrubbed clean and new. I suck in a lungful of cold sea air and give Lindy a small, genuine smile.

She stands and pulls me back to my feet, and we pick our way slowly down the beach. "Are you talking about that account?"

My nod is tight. "Turns out, Jasmine LeGrange started it."

Lindy winces. She knows Jasmine used to be one of my best friends.

"Yeah, which sucks. It made my mistake, I don't know, permanent. But only for me. That's the worst part. No one expects Tully to bear any responsibility for what happened. Did you know he spent the last year flying around on his parents' private jet, just hanging out?"

Lindy stops, her eyebrows creased. "Are you serious?"

I slap the driftwood against my palm, feeling every ounce of anger at the double standard in the sting of the wood against my skin. "Yup. I found out the night of the boat party, actually. You know, before—" I mime an explosion, and Lindy grimaces. "And I think that was the moment I started realizing it was all shit, you know? I've spent a year trying to prove to everyone I was worth a second chance while Tully's out there getting all the chances he wants without having to prove a damn thing."

"Look," Lindy says, "whether or not you get a second chance isn't up to them. If you only define your self-worth through everyone else, you'll always be disappointed."

It makes sense, what she's saying, and it's a truth I've been circling for a while, I realize. But also: "That sounds . . . really lonely."

I had the chance to define myself on my own terms in France, and I was a spectacular failure.

Lindy reaches out and grabs my hand, squeezing my fingers.

"I don't mean don't have any friends, just make sure the friends you have are there for the right reason."

Corinne. Ezra. Kat. Dammit, even Beth. Those are the people I want in my life, the ones I want to see happy and who I think want to see me happy. We reach the stairs, and we climb them together.

"You have me and Will too. You know that, right?"

I grin at her. "Nah, you're not really the vibe I'm going for."

She shoves me in the shoulder and rolls her eyes. "I'm pretty annoyed you pretended you didn't know us, Lo. We're cool!"

I groan, but I'm grinning even wider. "Oh my god, Lindy, you are so deeply uncool." I pause and sneak a look at my older sister. "I wouldn't want it any other way."

She hooks her arm through mine, and we continue down the path back toward The Shack. Lindy's words tumble through my thoughts like a rock being polished by the waves. Out over the ocean, the sun breaks through the heavy gray sky to spread gold across the water.

The lights from The Shack's wall of windows glow in the setting sun.

Lindy nudges my shoulder. "Can I acknowledge you're my sister now?"

"I hope you understand it's nothing personal. It's just that I'm very embarrassed of you and Will and your lifestyle choices. I once overheard you reading poetry aloud to him, and that's not the sort of thing I can support."

Lindy chokes back a laugh. "Oh, you'd hate to see us when we've had a few glasses of wine. Sometimes we dance together."

I gasp loudly. "I am so ashamed to know you."

She barks a laugh, and I can't help but join in. We take the steps up to the back porch, and through the giant windows I can see my crew sitting around the table with Will. It makes me pause, and Lindy stills beside me. Will they like me again? Will they be able to trust me? Georgia talks so much about how we need to trust each other when we're out on the trail, and I want them to know I'm in this, that I'll be right there beside them.

"What if they can't . . . ," I say, my voice soft on the wind.

My arm is still hooked through Lindy's, and she squeezes me close. "It might be hard, but I think they'll understand. Eventually. Just show them who you are, okay?"

Show them who I am. For so long, who I was depended on who was around me, how I could keep their attention. And look, the truth is, I like the attention. I like being in the center of it all, like Corinne said. But I think it's time to find that feeling on my own terms, not anyone else's.

A deep, steadying breath fills me up and pushes me forward. The door opens with a snick and seven pairs of eyes look up at me. Georgia and Will are seated side by side, and the rest of the group is spread out along either side of the big wooden table.

Beth's face is sharpened to a point when she looks at me, and Tavi doesn't look too pleased either. Priya looks down at her lap, and Mei's glance is fleeting. Only Corinne holds my gaze and gives me a little nod.

"So, hi, everyone," I say.

No one responds.

"I'd like to introduce my older sister Lindy. She's a big nerd, you'll love her."

At the other end of the table, Will drops his forehead into his hands and mutters, "Oh my god."

I raise my voice over him. "And Will is okay too. You wouldn't know it by looking at him, but he's actually, like, a nice, supportive dude."

Georgia joins Will, dropping her forehead to the table and rolling her head back and forth.

"Anyway, I'm happy to explain everything later, but for now . . . can I sit down with you guys?"

No one moves, but Corinne pulls out a chair next to her, and Beth doesn't swear at me when I sit down. Okay, so it's not a big, dramatic reunion, but I'll take it. I'll find a way to apologize for lying and I'll prove to them I deserve to be here.

TWENTY-SEVEN

BY BREAKFAST THE NEXT MORNING, I'm contemplating standing on the table just to get them to look at me.

It's perhaps not the most sophisticated idea. But proving myself without a flawless roller-skating routine and fireworks finale is hard! It's taking every ounce of self-control to be attentive, helpful, and genuine.

I wish I had Corinne to make all this easier, but she's been on the phone with her dad for the last half hour. I peer down the hallway toward the closed door of the den again, hoping everything's okay.

Without Corinne, chatting has been tissue-paper thin. Tavi asked if I was done in the bathroom, and Priya asked me to pass the milk, but most everyone has spent the morning treating me like a disease they don't want to catch. I'm getting a good six feet of dead air all around me.

No one has officially forgiven me by the time we pack all our gear back in the bus and gather in front of The Shack to say goodbye to Lindy and Will. Which is kind of annoying because I've taken Lindy's advice and forgiven myself for the whole "secret sister" thing. Okay, no. That's not quite the lesson I was supposed to take from all this. I want these people to be my true friends, so I need to be a true friend in return.

So new plan. Be on the lookout for demonstrative friendship opportunities.

Maybe I can get Will to give Beth a hug? She'd probably love that. Except when I try to gently shove him toward her, he recoils and spills coffee all down the front of his Patagonia zip-up. And Beth tries to . . . catch the coffee? . . . then burns her hand.

"I'll get ice!" I shout, like an innocent little lamb whose only goal in life is to gambol about a field and get ice for burn victims.

"No," Beth grunts. "Just. Don't."

Lindy looks at me with big eyes and throws her hands up in question. Yeah, I don't know why Beth didn't appreciate any of that either. But you can't win them all.

At last Corinne comes bustling out of the house, her big backpack bouncing.

"Everything okay?" I ask.

Corinne smiles big, but the corners of her eyes are tight. "Totally! He's just been busy, so we were catching up."

Right. Okay. Keep trying. Perhaps Priya needs me to fill her CamelBak? She says no. Or Mei wants her hair braided? Also no. This is going nowhere fast, and suddenly we're all piling into the van and headed back down the drive and I've demonstrated true friendship to exactly zero people.

And that . . . that . . . Shit, that *hurts*. I hunker down in my seat and wrap my arms around my stomach, but the pain just zigzags up to my brain. If they truly can't forgive me—because, let's face it here, I kind of really betrayed their trust—it will devastate me. I can't imagine Priya and Tavi and Mei and even Beth *not* in my life now.

I just need to try harder. The moment comes at the trailhead, when Tavi hoists her backpack onto her shoulders and her little metal cooking pot swings around and whacks her shoulder. "Ugh, this stupid thing," she says, flicking it back into place. "I couldn't get it to fit anywhere else."

"I'll take it." My backpack is still at my feet, and I look up at Tavi and smile.

She frowns at me.

"Really, I've got space."

She shrugs and swings her pack back to the ground. It takes some finagling, but I manage to use a bit of rope to hook the pot onto a loop on the outside of my pack.

"Thanks," Tavi says.

Mei is nearby watching us, so I nod at her. "My pack has a bit more room."

It doesn't, but I'm shivering with excitement when Mei hands over two ziplock bags of granola bars and a headlamp.

My pack weighs about the same as a small-to-medium-sized car, but I'm light as air as we set off down the trail. If I can show Tavi and Mei I'm reliable and devoted, maybe Priya and Beth will see it too. God, I hope so. We wouldn't be this crew without them.

The trail ahead of us is narrow, the close green forest still foggy this early in the morning. It's kind of magnificent, the way the air is shaded blue and the salt-tinged scent of the distant ocean mixes with the sharpness of the pine. We walk in silence, until the air brightens and the trees thin. And I know I still have so much to prove to these girls, but right now on this trail, I feel connected to them, part of this thing we're doing together.

I'm also, frankly, fizzing with excitement to see this famed waterfall near tonight's stop. Apparently it's gorgeous during sunset. I wonder how it will compare to the Almost-Kissing Waterfall and if I'll find another Ezra to kiss behind it. God, I really need to kiss him again.

But yeah, this waterfall. I'm excited. Which, look, two months ago I would have said that was how you'd know I was kidnapped. Did Lola just wax poetic about a freaking waterfall? That's the signal. Call the cops.

But before any waterfalls are in sight, Georgia leaps onto a rock and looks down at us. "Okay, girls! You've done an amazing job with full packs so far. How are you feeling?"

Beth sort of groans and takes the opportunity to slump against a tree. Mei says "Great?" with the conviction of Tully contemplating his first semester at UCLA.

"Let's take a break, have a snack. You've all earned it, and this is our last bit of cover for a while. It can get windy up on the bluffs."

I wriggle out of my backpack and sigh. It's this full-body relief that nearly makes me giggle at the sheer wonderfulness of it. We sit on rocks or bare patches of moss and pine needles and start digging into our packs. It's a mess of poorly packed lanterns and nylon stuff sacks and plastic bags of granola bars and dehydrated meal kits.

But it's even more of a mess over in the Beth section of the forest. She's rifling through her backpack, muttering to herself. Tavi furrows her brows at me, and I shrug.

"Uh, Beth?" I call. "How's it going over there?"

Beth's eyes are manic when she looks up. "I started my period. I can feel it. And I forgot to pack tampons." She starts practically shredding her first aid kit, searching for something to use. "I'm definitely going to be eaten by a bear."

Okay, so I no longer think the woods are, like, teeming with bloodthirsty bears who have a taste for human flesh, but . . . trailing the enticing scent of a wounded animal everywhere you go can't be a good thing, bear-attack-wise. I reach into my bag for a zippered pouch and toss it her way.

"I've got a period that's like the life of a medieval peasant, short and brutal," I say, nodding for her to help herself to my emergency tampons, "so I'm always prepared."

For the first time in about twenty-four hours, Beth looks at me without frowning. In fact, I'd say she's about one super plus tampon away from proposing.

She dashes off behind some bushes to bear-proof herself, and I'm hovering near her pack when she returns. It worked for Tavi and Mei, so might as well see if the others will bite.

"You've got a lot in your pack here. Anything I can take? I've got some room."

"Oh, I . . ." Beth rifles through her stuff, then shoves a handful of dehydrated meals my way. This inspires Priya to hand over her water purifier, and Corinne gives up eight pouches of oatmeal. By the time we're packing back up, I've got nearly all the food and a bunch of other essentials too. It's a little zing of pride mixed with relief that at least they still trust me enough to take the important stuff.

The next two miles are hard work, but my steps find a steady rhythm. The sky is a watery blue, the stubby plants a gradient of grays, greens, purples. We've been following a stream for a while now, the rush of water getting stronger until it dumps into a jewel-box lake that reflects the clouds. It's chilly, but the sun is warm on my face and my legs burn as the trail dips and climbs and wanders, almost like it was dragged across the ground by a giant snake and not made by man.

Sweat drips down the back of my neck, and I hope we're

stopping soon because I definitely need to repack some of this stuff. The weight is much heavier on one side, pressing down on my right shoulder and slowly grinding my hip to dust with each step. I keep switching my hiking stick from side to side, unable to figure out the best way to relieve the pressure.

Soon, we rejoin the river, faster and deeper and closer to the cliff edge now.

Up ahead, two thick logs are tipped over the water, forming a rudimentary bridge spanning a narrow river gully. Georgia goes across first, then it's my turn. The logs are shoved together, and they sort of dip in the middle from hundreds of feet marching across. Out to my left, the flat expanse rolls on for a few hundred yards before falling away over the cliff, and the crash of water hitting the beach is a low roar in my ears. Which, whoa. We're at the *top* of the waterfall we'll get to see later. It's kind of a weird thing to think about. I inch out over the logs, using my hiking stick for support.

Step over step, until I'm past the middle of the bridge, one arm thrown out for balance and leaning slightly to offset the uneven weight on my right. I look up at Georgia and grin. Only a few more steps and I'm—

My heels slip, and my stomach plummets. I've got just long enough to say "shiiiiiiiit" before my leg flies out into thin air.

Ohgodohgodohgod.

I'm going down like Will's boat.

My pack, which I failed to clip together at my waist, swings out with the momentum and drags me farther over the edge. There's no railing, nothing to grab, so I do the only thing I can possibly think of: I drop hard to one knee, drastically overcorrect, flail dramatically, and barely manage to grab the edge of the log as my body tilts over the opposite side of the bridge. Exactly as planned.

In the process, the backpack has jerked off one arm, so it's sideways across my back and tipping dangerously toward the river.

"Lola!" Georgia calls, and the other girls scream. And yeah, right there with you. I'm gripping the logs with all my strength, but my damned pack is now caught at my elbow and I'm like a sloth holding on for dear life. The logs shimmy and jump as Georgia crashes out onto the bridge, and one of my arms slips. The pack slides off my arm to my wrist so it's full-on hanging below me like a weight.

Crap. *Crap.* I've got my cheek pressed against the wood and my eyes shut tight, but I can feel the drag of the water against the pack, trying to tug me into the river.

Georgia's hand goes tight around my upper arm. "Let go, Lola. I've got you."

I scrape my cheek against the wood and hold on tighter.

"Come on, Lola, I've got you."

I crack open one eye and look up at her. She's on her knees, and her face is determined. Okay, I can do this. Let go. Just—

I let go of the log with one arm, and the bag drops into the water. Georgia drags me up onto the bridge and I lie there, panting. But only for a second. The pack bobs in the river, and the truth sucks out every last bit of air in my lungs.

"The food!"

I push up to my knees, scramble the rest of the way across the bridge back to dry land, and take off, dodging thistle plants and low bushes to follow the river. I've got to reach the pack before the waterfall. The pack, with all my stuff and everyone else's too. Oh my god, we're going to starve out here and it'll be all my fault.

I skid down the bank ahead of the pack and splash into the river. Which, oh shit, it's cold! What sort of frozen hellscape does this water come from? I hiss at the frigid water and wade in deeper. The water pushes at my knees, tugs at my ankles, and my sodden boots are like lifting cement blocks with every step. The pack is close now, bobbing along merrily like it doesn't hold the key to our survival.

I'm deeper now, nearly up to my hips, walking sideways across the river but losing ground as the water presses me closer and closer to the edge. The gush of the waterfall is louder. More like a promise than a pretty bit of landscape. It's so loud I barely hear my name, but suddenly a hand grabs hold of my wrist and I wrench around to look.

Beth's got my wrist, up to her thighs in the water. Behind her, Tavi's next in the chain, then Corinne. Beth passes me her walking stick and I stretch into the river as the pack floats closer, until I can practically . . . almost . . .

I surge forward and hook the pack through Beth's walking stick. Yes! Cheers erupt behind me and the girls reel me in toward the shore. I collapse back against the sandy embankment, the pack hugged to my chest. The girls surround me, a rush of voices that don't make much sense over the adrenaline-soaked blood hammering in my ears.

I can barely breathe past the jackrabbit that's taken up residence in my chest, but I tip my head back against the sand and stare up into the blue sky and golden sun and white clouds.

"You saved me," I say up at Beth, teeth chattering.

Beth holds out her hand once more and tugs me to my feet. "You're crew. That's what we do."

But her voice is flat, and as my heart slows, I look around to see everyone—*everyone*—is still glaring at me.

TWENTY-EIGHT

"*WHY* DID YOU THINK IT was a good idea to take everyone's gear, Lola?"

That's Georgia. But the same question has been posed by everyone else, even Corinne. I wring out my hair and try to think clearly.

"I was trying to help."

Tavi doesn't buy it. "You were *trying* to make us forget the stuff with your sister and brother-in-law."

I rub at my nose and focus on yanking my soaked boots off, but when I glance up, everyone's still staring.

"Okay, yes. I was hoping you'd stop being mad about Lindy and Will and—"

"And the fact that you didn't actually get into the program," Beth helpfully adds.

My face scrunches up with the effort of tugging my other shoe off. "Yeah, that too," I finally admit.

We're all still crowded on the steep embankment of the river, but Georgia motions for us to haul back up to the trail proper, where she's laid out my mess of a bag.

"Most of the food is okay," she says, surveying the damage.

But Tavi's cooking pot is gone, Mei's headlamp smashed on the bridge, Priya's water purifier snapped apart, and the oatmeal packets are waterlogged.

Oh yeah, and literally all my stuff is soaked. My clothes are drenched, and my sleeping bag has become a sponge. My lantern and headlamp have shorted out, and the fire-starter kit is destroyed. Cool. Cool cool cool.

"Okay, girls," Georgia says, taking charge. "I know you're angry, and we can all agree what Lola did was *extremely* short-sighted—"

Eyes bore into me, but I make myself accept the admonishment without shirking. Even if my skin prickles with cold and regret.

"But," Georgia continues, "the important thing now is to make sure our crew is okay. So that means . . . we're going to need to get everyone into dry clothes."

There's some grumbling, but I end up with borrowed clothes—even loaner underwear—and have never been so grateful to be dry and not voted off a cliff in my life.

"So," I say, readjusting the band of the shorts. They're Mei's and a little tight across the hips, but when I yank them up higher, a gentle breeze flutters against the bottom of my butt cheeks. "That was intense."

Tavi snorts out a laugh. "That was almost the first line of your obit."

I peer past Tavi, where the rush of the river disappears over the side of the cliff. The thunder of water tumbling against rocks reverberates in my bones.

"Right. And, I mean, if you all hadn't come in after me . . ."

Thank you feels like a not-strong-enough word for what they did for me.

"There'll be time for that later," Georgia says. "Let's get to camp and try to dry out your tent and sleeping bag or you're going to be awfully cold tonight."

She helps me into my still-damp pack and ties my sleeping bag so it's open and draped over the outside of the bag to dry in the sun. Gonna be honest, everything feels heavier and lopsided and bulging now, and that last half mile in borrowed Tevas saps every ounce of my energy. But I make it one step at a time.

The sun is dipping toward the Pacific when we finally reach the sandy hollow where we'll be camping. And by the time Georgia helps me shake out my nylon tent and spread my sleeping bag over a bush for a last few minutes of sunlight, it's too late to head down to the waterfall. Disappointment whispers through the girls, and more than a few glares are thrown my way. This disaster of a day is building like gunk in my system, fouling my mood layer by layer. Everything I did today was in vain. Every time I tried to force the girls to realize I was meant to be here, I demonstrated just how clearly I'm not.

It's tipping toward darkness by the time the fire is built and the tents arranged. Around me, the girls talk quietly, but I feel apart. Apart and unsure how to fix it without just making things worse. I'm so lost in thought that I startle a little when I notice Georgia beside me.

"So earlier," she says.

My shoulders sag.

"You showed a lot of bravery and determination out there . . ."

"But?" Because I know it's coming.

She looks at me. "But things happen out in the wild, and you have to do your best to be prepared. And you didn't. You endangered yourself, and that could have made everyone suffer."

"That'll be the title of my memoir . . . endangering myself and making everyone suffer," I mumble.

"Instead of feeling bad for yourself, learn from your mistakes."

I splutter and choke on her advice. "You think I'm not trying to do that? Jesus. It's a struggle every day, and a failure. Every. Day. I'm starting to think some of us are just meant to be disasters."

Georgia sighs, and the firelight flickers against her features when she looks at me. "You're not a disaster, Lola, so stop hiding behind that as an excuse. This summer isn't about changing who you are, just changing your focus."

But I can't. I just *can't* anymore with this day. I push off my knees and stand, looking down at Georgia.

"Cool, and maybe if I wasn't so tired and cold, I'd be down for some advice. But I'm not, so the only thing I'm going to focus on right now is giving up and going to bed."

I go to bed damp and bitter, and I wake up damp and bitter.

Georgia said this whole experience isn't about changing who I am, but if I were a different person, I bet I wouldn't be waking up in borrowed, too-tight shorts because I fell in a river *and* set a boat on fire. So yeah. Eff that noise about changing focus.

But the only thing I can focus on currently, besides how cold my toes are, is a certain poop shovel staring at me, waiting to be christened. I grab the shovel and unzip my tent, shivering in the gray morning. I let myself stall for a count to ten, then crawl out and thread through the scrubby coyote bush and blackberry brambles to a private corner. And you know . . . it's not terrible. I mean, I'm not about to start digging holes in the backyard to exclusively shit alfresco. But in a pinch, I could— Ugh, no. I'm not going to finish that. I still have some dignity.

Corinne is up when I get back, her voice croaky with sleep when she says good morning. I manage a smile, but then she holds up her finger and disappears back into her tent. She reemerges a minute later, holding out a fluffy green pullover, wool socks, and black sweats. "You look cold."

Pulling on Corinne's clothes is like sinking into a warm bath.

"Thank you," I breathe out, snuggling down into the pullover. My breathing slows; my emotions smooth. It's subtle, but suddenly things don't seem so hopeless.

We sit in silence and watch the gray dawn begin to glow. Georgia's advice turns over in my head, but in the clear light of morning, with a friend at my side, it maybe doesn't seem so wild, this idea of shifting my focus. It means I can see yesterday for what it was—some mistakes that taught me a lesson. Not gonna lie, it kind of makes me wish I had another chance at France. Because the truth is, I really wanted it to work out. I imagined swanning home all horribly French, which is honestly the best glow-up. You know, perfect crimson lip, devastating style that is equal parts effortless and "I could murder you in a pose-off if I cared," probably a smoking habit. Instead, the absolute second it became hard, all I could see was the work. It was so much easier to feel bad about my horrible luck and horrible relationships than try to push through and make the hard work worth it.

All around me, mist rises and blurs the world into golds, purples, and grays. It's hideous. I love it. And I'm not willing to give this up now. How could I, when I know this place and these people are out there?

"Come on," I say, standing and holding out a hand. "Let's make everyone coffee and go see this waterfall."

I haul Corinne to her feet, and soon we've got five mugs waiting for our crew. The scent of instant coffee pulls everyone from their tents in various stages of grumpiness, but before long, we've got everyone bundled and caffeinated.

The world sleeps as we start down the narrow path, and I'm struck with this sense of calm. Of possibility. We weave through the brush, the sound of the surf a slow, steady rhythm that draws us closer. Until the beach opens up before us, unfurls on either side like it goes on forever. Georgia nods toward the left, and we follow her in silence the last quarter mile down the beach.

Alamere Falls is supposed to be spectacular at sunset, but I don't know if I'd want to see it any other way than this. The sun rises behind the cascade, spilling over the edge and throwing warmth across my face. And it's *amazing*. The ocean at my back and the waterfall in front of me and this expansive sense of . . . of . . . god, I wish I paid attention more in English so I had a proper way to describe how it makes me feel. Like a million trillion points of light are pressing out against my skin, and a million trillion points of light are sinking into me at the same time. I want to show this place to Kat, hike it again with Ezra too. I want to see their faces as they stand on the cliffs looking out toward the sea in a place they can only access by their own two feet and a sense of will.

Priya comes to stand beside me, her camera around her neck and the mug of half-empty coffee nestled between her hands. "I'm going to remember this trip for a long time," she says, eyes on the waterfall.

Corinne and Mei come to stand on my other side; Beth and Tavi aren't far away.

"Yeah," Mei says. "You certainly know how to make things memorable."

I sketch a frilly bow. "It was the least I could do. Making a scene and practically dying in the process is, like, my go-to."

Corinne, standing next to me, bumps my shoulder. I feel something swelling in me, pushing out against my ribs and throat and teeth.

"That's actually," I say, confessions tumbling out of me like so many waterfalls over cliffs. "That's actually why I'm here. I, uh"—I scrunch up my nose for a second—"I accidentally burned down a boat? Like, a smallish yacht, actually. And, well, it was sort of Will's boat. And it wasn't the first big mistake I've made lately, so that's why I ended up in the program. And I, uh, I didn't want anyone to know all that stuff because even when I was trying to deny it, the truth is I wanted you all to become my friends. Like, my real friends. I . . . don't have a lot of those right now."

"Whoa," Tavi breathes out.

"So this isn't fake application padding for college," Beth says.

"More like semi-forced community service, except the community it's serving is me, and I was super into hating it no matter what, but I, um, don't anymore. So . . ."

Look, this is as close as I'm going to get to saying I love you to these girls, so I hope they can read between the lines here.

"So yeah, thanks for being patient with me and sticking around as I figured shit out."

"I'm happy you're here," Mei says. She reaches across Corinne to squeeze my hand. "I've gotten so many compliments on that lipstick, and that alone makes your complaining worth it."

"Hey! I've pretty much stopped complaining!"

Corinne lets loose a bark of laughter. "We love your complaints," she says. "Sometimes. It's all part of the Lola charm."

"Okay, enough deep thoughts." I stand and pull out my waterproof phone—truly, the best purchase of my life, apparently. "Everyone, gather around! Let's mark the occasion of this amazing waterfall and me not dying!"

We smash together and grin wide for a selfie. I pull it back and check it out, and it's perfect. My eyes are shut. And Tavi is half turned to Mei, saying something, and Corinne is making an exaggerated kissy face. Beth is swatting at a bug and Priya's big camera is half obscuring her face.

But dammit. It's perfect.

We break fast, break camp, and break out of the mist as we climb the headlands back toward the trailhead. There are five miles back to the orange VW. And, not gonna lie, as much as I've loved this, I also can't wait to lay waste to a Taco Bell.

We've hiked into the dark blue forest near the end of the trail when Georgia calls us to a stop again. Our packs are heavy and our legs tired, but I see my smile reflected on all the girls' faces.

"I am so proud of all of you. This was fantastic practice for our backpacking trip only a couple weeks from now, and I have to say, I think you all are ready. Today, we've got one more task, and this is it. I want you each to spread out—make sure you can either see me or the trail—and find a tree. Maybe it's a tree that calls to you or one that seems the most comfortable, but I want you to sit at the base of the tree and not think. For thirty minutes, I want you to simply exist in this forest."

Beth rubs a hand along the back of her neck. "Alone?"

"Utterly alone," Georgia specifies, which doesn't help Beth look more at ease.

"Do you need more tampons?" I whisper at her. She shakes her head no as Georgia continues.

"The point of this exercise is to let nature surround you, and to learn to actively not think while you're alone in the woods."

Okay, so I would rather poop in the woods for the next hundred years than be alone. But instead of complaining—see, Corinne, I don't always complain—I point my feet off the trail and walk into the woods. The trees all look the same. I don't feel one calling to me, which I'm going to say is a good thing because that's definitely how you end up devoured by a demon tree.

Ahead of me, a large fir stands at the edge of a clearing, the ground around the trunk soft with a bed of needles. I unclip my pack and slide it gratefully off my shoulders before sitting back against the tree and . . . nothing.

Perfecting Corinne's cat-eye.

A bean and cheese burrito.

An Ezra kiss.

The existential dread of being alone.

No, wait. Counting. Counting birds. And the number of trees I can see. And the severe lack of people around me that leads to my own thoughts pounding through my head and not being able to escape them.

Okay, breathing. In. Out. In. Out. Innnnnnn, two three four. Outtttttttt, two three four.

My focus shifts, and with every deepening breath, the oppressive sense of just how alone I am fades. I feel smaller and smaller, surrounded on all sides by trees that are bigger and taller and older than I am and will remain bigger and taller and older after I'm gone.

It's not an easy thought, but I'm struck by this strange, almost overwhelming sense of being one very, very small part of this environment. It makes me feel . . . connected. Part of something larger than myself. Lord, I'm three months from turning vegan and devoting eighty percent of my life to loudly telling people about it.

But also, alone doesn't need to mean lonely or hopeless. Alone can mean having the space and time to figure out who I want to be.

I press my fingers into the dirt and half imagine I can feel the beating heart of the forest. Above, the branches creak and rustle, and the ocean wind weaves through leaves and needles. Around me, birds call and answer, and ferns shiver with unseen creatures. I could add my voice to the chorus because I am as worthy of being heard as the trees and creatures. It's another shift in my heart and bones and lungs—I don't want to shout simply to be heard. I want to shout because I have important things to say.

"Girls!"

Georgia's voice echoes through the not-so-silent silence, and I blink fast. Why is she calling us back so early? We just settled in. But I glance at my phone and frown. That can't be right. A half hour has passed. Huh.

"Thanks, pal," I whisper to the tree with a gentle pat to its trunk. "You didn't suck. Or eat me."

An hour later, we pile into the orange VW, bubbling with talk and laughing when we realize how bad we probably all smell. I post the photo of us by the waterfall this morning and talk Georgia into going through a drive-through, which might be my very best decision of all.

Around me, the girls who've improbably become friends tuck into tacos while Georgia screeches from the front not to make a mess. We're quiet and close and loud and wonderful. So maybe the tacos weren't the only good decision I've made lately.

TWENTY-NINE

GOOD DECISIONS.

Decisions and choices swirl through my mind the rest of the drive home, and when Georgia drops me off, I can still hear the rest of the girls shouting their goodbyes as she drives away.

My cheeks hurt from smiling and I'm buoyant with the memories of the last couple of days. Or maybe I'm buoyant because my backpack is no longer strapped to my shoulders (and clipped responsibly at my waist—I'm not making that mistake again).

All I know is, I march straight into the house, past Mom and Dad asking me how it went with trepidation in their voices, and directly to Kat's room. She's doing a yoga video. If that yoga video is only shavasana and there's some light snoring involved.

For a second, I watch her, this girl I've known since the very beginning and want to learn to know again.

I've asked her seventeen times to talk to me and every time she says nothing. Up until a couple of months ago, that would have been seventeen more times than I'd ever asked someone else about their feelings.

But all I know is, I miss my twin. There's a hollow space inside that's always been reserved for her, and no other friend or sister or boy can take that hollowness away, only Kat. I pad into her room on bare feet and lie down next to her.

"You're snoring," I say gently to her.

She jerks slightly and says, eyes still closed, "It's part of the practice." There's a beat, then she wrinkles her nose. "You smell."

"Yeah, I know. How are you?"

Her mouth tightens, then she says, "How was camping?"

She's trying to change the subject. Things may have changed between us, but she still has her tells.

"Look," I say, staring up at the ceiling. I feel for her hand and clasp her fingers. "I want to be friends again. I want you to be the first person I go to with news, and I want you to do the same. I love you, okay?"

Kat rolls her head to the side to look at me. "What the hell has hiking done to you? I mean that in a good way."

"It's been terrible for my personal hygiene. I've sweat more in the last two months than I have in seventeen years. Like, my eyelids have gotten sweaty."

Kat smiles, small and pretty and so very her. She looks back up at the ceiling, so I scoot closer, our arms flush and our temples tipped together.

A little huff of air issues from her nose. "I don't know why this is so hard, but it's become, like, a thing. I separated my life from yours, and I'll have to work a little harder to put it back together, okay?"

I squeeze her fingers and roll over and stand. I pause again at her door and say, "Okay, well, whenever you're ready, you know where I'm at."

That perhaps wasn't *quite* the truth, because I doubt Kat would expect to find me at a nighttime food festival. And yet.

Yesterday, Ezra texted me a screenshot of the flyer at Basecamp, and after nearly two weeks of not seeing him, I would have said yes to a third-grade recorder concert.

The way I feel about Ezra is this strange combination of tingly anticipation and warmth and like my stomach is dropping out the bottom of my body. But it's not explosive, and I've always thought love was a pyrotechnic that burned bright and took down the mast of a yacht in its inevitable destruction. But I don't want to burn down a yacht for Ezra. I want to . . . talk to him. Learn everything about him. Go sit in the forest with him and see if he can feel the pulse of the earth like I did yesterday. And then make out with him. I mean, it's all so opposite of who I've always been, and that's more than a little terrifying.

But also . . . Even though I hope Kat and I are finding our

way back to each other, I still can't forget what she said to me in anger. That the only reason guys like me is because they don't have to live with me. If he were to get to know me beyond the flirting and the kissing and the big personality, be there for the moments when I cry and rage and decide at ten p.m. that I want to learn Spanish . . . he'd run.

I shake my head, shake her words out. Kat doesn't get to decide who I am. I can be bright and loud and sad and angry in equal measure without the force of one emotion becoming a tidal wave dragging the rest out to sea. I can use these powerful emotions for good.

And right now, I use those powerful emotions for cute animal GIFs. Ezra texts me that he's clocking out and headed toward Basecamp's side entrance to meet me, and I text him a GIF of a panda eating cake.

Definitely not because I'm afraid if I try to use words they'll be *I think I might be able to love you.*

I smooth out the accordion folds of my swirly gold lamé midi-skirt and walk fast toward the side entrance. I paired the skirt with a food-fest-appropriate tee (embroidered pink doughnut on the breast pocket), white sneakers, and some snake earrings to keep my ring company. As I round the corner, my heart jumps. Ezra's waiting for me, a chambray pulled over his Basecamp tee.

I slow, weirdly shy. His smile is tentative, and he hooks his palm behind his neck. There's a foot of space between us. I want so badly to kiss him. He licks his lips, stares at mine, and scrubs his hand across his cheek, where a hint of stubble darkens his jawline. He doesn't step closer, and I'm stuck somewhere between wanting to show him I've missed him and not wanting to scare him off.

The moment stretches toward awkwardness before he says lightly, "I feel like people only come here at night to be murdered."

I spin around and start walking next to him. "Well, you just ruined my surprise. I wore my murder skirt and everything."

The tension chips away, and little by little we remember how easy this is.

"We'll have to murder some doughnuts instead," he says.

I snort at him. "Did my dad give you that joke? That thing's got a mustache and opinions on teen driving."

We amble down the sidewalk toward old-timey lights that stretch overhead and a sign surrounded by white bulbs that announces "Midnight in the Garden of Good and Eatin'." A big arrow points into the trees.

"That's how they get you," he says, "with the puns. Then it's all murder."

"She lived as she died, searching out food she'd later regret."

Ezra holds out his arm toward me, and I slide my hand through the crook of his elbow. The grassy path is lined with lights, and lanterns are strung in the trees. It all leads to a large clearing, and the closer we get, the louder and more full of people the night becomes.

An intoxicating swirl of scents and sounds rushes around us as we step into the clearing, and I hold tighter to Ezra so we don't get lost in the push of people. There are close to a dozen food trucks circled up, with picnic tables spaced out in the middle. Doughnuts, street tacos, Korean barbecue, Ethiopian coffee, German sausages, and so much more. Spoking off the main clearing, bartenders mix drinks from behind wooden slabs held up by barrels, and ice cream is sold from handcarts.

We walk along the food truck options together and build a feast of bao buns, injera with misir wat, latkes, spicy giardiniera, and a dozen cinnamon doughnut holes. We squeeze into an open spot at the end of a red-painted picnic table and tuck in, trading forks and plates as we go.

"Oh my god," I say through a mouthful of the Ethiopian lentils sopped up with injera. "This is amazing."

Ezra swallows down a bite of the pork buns and takes a swig of Topo Chico. "I would willingly let you murder me after this food. Holy shit, it's good."

The doughnuts remind me of a seasonal confection Edie sells in her Sonoma Sugared bakery, and I go into a whole thing about her pistachio macarons while Ezra practically salivates. We have to shout to be heard, but the atmosphere sparks with laughter and joy, and I find myself bobbing my head to some unseen music curling through the crowd and reaching over Ezra to grab a pickled cauliflower or snatch the bubbly water. I'm effervescent with the feeling of it all.

"How was the hike?" Ezra asks sometime later, when our plates are scraped clean and we're down to the last few bite-sized doughnuts.

"Well, I nearly fell in a river and had to go rescue my pack from a waterfall, so you know, the usual."

Ezra's eyes go wide. The warm glow of the lights overhead gleam off his hair and eyelashes and pricks out the freckles across his cheeks. "Was everything okay?"

"Oh yeah. I mean, I had to wear borrowed underwear the rest of the trip, but other than that."

His cheeks go adorably pink at the word *underwear*, and I tip my knee against his under the table. He doesn't pull away, but scoots the tiniest bit so our calves slides together. My heart sings and warmth spreads deep within me from the point where our skin touches.

He runs his hand through his hair and picks at the last doughnut. "I did this hike with my cousins in Virginia once. My sister and I were the youngest of everyone and I had to cross a river holding both our backpacks literally above my head. And there were these creepy-ass dolls hanging from this tree way out in the forest. It was . . . not my favorite camping trip."

"Gah! Dolls! Why would you tell me that? Do you want me to swear off ever going into the woods again?"

He shakes his head and grins. "Nah. I showed you my favorite spot. You can't go back on nature now."

A smile tugs at one corner of my lips at the memory of that

spot. "Okay, fine. Secret waterfalls only. I'd go back there. And, um, oak trees at night."

Ezra's eyes find mine. "I would too."

My breath is tight in my throat, and I'm half tempted to kiss him right here, but an older lady catches my attention. She's holding two heaping plates of food and an impatient expression.

We gather up our things and compost all the plates, then wander toward the music. It's a trio of musicians—a violin, cello, and drum—and it takes me a second to realize they're playing covers of modern music on their very traditional instruments. It's fun and catchy, and I find myself tugging Ezra's hand toward the middle where people are dancing.

He resists. "There are people everywhere," he says, shifting his gaze around the dozen or so revelers watching the musicians.

"Yeah, that's what makes it fun!" I spin, my skirt whirling out around me, before dropping into a deep bow. "Dance with me, Ezra."

Ezra's shoulders droop, helpless to say no, and he lets me tug him into the middle. There's nothing slow about how we move. We spin and laugh and twirl. He grabs my hand and spins me out away from him, then back in toward his chest, and I bump hard into his body. But his arm is tight against my back and I fit snug against him and his breath is warm where it glances across my neck.

Our hips sway together, and where I grasp his wrist, his pulse jumps. I twirl out away from him again, my skirt catching up around my knees in a flash of gold.

Ezra laughs and tugs me close again, raising his voice to shout over the music. "You're amazing!"

Except he shouts it just as the music stops. His words echo out over the crowd, and a few people giggle. His cheeks flame red, but I drag him closer to the buskers to drop a twenty in the open violin case before hauling him away. We half run through the crowd and back out to the sidewalk, where we slow, our hands finding each other. Our fingers twine together, and my heart thumps with anticipation.

It's this sweet, warm promise all around us. The anticipation of what's to come. And I don't only mean tonight.

"Where are you parked?" Ezra's voice is low when he asks.

"Back at the store."

He nods, and we don't say any more until our cars come into view. I parked right next to his old Volvo, and the slim space between our cars is shadowy. He's the one who tugs me between the cars, and he's the one to kiss me first this time. He braces his hands against the car on either side of my shoulders and dips his mouth to mine, and it's exactly what I've been missing.

My fingers crawl up his side and sweep around to hold on to his shoulders, drag him closer. Kiss him deeper.

He's breathing hard when he pulls away, and I push up to my toes to press a kiss to the juncture of his neck and shoulder. "Do you want to go to the annual bonfire with me?"

It's an unofficial-official Crenshaw Day tradition to welcome in the new school year with a beach bonfire on August first. Which is only a couple days away.

Ezra stills, stands up taller, puts space between us. "You mean, the thing with all our classmates?"

Hurt tugs at my heart. "You don't want people to know we're . . ."

"What are we, Lola?"

There's hope in his voice, but fear too. My hand whispers up his stomach and chest, up his neck and jaw, to bury my fingers in the curls running roughshod over his forehead. I trace a line back down his face to the beautiful freckle at the corner of his lips, and he catches my fingertips and kisses them. It makes it very hard to breathe.

"I'd like it if we were together," I manage to get out past my fluttering heartbeat.

A sound rumbles through his chest, and he says, "You're sure? You don't think everyone will—"

I cut him off. "You are a fucking amazing person and, like, a disconcertingly good kisser, and I want to go to a beach bonfire with you."

The grin that lights up his face makes my knees go weak.

THIRTY

THE SKY IS BLAZING AS Kat and I pull up to the wide curve of beach. The headlands glow gold with sunset and the shark fin rock jutting up from the surf is a jagged shadow.

We were quiet on the long drive to the coast, but the mere fact that she agreed to drive with me instead of Wash and Joon settles my nerves. We've always had so much fun at the annual bonfire. We may be in a different place now, but I have to hope tonight will still be great, just maybe in a new way. The lot sits above the surf, so we can peer down on our classmates already there. There are coolers and blankets spread across the sand, and a giant stack of dry wood next to a ring of rocks.

We step out of the car, and the wind picks up the hem of my gauzy white tunic. I'm wearing a pair of faded black cutoffs underneath, and the tunic settles back against my thighs as the wind softens. I brush tangles of hair off my face and angle away from the sun to shut my door.

That's when I see Ezra. Leaning against the passenger side of his Volvo with his arms crossed and one ankle hooked over the other. Waiting for me.

"Hey, I'll meet you down there," Kat says, her gaze sliding to Ezra and back to me. I wonder if she's okay with this. She purses her lips in a small smile and waves me off.

Wash's Land Rover is parked in between us. I skirt the hood and stop a few feet away from Ezra. He's got dark sunglasses on, and the golden light has turned his light brown hair to something liquidy and bronzed. My breath lodges in my throat.

Ezra tilts his chin toward me, and I close the distance between us, leaning into him. His hand plays at the hem of my tunic, fingertips grazing my thigh. The breeze is cool, but my skin heats in the wake of his touch.

"You're sure about this?" he asks, voice soft.

I push up to my toes and kiss him quickly. "Honestly? Right now, I'm more concerned with how long I have to wait before I can kiss you again. But yeah, of course I'm sure."

Before I give in to this powerful need to push Ezra into the back seat of his car and defile his innocence, I step back and hold out my hand. He slips his fingers into mine, and we head toward the steps.

The beach is milling with people, but one voice carries up

over the sand and sea and makes my stomach churn. Even from the top of the low cliff, he's unmistakable. Can I get through a party with Tully without blowing up? Blowing up includes but is not limited to: my temper, my relationship, literal things. But if Hike Like a Girl has taught me anything, it's that I can do hard things.

Here's hoping.

Worry pricks my skin like a salt breeze heavy with an oncoming storm. But the horizon out at sea is clear. I brush it off and fix a smile onto my face.

I squeeze Ezra's hand and tug him down to the beach.

Meg is at the bottom of the stairs with a few other girls I used to count as friends, Grace and Verona. My stomach twists at the sight of her, and I'm ready to walk right by, but she detaches herself from them and calls my name.

Meg glances at Ezra before leaning closer to me and saying, "Just a warning, Jas is in a foul mood. Her dad is pissed that she let Tully on the new yacht after . . . you know."

Ezra's fingers are tight in mine. Behind Meg, her friends have their hands up to their mouths to hide their words, but their eyes flick between us.

"Thanks for the warning," I say, focusing back on Meg.

Meg frowns, then angles her back to Ezra, like she's trying to keep him from hearing us. "Um, and . . . about the other thing. I wish I could say I definitely didn't know, but I suspected." She picks at her thumbnail, and I refuse to fill the silence. "I don't

like how it all went down. Could we talk about it? Maybe . . .
maybe lunch in a couple days?"

Her admission soothes my skin, and even though we'll never
be what we were, maybe we can find a way to something new.
"Yeah, I'd like that."

Hope is golden and warm in my chest. I tug Ezra's hand, and
we weave through the crowd toward the edges, where it's not so
crushing and loud. Yet whispers follow us every step—the sound
of Ezra's name, and Tully's. When I peek up at Ezra, he's staring
straight ahead like he can't hear a thing.

"Hey," I say, stopping with my toes in the sand. He turns
toward me, his jaw clenched. So he *can* hear them. "We can
always leave."

He swallows. "You don't want—"

I stop his mouth with a kiss, and when I pull back, I notice a
blush and a smile blooming across his face. Maybe everything
will really be all right.

And that's the moment Jasmine finds us. She leers at Ezra
before swinging her attention to me and making a kissy face.
"Oh my god, Lo, I love this for you!"

"I mean, your opinion doesn't really matter, but thanks?"

She taps her chin. "I just wish I could figure out who it's a
step down for."

Ezra goes still beside me, but I give Jasmine's arm a little pat
and coo sweetly, "As long as it's far away from you."

She balks, but we leave her behind to join Wash and Joon,

who're already holding beers for us.

"I see you survived Jasmine," Wash says, pushing a beer toward Ezra. He pulls his hand from mine to open it and tips the lip of the can against Wash's as our friend says, "Cheers, I guess?"

Ezra laughs, but it fades to nothing fast, and he doesn't take my hand again. The golden hope dims, and doubt creeps in. But I paste on a smile and accept a beer from Joon. It's just like setting up my tent that first time. At first it felt impossible, but every time will be easier. Everyone seeing Ezra and me together will be just like that. Right?

For a little while, that feels true. As the light softens from orange to pink, we hang with Wash, Joon, and Kat. But then Wash and Kat volunteer to go buy s'mores stuff, and Joon runs off with a soccer ball. And Ezra and I stand there, nursing beers, watching the party. The space between us feeling a bit . . . *sticky.*

It probably doesn't help that the bluster and rumble of Tully's voice has been a constant background effect. But suddenly, it gets louder. Through a gap in the crowd, I watch him yank one of the giant branches from the dry stack of wood and start shaking it over his head like a Neanderthal. Definitely one who hasn't yet discovered fire or volume control.

"Time to light it up!" he bellows, then mimes knocking the heads off a couple guys with his branch. Their laughs are obligatory, and it hits me that these are the same classmates who heralded his return at the start of summer. The shine has worn off. Tully, though, doesn't notice and starts throwing branches together for the bonfire.

Except he's absolute crap at it. I watch as he keeps carelessly knocking over the teepee structure others are trying to build, and he grabs the long matches to try lighting it himself. He fails again. And again. He swears. He blames the matches, and the wood, and whoever set up the wood. It's, frankly, uncomfortable to watch.

After what feels like an entire Greek tragedy's worth of a wholly incapable man trying to accomplish a menial task, I can't take another second of his terrible mediocrity.

I tell Ezra to hold my beer and march over to Tully and hold out my hand. "Give me that."

His laugh is just the wrong side of desperate. "Like you can do any better."

I shake my palm at him, and he slaps the box of matches into it. I break up a few of the smaller pieces of wood to act as kindling, rearrange some of the logs, and hold the flame at the perfect spot. It does take some work and a few tries, but the spark catches, and I've soon got the bonfire blazing. When I look up in triumph, Tully's face is dark and sour. Jasmine, I notice, has taken up the space next to him, while Meg is across the fire with Joon.

"You're really becoming quite the little pyromaniac, aren't you, Lola?" Jasmine says. She searches the crowd. "Speaking of disasters. Where's Ezra? He already ditch you?"

Tully blanches—"Whoa, what? You weren't kidding about that, Jas?"—at the same moment Ezra threads through the crowd and stops beside me. He lifts his chin at Tully in a terse sort of hello.

"Wait. Shit," Tully says, frowning between us. "For real? Boo-ben and Lola?"

"Come on, Tully, you know his name," Joon says from across the fire.

Tully puffs up his chest. "I don't need to know his name."

"Yeah," I say with a laugh, "because you're not in high school anymore."

"I'm the best thing to happen to any of you this summer."

I've got an acid reply burning the tip of my tongue. But I swallow it down, and it doesn't taste nearly as sour as expected. Instead, I stand back and watch as the light of the bonfire throws Tully into caricature. Overblown movements. Loud laughs. Obnoxious and desperate.

And pathetic.

A nineteen-year-old guy who graduated more than a year ago hanging out with a bunch of high schoolers. I always thought we were the same and that made us invincible. A cataclysm that you can't help but marvel at.

But Tully's a destructive force that has no idea of what he's leaving in his wake. A hurricane that spins and spins and spins, thinking all the people sucked up into his storm are having a blast, but he can't hear them screaming under the sound of his own keening laughter.

I spent the last two years in that chaotic storm. Rather hold on tight to Tully than feel alone, right? He filled a void I was terrified to face. That was what went wrong in France. It wasn't the food or the people or the stumbling attempts at the language. It was me. I was truly alone for the first time in my entire life and realized I was shit company.

My hand finds Ezra's, and I hold him tight. Tully watches, his face twisting into something mean. He nods at Ezra, his eyes flicking back to where our hands are clasped. "Have fun with Lola, man. I hope you don't mind that your girlfriend is a whore."

The word punches through us, ripples outward. Someone behind me gasps.

But Ezra. Ezra's gone rigid, his fingers tight. He yanks away from me, and for one awful second, I'm afraid he's going to leave me.

But instead he lunges toward Tully, his elbow cocking back.

And he lands a punch to Tully's jaw so hard it knocks his head back and his ass to the ground all at once.

THIRTY-ONE

"WHAT THE HELL, EZRA!"

He stands over Tully, breathing hard. His shoulders expand with each big suck of air; his arms are still stiff at his sides. It's . . . kind of unbearably hot. But also, dammit, I told him I could stand up for myself all those weeks ago at Tully's party. And now he's done it again. Chosen my response for me.

Tully is still on the ground, moaning, and Jasmine kneels to check on him. Her eyes are narrowed when she glares up at me. "Guess you were right, huh, Lola? You really can make anyone popular." Her eyes cut to Ezra, and I feel him go very, very still next to me.

Even through the spike of anger at Ezra for clearly not listening to me, Jasmine's words cut at me. Poke at my fear that Ezra still considers me part of *them*.

Finally, he looks at me. And it's devastating. Full of pain and reckoning. He doesn't say a word, but he walks away. I can feel their eyes on me—all my classmates, the girls who gossip about me and the boys who try to get me to flirt with them. They're all watching. But this time, I don't run. I pick up Ezra's beer where it fell to the ground and stride across the sand toward his retreating back.

He's standing at the edge of the firelight, and he won't quite look at me, which only makes me angrier. I shove his half-empty, sandy beer at him. "I told you I can stand up for myself."

His eyebrows crawl high. "He called you . . . *that*."

"Yeah, I should have been the one to punch him. I don't need you to defend my honor, Ezra. I've told you that before."

He scrubs a hand down his face and groans. "Can we talk?"

My eyes narrow. "Is that not what we're doing?"

"I mean . . ." Ezra nods farther down the beach.

Irritation and dread churn through my gut, but I nod and follow him. The space between us feels thick. He walks away from the light of the fire into the soft gray night and sits down on a long piece of driftwood. His knees are wide, and he leans over and cradles his face in his hands.

I'm not going to lie, a very big part of me wants to ignore this. Push away my anger at him and pretend everything is fine and force him to pay attention to me. But how can I when I know what I'm capable of now?

I sit down hard and tug at his hand to inspect his knuckles. "Are you hurt? Not that you don't deserve it for punching him, but still."

He sighs and shakes his head, eyes still on the sand at our feet.

"Are you jealous of Tully? Is that it?"

Ezra jerks his chin up, a crease between his eyebrows when he looks at me. "Jesus. No. I'm not . . ." He roughs a hand through his hair and lets loose a shaky laugh. "I already told you, I don't want to be friends with these people."

These people. Just like before. I thought he'd started to look at me differently, started to care about more than who I'd been, but I guess not. And also: "You didn't seem to mind that much when you were on Jasmine's boat or in Tully's pool house." Because, yeah, it hasn't escaped my attention that he was apparently cool with them *those* times.

Ezra groans. "I didn't want to go then either. But if we're together, it'll . . ."

"It'll be up to us to decide together who we hang out with, what we do," I finish for him. "And the fact that you refuse to believe that is just . . . it sucks, Ez."

He stares down at his hands again where they're pressed together between his spread knees. I watch his profile, the way he swallows hard, the hitch of his chest when he sucks in a ragged breath.

"Is this the part where you tell me it's not gonna work?" I say the words to the ocean and hope the waves snatch them up and drag them back out to sea. But next to me, Ezra stills. He nods.

"I can't do this." His voice is too full and breaks at the edges. And it breaks me too. He sits up taller and works his jaw back and forth, like he's gathering courage, then he looks up at me with such horrible heartbreak that I want to grab him to my chest and never let him go. He takes a breath and says, "All of this. You. Me. It doesn't work."

It is at this terribly inconvenient moment that I realize I'm in love.

Dammit, I'm in love and I don't know how I can ever consider any other guy when Ezra Reuben is a possibility.

"It can," I try. My voice is so much steadier than I feel.

But Ezra shakes his head again. "We work in a vacuum, Lola. But back in school . . . I . . . I can't suddenly start hanging out with all the popular people because one of them is my girlfriend—"

"But I'm *not* popular anymore."

His laugh is a burst of air. "Yeah, you are. You might not be friends with Jasmine anymore, but you're still *Lola Barnes*. You're still the person no one can take their eyes off of. And I just . . . it's not worth it. One of us has to change to fit in with the other, and either I'll come to resent it or you will."

He stands up and walks away without saying goodbye, leaving me with nothing but the wind and sand and sea for company. I sit there for a very long time, watching the waves ceaselessly batter the shore. The water always wins in the end, but it's expected to keep trying for ages, to never give up for even an instant, before it claims any victory.

It's not worth it.

I'm. Not. Worth it.

His words are a virus I can't kick. They invade every part of me and grow, shift, spread.

So after everything. After trying to work on myself to be a better friend. After shifting focus to learn to love myself. After searching for something that feels genuine, not only chasing a reaction. After all that, I'm still not worth it.

Because it's like Kat said. The idea of me is a lot of fun. But the reality is a car crash. It's a boat-burning, boy-stealing, France-failing disaster that's doomed to destroy everything in its path and flame out utterly alone.

Cool. Perfect.

Behind me, back at the bonfire, laughs and shrieks volley over each other, climb higher on the wind.

If those words are a virus . . . back there, my old life . . . maybe it's the antidote. Because I might have secretly been lonely, but I was too busy to care. And you know what? Having convictions sucks. Bettering yourself is hard.

And like everyone says, I'm not made for hard work.

So I stand up, and I leave all that shit behind to sit on a log and contemplate how much life sucks. In its place, I'll have a party.

"What's up, assholes!" I shout as I get closer to the crowd.

A few people cheer and hold up beers. A few people shake their heads at me. But like I give a shit.

Across the fire, Joon catches my eyes. But he looks away fast and pulls out his phone. Nice. Call your boyfriend and gossip about how you all knew Lola couldn't really change in the end.

I grab a beer and a backup beer, but I never get a chance to crack open even one because Tully barrels into me and hoists me up high. He called me a whore like twenty minutes ago, but it's already forgotten. So I should forget it too. He spins me round and round, hollering as he goes. Until we're both so dizzy we tip straight into the sand and hit with a thud. But he's cackling with laughter, so I do too. Louder, like I mean it. Maybe in a second I will.

A hand extends, and I let it pull me up, but recoil. Meg's got me, and there's a frown digging a crevasse between her eyebrows. She's got great eyebrows like Corinne. But it's not like I'll be friends with Corinne after this summer. They all got to see the real me. And the real me sucks.

"Lola, please," Meg says, voice tight.

My heart twists, but I laugh in her face.

"Don't do this," she tries again.

Yeah, where was this concern when I was in France, when I came home and she spent six months ignoring me or letting Jasmine string me along.

"No thanks, Meg. I'm not here for your sudden discovery of a spine."

She blinks fast, but doesn't let go. "Come on, Lola. You don't want to do this."

"Do what?" Tully bellows, slinging a heavy arm around my shoulders. "Have fun?"

"Hell yeah, have fun!" I shout, tugging away from Meg and leaning into Tully instead. "How should we make these losers have fun?"

We spin again, and the faces watching us are a blur. But we'll suck them into our orbit soon enough. Tully roars and points at the fire.

"Let's jump."

My stomach tries to jump first. Like, out of my body.

"Oh shit," someone in the crowd whistles.

"Tully, that—" I try. My tongue sticks to the roof of my mouth.

He's got my arm tight in his giant paw and he drags me closer to the fire. I tug back, the heat of the flames licking at my face and sparking into the night sky. The bonfire has burned down but it still leaps as tall as my hips, reflects in Tully's eyes when he looks at me.

"Holy shit, this is gonna be epic," he yells.

All around us, a few people cheer. But more are watching open-mouthed, phones out to capture the disaster.

"Tully, no," I say.

But he's already backed up, a manic grin stretching his

mouth. He grunts and takes off, running by me with such force I feel the rush of wind in the ends of my hair. He leaps, stretches out, reaches across, strains to make it over the fire . . .

And crashes to the sand and rolls, just on the other side of safety.

Fear and adrenaline cascade from my scalp down to my soles. Tully jumps to his feet and absolutely screams with excitement.

His eyes find mine. "Do it, Lo! Do it!"

My feet shuffle back against the sand. The same distance Tully was. My heart is a deep, terrible boom in my chest, until it's all I hear.

It says *turn around*. It says *go home*.

It says *prove everyone wrong*.

"Dammit, Lo! Fucking do it!"

No.

"No," I mutter. Then again, louder, "No."

He growls.

I shake my head, harder, and it shakes loose this awful sensation, this need to be watched simply to be watched. Around me, phones are out, waiting. To see me fail. Because they don't care either way, they only want to be entertained.

"No," I shout back again. "It's stupid and dangerous. I'm not doing it."

He kicks the sand, a whiny kid not getting his way.

But I turn away. And see her, at the top of the stairs, a forgotten bag of marshmallows at her feet.

Kat.

She holds out her hand to me, and even though she's far away, it's a lifeline. I climb the steps to meet her and let her wrap me in her arms.

"Can you take me home?"

"Of course, Lo."

THIRTY-TWO

BEFORE KAT EVEN HAS THE passenger door open, someone shouts my name.

Tully comes huffing up the stairs, swinging his head to search for me. I close my eyes for a long second.

"Want me to tell him to fuck off?" Kat asks.

"Give me a minute."

I meet him at the top of the stairs. He leans against the post and pouts. It's honestly mind-boggling that I used to feel any affection for this poor, sad little rich boy; all I feel now is sorry for him.

"Why didn't you jump over the fire with me?" he asks, his voice sulky.

"Because it was dangerous and only for attention."

He lets out a big, blustery sigh, but winces and prods his jaw where Ezra landed that—let's be honest here, *iconic*—punch.

I sigh loudly and ask, "How's the face, Tulls?"

"That bastard hit me!" He grumbles like he still can't believe anyone called him on his shit. Oh, Tully.

"You called me a whore."

Tully grumps. "You know I didn't mean it."

"I mean, that's sort of the point. You still said it even if you didn't mean it."

"Why don't you want to hang out anymore?" Tully whines. "I thought I'd show up this summer and it'd be like it used to be. You know, you and me."

I blink at that. Does he . . . truly not remember what happened last time it was him and me? "Um, because you were cheating on your girlfriend and we both got suspended for fighting."

His face collapses in on itself, and he looks remarkably like my nephew when he's about to cry. "Yeah, but I wanted to break up with her anyway. And the food fight was funny!"

"It wasn't funny for me, Tully. I was crucified."

Tully looks at the ground. "I guess I didn't realize."

"You should have. You should have stood up for me, but you didn't." And yeah, I realize when I say it that I snapped at Ezra for doing basically that. Don't ask me to be consistent, I'm still learning how this whole "being a good person" thing works. I sigh and look at Tully. "People listen to you, Tulls. Maybe try thinking about how you use your voice."

Tully rolls his eyes with his whole body. "Ugh, Lo, you sound like my parents." He affects his mom's nasally tones. "'You have to go to college, Tully. You can't live in the pool house and expect us to finance your life, Tully.' It's so unfair."

His words are so petulant, so wrong-headed, that I start pacing. "That's such bullshit! I don't want to drift through life being handed everything and appreciating nothing."

Tully snorts. "Ugh, yeah, you do. Face it, Lola. We're alike, you and I."

"I don't want to be," I say quietly.

"Why fight it?" Tully says with a shrug. "This is who we are. All those people back at the beach, they're talking about us. They'll never forget us."

I shake my head, the realization of how Tully views his existence sitting uncomfortable against my skin. He'll be a miserable adult. Always straining for the limelight, but never for the right reasons. It hits me that it's not only that he faced no consequences for what we did a year ago. It's that he doesn't even comprehend that he should feel regret or guilt. I almost envy his total lack of reflection, but I don't want to live like that. I couldn't. Not now.

"No, Tully," I say, backing up a step. "No, I don't want that. I . . . Bye, Tulls."

I walk away from him and don't look back.

I'm still trying to sift through the wreckage of this evening when Kat pulls us into the circular drive in front of our house. Headlights swing across the back of our car, and my heart skips for a second with wild hope that it's Ezra.

But it's Wash and Joon, and anger flares in my belly that I was hoping for something—someone—else.

We climb out of our cars and sort of drift toward the bench hidden under the weeping branches of the California pepper tree at the corner of the house. I collapse onto one end, Kat onto the other, and the boys stand in front of us. Garden lights dot the edges of the driveway and front of the house, casting long shadows and turning expressions monstrous.

Or maybe that's just me. I certainly feel like a monster.

Joon eyes me warily, and disappointment hisses through me. "I'm sorry if you're upset I called them," he starts, nodding toward Wash and Kat, "but it seemed like . . ."

A sharp laugh scores my throat. "Like I was going off the rails? Yeah."

"What happened, Lola?" Kat asks. "It seemed like things were going okay when we left."

A shrug pulls at my shoulders, and part of me—okay, a big part—wants to say something shitty and pretend I don't care. But . . . but I do. I do care, and I want whatever I've been building with Wash and Joon and repairing with Kat to be constructed on a real foundation.

"Ezra broke up with me, even though now that I say it I guess we were never really, officially, like . . . together."

My voice fades and my throat grows hot.

"You were definitely together," Joon says fast. "Last time I saw him, I actually told him to shut up he was talking about you so much."

I have to swipe at my eyes with the back of my hand. "Really?"

"Really, love."

That helps to hear, except in all the ways it doesn't. But still, all these damn feelings. I wish I could pick a lane, instead of veering wildly between this aching sadness it's over and burning anger at how it all went down.

"Yeah, well," I say, voice thick. "Apparently it wasn't worth it."

Kat scoots closer and gently pulls my hand into her lap. "Is that what he said?"

I press my lips together and nod. "And that sucks, because I really like him! Like, a scary amount! And all he could see was the old version of me. And he said that wasn't worth it."

Wash shares a look with Joon and says, "I don't think it's you."

"I mean," I grind out, "it definitely is."

"Then that's his problem. Your job is to feel happy and comfortable with yourself, and others will accept that if they're worth your time."

Joon adds, "And if not, want me to slap him?"

I laugh thickly. "Yes. Yes, that's what I want." I pause, then say, "No, don't. If anyone's going to slap Ezra, it's me. Just as soon as I'm done crying over him."

THIRTY-THREE

THERE'S AN OLD ENGLISH PROVERB that says, the best way to get over a boy is a mani-pedi.

And if there isn't, there should be.

"Hi, Liz!" I raise my hand in hello as I enter the sunshiny salon tucked into a corner of the club's main building. My favorite nail tech is standing beside another chair, talking to a newer tech working on someone's feet. Liz turns when she hears my voice and smiles, but the grin slides from my face.

Jasmine is sitting in the massage chair.

I'm reminded of another old proverb: bitches get stitches. But I settle for a snarl and take the seat Liz has prepared. Somehow, I resist the urge to grab Jasmine's bottle of polish and dump it on her ridiculous Birkin bag (a hand-me-down from her mom, but still . . . not even my mom has a Birkin).

"I'm here for you, if you want to talk about Ezra breaking up with you in public," Jasmine says, her voice sickly sweet. She blinks at me, taking in my HLAG tee, still-wet hair, and worn-in Birkenstocks—I didn't even throw on my rose-gold pair, just plain old brown. "At least you seem to be taking it well, sweetie."

I grace her with my sharpest smile. "That's so sweet of you, Jas. But I'd literally rather die than talk to you ever again."

Liz pauses where she's trimming my nails, but dips her head and ignores us. Okay, just get through it. Get a pedicure and leave. Jasmine wants the reaction. The best thing I can do is not rise to it.

After a few tense minutes, Liz switches to my left foot, and Jasmine dips her feet into paraffin booties. I mean, it's a pedicure, but it's also basically torture. Yet the thing is, I'm going to have to get through it for the next year. Maybe longer, since our families circulate in the same South Bay society.

The nail tech sitting in front of Jasmine is massaging a pungent peppermint scrub into her legs, and Liz is finishing up on my heels. She squirts oil into her palms and starts kneading my feet and ankles. I ignore Jasmine and sit back, scrolling quickly through the last photos I have with Ezra and pausing instead on the shots from the Alamere Falls hike. The annual Hike Like a Family event is in just a few days, and I'm a mix of excited and terrified to see Mom out on the trail.

"I bet he'll start dating Jessica again," Jasmine says, interrupting my successful ignoring tactics and trying for a new angle to piss me the hell off. "She's *super* pretty. Oh, sorry, you probably don't want to—"

"I know it was you."

"What are you talking about?" Jasmine's words are dismissive, but fear jolts in her eyes.

I can see Liz sharing a look with the other nail tech, but I don't care. Jasmine wanted to poke at me, get the reaction so she can feel . . . I don't know, vindicated? Superior? A shock of emotion in her otherwise empty existence?

"The account," I say, letting my voice grow sharp and clear. "It was you."

She blinks fast, and I can't miss the way she swallows hard. I let her dangle there for a second, feel a perverse sort of power in the way her eyes dart, searching for a way out. Ha! Too late, sweetheart.

"It was a really shitty thing to do to someone you called a friend."

Her nostrils flare and her smile is thin when she says, voice tilted low, "I was only giving people an outlet for what they were already saying. You can hardly blame me for your choices."

And there it is. The truth. It whistles through me, blowing out any last bit of nostalgia I felt for this girl. Because it confirms what I think I've known all along—our secrets were never that. They were ammunition to use at a later date.

Before I do anything else, I lean down toward Liz. "This is on my parents' account, right?" When she nods, I grab two twenties floating in the bottom of my bag and make sure she sees me put them on the little table attached to my chair.

Pretty sure this pedicure is over.

I stand up, my oiled feet slick against the wood floors, and stare down at Jasmine. She's pinned to her seat like a bug. "You took intimate photos of me without my knowledge and put them online."

The woman next to Jasmine gasps and looks at her with big eyes.

"They weren't intimate, Lola. Don't be dramatic."

"It was me making out with a guy. His hands were on my butt. I was straddling him on a bench. I was sixteen, but you took several photos. You made an Insta account specifically so people could shame me."

The woman grabs her purse onto her lap, like Jasmine might also be into a little light larceny.

"Will you be quiet," Jasmine hisses.

"No, I won't be quiet," I say, letting my voice carry. "I want you to hear this, Jasmine. I regret what happened, and I deserved to face repercussions because of it, but you made sure I could never recover. You made sure that what happened was all on me, never on him. I was the slut, the ho, and even though he was older than me, he was the poor dumb guy I seduced. You did that. You should be ashamed of yourself."

"Me? That's so typical, Lola. Trying to pretend everyone else is to blame—"

"Oh, I accept the blame for what happened. No. You should be ashamed of yourself because you're a two-faced asshole who'll toss a decade of friendship out the window if it suits you. You're not a good friend, Jasmine LeGrange, and you sure as shit aren't mine anymore."

And then I grab her bright orange nail polish and smear the wand down her cheek, leaving a garish streak. Because, come on, I might be maturing, but I'm not dead.

"See you at school," I call back to her on my way out the door.

THIRTY-FOUR

"WHAT DO YOU MEAN, YOU can't come?"

Dad heaves a sigh that makes his broad shoulders sag. Early morning sunlight streams through my window, and I'm still in my pajamas, but Dad's fully dressed and is already carrying his old JanSport backpack even though Mom has tried for years to get him to upgrade to literally anything else. He crosses my room and kisses the top of my head.

"I know, and I'm sorry. Joss said the store POS system went down last night, and I'm the one who built it for them, so I've got to fix it. But if I go now, I may be able to be back in time to catch you guys on your hike."

I nod into his shoulders, dragging in the Dad Smell of sharp soap and this strange tinge of metal and wires that seems to follow him everywhere. Probably because he's always elbow deep in his second-favorite (after bird-watching) retirement hobby of taking apart old electrical equipment. Honestly, I don't know why I was scared of dating a major nerd when I come from one.

Dad pulls back and tucks hair behind my ear. "I'm really proud of all you've done this summer, my girl. I hope you know that."

A smile tugs at the corner of my mouth. "Maybe hold that pride until I successfully get Mom back in one piece."

"She's capable of more than you know. She has five daughters, after all."

Dad leaves, and I finish getting ready for Hike Like a Family, excitement kindling in my stomach. Maybe this is just the beginning; maybe I can convince them we should all start hiking together. It makes me giggle to think of it. Joss and Edie trying to wrangle the triplets, going on about "wanting to give them the freedom to express themselves" while the kids shriek and whack at trees like there's a personal vendetta involved. Lindy and Will with matching binoculars and pocket bird guides. Marnie coming prepped with a bunch of nature quotes from literature, and Kat choosing her outfit based on what's trending with the search #outdoorsy.

But more than anything, I want to share this sense of discovery and freedom with them.

I'm twisting the cap closed on the second water bottle to fit in my day pack when Kat calls down the hall for me. She asked yesterday if she could come with us, and it thrilled me way more than I want to admit.

But at this point, I'll just be thrilled if we all get there in time.

We're supposed to be at the trailhead in a little over an hour, and according to the text I got from Mom, we'll have to pick her up at the club on the way. Because nothing says "I'm ready to hike!" like a free Bloody Mary bar.

When I make it to Kat's room, it's to find her still in her pajama bottoms. She slumps onto her bed. "I don't know what to wear."

She's got a heap of leggings at her feet and a pile of tops behind her, including some cable knit and flannel even though it is literally August. It probably doesn't help that I definitely stole her favorite maroon leggings from the wash and am currently wearing them. Her hair's in an artfully messy fishtail braid that hangs over one shoulder and she's in a tie-dyed sports bra. I dig up a pair of black leggings and a plain white tee and hand them over.

"It's just hiking. The bears don't care what you're wearing."

Kat's mouth drops open. "Oh my god, are there going to be bears?"

"Don't worry, I'll push Mom at them."

My limbs feel light and bubbly, my heart full. Kat fiddles with her clothes and packs my mini Fjallraven with cans of club soda and totally inappropriate snacks. I'm talking a frozen burrito and a pack of gummy worms inappropriate. She finishes it all off with a handful of Taco Bell fire sauce packets. I make a mental note to teach her some survival skills at a later date.

She checks her reflection in the full-length mirror between the kitchen and dining room. "Do I really look okay?" She hooks her thumbs into the straps of the borrowed backpack and strikes a couple of poses.

"If anyone gives you shit, I'll make them my sworn enemy."

Kat pulls a face. "Lo, you already have like fifteen sworn enemies."

"I'm always accepting more applications."

We joke like normal as we climb into the car to go pick up Mom. For the first time in a while, I feel like things are going to be okay.

That's when Kat says, "Mom's not answering my texts."

I swing into the club driveway and pull up into the valet line but ignore the dude in the black vest. "Seriously?"

"Oh, wait," Kat adds, face toward her phone. "No, she says to come around to the patio. They just got their drinks."

"We're supposed to be there in a half hour!"

Kat shrugs and climbs out of the car.

Out on the shaded back patio, Mom sits at a table with Meg's mom and Susanna of the botched nose job. There's a flute brimming with mimosa before each of them.

"Mom!" She takes a sip before looking up at me. "We've got to go!"

"You just got here, darling!" She signals for Paolo to pull up a chair, but I shake my head at him. Mom takes another long drink and flutters a sigh. "You see the lengths I go," she says to the other women. Both nod in sympathy.

Mom takes another sip of her drink before finally—finally—gathering her things. She's in leopard-print leggings, a tight white tank top with "Dior" written along the chest in rhinestones, and a "utilitarian chic" green jacket with "Dior" brushed across the back in what looks like white paint. So there's that.

"Don't rush me, Lola," she admonishes when I try to grab her Armani clutch. She stops to speak to four other ladies on the way across the patio, and there's a scream locked in my throat that's so loud I'd probably trigger an earthquake if I let it loose.

"Don't you have a backpack?" I ask, assessing the clutch. She can't even fit a frozen burrito in there.

Mom waves at someone else. "Don't be silly! That'd ruin the lines of my jacket. I bought this outfit specially for today, you know."

I've got her to the gate that leads around the side of the club to the valet line. I can't risk her actually walking through the club or she'll decide she needs to nip in for another quick mani-pedi and abandon us again. "Do you have any water?" I ask.

"That's what the mimosas were for! I'm full of vitamins and minerals and ready for your little hike," she says, patting my cheek in a way that is surely justification for murder.

Okay, whatever. I hustle around to the car and jump in. Mom is not in a hurry. My phone says we've got twenty minutes to get to the trailhead that is twenty-five minutes away. Cool. Great.

I roll down the window. "Mom! Come on!"

"Don't rush me!"

I grip the steering wheel, and it somehow doesn't turn to ash in my hands.

Mom finally slides into the front seat after a bit of negotiation with Kat and a reminder that she practically got hip dysplasia carrying us to term. "I don't know why you're so upset, Lola. They'll wait for us."

My foot presses down on the accelerator, and we go careening out of the parking lot. "They shouldn't have to wait for us, Mom."

Mom readjusts all my settings on the AC, radio, and seating position before saying, "I'm your mother, Lola. They can wait."

Our car barrels down the freeway and nerves ping through me. Mom's in a mood. And when that happens, there's only one way to go from here. And it sure as shit isn't up.

We come screaming into the parking lot only three minutes late. According to Mom, my driving has taken fifteen years off her life. Promises, promises.

We're not the only ones running late, though. Standing a bit apart from the other families, Corinne leans against the back of her car with her eyes on the road and her phone in her hands. Without a word, Kat and I go stand with her.

"He said last night he had to change his flight because of

work stuff," she says, watching the traffic for her dad.

"He'll be here," I tell her, squeezing her shoulder.

We wait ten minutes, fifteen. Corinne drops her chin and stares at where her hands are worrying her phone from one palm to the other. No one has texted or called.

"Come on," she finally says, defeat threading through her voice. "He's not coming."

"We can wait longer," Kat says softly. "I know how much this means to you."

Corinne stands up and pulls her backpack on. "No, I'm not waiting any more for him. If he couldn't figure out how to be here on time, that's on him."

Together, we walk over to where Georgia chats with the other parents. She's offering thermoses of coffee from the back of her orange bus and special Hike Like a Family T-shirts. Corinne motions for her, and Georgia breaks away. Nearby, Mom watches Corinne and grumps. "You're fine waiting for her dad, but didn't think anyone should wait for me."

"Oh my god," Kat snaps. "Stop it, Mom."

Mom crosses her arms over her chest, and a tiny part of me hopes she scratches herself on those rhinestones. I suck in a long breath and remind myself she's out of her element here. (Her element being the club or the medical spa she calls "a retreat" in Carmel.) I mean, at least she's not Beth's parents. They showed up wearing tall brown socks, khaki-colored brimmed hats that have some sort of . . . flap? . . . at the back, and trekking poles.

It should be reiterated, we're doing a three-mile hike today. In the forest. With maybe fifty feet of gain. This isn't going to be a Chris McCandless situation. It's suddenly very obvious that eagerness runs in Beth's family.

Beth catches my eye and rolls hers, and it pulls a smile onto my face.

Georgia claps for our attention, and we round up. I tug on Corinne's wrist. "Hey, come hike with us. It'll be all hands on deck to keep Mom from walking over the side of a cliff on accident." Her brown eyes are drawn with sadness, but my pleading makes her grin, and after a moment she nods.

"Thank you all for coming today!" Georgia says. "This is always a special day for our crew, a chance to show you what we've come to love about this program."

Mei's dads clap and cheer, and her cheeks glow pink. They're both wearing the new Hike Like a Family T-shirts, which are the original logo, but with a second pair of hiking boots hanging off the corner of the *L*.

God, parents are the worst. And by the worst, I mean, sometimes the best?

"As you all know, we're one week away from our big hike! This crew has come so far, and I can't wait to share some of what they can do with you." She pauses. "That means you're all hitting the fifty-miler with us, right?"

A few of the parents laugh politely. Mom leans closer to me and declares in a voice that is not even in the same zip code as a whisper, "I won't be doing that."

I grimace. "Yes, Mom, we all know."

Georgia catches my eye and smiles, and I feel a peculiar sort of kinship with her. No one tell Will. She hands out water to anyone who needs it—Mom asks if she has sparkling and declines still when Georgia doesn't whip out a SodaStream for her gaseous water needs—and we head out on the trail.

It's slower going than I've become used to. Even with Tavi's parents in the lead (and they look the sort whose family traditions include running 5Ks before Thanksgiving) our pace is best described as ambling. Beth's mom keeps pausing to readjust her hiking poles, and Mei's dads are documenting every second with their phones. Priya's little brother keeps asking her to identify each plant, and I can hear the annoyance in her voice as she repeats, "I don't know." Her parents are behind already splitting granola bars even though I'm fairly sure I could still spot the cars in the parking lot if I squint through the trees.

And behind all that, we're bringing up the rear. I'm doing my best to stick with Mom even though Kat and Corinne are right behind us, laughing with the general joy and optimism of someone not saddled with the human equivalent of an HR complaint. Mom's noticed this special care and is eternally grateful. Oh, wait. Sorry. I mean she's sighing dramatically every few steps.

"There better be something spectacular at the end of this," she grumps.

I steady my breath and definitely don't imagine tying her to a tree and leaving. "Don't you think this is pretty? Look at those wildflowers!"

Trees are offering wonderful shade along the wide dirt trail as we curve around the rocky outcroppings of a hill, and we're surrounded by pale blue and delicate white flowers that cluster in the deep shade. Beyond, in a sunlit meadow, the last of the summer's poppies glow orange. Mom looks at all of this and shrugs.

"Do you remember those floral sculptures at the resort in Mexico? Now *that* was pretty."

Breathe. Breathe. "Yeah, that was pretty! Or that exhibit on the language of flowers Marnie dragged us all to a few years ago. Remember how interesting that was?"

"Your father bought me a bouquet of roses every day for a month after Invigor had their IPO," she says with a faraway smile. "Did you pack me any water? I'm thirsty."

Up ahead, Georgia is slowly making her way to each group of parents, talking to all of them, and I kind of can't wait for her to come chat with us. I wonder what she'll say about me? I wonder what Mom will think? I glance behind to see Kat and Corinne trailing farther behind and try to force some perspective. I mean, Mom did show up, after all. And yeah, she seems to be hating every second and just sucked down half my water even though I'd been under the impression that she was chock full of mimosa power, but she did the work of being here.

I sling my arm around her and squeeze her tight. "Thanks for coming, Mom."

She pats my arm but angles her cheek away from me. "Of course. But can you please not hug me? I'm already sweaty enough. Are you wearing that prescription deodorant I got you?"

Muuuuuuuurder.

"I'm going to go see what Kat and Corinne are doing." I turn away from Mom and realize I can't even spot them anymore. I jog down the trail toward a big bend hidden by craggy gray boulders. Jeez, is Kat really hiking that slowly? I mean, it's nice of Corinne to stick with her, but—

I round the corner and find them.

Find them kissing.

Like, full-on making out. My twin sister and my best friend. Kissing. When I am fairly positive only one of them likes girls, but I guess not? And, like, if my twin liked girls, why wouldn't she tell me? Why wouldn't we celebrate that together?

I drop my water bottle in shock, and they jump apart.

"Shit. Lola," Corinne says.

Kat is a statue, her eyes wide and staring.

"Why didn't— I mean, you both—"

My heart thunders in my chest, cracks against my ribs painfully. My fingers tingle at the ends, like all oxygen is being sucked from my blood. And I hate that I feel this. Hate that I can't just be happy for two people I love finding each other. But all I see is betrayal. All I feel is hurt and left out, because dammit, I don't want to be the third wheel! I don't want to be second choice. I'm always the second choice. I've never, ever been worth it enough for anyone to choose me. Not Tully, not Jasmine, not Ezra. And now not Corinne.

"You're supposed to be my friend," I snap at Corinne.

Her eyebrows scrunch together. "I still can be, right?"

"Were you pretending to be friends with me?"

"Lola, we truly didn't mean—" Corinne starts, holding a hand out toward me.

She said *we*. Is that why Kat wanted to come today? To be closer to Corinne even though she couldn't tell me—her sister—that she's gay?

"Stop," I shout. "How could you do this to me?"

Corinne's eyes squeeze shut, but Kat roars back to life. She lifts her chin at me and glares. She stomps closer and jams her finger toward my chest. "Holy shit, this isn't about you, Lola. My god, you can't let me have this one single fucking thing without trying to steal it from me."

We face off, inverse images of each other like we always have been. Kat's soft where I'm sharp, golden where I'm cool, smiling while I'm scowling. But now I can tell she matches every harsh angle of my sneer and glare. I nearly stumble back a step in the face of it, but make myself lean forward, press my sternum into her poking finger.

"I'm going to go," Corinne says softly.

Kat's eyes are still on me when she says to Corinne, "I'm sorry about her."

Corinne sighs. "Come on, Kat. I—"

"I'll find you later," Kat cuts her off. She doesn't add *after I bury the body*, but it's implied. Well, not if I murder her first. "You're so selfish!"

"You're the one who's stealing my friend! And after you made such a big damn deal about staying away from *your* friends."

Kat rolls her eyes. "Jesus, she's not a purse, Lola. She can be two different things to us if that's what she wants."

"Oh my god!" The words tear out of me, and they taste horribly bitter. But it's like this explosion inside me, and it's got to go somewhere. So I direct all my hatred at my sister. "Stop trying to consider every single thing I say in the worst possible way. Why do you do that? You act like I'd drop Ezra if Jasmine asked and assume it's all my fault that shit went wrong in France. It sucks!"

Kat laughs at me. "And there it is, blaming everything on France again. You know what an amazing opportunity it was? And like always, you completely squandered it."

"No one would talk to me. No one wanted to be my friend. Do you have any idea how many times I asked people to go shopping or go get coffee or, god, even study together? I was lonely and homesick and all I wanted was you there with me, but every time I tried talking to you, you were busy or going on about people I barely knew. So yeah, I came home acting like a shit because I was humiliated. There. Is that what you wanted to hear? I was a failure."

It all pours out of me, and I swipe away angry tears. Kat's features crumple; she steps closer. But at that moment somewhere in the forest, someone shrieks.

THIRTY-FIVE

MOM IS SPLAYED OUT ON the ground like roadkill.

I run to her side and kneel next to her. The other girls and their families are gathered around in a tight circle, which is absolutely the last thing that should be happening. When Mom is truly upset or hurt, she wants to be left alone. All these people staring at her will only make it worse. "Hey, guys, can we have a little space?"

Everyone backs up a step, but continues to stare. And I still can't tell how Mom's hurt. I mean, everything seems to be attached and at the normal angles.

"Julia, are you okay?" Georgia asks, squatting down next to me.

Mom pushes up to her elbows and moans like she's getting a

leg amputated sans drugs. "No, I am not okay. I think I twisted my ankle on that horrible tree root. You shouldn't have dragged us on this awful hike that is not suited to our abilities!"

Her cheeks are red, but probably more from humiliation than exertion. She juts her lower lip. "And now everyone is looking at me."

Everyone turns away and pretends to be super interested in the trees.

I hand Mom more water. "You should see the trail we did to Alamere Falls!" I'm trying to distract her. She's not here for it.

"I don't care about your other hikes, Lola. I'm hurt and you're not even checking on me."

I bite back every rude thing I want to shout.

"Mom, Lola?" Kat says quietly behind us. "Can I help?"

I twist to look up at her and set my mouth in a hard line. She shouldn't even be here. Mom wouldn't have even gotten hurt if I hadn't run back to see where the hell Kat had disappeared to. "You can't." I turn back to Mom and try to put on my most gentle voice as I ask to see her leg. She's got a scrape on her shin, but her ankle isn't swollen, and she doesn't flinch when I lightly press on it.

"I'll get my first aid kit," Georgia says, swinging her backpack off one shoulder. "We'll have you good as new and enjoying the hike in no time, Julia."

Mom tugs her ankle away from me and crosses her arms. "No, go on without me. I'm obviously a drag on everyone else."

The other parents make noise about her not being a drag, and that perks Mom up a bit.

Until Beth's mom tries to help by offering her the hiking poles—"since you didn't come prepared," she says—and Mom's mood darkens like a lunar eclipse.

"You're right, I'm not prepared. I'm holding everyone back. Just leave me."

A great, weary sigh blows out of my nose. "Come on, Mom. I'll go back with you."

"I can," Kat attempts.

I ignore her and help Mom to her feet. She's suddenly favoring the wrong ankle and I earn a lifetime pass to commit a TBD major crime by not pointing it out.

Behind me, Kat calls my name.

I keep walking.

Mom and I slowly hobble back to the cars, and she moans and groans nearly all the way home until we pass a Starbucks and she requests a blended iced coffee with three pumps of sugar-free vanilla, whipped cream, and chocolate sprinkles.

It's very similar to Kat's order. I push all thought of my sister aside. Maybe she can totally replace me in HLAG and tell me none of those girls like me either.

Instead, I focus on Mom. She's slurping up her drink and staring out the window. "I was really looking forward to doing that hike with you," I say to her.

She swallows. "Oh, there'll be others."

My fingers tighten against the steering wheel. "No, there won't be. This was important to me, and I wish you would have kept going."

Mom sighs and plays with the zipper on her jacket. "I was very uncomfortable. I didn't grow up hiking, you know. Your grandparents were more about hot tubs and golf courses, so this"—she waves her hand out the window; I note that we're passing the manicured entrance to a gated community—"it makes me nervous."

"It's the outdoors, Mom, not a colonoscopy."

"Why would you bring up my colonoscopy?"

"What I mean is," I say, using every last bit of calm I possess, "I wanted to share this with you today, because I actually really love it. Like, hiking and nature and stuff. And I love you, so I thought . . ." My voice fades.

Mom, I realize, is a lot like Tully. She's lived a lot of her life without real consequence. I know she worked hard before we were born, and she was the one supporting the family before Dad made it in tech. Yet all I've ever known is the woman she is now.

But I guess like Dad said, she has raised five daughters, and we're not so bad. Objectively, I'm the worst of us, and even I am coming around, so I need to give her some credit. I've spent years pressing Mom's buttons since I knew that's how I'd get attention, but I don't want to do that anymore.

And even though this hike didn't go exactly to plan, she *was* there. My mind drifts to Corinne, waiting for her dad to show up, and my heart squeezes. And it's not like Mom was the entire reason today didn't go to plan. I'm livid at Kat for not just *talking* to me. I would have supported her coming out! I mean, jeez, we were flower girls in Joss's wedding to Edie!

Mom sighs loudly, pulling my attention back to her. "I don't understand what you like about hiking," she says, staring out the window.

"Do you have to? Can't you just be happy for me?"

She doesn't have a response to that.

It rustles through me, disappointment that she's unwilling to try to understand what this summer meant to me. Maybe she never will. And I have to be okay with that. I pull into the driveway and help Mom to her room to lie down, my mind whirring. She's difficult and she's an agent of chaos, but so am I sometimes.

I shut her bedroom door and lean against it, the house entirely too big and quiet. And in that silence, all I can think of is my sister. What if that was it? The final break?

All I know is, I'm terrified to find out. I walk right back out of the house. My hands shake when I wrench my car door open, but I start the engine and take off. I drive until I don't know where I am, which, as we've established, doesn't take much. I pull over into a dark, empty parking lot hours later and call, of all people, Georgia.

THIRTY-SIX

PERHAPS THE MOST SHOCKING REVELATION about this entire night is that Georgia doesn't live at a campground. Following the voice on my turn-by-turn directions, I take a right into a little neighborhood of bungalows southwest of San Jose.

Georgia's cottage is a confection of white stucco and red tiles, with a Creamsicle-orange front door and a massive eucalyptus tree framing the front yard. Huh.

My stomach churns so violently, I'm afraid I may be sick all over her cute front porch, but she swings the door open, and the sight of her looking so normal soothes me the tiniest bit. She's in a HLAG tee and a pair of yellow pajama pants covered in daisies, her thick hair piled into a bun and the wisps held back by a stretchy black headband.

She takes one look at me and opens the door wider. "Come on in, Lola."

"Thank you. I'm sorry."

"Don't apologize for needing help," she says back.

Her home is compact and sunny, with a place for every little thing. It reminds me a lot of her VW bus, like a very organized citrus grove. "So I definitely thought you lived in your van."

Georgia smiles and disappears behind the half wall separating her living room from her small kitchen. She turns on an electric kettle and busies her hands scooping out loose leaf chamomile tea into infusers shaped like manatees. This is my life now, I guess. Reusable mana-teas. But also Georgia. I wonder how I got so lucky.

"I lived in the van while I was exploring the national parks." The water boils, and she pours us both a mug and leads me over to the living room. I sink back into a vintage-looking cream armchair backed with an embroidered sherbet orange pillow. "I'd had a bad breakup and lost my job all in the space of two months and everything felt so . . . empty. Being alone with my own thoughts helped me fill that void from within, you know?"

Honestly, I don't know if I know. But I think I want to.

"Are you saying I need to buy a van and live life on the road?"

"No, Lola," she says, but she's smiling. "I think you should at least finish high school first."

"When did you do it?"

"I was twenty-five," she says.

"God," I say with a grimace. "How old are you now?"

"Hey! I'm over here trying to give you sage advice. Don't give me shit about being old."

"Okay, granny, calm down. I won't keep you from *Murder, She Wrote*." I hide my grin by taking a sip of my chamomile tea.

She pulls her legs up under her and regards me. "Do you want to talk about whatever's going on? You were pretty vague when you called, despite all the screeching."

A weary sigh blusters past my lips, and I shrug. "I screwed up. Like, basically had the totally opposite reaction to something than I should have had and now I've got to figure out how to make it right, but I'm also still pretty upset?"

"Is this about . . . a boy?"

"Ugh, I wish. That'd be easier to sort out. No, it's about Kat."

"Ah," she says, nodding. "You know, being Will's little sister has taught me that having a sibling can be equal parts amazing and awful. Sometimes at the same time. It was actually him who bought me the van. He picked me up when I was also being very vague and screechy, though in my case, he literally picked me up off the floor of a dive bar in Oakland. He took me to an all-night diner and forced me to eat pancakes and sausage until I'd told him everything."

"God, what an asshole."

Georgia grins. "He was like that from the time I was little, always wanting to figure out people's problems. One time—" She breaks off and laughs at some memory. "One time he thought he'd help our neighbors figure out why their house alarm kept going off during the day and discovered the wife was having an affair."

"Gah! What happened?"

"They divorced and a decade later the husband actually gave Will the seed money he needed to start his company."

"I picture him, like, alphabetizing his picture books as a kid."

"Yeah, something like that."

I spin the mug around in my hands, my palms warm. "I'm hurt that Kat didn't think she could tell me something really big about her identity. It just . . . it feels like Kat doesn't have room in her life for me. It's lonely."

"You two fought. And if I've learned anything about you, I'm guessing you said some things you probably regret—"

A harsh laugh punches out of me.

"You know, not all siblings are close like I am with Will and you are with your sisters. If you take it for granted, it'll go away. Maybe you haven't worked at your relationship with Kat because you assumed it'd always be there, but that's never a guarantee."

The thought of Kat no longer being the most important thing in my life is a physical pain like losing a limb. I have to blink fast to keep fresh tears from coming.

Georgia must see the state of my emotions, because she adds quickly, "All that means is, if it's so important to you, you have to work at it like everything else. And if I've learned anything *else* about you this summer, it's that you're not afraid to work for what you want." She stands up and stretches. "Stay here tonight, sleep in. I'm meeting friends for a day hike tomorrow morning, but you can let yourself out when you wake up. Before you go home and apologize—really apologize—I want you to go clear your head in nature. You can't fill that hollowness in you with anybody or anything. It can only come from you."

She lets me borrow another HLAG tee, an old pair of athletic shorts, and a toothbrush before leading me to a tiny guest room filled with a double bed. I sink into the fluffy down comforter and am asleep before my head hits the pillow.

Warmth stripes my face.

The early afternoon sun is being shy today, scuttling behind clouds and flirting with the trees. When it does peek out, I lift my chin and let it wash over me.

This morning when I finally woke up, Georgia was long gone, but she'd left me a bagel on the counter and instructions for finding her toaster and more tea. I stayed in the borrowed clothes and also plucked a pair of low-top summer hiking boots I found near the door and replaced them with my gold lamé high-tops. I left a sticky note on the toe: *I'm going to want these back, but you can borrow them if you want. They'd look fantastic with your black jeans and oxblood moto jacket.* Georgia will definitely not appreciate my note, or the fact that I riffled through her closet before leaving.

Coming full circle—my god, look at me on this journey of

self-discovery—I drove back to that very first trail where Kat and I failed. The difference in my strength and stamina after just six weeks kind of blows my mind, and I find I'm thinking ahead . . . imagining new hikes to try, new places to adventure. Old Lola would gasp and slap me across the cheek so hard if she could see me right now.

Up ahead on the trail, a couple in regular sneakers with only one water bottle between them is standing at that confusing wooden sign. The fork in the trail that tripped us up before. I can hear the guy, trying to sound super confident that he knows the right way.

"It's this way," I volunteer, pointing down the well-trodden path.

"See?" the woman says. "I told you."

"Is it cool?" the guy asks. "The view from the top?"

The thing is, I have no idea. But I do know this: "It's worth it."

I leave them behind and continue down the path, letting the sensations wash over me and away. The rubbery sort of dull ache in my thighs and the heaviness of my breath. The beads of sweat along my hairline and the soreness in my shoulders. Finally, I pause at the edge of the trees and smile up at the ridge that I never had the confidence to face before.

Two months ago, I stood in this exact spot and wanted to cry. I wanted to blame anyone else for my predicament and take the easiest way out. Now I see the challenge and face it. I take a sip of water and start the climb. My thighs burn and my calves warm with the effort, but the only way forward is to put one foot in front of the other. The wind is dry and smells of sage, like herbs baking in the sun.

I push up, and up, and up until the top of the ridge comes into view and I crest the hill. A carefully stacked tower of stones—a cairn—perches at the highest point of the peak, and I add one minuscule pebble to the top.

The views stretch for miles, hills and trees and meadows. And there, at the very edge of it all, the blue smudge of the sea. If I close my eyes, I pretend I can hear it on the wind. I sit and take it all in, appreciate the chance I have to see these views and feel this world all around me.

After a handful of minutes, the couple appear at the top and high-five each other. Nerds. I brush dirt off my hands as they're trying to get the view in their selfie and offer to take a photo of them.

I stand at the top of the ridge for another a minute before heading back down. The ease of the downhill feels that much better because I know what it took to reach the top. Back in the woods, I amble down the trail for nearly a mile before I spot the perfect tree. It's standing a little apart from its friends, and when I peer up for the crown, it's head and shoulders above the others. I sit with my back to the warm bark and my legs stretched out.

Something Ezra said catches at my mind. That there's always hope. It still hurts to think about him, but those words are important. My eyes are closed, but I reach for my serpent ring and smooth it in a circle around my finger. It was my one good day in France, and weirdly enough, I was alone. It'd been sunny and warm for early October, and I'd struck out from the school toward Rouen to check out a monthly vintage market. I'd found this ring in a box jumbled with other old jewelry, and I'd even spoken entirely in French to buy it. The woman working the booth had this amazing blunt bob, not sleek but kind of messy and carefree, and I knew right then that I was going to chop off my hair. Later, I'd seen that same woman in a café and we'd chatted for a bit before she had to go. But it'd been one good day, and this ring reminds me of it. Maybe, sometimes, focusing on that one good day is enough to carry you through to the next one.

I feel oddly hopeful in this moment. For so long, I could only see the single second I was in, but now I don't feel so much adrift in time as rooted, with a past that I'm not afraid to examine and a future that holds hope. And a present that I appreciate. Birds call from the branches, and others respond from deeper into the trees. The leaves whisper to each other, the sound shivering down around me. It's simple and peaceful. I tip my head back against the tree and let my eyes drop closed.

I am one small blip in this wild, wonderful world. Why would I ever let anyone else determine who I am and what I want with this life of mine?

It's a long time later when I blink my eyes open and sigh a big breath out into the forest. I'd like to think the trees hear me and answer in their own way.

I know how I want to apologize to both my sister and my friend. And I know whatever grows between them has nothing to do with me. I can exist outside it, and that's okay. But I love them both, and I want them to be happy.

And I love me, and I want myself to be happy too. Happy long-term. The sort of happiness that can sustain and support all the big things about me—my voice and my emotions and my confidence. The sort of happiness that doesn't hinge on reactions. And I think—I hope—that I'm finding that.

Two roads diverged in a wood. And I chose the one that led to me.

THIRTY-SEVEN

OKAY, SO IT ISN'T UP to me what happens next for Kat and Corinne, but that doesn't mean I can't give them a little nudge along the way.

By the time I get back to my car, the sun is melting into that late-afternoon liquid gold that turns everything into the perfect Insta filter. And yeah, fine, I definitely take some selfies.

Once I get home, Kat is already in her room. I leave her be and shower before actually going to sleep early.

The next morning, I get up before anyone else and make coffee. I pad down the hallway and knock on Kat's door before cracking it open and leaving the coffee inside her room.

"I, uh, left you coffee there. I already put the hazelnut creamer in it. Can you come meet me in the old tree house?"

I take my own coffee and a fuzzy gray blanket from the back of the couch and slip across the patch of grass beyond the large deck. The dew is cool where it clings to my bare feet, and I breathe in the fresh morning. I'm not about to become, like, a morning person, but this doesn't suck.

Up in the tree house, I wrap my legs in the blanket and sip my coffee. It's a long time before Kat joins me, but the fact that she comes to talk is sunshine in my chest.

"I'm so sorry," I say as she sits cross-legged against the wooden boards framing the tree house. "How I acted on the hike was terrible and . . . and not who I am. Do you, uh, want to tell me about it?"

My sister stares down into her cup of coffee, and I can see her lips rolling together. She stays silent.

"Kat, I'm sorry I never told you how lonely I was in France. And I'm sorry that I expected you to make me feel better when I got home, but yeah. I did feel bad for myself. I mean, I wanted to be, like, so effing awesome at living abroad, but I wasn't and it just . . . it was hard. And it was harder to come home and realize you had stopped wanting to be around me."

"Because I was angry," Kat finally says. She looks up at me and sighs. "I was angry that you expected me to be your support while you were away, but offered nothing in return. And then you got home and tried pretending what went wrong overseas was everyone else's fault. I thought it was happening all over again with Ezra and with Hike Like a Girl, so that pissed me off too, and I think it kind of clouded my ability to see that you were working and changing."

She pauses, takes a sip of her coffee, and I stay silent.

"But," Kat adds. "Um, more than that. Last year when you were gone . . ."

I wriggle one foot out from under the blanket and nudge the knee of her joggers. "Yeah, turns out you're gay?"

Kat sighs again. "I still like guys, but also girls too. So I think I'm bi, but it's still all so new."

It hits me, what she's saying. "Corinne isn't your first girlfriend."

She shakes her head. "While you were gone, and it all happened so fast. I suddenly found myself sneaking into closets during debate prep with a girl, but I didn't have anyone to talk about it with as I was navigating a whole new world."

It should demonstrate the strength of my character and commitment to Kat that I don't break into a Disney song right now.

"But Joss figured it out, and it was this giant relief to finally have someone who would listen. So I kind of . . . stopped trying to tell you."

I tilt my chin, remembering the order of events last October when I left France. "But you quit debate right after I got home."

Kat groans. "Well, one. I was pretty terrible at it. I kept agreeing with all the arguments." That draws a smile from me, but she rolls her eyes and keeps going. "And two, she broke up with me the day you got home. I was miserable, and suddenly you were there and it was all about your problems and your life. I wanted to tell you, Lo, I did. But every time I tried bringing it up, it was like you weren't even listening. Or worse, you would say things in passing about how I needed a new guy or that you missed the old me. I know you didn't understand how it hurt, but . . ."

"But it did."

She nods.

"We should have had a big blowup when I got home and figured this shit out, like, months ago." I press my lips together and eye my sister and say, "So your first girlfriend . . . was she cute?"

"Less cute after she broke up with me." She bites down on a grin. "And Corinne's way cuter."

I take a sip of my coffee. "Does this mean I can score some more free C.Rahmani makeup? There's this new—"

"Oh my god, Lola."

I scoot over so we've both got our backs to the tree house wall and spread the fuzzy blanket over our laps. For a minute, we simply drink our coffee. "I really am sorry for freaking out about you and Corinne," I say quietly. "I've recently come to the realization that I, uh, don't have a lot of true friends, but Corinne feels like one. I don't want either of you to think I was angry because you're bi." I pick at the fibers of the blanket and mumble to my lap. "I'm just afraid of being left out."

Kat nudges my shoulder. "But you will be left out sometimes. That's okay. That doesn't mean that I don't love you or that Corinne doesn't think you're super rad. That's actually what we bonded over at first, you know. Talking about how funny and bold you are."

A sly smile tugs at my lips. "Does that mean I can be your third wheel?"

"Sometimes."

"Okay," I concede, and clink the edge of my mug to hers. "I'll take sometimes." I lean my head onto her shoulder. "I love you."

Kat reaches her hand up to pat the side of my head. "Love you too, Lo. And really, this summer . . . I don't know if Georgia is, like, a witch or something, but you've changed. In a good way, I mean. I'd never be happy if you suddenly got quiet or meek. But now you're like Lola Plus."

Lola Plus. I'll take it.

An hour later, I'm back at Kat's bedroom door, knocking again.

"Hurry up," I command through the door. I check my phone, but I still haven't had a response to the series of texts I sent earlier, the apology ones or the idea ones. But I have to hope this will work out.

Kat pulls the door open. "Do I look okay?"

She's re-confiscated her favorite maroon leggings and has paired them with black running shoes, a visible floral sports bra, and a loose black tank she's knotted just above her belly button, showing a sliver of stomach above the band of her leggings.

"You're gorgeous, like always."

She fluffs at her hair, in a high ponytail today, and tugs at the simple gold studs in her ears. She asks for the fortieth time where we're going as I pull out of our driveway, but I stay mum. I don't want her to be disappointed if this doesn't work.

We wind through the hills and finally approach the dusty, nondescript trailhead Ezra brought me to weeks ago. The one with the perfect kissing spot. My chest aches with the memory of him, but I breathe around it.

Corinne's there. My heart skips, and I bite back a grin as Kat swivels her head from Corinne's car to me and back again. We pull up next to her, and I only sort of hit the wood fencing separating the lot from the trail. I'm getting really good at driving this summer.

I climb out of the car and face Corinne, a tentative smile spreading across my face. "Are we okay?"

Corinne presses her lips together and nods. "We're good, Lola. Thank you for apologizing."

"The first of many apologies, probably," I admit.

That pulls a light laugh from my friend. "Oh, I'm sure." But she crosses and scoops me up into a hug. When she pulls back, her eyes go to Kat, who's fiddling with her hair and outfit on the other side of the car. "But seriously, I want you to know. I mean, I thought she was gorgeous, but I didn't even know for sure that she was bi until she started kissing me."

My head whips to my sister, who's obviously listening because her cheeks flare pink.

"Ooh, I didn't know she kissed you. Get it, girl." I grin as Kat rolls her eyes. "She gets all her boldness from me. As the older twin—"

"By two minutes," Kat interjects.

I ignore her. "As the older twin, she's always looked up to me as a role model."

"Oh my god, Lo." But Kat is smiling as she walks around the back of the car and joins us. She stands a bit closer to me than Corinne and looks at her shyly. It's so damned adorable I may melt into a puddle right here.

"So, uh, we're hiking?" Corinne asks, biting on a smile.

"You're hiking," I correct her. I reach into the back seat and pull out the backpack I've prepared for Kat with all the essentials. Meaning, no frozen burritos. "I'm going through the Taco Bell drive-through and ordering my weight in Taco Supremes. You'll get her home at a reasonable hour?"

"Yes, Mom."

But Kat and Corinne look at each other, all smiles. I should become, like, a professional matchmaker for sure.

"Oh," I add. "And there's a waterfall at the end with a surprise behind it. You'll have to walk through the water to find it, but trust me, it's worth it." I waggle my eyebrows at them in case I'm not being obvious enough. Then add, "For kissing."

Kat's face burns red and Corinne drops her chin to hide the way she's grinning. My work here is done. But before they go, Kat grabs my hand.

"Ezra's miserable without you," she says quickly. "Joon said he's been moping around trying to figure out how to apologize to you all week. I think you should . . . you know, grand romantic gesture that shit."

I smile at her, but I'm pretty sure she's just saying this to make me feel better. Ezra and I are over. And that's hard and it still hurts to think about, but it'll eventually be okay.

Except when I get home, I find Marnie sitting at the kitchen table with one of Edie's Sonoma Sugared bakery boxes in front of her.

"Hey, this was left on the front porch for you." She pushes the box toward me, and I see a lineup of pistachio macarons. "There's a note too. I didn't read the note, but I did take a macaron."

Frowning, I lift the box. "Thanks, Mar."

She goes back to her book, and I take the box back to my room. I lift the lid and find a folded piece of paper tucked into the side. I sit back on my bed, unfold the letter—which, hello, Medieval Times—and start reading.

Lola—

There's a couple things I need to say, but the first is this: I was an idiot. A complete and utter idiot. I will do whatever I need to prove to you that you're worth it. Because you are. I realized pretty much immediately that I'd be happy to deal with all of it, if only it meant I'd get to do it with you. Am I being too vague? I think I'm being too vague. But I'm sitting in my car outside your house (not in a creeper way!) and I've only got this one piece of paper, so it's gonna have to work.

So here it is: I'm in love with you. I fell in love with you in about two seconds freshman year when you worried the FlyNap we were using was going to give the fruit flies bad dreams. You're just so wholly YOU, and it was basically impossible not to fall for you. But that was years ago, and I definitely DO sound like a creeper. Damn. This isn't going well. What I mean is, I was in love with you then, and being with you this summer has confirmed that I'm done for. You're it for me. I'm afraid to say I'm going to love you forever. I hope that's okay.

—Ezra

THIRTY-EIGHT

NERVES HAVE NEVER BEEN MY companion.

But right now, staring up at the stack of shipping containers that is Basecamp, my stomach is bubbling with them. I toe
the concrete sidewalk with my leopard-print canvas sneaker
and worry my serpent ring back and forth, back and forth. I'm
in slim-cut black linen joggers I snuck out of Kat's room while
she was showering this morning and a boxy tee that tickles the
bottom of my ribs. I'd tied my faded pink hair back into a pony
earlier and start nervously twirling the pieces that have come
loose.

Okay, stop freaking out, Lola. Ezra wrote me a note that I've
read thirty thousand times in the last twenty-four hours. He
was vulnerable with me, so he's earned a little vulnerability in
return. I'm pretty sure I'm not about to get publicly mocked.

But also, there's still this bead of anxiety inside of me that it'll be too much. That I'm too much.

No. Stop. I'm Lola Plus, right?

Lola + boldness.

Lola + confidence.

Lola + Ezra?

Fingers crossed, because I really want to kiss him again. And talk to him. And make him laugh. And hear his opinions on, like, all manner of stuff that I never really thought I cared about but maybe I do? Books and movies and college applications and road trips and hiking and pizza toppings. I want it all.

But first, I need to open this door and walk down the hallway and into Basecamp and, like, throw him in that tent display and have my way with him. Or talk to him. Yeah, I should probably talk to him first.

Before me, someone clears their throat. I pull my focus back to the task at hand and see a woman holding the door open for me. "Are you coming in?"

Yes. Or should I text him first? You know, test the waters to see if we're okay with showing up at your employer to declare my affection? No. Yes.

"Yes."

She holds the door wider and ushers me into the dim forest, and just hearing those manufactured bird chirps being pumped in among the trees calms my heartbeat by the tiniest bit. God, I've officially drunk the illegal kombucha, haven't I? And dammit, it's tasty. There are caps hanging from the fake aspen branches today. Ooh, that one is actually kind of cool. It's a washed-out green with a wide, flat brim and—

"No, Lola," I admonish myself. Enough stalling.

I march down the hall and into the atrium, searching for Ezra. I . . . hadn't actually considered how I'd track him down. Maybe I can commandeer the speaker system and announce that he's needed in Aisle Lola? But the Basecamp gods smile down, because I spot him almost immediately.

And he's about thirty feet off the ground.

There's a guy belaying for him at the bottom of the rock wall, and Sheena's nearby smiling rabidly at anyone who comes too close.

But whatever. Sheena's not going to kill my vibe right now with her smiles and enthusiasm. I stride across the floor to the climbing area and skirt the lower walls separating it from the rest of the floor. The ground is rubbery and soft, and Sheena's on me in an instant.

"You again. What are you—"

I crane my neck to stare up at Ezra. "Hey, nice ass!" I shout it up at him, and he slips off the wall and jolts to a stop in his harness.

Oops?

"Listen," Sheena hisses, "this isn't—"

But I've only got eyes for the guy hanging above my head. He wipes his hands together, and chalk dust puffs into the air. Even from down here, it's impossible to miss the way he's smiling.

"What are you doing here?" He stretches his legs out to push off the wall and gains some momentum, swinging back and forth a few times before he reaches out and grabs hold of a big, bright blue handhold. He places his feet back on the wall and twists to look down at me.

"I'm just here for the view."

He shakes his head at me and starts climbing slowly as Sheena tries again. "Miss, you can't—"

"Ugh, fine. Can I climb?"

Her lips purse. "There's a beginner—"

I walk away from her and step into a climbing harness, kicking off my shoes for the grippy climbing slippers sticking out from a cubby (and ignore Sheena telling me they're hers). I clip myself onto the belay line and turn to her. "Are you going to belay for me, or should I use a top rope?"

Okay, yeah, I've been climbing a few more times with Mei and Tavi and feel very proud of myself for pulling out my climbing knowledge on ol' Sheena here. Her pursed lips flatten to a slit, but she grabs hold of the line and I stare up at the wall, choosing my route.

I'm jittery with the effort of staying on the wall, but it pushes out the jitters of talking to Ezra. I climb fast, until I'm nearly level with him, though he is definitely following a harder line than me. I glance over at him, the way his forearm flexes as he holds on to the wall and the concentration tightening his jawline as he tries to muscle his way over to another toehold.

"What's hanging?" I say totally nonchalantly, and Ezra startles. He whips his head between the ground where I had been standing to the face of the rock wall where I'm currently chilling. I'm basically *Free Solo* over here.

"Holy shit, Lola. You are . . ."

I'm hoping he's thinking amazing, surprising, imbued with inner strength I never fully appreciated instead of something like . . . too much. But then the most gorgeous smile tugs his lips upward, carving dimples into his cheeks, and I nearly swoon right off this wall.

"There's a better toehold if you come this way a couple inches," I tell him.

He glances to where I'm pointing and frowns. "I can't see it."

"Trust me," I say. "Right foot, over toward me by about a foot and up a couple inches." He points his toe, feeling for the hold that's sort of hidden under a ridge of molded "rock." I can see the second he finds his footing, and he pushes his weight to his right. It brings him closer to me, close enough to see the scattered freckles dusting his nose and that effing adorable one at the corner of his mouth. My heart crashes around my chest, shrieking in delight and basically losing its shit.

I grin at him, take a deep breath, and say, "Race you to the top?"

The bastard barks a laugh and starts freaking hauling himself up the rock face, and it's all I can do to keep up. Oh, he's good at this. It makes warmth pool in my stomach and adrena-line spike in my veins because, dammit, I really wanted to beat him. But he's the first to slap the top of the wall, and I'm a few feet behind him.

And yeah, kissing at the top of the rock wall sounds kind of fun, but I'm sure Sheena would have something to say about that and I kind of don't want any witnesses for our reunion. Ezra must agree, because he presses his lips together and nods toward the ground. I nod and follow. Sheena lets me drop the last foot, and I want to glare, but also, I have to admire the pettiness.

We step out of our harnesses and change our shoes in silence. Ezra leads me toward a back exit, and we walk out of Basecamp straight onto the sidewalk along the river in the park. There's a coffee stand set up a few yards away, so we order an iced latte for me and a cold brew for him. And still, we don't talk.

A few months ago, the silence would have rubbed me raw. I would have bristled and fought against it. But instead, I force myself to simply appreciate the sensation of walking next to Ezra. Of the way the green wall of trees bordering the river shivers in the late-afternoon breeze and the way the cold coffee tastes on my tongue.

Ezra heads down a side path that I realize after a second is the same way we walked to get to the night market. It's cooler in the shade, and our steps are soft against the short grass. Tucked into a copse of sturdy, tall trees, we find a bench and sit. Beyond us, I can hear kids running around the playground and screaming in delight, and out on the main path a couple strolls eating ice cream. But here on our bench, it feels secluded.

I break the silence first. "So obviously, I've handed your letter over to the FBI, stalking division."

His cheeks flare red and he twists on the bench to face me. His knee brushes against my thigh and I sort of die. Bring on the smelling salts.

"I'm sorry," he finally says, his voice low and a little rough. "I . . . kind of freaked out at the bonfire and I'm . . . I never thought someone like you would ever look at someone like me, and I got in my own head about it. Convinced myself there was no way it'd actually work in the real world. Which is—"

He breaks off and runs a hand through his hair, making the curls stand on end, and gives me this sort of sheepish smile. I'm basically turning into an ice cream cone left out in the sun. So much melting over here.

"It's bananas, is what it is," I assure him. "Because, like, this is the real world. And we really work."

"Yeah, I know." His voice is soft, and I face him, hooking one leg under the other. He's amazing and cute and kind. So I tell him that.

"And," I continue, "I just like to talk to you, Ez. Like, I want to know your top three pizza toppings and your favorite vacation spot and everything else. But, I mean. Also. The way you kiss, dude. It makes me pretty interested in experiencing how you do other things."

Ezra straight-up chokes on his coffee. His cheeks prick pink, and I realize maybe I shouldn't have said that last part out loud. But, I mean, Lola gonna Lola.

"Um, yeah . . . ," Ezra manages. He sets his coffee at his feet and his voice creaks before he elaborates. "I mean, I haven't really . . ."

My smile could be safely described as devilish when I practically growl, "There's one way to remedy that." His pink cheeks burn red, and I soften my smile. "You're irresistible when you're flustered."

I'm about to say more, tell him I'm joking and we really don't need to do anything more, when he seizes me in a kiss.

His sure fingers cup the sides of my face, and he pulls my mouth to his. My skin tingles with electricity where he touches me, flooding my body with warmth that pools and simmers. His kiss shows just how much he's missed me, and I press back, showing just how much I've missed him too. After a moment, he softens, becomes less urgent and more languid. And oh god, this is wonderful too. The way he seems to love exploring my lips and mouth and tongue with his own. His fingers drift to the strands escaping my pony and thread into my hair at the base of my neck.

When we finally pull back, I breathe out his name on a sigh. My skin is hot . . . all of me feels hot. I have to swallow hard and will my heart to slow before I can properly speak again. I play my fingers across his cheek, his jaw. He catches my hand and presses a kiss to the tip of my middle finger, and my heart pulses with the sensation of it.

"And the other thing you said in your letter," I say, chewing on my lip. I feel so weirdly shy about this part. Kissing I can handle. Emotional maturity . . . less so.

Ezra plays with the hem of my shirt idly, his fingers brushing along the skin of my stomach. "Ah, yes. Because every grand declaration should include talk of fruit flies."

That pulls a rush of laughter from me, and I scoot closer to him, my hand on his thigh. He glances from my hand braced on his leg up to my face, his eyes so full of hope that I can barely stand it.

"I . . . I haven't actually ever . . . said that to a guy before. But . . . same."

A smile breaks across his face and sends cartoon rainbows arcing across my heart. "Really?"

"Really, Ez. I want to be with you."

He doesn't answer for a moment, but tips his forehead to mine and twines our fingers together between us. "And I want to be with you too."

I kiss him softly, then pull back. "So we're doing this?"

He laughs low in his throat. "God, I hope so."

He leans close again, but I push my palms gently against his chest. "But we don't have to do anything else but date, if you want. I don't want to force you into anything physical before you're ready."

Ezra groans, his shoulders falling. "I'm going to regret this in two seconds, but thank you. That means a lot to me."

He stands and holds out his hand to me. I let him pull me to my feet, but before I can stop myself, I reach back and slap his butt. "But I can still appreciate that ass, okay?"

He nudges his hip to mine and wraps his arm around my waist. "Obviously."

We drop our empty cups in the compost bins and walk hand in hand. "Dinner?" I ask.

Ezra nods. "That sounds fantastic." And we keep walking together into the gathering dusk.

THIRTY-NINE

DAD'S TESLA IS PACKED WITH people and gear. He and Mom are in the front seat; Kat sits beside me. In the back, my internal frame pack has been loaded with all my equipment and enough food and water to last two days until we reach the first cache of supplies.

I lean back against the headrest and watch the trees zoom by, lost in thought about two nights ago with Ezra.

It wasn't that, pervs. I really am serious about waiting until he's ready. Though, man, every time I think about what sharing that with him might mean. Ahem.

Anyway. We hung out in the backyard with Kat and Corinne, lounging on the pool floats and watching an old movie projected onto the portable screen. It was laid-back and fun and felt so much like a promise of what could be ahead for us.

And yesterday, Dad, Mom, Kat, and I packed into the car and headed out toward the trailhead four hours away, stopping for the night at a little roadside motel in Downieville. It was actually super fun to pile into one room and eat pizza and watch TV together. This morning, we only had a half hour drive to reach the meeting point deep in the Sierra Nevadas.

The trees outside my window suddenly pull into sharper focus as Dad slows, and a zing of anticipation and a little bit of fear ricochet down my skin. I sit forward and peer between the front seats to see Georgia's VW bus parked in a little lot and a bunch of activity. Parents taking photos, my friends standing next to packs that are half as tall as they are, Georgia handing out printouts of PCT California Section L guides to the anxious parents.

I can't help it; I vault out of the car and stride to the back, a surge of excitement helping me lift my heavy pack up and out, like it weighs nothing. Even though—let me be clear—this shit is heavy. On our last few hikes we've added weight to our packs to prep for multiple days with a full pack, but thirty extra pounds strapped to my back (and belted in properly, of course) still feels like a lot.

Over the course of the next six days, our crew will hike fifty-six miles of the Pacific Crest Trail, from Sierra City south to Olympic Valley just west of Lake Tahoe. And yeah, I have convinced Mom and Dad they should rent a mountain house in Tahoe for us to stay in when they pick me up because I'm starting to realize I'm a bit smarter than I give myself credit for. I plan on doing so many spa treatments. In fact, we've gone all in, and the entire family is coming for a week off to relax. Edie even said she'd make some Lola-Slayed-the-PCT-themed desserts for the occasion.

Of course, Mom did have to make a comment this morning that drew a storm cloud over things. She told me it was okay if I didn't do the hike, that we'd still stay in Tahoe. It's this weird hurt in the center of my chest that even after everything I've done this summer, she still can't wrap her head around the fact that I want this. But I do. Want this. And I have to hope that someday she'll understand.

I push the hurt aside and peer around. The pines are thick and green, the sun a dollop of pure gold in a bluebird sky. All around us, the scent of earth and trees makes my heart skip a beat. We truly are headed into the wild. Mom might never understand, but I cannot freaking wait.

Before me, my crew stands with their families and goes through final checks of their gear. Beth resists a horrific floppy hat from her mom but relents and lets her spray her down with sunscreen. I've come to realize that, like me, Beth uses bravado to cover any insecurities. Priya's wearing yet another science-themed shirt, and I notice her little brother is too. This one says "Pluto—Rotate In Peace." I'm fairly certain she's going to, like, discover a new solar system someday.

Tavi's mom, who is as tall as her daughter, is holding both sides of Tavi's face and looks like she's deep into minute three of a five-minute motivational speech. Her dad, meanwhile, is double- and triple-checking her pack for supplies even though Tavi keeps interrupting her mom to reassure him she's got everything. Mei is posing for selfies with her dads, each of them making the same cheese face. She catches me smiling at them and skips over to hand me a rose-tinted C.Rahmani matte lipstick she knows I've wanted.

Speaking of C.Rahmani. Corinne and her mom have joined my little group, giving hugs and—in Colette's case—double cheek kisses all around. Mom may faint from the poshness of it all.

"Are you girls ready?" Colette asks, her French accent curling the edges of her deep voice. She's wearing wide-legged sailor pants and black leather ballet flats. I mean, speaking of fainting because of the poshness of it all. I'm about to declare my love and ask her to run away with me.

I shake myself. The start of our adventure is only a few yards—a few minutes—away. I peer down the path, but it twists away into something unknown. I catch Corinne's eyes.

"I can't wait," I answer.

"Same," Corinne echoes.

Colette pats her daughter's curls. "How about when you girls get home, you come over and check out the new palettes I'm playing with in the studio. Kat, you too, of course." And by the indulgent smile she gives my twin, it's pretty clear Corinne hasn't kept their budding relationship a secret from her mom.

"Ohmygodyesplease," I say in a big rush of words, pulling a husky laugh from Colette.

Kat squeezes my wrist, her patented *shut up now* gesture that I know so well. "We'd love that, Ms. Rahmani."

All too soon, Georgia claps for our attention. She addresses the parents first, telling them how they can check in on our progress and also showing them the enormous satellite phone she carries on her and exactly where we'll be meeting them.

With the parents appropriately reassured that this isn't going to turn into a Donner Party situation (because, I'm not lying, we're going over Donner Pass on this hike), she says it's time to gear up and go. Mom lunges at me and wrenches me into a tight hug.

"Don't get eaten by a bear."

"Mom, that's what the bear canister is for," I remind her. She ignores me.

"Did you pack enough underwear? I once completely forgot to pack underwear for our trip to Greece and had to buy a whole set at the resort gift shop!"

"Julia," Dad interrupts.

Mom pulls back and smiles. She smooths my hair behind my ear and looks alarmingly like she might cry. "Please be careful. Don't eat any mushrooms. I love you."

Dad takes a turn next, gruffly hugging me and slapping my

back, before Kat buries her face in my shoulder. "I'm so proud of you," she cries, her voice muffled. "You're, like, actually doing it."

Gently, I un-barnacle her from my shoulder and smile. "I'm actually doing it. And when I actually get to Tahoe, I am actually eating candy for every meal and actually pooping in only the finest flush toilets."

"Toilets made of solid gold."

"Those toilets with the seat warmers that'll give my butt a little spray-down!"

Kat laughs. "God, it's going to be the best."

My fingers squeeze her arms. "You're the best. Thank you for putting up with me all these years. I'm glad I didn't absorb you in the womb."

Kat presses her lips together and sniffs. "And I'm glad I've had you as my built-in best friend. I can't wait to hear all about it, okay?"

The families leave, and it's just us. My crew, ready for the adventure of a lifetime. I shoulder my pack and put one foot in front of the other.

All I can see, in any direction, is wilderness. The pale ribbon of the trail stretches out before me, a twisting path that follows the natural curves of the world as it climbs and descends, plunges into pine forests and whispers through meadows of hardy wildflowers. My hiking stick is sturdy under my palm, helping me find my way.

It's expansive, like I hold a universe within my body. And it's intimate, feeling like one small speck in this amazing place. It fills me with awe that all this—*all this*—is waiting for me if I only open the front door and walk outside. What else will I discover in this big, wonderful world? God, I can't wait to find out.

We've hiked all day, stopping a lot at first to acclimate to the elevation and the reality of full packs. The sun has arced overhead, tracking our progress through these amazing mountains. Dotted below, we've spied alpine lakes, and above us we've marveled at snowpack still clinging to the shady spaces.

But now, with the sun starting to tuck itself into the west, we leave the trail for a patch of flat ground to make camp for the night. The first big sigh without the pack on my shoulders is one hundred percent the most amazing thing I've ever experienced in my life. Second only to taking my shoes off and wiggling my toes.

Working quickly and quietly, we pitch our tiny tents and arrange sleeping pads and bags. I don't even need help setting up my tent anymore. Georgia looks like she's got another ten miles in her, but honestly, I'm glad we're spreading these miles over six days. Already I feel coated with dust and sweat, and I'm thanking every god out there that I listened to Joss's suggestion to pack baby wipes.

The sky streaks pink as we get camp stoves going and vote on tonight's meal, herbed mushroom risotto. And finally, after

we're full of food and stretched out, we start talking. Little snippets of conversation and laughter ebb and flow around me, and I
simply absorb it all, happy to be one part of this amazing group.
Beyond our campfire, the glow of the flames illuminates seven
different hiking sticks, each one wrapped in multicolored soft
leather, but each unique. Even from here, I can spot mine.

As the first stars blink into existence, we crawl into our tents,
curl up, and fall into the sort of sleep that comes after a day on
the trail. I dream of hamburgers and tacos and Ezra and kisses
and more tacos.

Georgia packed instant coffee for the morning, and that
right there seals her as winner of Best Georgia Ever, Yes,
Including States and Countries. My eyes are still puffy with
morning, and the air bites every bit of exposed skin it can
find, but the sun sneaks across the ground, filling up the new
day with warmth.

The days are steady, and every mile down feels like an
accomplishment, until I'm realizing I've hiked twenty, thirty,
forty miles. We even spot a bear snuffling through a valley
below us on day three! I am definitely going to tell Mom it ate
me and she's actually welcoming home the ghost of her daughter, and I kind of can't wait to see her reaction. I'll give her
the smelliest hug in history and hold her tight even when she
screeches in disgust about the lack of prescription-strength
deodorant.

My feet ache, my hair is atrocious, and I've rounded the bend from "stinky" to "so stinky I can't even register the scent anymore." But I'm not sure I've ever smiled so much. I've learned that sometimes I laugh so long and loud that I snort, but maybe that's only when Tavi tells the story of the time they were running the annual Turkey Trot—ha! I knew it!—and her dad got stuck in his roast turkey costume.

Tomorrow is a light day, only five miles to Georgia's waiting van in Olympic Valley before it's hello, fancy flush toilet. So tonight, we stop early near the shores of a small, nameless lake. It's a deep jewel blue, nestled high in an alpine meadow, fringed on one side by stubby grasses and on the other by a steep slope of boulders and trees backed by a ridge of rocky peaks.

For the past five days, I've kept a secret in my pack, but tonight, with the warmth still at our backs and the cool waters of the little mountain lake calling to us, it feels perfect.

The perfect, perfectly Lola end to a journey I never could have imagined three months ago.

Tomorrow, once our parents pick us up, it will officially be the end of Hike Like a Girl. But I can't imagine not seeing these girls, not calling them my friends. Already, we've started brainstorming new adventures together. Not all hiking, but a little something for everyone. A theme park for Beth, who it turns out is a secret Disney fangirl. More hiking for Corinne, because she really does love this. Rock climbing for me, Tavi, and Mei. Mei has even researched some good spots to try climbing outdoors! I can't wait to talk to Ez about it. And—in a surprise twist—a night out at the opening of Priya's first photography exhibit at a small gallery in Oakland.

The work has been hard out on the trail, but my god has it been worth it. Every step feels earned, every new vista a reward. Every new challenge a chance to prove to myself that I'm worth it.

FORTY

THE TENTS ARE ARRANGED. THE shoes off. The dinner chosen. (Chicken alfredo tonight.)

I unzip the pouch I've been carrying in my backpack and clear my throat.

"A surprise," I say, "for everyone, but especially for Georgia."

Then, with a flourish—because, seriously, I have carried this stuff across fifty miles—I produce seven coconut macaroons coated in dark chocolate, a birthday candle, and seven paper crowns.

Georgia's eyes go wide, and she even gasps a little. Will told me she'd be turning thirty while we were on the trail and that she loved coconut cake, so I had Edie make these cookies for me with a special tempered chocolate coating to keep them from melting.

"Happy birthday, Georgia. Despite every effort, I have come to realize you're exactly the sort of badass I'd love to become someday. Like, to be clear, many years in the future, because you're ancient."

She pushes a hand to her mouth to cover a laugh that sounds suspiciously like it's turning into a sob, and she rushes over and seizes me in a hug. "Thank you," she says into my disgustingly dirty hair. "You didn't have to do this."

I pull back and shrug. "It seemed only fair. You changed my life. I brought you dessert. Now we're even."

She shakes her head, still laughing, eyes bright, before divvying up the indulgence. We all put on the party crowns and sing to Georgia around her lighted birthday cookie, then tuck in. And oh, holy god, they are delicious. Possibly the best thing I've ever tasted in my entire life, and I don't think I'm saying that because all I've eaten for the last several days are rehydrated meal packets and oatmeal. I swear I can taste the butter—real butter!—and the way the chocolate melts on my tongue. It's a real taste sensation happening over here.

I lick my fingers in case there's any coconut flakes clinging and sigh in contentment.

But not in too much contentment. A handful of yards away, the small jewel-box lake catches the glint of the setting sun, and I'm overcome with a sudden, irrepressible need to feel the water. I catch Tavi's eyes.

"Race you to the lake," I say.

She lets loose a punch of laughter and takes off like a shot. I'm woefully slow, and even Beth passes me running toward the lake. A marmot warming itself on a rock squeaks and hurtles into its den, and a flock of birds scatter. The first splash of water against my bare skin makes me shriek.

"Oh fuck!" Georgia shouts, barreling in after us. "That's cold!"

Laughter swirls around me, and a whole lot of swearing because, holy shit, it is frigid. But out here, alone in the vastness of this world, we don't feel any need to quiet down or watch our language or be any of the hundreds of things people think we should be. We're simply seven amazing women standing up to their calves in ice-cold water, full of coconut cookies and watching the sun dip behind the mountains.

A hush ripples through us, and silently I link arms with Priya on one side and Georgia on the other. We stand there, the last fingers of warmth streaking down our faces and pooling inside, saved up until the new day. The last day.

I can feel that warmth swirl within me and without. A connection to the sun and to myself and to the women standing alongside me. I can feel the chase of that warmth propel me ever onward. To see what's around the bend. What's beyond the horizon. I've never been destined for a small life, but in this moment I feel infinite.

I tip back my chin, open my throat, and howl at the sky. It's a glory of pink and orange and purple overhead, and soon my voice mixes with those of my friends as we howl down the moon. We've stored the sun for another day.

Our shouts echo and curve back around us, mixing with the wind in the grasses and the water lapping at our legs. It's a connection that weaves in and out of the earth and sky and seven unique women.

I watch the last sliver of sunlight give way to a starry night, and I smile.

Acknowledgments

Hello! It's me again. And I'm here to say *thank you*. Thank you for reading. Thank you for letting me write more books. Thank you for suffering through probably one-too-many asides about going to the bathroom in the woods.

So many folks made this book possible. To my insightful editor, Alice Jerman, and hugely supportive agent, Amy Bishop—this book would be *so* different without you both. (My very favorite chapter was born thanks to an edit note!) To Clare Vaughn for once again coming up with the perfect tagline. To artist Karina Perez and designers Catherine Lee and Jenna Stempel-Lobell for my amazing cover—they so perfectly captured Lola's energy. To the rest of the Harper team: Alexandra Rakaczki, James Neel, Kristen Eckhardt.

This book is, at its heart, about the bond of sisters. So a huge thank-you to mine for enduring my childhood stories without too much lasting damage. Ask me about Murray the Man-Eating Sea Bass for a great example of what a terrible big sister I was. You've definitely earned this dedication, Jackie.

Several other people have had a hand in shaping *Lola*, shaping me, or just generally being fantastic. Thanks to the MUGsters—Taylor L.W. Ross, Ana Ellickson, Genevieve Sinha, Aleese Lin—for the edits, friendship, and excuses to get away for writing retreats. A forever thank-you to Carrie S. Allen and Sabrina Lotfi for their care and support . . . which makes me sound like a finicky succulent, but *it's not wrong.* To the support (and commiseration!) of my fellow 2022 debuts. To the Denver chapter of Forever Young Adult—especially our leader, Annie. To Cory for the writing dates and brainstorming. And thanks to my nonwriter friends and family for cheering me on: my kids, Nico and Gus; my family, Steve and Teri, Kim and Michael; my friends Megan, Traci, Haley, Liz, and everyone else who is endlessly supportive.

And now, a story. When we first started dating, Ian and I went camping. We were still in the "trying to impress" stage, so I totally pretended to be a camping expert. And Ian, as we walked in the dark to the vault toilet, nonchalantly said, "Don't forget to tap the toilet to knock off any spiders." Reader, I died. And that was the moment we really got to know each other thanks to a vault toilet and my terrified insistence that he stay with me, flashlight on, so I wouldn't fall in and be devoured by the toilet spiders. True love! Years—*years!*—later, there is still no one else I'd rather adventure with.

I never imagined, when I wrote *Being Mary Bennet*, that I'd get to spend more time with my version of the Bennets. But, I mean, you've met Lola now. She refuses to be a side character. Yet, this is where I leave the Barnes family. I am so thankful that I was able to spend two whole books with this ridiculous, loving, exasperating, wonderful family.

And finally to you, readers, for going on this journey with Lola. See you on the trail.

flashlight on, so I wouldn't fall in and be devoured by the toilet spiders. True love! Years—*years!*—later, there is still no one else I'd rather adventure with.

I never imagined, when I wrote *Being Mary Bennet*, that I'd get to spend more time with my version of the Bennets. But, I mean, you've met Lola now. She refuses to be a side character. Yet, this is where I leave the Barnes family. I am so thankful that I was able to spend two whole books with this ridiculous, loving, exasperating, wonderful family.

And finally to you, readers, for going on this journey with Lola. See you on the trail.